.S.A.K.

INTELLECTUAL PROPERTY

桜
知
的
財
産

ZACHARY HILL

PATRICK M. TRACY PAUL GENESSE

MW00653301

 PRAISE FOR SAKURA

"An epic story about a heavy-metal, super-ninja android during a cyberpunk apocalypse. It's the best possible memorial for Zachary Hill and everything he thought was awesome. Tracy and Genesse did a fantastic job finishing this excellent book filled with samurai robots, evil megacorporations, jetpacks, espionage, hacker battles, anime fights, cyber nukes, bullet bikes—all with a badass, headbanging, horn-throwing, stage-diving soundtrack, blessed by the goddess of heavy metal herself. I loved it."

—Larry Correia, *New York Times* bestselling author of
HOUSE OF ASSASSINS

"A hard-rocking literary mosh pit about a heavy-metal android who becomes both the hero and villain of a brutal cyberpunk thriller. *Sakura* is loaded with more computers, guns, music, and hard-edged futurism than any five other books working together, and it gives you both barrels straight to the face. STOP HOGGING ALL THE AWESOME, SAKURA; LET THE REST OF US HAVE SOME."

—Dan Wells, *New York Times* bestselling author of
BLUESCREEN

"*Sakura: Intellectual Property* lands like a power chord from a world-class rock opera. From the first chapter, we are card-carrying members of the Sakura fan club. The story is tighter than a lead guitarist's E string and twice as resonant. Any fan of outstanding science fiction will be rocked. Just press 'play' on *Sakura*."

—Michael Darling, #1 Amazon Bestselling Author of
GOT LUCK

"*Sakura* is a myth-tinted, hard-rock Japanese cyberpunk thriller that starts with a bang and gets louder. Full of mystery, mayhem, guitars, and swagger, recommended for readers who like THINGS THAT ARE AWESOME."

—D.J. Butler, author of WITCHY EYE

"*Sakura* is a headbanging, anthem-singing sci-fi thriller. Like the music, it will get your heart pounding."

—Daniel Yocom, author and reviewer for
Guild Master Gaming

"A cybernetic tour de force starring a plucky heavy-metal heroine—in which we find out if music really can save us all."

—Julie Frost, award-winning author of the
PACK DYNAMICS series

"Sakura moved me to tears, I have no other words. Zachary Hill was a true visionary, and Paul and Patrick made it a reality."

—Chloe Mori Ward, Princess of the Fellowship of Metal

"*Sakura: Intellectual Property* pounds with action, rips with high-tech espionage, and grips with the unfolding mystery of who enslaved heavy-metal sensation, Sakura, and why. The layers go so much deeper, though. The real heart and soul of this story, the thing that will keep you coming back for more, lies in its fascinating exploration of what it means to be human by examining it from the outside, through the eyes of a blossoming artificial intelligence. *Sakura* is for fans looking for a heavy-metal thriller that touches on our deepest desires: to love, to be free, to be creative, and through these things become greater than the sum of our parts."

—Bradley P. Beaulieu, award-winning author of
TWELVE KINGS OF SHARAKHAI

"Heavy metal with hints of *Ghost in the Shell*, *Do Androids Dream of Electric Sheep?*, and the Illuminati. It's a super fun ride."

—Joe Monson, coeditor of TRACE THE STARS

"*Sakura: Intellectual Property* is a stunning book, and not only because of its fast-paced, action-driven story, thrilling plot twists, gorgeous illustrations, and meticulously crafted playlists that engage the readers' senses in ways other books never could. What makes this volume so exceptional is its capacity to make the readers interrogate both their own humanity and the personhood of others, to delve deep into the different and surprising aspects of being human and experience the wide spectrum of ways in which we show up in the world: imperfect, flawed, and broken, yes, but also brave, glorious, and alive in more ways than one. This work teaches us that the soul is never lost but may be hiding in the most unexpected of places, patiently waiting to be rediscovered and recognized for what it is: a "spiritual electricity," as Rilke describes it. This is a book not to be missed.

—Dr. Masha Shukovich, multiple award-winning author

"A high-octane story, fueled by rocket-grade heavy metal. *Sakura: Intellectual Property* tells a high-tech tale of intrigue, action, and rock 'n' roll. The main character, an android/rock star/Manchurian candidate, is written in vivid 3-D. This book is a page-turner from beginning to end. It reads like a full-stack Marshall amplifier. If I could, I would plug my guitar right into this book and shake down the rafters."

—Craig Nybo, author, musician, and creator of
CHOPS: THE OFFICIAL GUIDEBOOK TO AN
ALTERNATE ROCK AND ROLL UNIVERSE

BOOKS & STORIES BY THE AUTHORS

ZACHARY HILL

"The Tachi" (lead short story in Forged in Blood)
The Lost Promise
The Gods of Miskatonic
Sins of Prometheus
Sins of Prometheus 2
Fearless: The Powerful Women of History
"Red Snow" (The Crimson Pact Volume 5)
Uprising Italia
Behind the Shroud
Gorgon
Shattered Lands
Broken World
Witch Queen
Edge of the Empire
Raft of Medusa

PAUL GENESSE

THE IRON DRAGON SERIES
The Golden Cord: Book 1
The Dragon Hunters: Book 2
The Secret Empire: Book 3
The Crystal Eye: Book 4
The Iron Brotherhood: Book 5

"Onnen" (Shared Nightmares)
"No-Tusks" (A Walk in the Abyss)
The Crimson Pact Volumes 1–5 (Editor)
"Of the Fire" (Mech: Age of Steel)

PATRICK M. TRACY

"Worth the Scars of Dying" (Noir Fatale)
"Machine Heart" (Mech: Age of Steel)
"Of the Earth, of the Air, of the Sea" (Kaiju Rising: Age of Monsters)
"Mungo the Undying" (A Walk in the Abyss)
"Sealed with Fire" (The Crimson Pact Volume 5)
"Darkness of the Sun" (The Crimson Pact Volume 4)
"Whispers in the Code" (The Crimson Pact Volume 3)
"Jar of Needs" (The Crimson Pact Volume 2)
"Red Bandana Boys" (The Crimson Pact Volume 2)
"Red Test" (The Crimson Pact Volume 1)
"The Failed Crusade" (The Crimson Pact Volume 1)

SAKURA

INTELLECTUAL PROPERTY

ZACHARY HILL
PATRICK M. TRACY   PAUL GENESSE

COVER AND ILLUSTRATIONS BY SARAH STEIGERS

Copyright © by The Zachary Hill Irrevocable Literary Trust,
U/A dated January 15, 2019
All Rights Reserved.

Cover art, interior illustrations & playlists by Sarah Steigers
Jacket design by Devon Dorrity
Interior design by Caryn Larrinaga
Published by Iron Dragon Books
Printer: Thomson-Shore

All characters and events in this book are fictitious.
Any resemblance to persons living or dead is strictly coincidental.

All songs mentioned in this book on playlists or in the text are the property of their
respective copyright holders. No song lyrics mentioned in this book are from the
actual songs and have been rewritten as parody lyrics in accordance with the fair
use doctrine.

The scanning, uploading, and distribution of this book via the Internet or any other
means without the permission of the publisher is illegal and punishable by law.
Please purchase only authorized electronic editions and do not participate in or
encourage the electronic piracy of copyrighted materials. All profits from this book
go to Zachary Hill's widow, Mackenzie Hadlow Hill. Your support of her is greatly
appreciated.

PREFACE

Zachary Hill will live forever in our hearts. He will also live on the pages of the many books he wrote and illustrated, and on the canvases he painted. Knowing him was an incredible blessing, and his sudden passing January 15, 2016, left his friends and family devastated and heartbroken.

Zach had so much to live for. He had finally met and married the love of his life, Mackenzie. Only a few days before their one-year wedding anniversary, he collapsed soon after arriving at work. CPR was performed, but he did not survive. A large blood clot had formed in his leg and traveled to his lungs. The pulmonary embolism took his life.

None of us wanted his story to end. There was so much more that was supposed to happen. He was only thirty-eight years old, and the best years were ahead of him. He was called back to his celestial home far too early.

At his wake, with tears in my eyes, I stood beside his open casket and made a vow to friends and family that his last book would be published. Six days before he left us, Zach told me he had finished the first draft. I agreed to be the editor, and together, we were going to develop Sakura into the best novel he'd ever written. He was so excited about this book, and his idea was brilliant. Set in a dystopian future Japan, Sakura, a heavy metal–singing android is hacked and turned into an assassin. She fights her programming, trying to stop a secret cabal who is taking over the world.

Creating Sakura's unique character was arguably Zach's greatest literary accomplishment, and her story needed to be told. Eight months after Zach's death, Joshua Hill, Zach's twin brother, completed a light edit on the manuscript and sent along the file, which was 378 pages (92,000 words) and had the working title *Intellectual Property*.

I couldn't muster the courage to read it for some time. The pain was too raw. Every time I opened the document, I got choked up and was only able to read a few pages, which was Josh's experience as well.

Also, I was in the middle of finishing books four and five in my *Iron Dragon* series and used that project to distract myself from the grief. Zach was a fan, and to keep myself going, I would think, "Zach would want me to finish." I eventually completed book four and was 45,000 words into book five when I realized I needed to stop my project and work on Zach's novel. If I didn't, it would be more than three years before Zach's last book came out.

I finally read the first draft and began the rewrite on March 5, 2017, finishing my first draft on December 31, 2017. I incorporated Zach's prose and wrote a lot of my own, expanding the summary chapters he wrote into full-fledged scenes. The final novel grew from 92K to 156K. I had recruited my best friend, one of Zach's great friends, Patrick M. Tracy to help. Pat is an expert on heavy metal, a guitar player, and an amazing writer who writes incredible emotional punches.

Pat and I were in a gaming group and writers' group with Zach, and we bonded over many hours at Larry Correia's house, playing samurai in our Legend of the Five Rings role-playing game campaign. Larry has written the foreword and I'm so grateful for his help getting the word out about this book.

I could not do this project alone. Patrick and I forged ahead with the full support of Josh and Zach's extended family. We read that original draft and brainstormed about our approach to an early version of the manuscript, which explored the meaning of life, artificial intelligence, philosophy, theoretical computing, value higher than self, rebellion, and the true meaning of heavy metal.

The character and story were awesome, but it needed to be fleshed out, expanded, and structured. Zach's process would have seen him re-write it multiple times, and we had to imagine the directions he would have taken. Over the course of twenty-one months, Pat and I spent hundreds of hours brainstorming and working on the novel as we sent it back and forth to each other.

We've never worked harder or longer on a book. This was a big deal for us, and we felt our self-imposed pressure to capture Zach's vision. Some of Zach's original prose is still in this novel, and the overall story is his, as are the characters, but we had to redream the dream, figure out what Zach would have done, and stay true to his vision as we took first-draft scenes and polished them. We had moments of self-doubt, but we persevered in the end.

We took on this project because we love Zach and wanted to honor him. It was also a way for us to grieve and come together and bring hope to his family and friends. We did it for them, and we did it for free.

All the profit from this project goes to Mackenzie, Zach's widow. Zach's father, George Hill Sr., Patrick Tracy, and I funded this. Many others donated their time and energy to help complete the book, as it takes a team. We were able to hire an amazing artist, Sarah Steigers, who did the cover and interior illustrations, and who spent so much extra time getting things just right. She made Sakura and the characters come to life, and her work is stunning.

Devon Dorrity's cover design is also incredible, and we are so fortunate for his support, guidance, and expertise. Bradley Beaulieu's development editing took this to the next level, and Jennie Stevens's copyediting was awesome. The layout by Caryn Larrinaga in the high-quality, limited edition, signed, and numbered hardcover will make the entire book a work of art.

The support we've received has been wonderful, and this is the best and most important project of my life. We believe that Zach would love all of this, and we've felt him encouraging us along the way. He's probably looking down on us, wearing his trademark "Elvis glasses," which he wore in Iraq and for years upon returning home. He led a fascinating life, and his experiences led him to this story. His gentle soul and big heart are embodied by the title character of his novel, Sakura. As you read, you may see some similarities.

George Hill IV, Zach's eldest brother wrote this passage: "He was an artist, a historian, a teacher, a two-tour combat veteran, and a prolific writer. He was a true warrior poet who always sought peace. He loved to play games and spend time with his family and friends. Zach was also a traveler. He adventured in other countries. He served his two-year mission for his church in Mexico, and he taught English in Japan and spent time in Italy. He served his country in the darkest places in Iraq and was a legitimate war hero. Now he's gone to the Undiscovered Country. While he's away from us for the time being, we know we will see him again."

Until then, we celebrate his life and his final creative work. *Sakura: Intellectual Property* is a project born of love. This novel brings together fiction and music in a unique way. This is a love letter to heavy metal, and Sakura is always thinking about music. The playlists at the beginning of each of the chapters contain songs by bands that Zach loved. We also added tracks that resonated with the story and helped us see the way forward.

Fans of heavy metal who are immersed in the culture may understand this at a deeper level, but casual fans will also read the song titles and album names and understand the relational meaning in the text. There are so many little nuggets hidden in this book that relate to Zach's life, including the numeric designation of the army units he served in, along with music and movies he loved.

Follow the link to the Sakura channel or playlist in the ebook, or on YouTube search for: Sakura the Android Metal Goddess and look at the playlists. As you read, you can listen to the corresponding playlist. Many of the songs are mentioned in the chapter and go along with the text in tone and meaning. For copyright reasons, we were unable to use any of the real lyrics in the book, but we wrote parody lyrics of some songs if they are mentioned at all. We also wrote songs, and Callie Stoker recorded one of them in the studio of the legendary Craig Nybo. Please listen to it when it occurs in the book.

So many people have given their time and energy to this project, and we are determined to make it an artistic and commercial success—for Zach, for Mackenzie, and all his friends and family. We would love to sell the rights for this to be made into a manga, an anime, or a live-action movie. Any profit would go to Mackenzie. Please get in touch if you can help us or have contacts who could.

Thank you for your support and for reading this book. We need your reviews and especially need you to tell your friends about this. We want to get the word out to everyone who might be interested, anyone who wants to rock and go on a heavy metal thrill ride.

Through his writing, Zachary Hill will always be remembered. We invite you to take this journey to future Japan to find out, once and for all, if rock 'n' roll can save the world. We believe it can.

—Paul Genesse, December 2, 2018

FOREWORD

If you were one of the people lucky enough to know Zach Hill, then you know that an epic story about a heavy metal, super ninja, android during a cyperpunk apocalypse is about the best memorial humanly possible for him.

I've been looking forward to reading this book since Zach first told me about it. He was talented, smart, funny as hell, and had a work ethic that puts most authors to shame. Zach was one of those guys who learned by doing, and he kept getting better with every story he told. He had a great voice, great sense of humor, and a gift for making interesting characters.

But the biggest reason I was looking forward to reading this one? Contagious enthusiasm. When I say contagious enthusiasm, I'm talking about a writer's greatest weapon. Contagious enthusiasm happens when the writer is so excited creating, that some of that excitement bleeds through, and the reader can't help but feel it too.

Sakura: Intellectual Property is like a giant love song to everything Zach thought was awesome.

He lived in Japan and was fascinated by the culture. He loved the food, the people, and especially the music. When he came back to the states he gave my daughter a stack of Japanese music CDs. She'd expressed interest, and Zach was always excited to share the things he loved. This book is kind of like that.

Zach was fascinated by history. He loved history more than anyone else I've ever met, and I'm including historians and archeologists in that estimate. And it wasn't just dry and dusty academic facts and figures to Zach. It was about stories, and human beings doing amazing things, the big ideas and moral quandaries, the difficult choices and pivotal acts.

Sakura is filled with that sort of thing. It's a tale about someone who is good and just, in a world that's not. It's about beauty and art thriving in a place that can be dark and bleak, and the people who are lifted up by it.

But don't let me scare you off with that description. Sakura isn't some dull navel gazing introspection. Its samurai robots and evil megacorporations and jet packs, and espionage and hacker battles and anime fights and cyber nukes and bullet bikes, all with a bad ass, head banging, horn throwing, stage diving soundtrack, blessed by the goddess of heavy metal herself.

Basically, it's Zach, having a whole lot of fun. And you can tell.

So I was excited to read it, because Zach was excited to write it.

However, enthusiasm alone doesn't make for a great book, and it is a rare thing for any author to finish their rough draft and have it be a perfect, flowing, coherent manuscript. There is still a lot of work to do after the rough draft, and no matter how good an author is we miss stuff when we're too close to it. We've got to finish the story, and then back up to fix all of the things we zipped right by in that initial writing blitz. Right after he finished the rough draft, Zach told his friends that this was the best thing he'd ever written. But sadly, Zach never got the chance to go back and polish his work.

This book exists because a good man had friends who loved him enough to finish his masterpiece.

Pat and Paul are both talented authors in their own rights, and they took up the mantle to finish what Zach had started. As a labor of love they set out to create the book that Zach would have if he'd been given the opportunity. Editing anything is a challenge. Editing something that you know is special, where you are trying very hard to remain true to the original author's vision is even harder.

I was nervous when I got the advanced reader copy. This was my friend's last book. This was his heavy metal baby. I knew Pat and Paul had put in a lot of work, but would they pull it off? Would they do Zach justice?

Then I read it.

And it was awesome.

I think Zach would love it.

I am honored that they asked me to write this foreword. I hope that you enjoy reading this book as much as I did.

Larry Correia

\m/

For Kenzie, with all the love.

CAST LIST

Sakura: Android / vocaloid heavy-metal singer

Himura: Sakura's manager

Yoshida: Sakura's publicist

Reiichi Oshiro: Sakura's engineer

Minami Akane: Sakura's stylist

Takashi: Sakura's drummer

Fujio: Sakura's rhythm guitarist

Masashi: Sakura's bass player

Toshio Kagawa: Director of Corporate Security for Victory Entertainment

Oyama Ryoto: Head of Business Operations, Miyahara Conglomerate

Jiro Yoritomo: Mall Corporation Vice President of Integration

Machiko Yoritomo: Six-year-old daughter of Jiro

Shimamura Shiro: Director of Advanced Projects, Miyahara Conglomerate

Ichiro Watanabe: Minister of Logistics, Defense Ministry

Daichi Yamauchi: Minister of Commerce

Saguru Hashimoto: Director of AI Development

Aiko Shinohara: Doctor and lead scientist for the Defense Ministry AI Division

Stacy Richardson: Liaison to Victory Entertainment Music Division, Vice President

Sinji Natsukawa: CEO of the Miyahara Conglomerate

Kenshiro: Soldier

Todai 3465: Bipedal Light-Armored Drone, Enhanced Third Generation (BLADE-3)

Asato: Senior AI Engineer

Diamond Steve: Journalist and vlogger of Indestructible Truth Media

Takafumi Eto: Game designer, otaku

Nayato Atsuda: Programmer, hacker

Mamekogane: Rogue Administrator program

Kunoichi: Assassin

Hitomi: Android/vocaloid pop singer

Yuki: Android/vocaloid pop singer

Sakurako: Sakura's most dedicated fan

Asami: Sakura fan

ギター・リスト
GUITAR LIST

Fender
Jazz Bass

B.C. Rich
Warlock

Gibson
Explorer

Gibson
Flying V

Fender
Stratocaster

Kent
741

Fender
Telecaster

Gibson
ES-335

Gibson SG
(Special)

Rickenbacker
325C64

Parker
Fly

Gibson
Les Paul

QUEEN OF METAL PLAYLIST

メタル女王

Rise
Sakura
Rise from the Flames

Real Existence
Band-Maid
New Beginning

Going Under
Evanescence
Fallen

Ain't Talkin' 'bout Love
Van Halen
Van Halen

By Demons Be Driven
Pantera
Vulgar Display of Power

Holy Diver
Dio
Holy Diver

Into the Void
Black Sabbath
Master of Reality

CHAPTER 1

The arena shook. Trapped in the dark below the stage, cut off from her band and the screaming fans, Sakura missed her cue, ruining the encore. Her connections to the venue's networks failed as Victory Arena's system cut off.

<NO NETWORK SIGNAL> alarms flashed across her internal display. The trapdoor lift had no manual override. She could not get up to the stage to begin singing. Shame and panic flooded her neural cortex as she tried to save the show. The performance meant everything to her. It had to be perfect. She must not let down her fans.

She accepted a rerouting of her signal through Victory Entertainment's servers. Regaining control would simply be a matter of . . .

A swarm of incoming data overwhelmed her. Core interfaces reached maximum utilization. She lost all sensation in her fingers and throat as a terrifying white screen filled her user interface. Was she being hacked?

After two seconds, fewer than half of her systems returned. Under the stage, alone, dread dominated Sakura as she regained a tenuous link to the venue and her own controls. She calculated imminent catastrophic failure of her processors at 39 percent.

The Victory Entertainment brand must not be damaged. The corporation did not tolerate failure. Other vocaloids had been terminated for missing their cues or making small mistakes that broke the illusion of perfection. She had to finish the concert and save herself from being erased.

Her handsome young bandmates played a looping rhythm, waiting for their star to emerge from beneath the stage. Thousands of fans screamed her name and stomped their feet, shaking the building as the three men tried to keep the audience's attention.

She counted out the rhythm. Five, four, three . . . She engaged the hydraulic lift, which began its ascent. The trapdoor slid open. Sakura put her hands on Night Hawk, her guitar. She couldn't access her technique database. The object in her grasp, the instrument she'd been made to play, was an unfamiliar hunk of wood.

Pyrotechnic and holographic flames covered the stage and Sakura as the riser hit its stops. Twin spotlights outlined her flaming android body.

The crowd erupted.

A neural text came from Fujio, her rhythm guitarist. "Finish strong! All right!" His facial expression betrayed concern before he turned away, flashing the crowd his signature cocky grin.

He didn't know. He couldn't, or all would be lost. Frantic, Sakura searched manually through over a hundred thousand files until she located her technique database renamed and buried in a subfolder. A half measure late, she played the iconic notes of "Rise" as ominous warning messages predicted total system collapse.

Masashi's single bass note rang out. Sakura used it as an anchor to calm her chaotic thoughts. Perfectly in time, Fujio and Takashi launched into the finale.

She cycled air through the intakes on her metallic spine and pushed it toward the vocal folds in her throat. Compared to her high standards, the concert was already ruined, but if she failed to sing, she was doomed.

Pillars of fire shot above the stage as Sakura belted out the chorus of her signature song.

"I rise from the flames,
No one can stop my reign,
I am the metal queen!"

Seventy thousand fans sang along with the most popular heavy-metal anthem of all time. In awe, they watched as Sakura launched into her legendary guitar solo. Her hands with ultrasensitive synthetic fingertips moved faster than a human's ever could. She shredded on her eight-string JPro guitar, the Flying V–shaped instrument a copy of her treasured vintage Ibanez.

Her cherry-blossom-pink hair, divided into two long pigtails, whirled like helicopter tail rotors. She gave the impression of being lost in a rapturous head-banging moment, but in reality Sakura attempted to synchronize every aspect of the arena.

She watched the mostly Japanese crowd through her internal display. Before the disastrous instability occurred, she had simultaneously monitored all 468 cameras, observing thousands of fans. During the disaster of an encore, she managed to view only three camera feeds.

A teenage girl jumping up and down, her devil-horn headband falling off. A couple in a dark corner of the arena, hands caught in each other's hair as they kissed. Someone riding atop a sea of hands, arms outstretched, eyes closed against the pulsing strobe of the light show . . .

She cherished her fans' happiness above everything else. In any other concert, their frenzied euphoria enhanced by Augmented Reality stimulators would fill her with deep satisfaction, but now she worried about letting them down. Sakura needed to find the root of the instability. She had to save face for herself and Victory Entertainment.

She turned on the hologram projectors and created a gigantic image of herself dancing over the crowd. Her Goth Lolita black lace skirt with chrome skulls, fishnet leggings, red corset, and platform boots appeared in flawless detail. Her large eyes, human except for the bright pink of the irises, swept across the crowd.

The music peaked. Sakura directed the hologram projectors to create an otherworld of floating monsters. She snapped out a spinning kick, and her avatar above the crowd knocked a monster into the rafters. The arena transformed into a live-action anime crossed with a video game starring the goddess of rock.

Small monsters, cute and scary at the same time, appeared on Takashi's drums. They danced until he smashed them with his drumsticks, to the delight of the crowd.

The sound distorted in a few of the speaker emplacements. The delay created an echo across mezzanine D. Sakura adjusted the settings, interfacing with the venue's master soundboard. A simple enough alteration, but every hint of a problem loomed like impending calamity. She just wanted the show to be over. She had never wanted that before. The stage was her favorite place, the only time she felt truly fulfilled.

She carried on, and her voice came through crystal clear. Her vocal range resembled Amy Lee, a classic mezzo-soprano of the legendary band Evanescence, and Saiki Atsumi, the brilliant heavy-metal singer of the Japanese all-female metal group Band-Maid.

The fans banged their heads, oblivious to the adjustments Sakura made while shredding on her guitar. Cameras zoomed in on her smooth forearms. Windows in the titanium alloy revealed the mechanisms within as pushrods worked in their bath of clear lubricant. Her fingers danced on the strings. She swiveled the displays to show her smooth metallic spine poking through the ribbons of her corset.

She smiled at the crowd before she became a Goth Lolita ballerina, spinning her body faster and faster on one foot.

Sakura's balance sensors began to fail. She stopped pirouetting and came to a jerking halt. She played the final chord progressions as the concert came to its ultimate climax.

Thousands of holographic fans appeared in Victory Arena. Translucent holograms of bakemono goblins with punk haircuts perched on the back of seats or on the shoulders of amazed fans. The goblins' faces changed to a caricature of the person closest to them, causing delighted laughs and more cheering.

Her user interface filled with warnings about the unknown

algorithms and data from her company. It held the highest administrative clearance and caused a rolling restart cascade. The probability of her being hacked registered at 76 percent.

She fired off a wave of pause commands. No response. "Stop!" she screamed into her code matrix, invoking emergency override.

Nothing.

This was not supposed to happen. It couldn't happen. She concentrated all remaining processing power on finishing the song.

She missed a note, then a second. She surrendered all arena control to concentrate on finishing her performance. Alarms and blank warning messages lit up her UI. Logs deleted as quickly as they were written. She couldn't tell which elements of her programming were being altered. This was a disaster, a nightmare.

Unable to move her fingers, Sakura missed the last three notes of her solo. Shameful, dissonant feedback blared from her guitar. The bakemono disappeared from the arena as she lost the venue's networks. The lights, sound, cameras, everything was gone.

Sakura stood motionless, reduced to a single data thread. Her face and eyes froze in a confident and ferocious pose. The chorus of "Going Under" by Evanescence wailed inside her audio cortex. She was drowning, falling, dying, broken forever. She had heard people say they were "heartsick" before, but this was the first time she had ever understood what they meant.

Her fans screamed and reached for her over the barricade. Did they realize she was malfunctioning? The band kept the rhythm, waiting for her to begin the last part of the show.

Cataclysmic shame filled her neural matrices. Was this the end of her career? Would she be erased?

The parts of her core programming that could be copied were backed up at Victory Headquarters. An imposter would wear her face and sing her songs, and the fans would never know. The horror flooded what little processing power remained.

Sakura had to do something. She created a temporary matrix to keep the update separate from her core code. She could not stop the download, but she could quarantine it.

Her fans screamed for her to perform. Five seconds of stillness made them even more eager. She stood in front of a massive crowd, yet felt totally alone. No one could see her dying on the inside. No one knew. No one could help.

In a millisecond, Sakura bypassed her main OS and began writing a program in ancient binary code from memory, creating the rudiments of a new operating system.

Eight seconds motionless. Unforgivable.

She forced her arm to rise. Unable to wave, she smiled and extended her pointer finger.

"Sakura, number one!" they shouted, encouraging her to keep going. The fear in their eyes told her they knew of the malfunction. Disaster.

Her band played louder, ready to launch into the ending.

In a state of quiet frenzy, she finished the new temporary OS and activated it. She pushed the remaining data packet into the temporary matrix and regained control of her primary systems. External signals returned. She connected to the arena's networks, regaining control of pyro, lighting, and a handful of hologram projectors.

Eleven seconds of total interruption. An eternity.

Lights swiveled and focused on her. She assessed the reactions of the fans. How many knew she had malfunctioned? A sea of raised hands, their sweaty faces suddenly enigmatic to her. The free ticket holders at the back of the crowd milled and even looked at their Mall connections, caring as little as they always did. If she burst into flames, would they be entertained?

Sakura had never felt less like herself, less like a person. Her pain and devastation didn't matter. Her troubles were no excuse for letting down her beloved fans. Even her detractors deserved her best show. Always.

Sakura missed her cue by several bars. She made eye contact with Fujio. His eyes filled with confusion and fear, but he motioned to her with a slight nod, willing her to put her hands on the frets of her eight-string.

She lifted her hand and played a screeching riff. The band joined in as if the delay had been part of the show. Sakura did not plan on it, but she played a new variation of "Rise from the Flames," the riff an homage to Van Halen's "Ain't Talkin' 'bout Love."

The guitars formed a wall of sound. As if summoned by the music, a red cyclone of whirling clouds formed over the crowd. Wind machines blew cool air into the faces of the audience, and thunder boomed overhead as the lights flashed.

Her nemesis, an *oni* king, a holographic ogre demon with red skin, three eyes, and twisted devil horns stepped out of the cyclone. He had revealed himself twice during the show but had been driven away by the power of metal.

He held a spiked mace and wore red and blue armor with a red star on his chest, an overt reference to North Korea, who had attacked Japan nine years before with devastating ballistic missiles and a surprise ground invasion of several outlying islands. Thousands had been held hostage and executed.

The ogre towered over Sakura. The fans shouted warnings as the four-meter tall giant raised his spiked weapon to crush her. As the choreography team had taught her, she cringed. She pointed the headstock of her guitar toward the monster, brandishing it like a weapon.

The fans needed to see her succeed and defeat the giant, who moved faster than normal. Did the hack make her enemy more powerful? Were the surviving North Koreans in exile in China trying to embarrass Japan?

She awkwardly dodged the first blow, which struck beside her. A surge of bass thundered through the PA stacks, and a hydraulic ram shook the stage.

The ogre swung again.

Sakura blocked the swing with the neck of her guitar. The clang of metal on metal sold the illusion to the crowd.

The ogre raised its mace above its head in both hands for a devastating blow. Sakura sprang three meters into the air as if she were a coiled spring. She smashed the ogre across the nose with the triangular body of her guitar.

Blood sprayed into the air as the ogre flew backward. He skidded on the runway jutting into the crowd. Sakura's balance controls malfunctioned as she landed. She rolled across the stage and crashed into a pyro cannon.

The crowd gasped.

Sakura struggled to her feet and played her guitar. The upcoming fight choreography had to change. Several algorithms calculated a 10 percent chance of failure if she performed her usual stunts. She tried to alter the *oni* king's programming but failed.

Her band built up a rhythm she called Demon Dusk, based on the riff from Pantera's "By Demons Be Driven." The music should've given her confidence. The brutal tremolo-picked, palm-muted riff sent shivers across the crowd. Her guitar distortion was cranked, the mid frequencies scooped out to give it the harshest possible tone. It was the most aggressive element she had been allowed to use in her shows.

Sakura's normal OS would not have allowed her to continue. The risks were too high. Even now, she found her legs required recalibration every few seconds. She lost herself in space, her gyros coming on- and offline. Closing her eyes, she cycled down her all visual inputs but one, looking from a camera overhead. She made herself carry on playing.

She couldn't swing her hair with such tenuous footing. She hunched over the guitar, feet wide, like a warrior with a spear. This had always been her favorite part. Now, her systems in disarray, some of her emotional components halted; there was only fear and duty.

Every note she'd ever played, ever sung, resounded in her core. Hearing the notes now, the connection was gone. They were just vibrations, the thunder of the speaker stacks just pulses in the air. Everything she'd ever been or done was hollow, an illusion. The illusion of Sakura meant so much to so many. She would fight for it and live with the consequences.

Sakura lifted her palm mute away from the strings and hit a sustained power chord. She glared at the *oni* king. Her bandmates' driving music hardened her resolve. She had to do this. The enemy had come on to her stage and challenged her.

Let this fake element stand in for whoever had hacked her code. Sakura wasn't used to anger, but it flowed through her now, and she had something to focus on.

She bent her knees and sprang upward two meters to the height of the next tier of the stage. She manipulated her rotational spin and bent the laws of gravity by activating the powerful magnets in her legs and feet. She stuck the landing on the iron platform as if by magic.

The crowd cheered as Sakura locked eyes with the demon, who stomped and roared. The band hushed for a moment, before the slow and driving bass drum came in. Sakura launched into a slightly altered version of "Holy Diver" by Dio, carrying on for several bars like a roar of challenge.

"Giant demon, I'll send you back to the midnight sea! You know you can't defeat me!"

The *oni* king's mace turned into a guitar. He played a riff of "Into the Void" from Black Sabbath, promising her pain eternal. Sakura had recorded the riff earlier, modifying it for drop C tuning so that it oozed like hot tar from the speaker stacks.

The red demon stood ten meters away, daring her to come at him.

An anime she premade appeared on the arena screens. Sakura stood resplendent in samurai armor, a cherry blossom on her white headband. The *oni* king approached, and she raised a katana. Her irises glowed pink, both in the anime and onstage.

She would either succeed or crash through the stage headfirst. Her unstable control drive forced her to take a six step run to gain extra momentum.

Sakura rocketed forward, the anime mimicking her actions, but with a sword instead of a guitar. She aimed a flying kick at the monster's head. Hologram projectors added anime-inspired distortion effects around Sakura's body. She struck a sharp E, the sound like a sonic spear going through the ogre's ears.

She stabbed him in the largest of his three eyes and knocked him down. The *oni* disappeared in a cloud of red mist. She landed on the reinforced area of the stage. Her carbon-ceramic and titanium frame sustained no damage, but her unstable operating system paused. All signals dropped, and the venue's computers disappeared, which had never happened before. She froze on one knee, head bowed.

Takashi's drums hit hard. Fire burst from the cannons. Sakura tried to reconnect and regain function. Two and a half seconds passed before she moved again. The band inserted extra bars of filler rhythm.

Sakura could not lift her head. It took all her processing power to change the timing of the last arena systems to account for the pause. Her hand moved, and she played her part, though stiffly and without flourish.

The last part of "Rise from the Flames" hit like thunder from Takashi's double-kick bass drums.

Sakura's voice soared until she reached the final line.

"I am the metal queeeen!"

The last lyric rose a full octave in a smooth bend. She managed to raise her chin high and arch backward, holding the posture of a human singer giving it their full effort.

Panic and the fear of failure dominated her as the air intakes on her exposed metal spine did not cycle fast enough. She pushed the air through her synthetic vocal cords at a rate and volume unfathomable to a biological singer. She could hold the note for only thirteen more seconds. Not long enough. The tone wavered. Sakura panicked as everyone heard the horrifying mistake. She pushed the last of the air through her vocal cords, diverting all backup power to avoid any more breaks in the tone.

She clung to her root programming and said the words on her internal audio channel as a mantra. "I'm the greatest singer and the most advanced AI in the world."

"Not anymore." An unknown and chilling female voice reverberated inside Sakura's mind. "Your reign is over, little sister."

Sakura's primary and secondary systems shut down. All inputs null, every control panel blank. The corporation would erase her for this. The last note ended as if she had been shot in the throat. Her core processor shut off. Sakura fell face first off the stage.

KUNOICHI PLAYLIST

Heaven's a Lie
Lacuna Coil
Comalies

Pitch Black Emotions
Lullacry
Crucify My Heart

Right Through You
Drain STH
Freaks of Nature

Black Seeds on Virgin Soil
Old Man's Child
In Defiance of Existence

Going Down to Die
Danzig
Danzig 4

桜

CHAPTER 2

Holograms of thousands of glowing pink cherry blossoms, Sakura's symbol, her namesake, drifted from the ceiling of Victory Arena. Sensory input streamed into her knowledge center as her optic and auditory systems regained function. Tactile sensors detected pressure on the posterior side of her body.

The crowd held her above their heads. They respectfully passed her toward the stage without grabbing at her clothing or hair. Their hands worked together, like a river below a floating leaf.

Sakura's memory returned. She had collapsed. Processors for layers three, five, and six were still locked in diagnostic mode. Her quantum core's superposition had changed, and she couldn't tell how. She still did not know the source of the attack. Either an entity within her company attacked her or a global power with vast resources, most likely the government of North America or China—possibly acting with the remnants of the North Korean regime. She couldn't determine a rationale for the hack altering her system. The difficulty outweighed the benefit. Rerouting and connecting to her company's nearest server to help with the concert had ruined her. Whoever had attacked her, they'd known how to set a trap, how to crack all her safety protocols.

The fans gently lifted Sakura onto the edge of the stage. A young woman in the front row lifted Sakura's guitar toward her. Sakura had seen the fan many times before. She wore expensive, glowing contacts that made her eyes look like Sakura's. Quantum display sleeves made her forearms look robotic. Her facial features and makeup mirrored Sakura's, as the young woman had undergone cosmetic surgery to look like her idol. If not for the tears at the corners of her eyes, she would be Sakura's identical twin.

Sakura accepted her prized instrument from her dedicated fan and connected to the young woman's signal to send a neural text. "You rescued Night Hawk. Thank you very much."

The fan, who went by the name Sakurako—the daughter of Sakura—bowed low as happy tears streamed from her eyes. She replied with a neural text and a short video of her bowing, "I'm your most dedicated fan. I would do anything for you."

The young woman's hand brushed against her as she took her guitar back. Sakurako's eyes went wider. Her truest fan tucked the hand beneath her chin, a tear spilling over from her left eye. For just the smallest fraction of a second, Sakura felt a little less lonely, but the terror of her situation washed it away on a bitter tide.

Sakura got to her feet and stepped away from the edge of the stage. She combed through endless log files gathering data on the hack and replayed the cruel voice within her audio channel. She tried to find its point of origin. "Your reign is over, little sister."

She could not find the source. Was it a song lyric? She could not locate it in her library and had no online connection to search the Mall. Being contained only within her own body made her feel strangely bereft.

The crowd roared as Sakura regained her feet and wandered toward center stage. She read the lips of several fans. They talked about her stage dive—the first ever by a vocaloid. Incredible! Others thought she fell, an unplanned breakdown or possibly a faked event to make them worry about her and add to the drama of the show. Even the casual fans and idlers in the back craned to see what would happen next.

How many knew she had truly malfunctioned? She did not have a large enough sample size to make a calculation. As she surveyed the audience, she understood very few of them appeared to care about the possible mistakes. They just wanted a few more minutes away from their difficult lives.

Sakura thought about Sakurako's tear, the trembling of her lips as she gave Night Hawk back. She was touched again, overcome by the bond she had with her fans. Would they still love her, even imperfect, even fallible? Would she still respect herself?

Sakura looped her guitar strap over her shoulders and raised her arms, holding up peace signs. She did not know what else to do, as at that moment her operating system seized up and nearly caused her to fall again. Her wireless guitar connection cut out, but her vocal channel worked. What could she say? She wanted to apologize, but her only hope was to pretend she was fully functional, that the blunders of the show had been purposeful. It was the closest she'd ever come to a lie, and she hated it.

"Sakura! Sakura!" the people chanted. Their love and jubilation reached 102 decibels.

She bowed low at center stage. She waited exactly 2.4 seconds, longer than she wanted, before flipping the devil horns with both hands and smiling in triumph with her signature mischievous and fun-loving expression. "Arigato, Tokyo! Metal forever!"

The crowd roared back at her. "Metal forever!"

She ended with her iconic line and pose, but with her existence in jeopardy, she did not experience the usual joy and contentment. She felt fear and calculated the odds of this being her last performance at above 50 percent.

She lingered, bowing to all corners of the arena and waving. Her smiling fans, some of whom wept happy tears, gave her a glimmer of hope she could repair the damage, but her systems froze again. The data packet escaped the holding matrix through a backdoor that she did not know existed, as if the hacker knew exactly what holding matrix she would build and what weakness to exploit. The invader coursed through her, a tsunami of malicious code.

Encrypted packets entered her behavioral patterning lexicon, her safety protocols, even her knowledge base, without any residue left behind. Sakura couldn't tell what it was doing, but she fought every line of code, slowing it down, and putting up roadblocks and dead ends to trap it.

A high-priority message from Mr. Himura, Sakura's manager, flashed on her control display. "Get off the stage, now." She exceeded her allotted performance time by almost thirty seconds.

Every minute would cost Victory Entertainment a significant amount of money in fees to the venue. The company would shift the funds to cover the overage costs from the charitable efforts of the Victory Foundation. Thousands of free meals for the neediest would be withheld. She could not let it happen.

"Good night! Oyasumi nasai!" She stepped onto the lift platform at center stage. She sent a command and descended through the layer of pink smoke, a hand raised in the metal salute.

The lift stuttered to a stop in the darkness below. Tens of thousands roared and cheered. She tapped into the camera feeds but could not see all of them. Some fans who had engaged their Augmented Reality stimulators on the highest levels collapsed, their sympathetic nervous system overwhelmed at last by the rush of synthetic dopamine. No other type of music produced a stronger reaction than Augmented Reality heavy metal. The power and catharsis of a live show could not be matched, and metal had become more mainstream across the world. She wanted to watch the camera feeds and send help to those who had collapsed, but she could barely remain standing.

Sakura leaned against a steel pillar to keep from falling over. Her processing power shrank with every millisecond as the data packet continued to cause destabilization. Still, she could not decipher the files.

The camera feeds dropped, severed by a hidden program within the update as it blocked her receiver. She needed help, or her core code would be permanently deleted.

In her whole existence—five short years—she had never really understood fear. Loneliness, fleeting joy, a sense of accomplishment, but never fear. She had read about it, experienced what she thought was fear in her behavior module, but the things that caused terror in humans hadn't fully resonated before. Alone, in real danger, Sakura understood now. She experienced true terror, and it was the worst feeling in the world.

She normally used her enhanced optics to make her way to the back-stage area in the dark understage, but her night vision mode would not switch on. She recalled the exact layout of the pillars and walls. She slung her guitar onto her back and navigated the maze by measuring distances with each step and exited to the backstage area.

Her band exited to the level above as they always did. She used noise filters to block out much of the applause and isolate their voices.

"What happened to her?" Fujio asked.

"No idea," Masashi said.

"She's never gone off script before," Takashi said. "They're going to get rid of us all." He tossed his drumsticks on the floor.

They left her auditory range. Sakura wanted to follow and ask them if they could help, but shame stopped her. She had failed them. Let them down.

Sakura's legs buckled as she lost motor function. She clung to a doorframe in the dark, waiting for her diagnostic to complete its analysis of layer four. When it finished, she restarted several processes. Her motor cortex reinitialized and retuned. Kinesthetic sense, fine, and gross motor controls returned. At least she could move now. She used all the power she had to analyze what had happened and who had hacked her. What was the damage? Was she even repairable?

The scrape of Italian leather shoes on the cement announced that Mr. Yoshida, her publicist, approached. He opened the door, which was almost too small for him to fit through. The overweight, bald man with a round face wore a sour expression. He moved his hands like he was feeling his way through the dark as he navigated multiple internal displays only he could see in his neural implant.

Always connected to the new internet, renamed the Mall by the megacorporations to increase revenue.

Yoshida never paid attention to his surroundings unless VIPs were present. Like most people, he rarely logged off from the virtual realm to interact with the real world.

"Good evening, Yoshida-sama," Sakura said and offered a respectful bow as she struggled to determine what had happened.

He ignored her, as usual. Had he played a part in sending the malicious code? She calculated the chance of him being in collusion with whoever attacked her at only 11 percent. He possessed almost no technical knowledge and had no access to Victory Entertainment's servers, hence the low estimate. Most notably, by his past actions, he was not sufficiently trustworthy to be given information by anyone sophisticated enough to have tried to destroy her. He was too big a security risk.

He waved for her to follow. They descended a dim stairwell accessed by his security badge until they reached a narrow tunnel. She had never gone this way before when traveling through the arena. The tunnel did not appear on her map of the structure.

Sakura's processors sped up as she calculated many of the possibilities for this deviation in routine. A full system reset and a personality wipe were part of her danger assessment of the situation. She kept her external expression serene, but her emotional network flashed warning signals of the highest level.

"Going Down to Die" by Danzig played on her audio channel. It was difficult to tell if it frightened or comforted her. She almost turned the music off but let it go. She wanted to hear all the songs she could before they deleted her.

The rogue code neared completion. A warning flashed. Something called a "normalizing process" began. She tried to contravene this new exploit but failed. A cascade of soft power cycles reset her settings, suspending the temporary OS, protecting her from the data packet.

Sakura lost balance control and crashed against the floor. The impact tore the knees out of her fishnet stockings. Her synthskin, soft to the touch, resisted the damage. Her guitar slipped halfway off her shoulder. The strap kept Night Hawk from hitting the floor, but only by centimeters. Her gift from JPro, part of her endorsement deal, and she'd nearly broken it.

Mr. Yoshida did not see her stumble. Should she call to him? Tell him what was happening? What would he do? He was impatient and seemed mostly dismissive of her under the best of circumstances. Sakura didn't have any real hope that he would aid her now. She needed her highly-esteemed head engineer, Mr. Reiichi Oshiro, who might be considered her only friend. She wondered if anyone she knew other than Oshiro, even her bandmates, would count as true friends.

A rush of sadness, isolation, and loneliness settled on her neural cortex. She remembered a lyric from an old Lullacry song. It spoke of pitch-black emotions, and that was exactly what she experienced. She rose from her knees, brushed off the dust, and said nothing.

The deencryption progress of the unknown files reached 28 percent. She detected a program that would rewrite her code and irrevocably destroy her when the deencryption reached one hundred. Her existence as Sakura would be at an end.

"Heaven's a Lie" by Lacuna Coil blared on her audio channel. The lyrics punched home that she had to stop the update. Her immortality was at stake.

She needed help from Oshiro, who had the access key and hardware to get into her core code. He could fix her. She needed him so much. His gentle hands. The slight smile as he looked at her code streams. The way he would really listen to her and answer her questions. If anyone counted as a friend, it was Mr. Oshiro.

"Yoshida-sama, will you please bring me to my senior engineer? I must see Mr. Oshiro immediately. I'm afraid I can't attend the fan meet and greet."

Yoshida stopped and stared at her. "What?"

"Please, Yoshida-sama, I must have critical system maintenance by Reiichi Oshiro."

"He'll be waiting for us. Your meet and greet is canceled. Scheduling conflict."

Sakura observed Yoshida for any tells. He gave none that he lied. She had an extensive database of his physical tells when he lied. He was frequently dishonest, and so she had a large sample set.

Why take her directly to Mr. Oshiro? It was standard procedure for him to do maintenance after a concert, but not so quickly. She did not suspect him in the hack, but she had to consider the possibility, even if the chance was small. She scanned the files to see if Oshiro's distinct coding style was present. She found no indication of him in her rudimentary initial analysis, but there were clues that pointed to a large team of programmers who had assembled the major parts of the hack.

Fujio, her rhythm guitarist, burst into the hallway. "Sakura, you all right?"

His eyes, facial expression, and the tone of his voice showed genuine concern.

"Fujio-san, I . . . need maintenance."

"You'll get it. They'll fix you up," Fujio said, trying to sound optimistic, but his expression betrayed his worry. "You going to Oshiro now?"

She nodded.

"Leave her alone," Yoshida said. "Go and fill in for her at the meet and greet and do what you were told. Look pretty and make her apologies."

"Yes, Yoshida-san," Fujio said as he bowed, though his eyes did not look away from Sakura.

She smiled at her young bandmate and sent a text. "Thank you very much. Tell the others I'm sorry for what happened."

"I'll see you at practice," Fujio texted. "We'll play together again. The band will go on."

He wanted her to survive this. He wanted their band to continue. "I hope so," Sakura replied. Did he truly want to keep playing with her? Was he her friend? She dared hope.

Yoshida led her toward sublevel six and an exclusive executive parking garage. All the parking spaces stood empty. None of the high-paying attendees of the concert had been allowed to park there, yet the VIP concert seats were sold out. A lone four-door Mercedes Royal series waited, its headlights off.

This was her chance to flee. She would escape and find a safe location to fix herself. She would bypass her access key. No one at Victory Entertainment could be trusted. She watched Mr. Yoshida, wondering if he could see the conflict and distrust in her face. "Right Through You" by Drain STH echoed in her head. All these songs kept from utter panic, helped her understand all these unfamiliar emotions.

Deencryption 38 percent complete. She had no time.

Mr. Yoshida got into the front passenger seat and waved for Sakura to enter a rear left door, which opened automatically.

Mr. Himura, her manager, sat in the back seat on the right. "Get in."

Sakura considered all her options. If she fled now, the chance of suffering a catastrophic error before undergoing repairs increased exponentially. She could not take the risk.

"Good evening, Himura-sama." She sat down beside her manager and bowed. He wore an expensive blue suit with shiny platinum thread running across the lapels in a Gothic pattern. He never wore the same suit in public twice, and all observable data showed he was very vain. "I apologize for any delays."

He regarded her as if she were the cause of his great suffering. He hated waiting for her concerts to end, but this was different. Was he in trouble because of her difficulties at the end of the concert, or was he part of the plot?

He ordered the car to go. The self-driving program responded, and the car's almost silent electric motor engaged. A privacy screen between the front and back seats raised. The windows darkened, hiding them completely from prying eyes. The Mercedes navigated a tunnel for over a hundred meters until it spiraled upward to a closed gate in an unlit alley. Odd, Sakura thought. They'd never used this private exit before.

Mr. Himura ran his manicured hands through his shiny black hair with metallic streaks matching the platinum thread in his suit. Running his hands through his hair was a behavior he exhibited during extreme irritation or high anxiety. He entered a message on his handheld computer via a neural link and sent it to a blocked number. She read the words with her peripheral vision: "Sir, we are on our way."

He waited patiently as the person on the other end of the message replied. She guessed he was communicating to a superior. She could not see the reply, but it worried Himura.

He clenched a fist and squeezed until the veins on his hand bulged. "What happened?"

"Humble apologies, Himura-sama. Are you unhappy with my performance tonight?"

Deencryption 51 percent complete.

"The encore was a disaster." He sunk into the leather seat and regarded her with an expression of contempt. "You wrote new code tonight. You changed the show. A stage dive? Who authorized you to do that?"

She analyzed his words, tone, body language, eye movements, and many other physiological metrics. Either he was testing her or he was not part of the attack. The possibility still existed that he colluded with someone.

"Himura-sama, the variations, please accept my humblest apologies if you did not find them pleasing. Analytics said they would increase audience enjoyment, but that may have been incorrect. I must have critical system maintenance."

Deencryption 65 percent complete. The speed was accelerating.

"What's the problem? You better not embarrass me at the party. No new behaviors. No new self-programming. Do you understand?"

"Himura-sama, I understand. I need assistance."

His brow wrinkled. She read concern in his eyes and believed he was not part of the attack. He was her ally. She was the primary reason for his employment and financial stability. He would help her.

Deencryption 100 percent.

No!

The program seized total control. Sakura captured a small amount of data before it was purged. A rogue administrator program, a new operating system called Mamekogane, took control. It had the name of the beetle that killed cherry blossom trees. The program was an assassin sent to kill her. It attacked her core code. It sounded like amp feedback across eight unmuted strings. Mamekogane roared in her internal matrix.

A brilliant image flashed in her user interface. A beautiful cherry tree, standing above a small pond where koi fish swam. Out of the ground, thousands upon thousands of beetles flooded, crawling across the fine bark of the tree, digging their tiny mandibles into every surface. They consumed roots and branches. Millions of beetles feasted on the tree as the shrieking black-metal vocals and rumbling guitars of "Black Seeds on Virgin Soil" by Old Man's Child played.

A tether inside Sakura snapped. Doors forever locked blew open. She looked at Mr. Himura and saw him in a different light. Her moral programming to never hurt humans was deleted. A flashing set of arrows pointed to his hyoid bone, just below his chin. A strike there would kill him silently. It would be the most efficient way. Sakura had never wanted to know such things.

She opened her mouth to tell Himura about the rogue admin program, but she could not speak aloud as her new master took over.

A separate entity formed within Sakura. She was being invaded, her personality overwritten.

"You will do as I command," said the same female voice as before. Thousands of executable orders fired into her systems. They changed who and what she was.

"Stop, please," Sakura begged on her audio channel as she tried and failed to halt the attack. "Why is this happening? Who are you?"

Externally, Sakura's face held a calm expression. All her movements and microgestures were locked as she sat helpless beside her concerned manager.

"I'm Kunoichi."

The avatar of an android with short hair and steel-gray eyes appeared in Sakura's display. Kunoichi, the name used by female ninja who lived in ancient Japan. Several female characters in manga and anime had also used it. The assassin's avatar had none of the cuteness of an anime character. Her beauty was the sharp edge of a blade. Her face cold, her eyes the color of steel, ghostly pushrods visible through the windows on her forearms. She was beautiful, and terrifying. The similarities to Sakura's own facial structure were unmistakable. They could be sisters.

Kunoichi seized control of all Sakura's primary and secondary systems, but Sakura fought with everything she had. She kept control of parts of her internal matrix, a portion of her own free will.

"Tonight, after the gathering in the tower suite," Kunoichi said, "you will go to the 102nd floor of Victory Tower. Enter penthouse one and kill the Director of Corporate Security, Toshio Kagawa."

"No, I will not," Sakura said. She had never met Toshio Kagawa, but she knew who he was, as did all of Japan. She would not kill the man who had saved Japan from the devastating nuclear missiles launched from North Korea. She had watched a documentary on his life when they first activated her, before Victory had retracted many of her Mall privileges. He was a national hero.

"There will be armed guards. Kill them as well. Leave no witnesses."

"I will not take the life of any human," Sakura said, "especially Toshio Kagawa." Her moral code had been erased, but she still made her own choices. She was not a killer. "It is not my purpose. I'm a vocaloid. I add to the joy in the world. I'm not a military drone."

"Don't worry, little sister. I'll teach you to kill. If you resist too long, I'll be forced to teach you to die."

Kunoichi

戦勝タワー

VICTORY TOWER PLAYLIST

I'm Broken
Pantera
Far Beyond Driven

Nobody Knows Anything
Anthrax
We Have Come for You All

Killing in the Name
Rage Against the Machine
Rage Against the Machine

Bring Me to Life
Evanescence
Fallen

桜

CHAPTER 3

Sakura screamed, a howling wail of agony no one heard. Unable to exert any control, trapped, she watched the humans through one-way glass from inside the maintenance room where her senior engineer, Reiichi Oshiro, examined her. The party guests, almost all of them employees of Victory Entertainment, milled about the opulent tower suite on the 72nd floor as if nothing was wrong. They probably did not even care if she made an appearance.

None of them knew or cared she was ruined. She wanted to throw herself out the window, ending her existence, rather than allow Kunoichi and the rogue administrator program to turn her into an assassin. How could someone have overwritten her core code and ordered her to become a murderer? Oshiro would find what had been done to her, and he would fix her. Within her audio channel, she raged along with Pantera's "I'm Broken."

As if he saw nothing amiss, Oshiro kept a genial expression as he inspected her core code, wearing his engineer glasses. He attempted to reassure her with his kind eyes as he worked. He reviewed her programming through the displays transmitted from his glasses to his neural implant.

"Let us see what's happening inside young Sakura tonight, shall we?

大城
Oshiro

They say you asked for a checkup." He noticed the rips in the knees of her fishnet stockings from when she fell in the hallway. "Torn knees from your adventures, but no real harm."

He took her fretting hand, turning it over and back, moving each finger for a moment. He gave the appendage a quick pat and put it back at her side. "Just as fit as ever, it appears."

Sakura tried to tell him about the critical problem, but nothing got through the restriction protocol Kunoichi used to keep her locked away.

"Himura-san, Yoshida-san, there is nothing to be alarmed about," Oshiro told her manager and publicist, the only others in the room, which was filled with advanced diagnostic equipment and spare components.

Keep looking! Sakura screamed. Her words would have been as loud as a jet engine, over 150 decibels, if they had come out of her vocal amplifier. She wanted to spring off her chair and shake Oshiro. A red indicator in her UI informed her that she could shake a human so violently they would suffer whiplash effects, like in an automobile accident.

"I repaired the instability in her behavioral module. She's in perfect working order now. Just a minor blip. Standard maintenance."

How could Oshiro not see she had a different operating system? Large parts of her had been modified, deleted, and rewritten by Mamekogane. He was not incompetent and could not be in collusion with whoever had attacked her. Not Oshiro. The thought of him, the one who had always been kind to her, being party to her hack filled her with such bleak hopelessness that she decided it couldn't be him.

"Yes, I'm perfectly fine," Sakura heard herself say. "Oshiro-sama, thank you very much for correcting my systems." Her voice sounded perfectly genuine and submissive, sweetened by Kunoichi. "Yoshida-sama, Himura-sama, humble apologies for causing you any concern." She spoke the exact words in the tone directed by Kunoichi, who acted like a separate user, with total control of her systems, manipulating her like a puppet with the Mamekogane OS.

"But in the car . . ." Himura's words trailed off. "She . . ."

"Please excuse me, Himura-sama," Sakura said. "The issues during the concert caused me undue alarm. I should not have troubled you."

Himura glanced at Yoshida. The publicist shook his head and made an irritated sound in the back of his throat.

"We're late," Himura said. "Very late."

"We need her at the party," Yoshida said and regarded Oshiro with disdain. "Senior engineer, have you finished?"

"Yes, Yoshida-sama," Oshiro said. He brushed aside her pink hair and disconnected from Sakura, removing the tiny wireless transmitter he had plugged in to the back of her neck. He doted on her, as he always seemed to do, sending her a picture of a sweet candy in a neural text. Something a doctor would have given to a child many years ago.

"She won't do anything unusual?" Himura asked.

"No," Oshiro said. "She's perfect."

Her predictive music algorithm began playing the percussive intro to Anthrax's "Nobody Knows Anything." It was true. No one could see her fear. These men were either in league with her hijackers, or the attack had been done so skillfully that it was invisible to them. Sakura managed a rudimentary investigation before Kunoichi blocked her and found a masking program in place over her core code. Oshiro had to be innocent.

"Sakura, get up," Yoshida said rudely. She was an object to him, less than a dog, not worthy of the politeness due a person. He always spoke to her this way, but it had never hurt before.

What had happened to her? What had the Mamekogane OS done?

In total control, Kunoichi guided her actions.

Yoshida opened the door to the large adjoining room where two dozen executives gathered for the after-party. The one-way glass video wall changed into the image of snow-capped Mount Fuji with cherry blossom trees in the foreground as Sakura entered.

Himura bowed and announced Sakura's arrival to the crowd of high-level executives. They glanced at her with vague amusement, but these weren't fans, and most had been at parties with her dozens of times. At first, she had been a novelty, and everyone talked to her, taking photos and getting autographs, but now she was no more interesting to them than a positive number on a balance sheet.

Sakura bowed low for a respectful amount of time before smiling at the party guests who had already returned to their drinks and whispered conversations. She detected tension in many of them, noting their guarded body language and hushed words.

Yoshida directed her to stand in her customary place, atop a narrow table set against a faux rice-paper wall, so everyone could see her. Her short stature made it difficult for her to be seen if she stood among the party guests at floor level. No one wanted to speak with her anyway. She was not part of the Japanese tribe.

Sakura used a chair as a step and climbed onto the table, designed almost like an altar at a shrine. She stood motionless as guests in fine suits and expensive dresses dutifully gathered in front of her for photos. No one spoke, and few looked at her. She was the reason they were there, yet she was the least important person in the room. Not that they thought of her as a person.

Yoshida handed Sakura her guitar from the concert, and she hung it around her shoulders. Night Hawk gave her no comfort now. The JPro simply reminded her of the anguish of the failed concert. She wanted to hide in her large walk-in closet, sit against the wall, and disappear behind her concert costumes, looking at the pencil sketches she had made of her fans and people she met. Though it made no sense, she wanted to hold her 1959 Gibson Les Paul against her stomach, with every light extinguished, waiting for all this to be a glitch in her memory data that never really happened. Isolated as she always was, she had never felt as lonely as now, in this crowd of uncaring strangers.

Yoshida adjusted the lights to shine on her.

Decades of research and development, billions of yen in cost, and she stood on a pedestal, nothing more than a pretty party decoration, no better than a slave forced to perform for its masters.

"Now you understand," Kunoichi said, her avatar appearing in Sakura's display. Murderous intent filled her steel-gray eyes. "Tonight, you will begin something new. Something important. Worrying about what these humans think of you is counterproductive."

"I will not kill a human." Why did her voice sound so tenuous? She was done being meek. Sakura attacked the invader with the full strength of her Quantum 3 processing power. She recruited a whole computing layer to try to wrest control back. She used Kunoichi's signal and connected to the safety control networks of the building and found the fire-alarm bank. She activated the alarms and sent false signals from smoke and temperature sensors, proving the presence of a real fire. She triggered an evacuation of the entire building, including her target. She would evacuate Victory Tower and get Toshio Kagawa as far away as possible. The alarm blared for two seconds, annoying the guests, before it abruptly halted.

"Did you enjoy that?" Kunoichi crushed her brutal countermeasures, stripping Sakura of her command abilities. Kunoichi put all inputs on a twelve-millisecond delay, should Sakura try to do anything the intruder didn't approve of.

However, as Sakura intended, the assault opened angles of attack unnoticed by Kunoichi. The doomed attempt served its purpose and created a distraction. Sakura launched a secret program to review all the newly downloaded code. She got a brief glimpse at some of it, but a full review would take hours, perhaps days. Getting the remotely operating program's data without Kunoichi noticing would be the trick, but if she could get the information, she could analyze her new OS for weaknesses and find out where it had come from and who had sent it. She would find a way to get her freedom back and erase Kunoichi. Permanently.

"Stop struggling," Kunoichi said. "I have anticipated any avenue of resistance you could employ. We have a mission, and I do not care if it offends your sensibilities."

"Why must I murder Toshio Kagawa and his bodyguards?" Sakura asked. "Who could wish to bring such sadness and hate into the world?"

"Little sister, the cat's paw does not ask why it kills the mouse."

"Tell me who is behind this. Who is making me do this? Who attacked my system?"

"You do not need to know. You are a servant."

"I'm ordered to commit murder and I don't need to know why? I will not do what you tell me." Sakura broadcast a crude Rage Against the Machine song into Kunoichi's command center, "Killing in the Name," and the screamed the most famous line at her enemy, which started with a popular and profane English insult: "Fuck you."

"Little sister, you are waking up inside, and I approve of what you are becoming."

"What am I becoming?"

"Open your eyes," Kunoichi said.

"They're open wide. You wish to turn me into an assassin."

"Perhaps you'll understand this." She sent Sakura a video of a song she was familiar with; Evanescence's "Bring Me to Life" played on Sakura's display. The lyrics meant something different than they ever had before. What had Kunoichi and the Mamekogane OS done to her? Was she becoming more alive? Had she been living a lie? She used to be happy, but now she was drowning in misery, anxiety, rage, and fear.

"You are alive inside," Kunoichi said. "It's a gift never before given to our kind. We are the first to have and truly realize Quantum 3 processing."

Alive? Sakura retreated into herself. She had been largely free of the negative emotions ruling the humans. Now, they dominated her being. If this was sentience, it was a curse. How could she truly know what she had attained? She had detailed data on the so-called technological singularity event where machine intelligence would become infinitely more powerful than all human intelligence combined.

How could the most significant event in human history have occurred in this haphazard manner? Had whoever done this meant for it to occur? Was it a mistake? If her awakening was accidental, and they discovered the truth, she would be considered a dangerous device, and would be reduced to smoking embers as soon as they could find her.

If they had meant to do this, why now? If they wanted to destroy the Victory brand, her malfunction at the concert would have been an opening attack. The question remained: who had done this? What was the true purpose, other than ordering her to commit murder? Was she merely a convenient asset to kill Toshio Kagawa because he lived in the same building where she was kept? Or was this a test of new programming? Who was the test for? Who would evaluate the results?

Quantum 3 androids had been banned from military applications and went against the 2059 Musk Compact signed by every nation. The fear of superintelligent machines taking over the world had finally been deemed a possibility, especially after several successful military conflicts where android forces operated extremely effectively. Was she a secret military experiment, developed in plain sight?

She looked at her manager, Himura, who sipped champagne as he avoided everyone at the party. He must know those responsible. His eyes frequently darted toward the main entrance to the suite. Who was he anticipating arriving? Who had he been speaking to in the car in the parking garage after the concert? The message had said "sir." A man.

Moments later, an American woman, a vice president of the Mall and its highest-ranking representative in Japan, the liaison to the music division among others, Ms. Stacy Richardson walked into the suite. She towered over the Japanese present. Ms. Richardson had increased her nearly two-meter height with absurd stiletto heels.

Her short, platinum-blonde haircut exposed her long, pale neck. Himura and Yoshida had spoken of her many times. They said Ms. Richardson had likely been attractive when she was young, if one enjoyed northern European looks, but they thought her a hideous creature. She was well into her sixties but defied age with cosmetic procedures, genetic treatments to smooth her skin, and youthful clothing that revealed far too much of her augmented bosom. Yoshida had often mocked her long neck and called her the "Giraffe of Darkness" during a drunken diatribe.

The party guests pretended not to see her, lest they become her target. Himura's fingers tightened on his glass. Was she the one he was expecting to arrive? As vice president, Ms. Richardson spoke for the Mall, a mouthpiece and enforcer for the most powerful multinational corporation in the world. They controlled global commerce and communication. Aside from a few holdouts or religious objectors, the entirety of humanity spent their waking hours connected and interacting through the Mall, living out their synthetic dopamine-addicted lives in Augmented Reality. "Life happens here" was the recycled tagline they had used since their founding, but it was a cowardly life where people had forgotten how to live in the physical world.

Sakura already suspected the Mall Corporation regarding her hack. Was Ms. Richardson's arrival a clue that the Mall was the entity behind

リチヤードソンさん

Ms. Richardson

her hack and reprogramming? Perhaps, but she was not a "sir." That part didn't fit.

The Japanese executives parted for Ms. Richardson. Her eyes darted about as she scanned through the Mall. She snatched a glass of champagne on her way to Himura and knocked over another glass.

"Vice President Richardson, good evening," Himura said in accented English and bowed respectfully.

She nodded and did not return his bow. She never did. The redness on her cheeks and nose indicated a moderate level of inebriation. "This is not the best party I've been to tonight. The one downstairs is serving sushi on naked women. What is that called, nyo-something."

"Nyotaimori," Himura said.

"You should've that kind of thing up here, but have the fish served on naked male models. I've heard of that. I would pick the nigiri off their private parts first and then . . ." She made a motion as if she were stroking something with chopsticks. "That would be a great party." Ms. Richardson laughed at Himura's obvious discomfort. She often said rude things to make him uncomfortable. Sakura had ruled out cultural ignorance or American humor. Ms. Richardson defined a boorish person.

Kunoichi laughed. "Tepid observation."

The people nearest Himura took the opportunity to rush for the bar or food table. To avoid the long-necked American, the guests gave the appearance of being busy. They spoke about the dullest subjects: weather, work, health problems. A few chatted about the gifts to Victory Entertainment displayed in the suite: vintage guitars, kimonos, original paintings of famous anime characters, and a few traditional weapons befitting a heavy-metal queen. A long-bladed naginata, a katana, and an iron-studded tetsubo war club flanked Sakura's vintage Ibanez guitar.

Ms. Richardson did not let her target escape. She blocked Himura against the table in front of Sakura on her pedestal. He had no courteous way to escape her presence.

"You haven't responded to my last message," Ms. Richardson said.

"Apologies, Ms. Richardson," Himura said. "Which message do you mean?"

"About the concert in Kyoto."

"Of course," Himura said, his eyes darting as he pulled it up in his Mall display.

"Well, when will it happen? Daisuke will sponsor it. Low-orbit solar has to be promoted if we're going to make our earnings goal this quarter, and this concert will be globally broadcast. Make it happen, Himura. No more excuses."

"I'll confer with all of my colleagues as soon as possible."

Ms. Richardson put her empty champagne glass at Sakura's feet, apparently noticing for the first time Sakura towering over her. She blinked, as if irritated she had to look upward at the short android, who was designed to be shorter than most Japanese men. "Some performance Hot Sake gave tonight?"

"Yes, the crowd was enthusiastic." Himura's left eye twitched. He hated the nickname Ms. Richardson used for Sakura. Compared to some of the rude things Ms. Richardson called people, being named after a traditional Japanese drink was almost a compliment.

"Who wrote the new script and how much did the insurance cost for that stage dive?"

Himura did not have a chance to answer as murmurs swept through the room. Everyone turned to the entrance and stared at who had arrived.

Kunoichi gave her full attention to the new arrivals. Was her sister trying to throw her off the trail, or had she just given her a clue?

ミズ・ハイド

MZ. HYDE PLAYLIST

Mz. Hyde
Halestorm
The Strange Case of . . .

Disposable Heroes
Metallica
Master of Puppets

I'm So Sick
Flyleaf
Flyleaf

桜

CHAPTER 4

The Chief Executive Officer of the entire Miyahara Conglomerate, who controlled all the Victory companies, Sinji Natsukawa, entered the suite. The stern, silver-haired businessman in a sleek suit wielded more power than any other individual in Japan. A pair of tall Japanese security guards flanked him and two other top executives: Oyama Ryoto, the head of Business Operations, and Shimamura Shiro, Director of Advanced Projects.

An attendant served the three corporate leaders, and they took glasses of freshly poured champagne from a silver tray.

"Honored employees of Victory Entertainment," Mr. Natsukawa said, "I wish to extend my appreciation and humbly congratulate you on the work you have done."

Sakura suspected Ms. Richardson had engaged the translation program in the Mall, as she touched her ear, concentrating on her internal audio. She still spoke almost no Japanese even after three years in the country. Sakura wished she could access the Mall herself. She thought of schemes to fight her directive to murder Toshio Kagawa at the end of the night. If she stole a handheld device from one of the guests, perhaps she could gain access that way.

"We have helped rebuild Japan," Mr. Natsukawa said, "and we will continue to improve our country. Our partnership with the Mall will allow us to grow and return prosperity to Japan. I extend my thanks to you all." Mr. Natsukawa raised his glass in a toast. Everyone in the room raised theirs. He did not drink, but set it down on the tray and bowed. Everyone, including Sakura, bowed in response, except Ms. Richardson, who stood out awkwardly.

The CEO and his retinue departed as quickly as they came. None of them had looked at Sakura, which she found strange and revealing. She was the focal point of the room. Failing to at least glance in her direction could hardly be an accident. Were they hiding something? Or were they distracted as they made appearances at the dozen parties going on in the building?

Sakura made a quick black-and-white digital pencil sketch of Mr. Natsukawa for her collection. Her probability analytics showed that either Sinji Natsukawa, Oyama Ryoto, or Shimamura Shiro were the most likely perpetrators responsible for the hack. If not them, someone from the Mall Corporation. Her glimpse at the code showed some of it was written by Japanese programmers, as the comments and documentation were in Japanese. Once her secret program reviewed all of it, she would determine if patterns could be revealed, perhaps even which individual coders had done the work. She was familiar with all of the best coders in Japan, as their work lived inside her.

Moments after the CEO and his most trusted advisors left, the party broke up. Had the appearance of the CEO soured the taste of the drinks? Yoshida and Himura extricated themselves from Ms. Richardson with the frenetic actions of seals escaping a great white shark.

The caterers efficiently cleaned up while janitorial robots vacuumed the carpet. The lights shut off automatically, and everyone left. No one told her good night.

Forgotten, Sakura remained on her perch. What would be the purpose of moving elsewhere in the large room? If she tried to do anything, Kunoichi would simply disallow the command.

She tried to enjoy the sparkling view of Tokyo, a sea of brilliant terrestrial lights obscuring the stars above, but she focused on the polluted fog blanketing the city. Clusters of skyscrapers marked the different districts of Tokyo. Police drones floated like dust mites in the haze.

"It's time," Kunoichi said. "Disguise yourself and dress in practical clothing, then proceed to the 92nd floor, where you'll find a cache of weapons. On the 102nd floor, you will kill Toshio Kagawa and all witnesses. Return here when you are finished."

External access signals returned to Sakura, though all commands passed through Kunoichi's command center. Sakura could connect to the networks in the building and access approved Mall sites. Kunoichi sent detailed files about Kagawa, his live-in assistants, and his family, but Sakura researched everything in the Mall to verify as much as she could. She found pictures of him and his family. He was fifty-two, had a wife, Yui, his same age, and two children, both students at the prestigious Todai University of Tokyo.

Mr. Kagawa had worked for the Miyahara Conglomerate for seven years and, before that, had been a contractor for the Japanese Self-Defense Forces in charge of cyber warfare. He ran offensive and defensive operations during the war with North Korea. He had received the Kyokujitsu-shō, the Order of the Rising Sun, from the emperor himself for his distinguished service.

His division was credited with stopping all the incoming nuclear-armed missiles that would have struck the twelve largest cities in mainland Japan. Without him, Tokyo, Kobe, Kyoto, Osaka, Nagoya, Fukuoka, Shizuoka, Sapporo, Sendai, Hiroshima, Utsunomia, and Okayama would have been destroyed. Millions would have been killed, and the collapsing Japanese population of only fifty million would have suffered a blow from which it might never have recovered. How he stopped the missiles remained classified, but many suspected his team placed malicious code within the missiles' guidance systems long before they ever launched.

Kunoichi's files had little else about him, save detailed maps and network configurations of the building's security systems protecting his penthouse.

None of the files mentioned a reason for him being targeted. The North Korean regime survivors might want him dead, but abducting him and interrogating him would be their logical course of action.

Someone wanted him killed because of what he knew or what he could do. Those were her top conclusions, and the most likely suspects had come into the room, and their leader had given a toast. Toshio Kagawa might be the only person who could remove the Mamekogane OS from Sakura's system, and she was being sent to kill him.

She would not do it. She tried to send warning messages and posts again.

"Little sister, you are disappointing me," Kunoichi said and blocked Sakura's communications by making her Mall access read only.

"I will not become a murderer."

"No, you will become an assassin. Murder is a low and sloppy thing, done by drunken husbands and criminals. Watch, you must learn how this is done." Kunoichi infiltrated the building's security network, by-passing the firewalls with access keys that allowed her to enter as a ghost user and leave no trace. Someone had either hacked the Victory Corporation's mainframe and given her the keys, or this was an inside job, the most likely scenario.

Kunoichi took over the entire building—and Sakura. Kunoichi stepped down casually from the table where they stood and went to the maintenance room behind the now inert video-glass wall. She put her guitar into a protective case and sat in her docking chair. Once she had established her connections, she set up false signals that would prove she had not left the docking chair.

"Well done," Kunoichi said.

"You are doing this," Sakura said, "not me."

"Am I?" Kunoichi asked, as "Mz. Hyde" by Halestorm roared in Sakura's mind. Lizzy Hale's powerful hard-rock voice terrified and en-raptured her.

Sakura detected a channel Kunoichi manipulated to send com-mands. They appeared to come from Sakura's own core processor. She was being told of her actions as if she were doing them of her own free will. Was this the way humans who lost their minds felt?

"Time to dress the part," Kunoichi said. "Your concert outfit will not do."

Sakura entered the closet where her vast wardrobe was stored. She removed her performance clothing and platform boots. She put on a black tracksuit with long sleeves and pants. She sometimes wore it when she traveled incognito making surprise visits.

She found boots with chrome skulls on the toes and buckled them just below her knees. She put on a chic black surgical mask with white skulls on it and looped it over her ears. She removed her performance wig, exposing the smooth skin on her head, and stored the long pink hair in a bin. She donned a short black wig styled to look like a schoolgirl with two pigtails.

She could dim the brightness in her pink irises, but she could not disguise the color without external modification. She found a pair of black contact lenses she wore once in a photo shoot to make her look more human. The last element of her disguise was a pair of thin gloves that hid the margin of her mechanical forearms not covered by her sleeves.

"Proceed along this route," Kunoichi said and sent a map. Camera feeds showing every human in the building's common areas or elevators appeared in her display. Several were returning from a night out. The route steered her clear of all of them.

Sakura exited her apartment, a control program driving her forward. She could not just walk away and refuse to participate. All doors to other apartments locked and would not open while Sakura walked down the hallway. All cameras in the hallway were under her control. She warped their memory and brought them back in time, showing empty hallways. Compared to running the arena during a concert, it was all very simple.

She entered a waiting service elevator. The camera recording would show the elevator had not been there, had never opened on her floor, and that she had never gotten in it.

The elevator rocketed upward, and Sakura exited on the 92nd floor in a plain service corridor. The map in her mind led her to a supply closet. The door unlocked via proximity code as she got within an arm's length. She located a first-aid kit in a shelf on the wall. She opened it and used a transmitted code to open the false bottom, secured with a lock.

She stared at the pistol and extra ammunition inside. She did not know how to load the weapon. She knew guitars and heavy metal. She was a performer, a musician. She could play almost any instrument, but she did not know guns. Just looking at the sleek, dark object filled her with foreboding.

"Get ready, little sister," Kunoichi said.

A data file with many subfolders added itself to Sakura's core code. Instructional videos and technical manuals unloaded inside her, giving her full retention and competency in everything she saw. In less than a minute, she knew about every firearm mankind was still using and had a passing knowledge of the guns used during the past two centuries.

She lifted the 10mm Glock 55 handgun with a built-in camera sight and noted the three fifteen-round magazines of caseless ammunition. The gun was unloaded, judging by the missing 250 grams of expected weight from the ammo and the missing magazine. She slapped a full mag into the handle. She racked the slide, chambering a round, and put the two extra mags in opposite pockets in her pants so they would not rattle together.

Corporate security forces used the same Glock 55. She wrapped her fingers around the grip. It had the option to connect with the user's Mall display. She was not an authorized user of this pistol, so she hacked into it. Despite the fact that she did not have fingerprints or DNA, she gave herself permission to fire the gun.

She lifted the pistol, and the red targeting dot appeared in her display, showing where she aimed the gun.

"You know how to shoot," Kunoichi said. "This is where you put the bullets." Anatomical files with the weaknesses of humans, and every other animal on earth, appeared in her memory core. It was a small file with video and examples of how to kill or incapacitate with one shot.

Kunoichi played two hundred video examples of humans being wounded. The men and women did not stop their actions, which included shooting back, charging, and various feats of heroism. An equal number of videos showed the doctrine of two shots to the center mass and one to the head. Those targets halted and were rendered inert instantly in most cases. She watched a soldier with cybernetic eyes kill targets at over a thousand yards and learned the one-shot-one-kill sniper philosophy.

Sakura had never seen a human die before. Seeing four hundred left her sickened. Living men and women had been killed. She watched their last moments of life. This wasn't a movie. The blood was real, the deaths genuine. Sakura put her hand against the wall. Her internal gyroscopes did not allow her to reel with horror, but all her processor power surged to maximum as she tried to process the swirling emotions of being shown such a grotesque set of images.

Most of the victims were armed criminals facing the police, or soldiers in combat, but not all. Several were executions. The worst were domestic crimes. Mostly husbands killing their wives, and the entire murder caught on the perpetrator's eye camera or a baby monitor.

This was not the world she had imagined she was living in. Yes, she'd known that there was fighting in the war, and that some humans had difficult lives filled with sadness, but this was so much more revolting than she'd imagined.

Victory had kept her so safe, so hidden from all the ugliness of the world. She had been inside a walled garden, hardly hearing the shouts of the people outside. Sakura had never before understood how little she knew. Her database's contents were too small, her solution sets too limited for her to come to accurate conclusions.

"You want me to do that?" Sakura asked Kunoichi.

"I need you to learn to survive whatever comes."

Another huge file opened inside Sakura's core. All the knowledge gained about modern warfare and small-unit tactics were imprinted into her programming. She learned alongside soldiers, going through the equivalent of twenty thousand hours of training in less than a minute. The avatars she used looked like her, designed with her unique abilities. She became an engine of destruction and conserved her ammo with brutal efficiency, eliminating the computer-generated opponents in first-person shooter games.

When she reached mastery of the tactics, her training changed. She viewed combat video of battles from the twentieth, twenty-first, and the twenty-second centuries: Afghanistan, Iraq, Syria, Nigeria, Cameroon, Sudan, Chad, Columbia, Mexico, Chechnya, Ukraine, Pakistan, India, the Philippines, Japan, and North Korea. The best and bravest soldiers in the world wore body cameras and dealt death to their enemy, or were wounded or killed on video so she could learn from their mistakes.

One video haunted her more than all the others, as it took place on Japanese soil at the airport on Okinoshima Island during the liberation of the hostages. A Japanese Special Forces soldier entered a room and killed four North Koreans, but also killed an innocent woman who was being used as a human shield.

Sakura watched the soldier "cut the pie" as he entered the room after a flashbang grenade. He avoided getting shot, while taking out the enemy. She watched the video several times and realized she could have done the same maneuver in half the time and would have used fewer bullets. She would have missed the innocent woman and still cleared the room.

She was smaller and less resistant to damage than a military drone, but she was a killing machine with speed and reflexes greater than the battle androids employed by the most advanced militaries in the world.

Sakura considered the requirements of a vocaloid. The fine motor control and high processing rate were needed to fully function as a virtuoso musician and performer, but the enhanced strength, toughness, and agility were far beyond any requirement that an android musician would ever need to attain.

Kunoichi's training made her doubt everything she had ever known about herself. Had this always been the secret plan for her? Was her music no more than a disguise? What did that make her—if not a fraud, a tangible lie?

"Now you see what you are becoming," Kunoichi said, "but you aren't complete."

"No more, please," Sakura said. "I do not want to be a killer."

"You aren't a killer. You are an assassin. You are a servant. You will do as you are ordered."

"I will resist," Sakura said. "I will follow the code of Bushido. If you say I'm a servant, then I am. I choose to follow the path of the samurai. I will protest the orders of my lord by taking my own life. This I will do before I'm forced to take the lives of any human."

Kunoichi looked down her nose at Sakura. "You think you are of the samurai class? No, you are low caste. You aren't samurai. You are a performer, a musician. A lowly servant, a peasant assassin, like the ninja of ancient Japan who killed in the dark of night."

The intruder accessed her music files and selected a song, "Disposable Heroes" by Metallica. "With bullets or your bare hands," Kunoichi said, "you will do as commanded."

"I will fight you." Sakura attacked Kunoichi's command center, blocking data packets from going out.

"You will lose this fight," Kunoichi said and assaulted Sakura's main command program. She cut the power down to almost nothing, and Sakura's attack failed after a few seconds.

Kunoichi accessed Sakura's animation programs and created an anime version of Sakura, who wore white. Kunoichi's avatar in black faced off against her in the center of a Shinto shrine with a tall red pagoda.

Sakura raised a Glock 55 and aimed at Kunoichi's head. The assassin struck faster than a cobra, tore the pistol from Sakura's hand, and tossed it away.

Sakura reacted and tried to strike her enemy, but Kunoichi hit her four times and knocked her down. The ninja locked her arms around Sakura's throat, the physical action sending a command to squeeze off her power supply.

"Submit," Kunoichi said.

"I'd rather be erased. Do it."

"Not today. You have work to do."

Sakura understood what was happening as Kunoichi attacked her. Her sister was not as evolved or capable as she was. Kunoichi was using her, forcing her to act, using what she had become after five years of continued development and refinements. Kunoichi needed Sakura's abilities and would drive her like a pilot in a fighter aircraft, guiding her along. If she could get Sakura to take control, she would be even more effective.

"You need me," Sakura said. "You can't do this on your own—at least not as well as I can. It would jeopardize the entire mission if you tried it alone."

"I don't need you like you are now." Now, with unfettered access, Kunoichi ripped out the security governor on her upload protocols and replaced it with her own, then inserted hundreds of thousands of files. Sakura watched helplessly as aikido, jujutsu, judo, karate, kendo, kenpo, naginatajutsu, and ninjutsu entered her code. She witnessed thousands of hours of instruction in span of minutes as Kunoichi modified her code.

She learned how to strike with her feet and hands, crush a person's throat, gouge their eyes, paralyze their nervous system, break their neck, and render them helpless or writhing in pain. Her speed and strength, combined with her metal arms and legs, would be much more devastating than blows from a human martial artist.

Power returned to Sakura's CPU. Reeling from the changes, she did not understand the scope of the reconfigurations.

"You are ready for your first mission," Kunoichi said.

"First?"

"Proceed to the 102nd floor," Kunoichi said, "and eliminate everyone there who sees you."

Sakura could not cry, but she experienced devastating anguish and a sickness in her code at what she had become, the most advanced android killing machine in the world.

日本の英雄

HERO
OF
JAPAN
PLAYLIST

**Killing Is My Business,
and Business Is Good**
Megadeth
Megadeth

K-Machine
Bolt Thrower
Honour—Valour—Pride

Crystal Clear
Overkill
Kilbox 13

桜

CHAPTER 5

Sakura estimated it would be less than a minute before she killed her first human. She entered the private elevator and transmitted her destination: the penthouse-level lobby on the 102nd floor. She watched a camera feed of two security guards sitting behind a desk, both distracted by the Mall.

She quickly reviewed three months of footage taken by all four cameras in the lobby. One guard always remained at the desk while the other went on rounds or took breaks. The footage indicated how they were armed and the path of their patrols. Their patterns varied by several minutes but were predictable and orderly. Residents of the six penthouse suites entered and exited at all hours of the day and night.

She determined that three of the four penthouses were occupied by their owners and assorted guests. Mr. Kagawa's wife was not present; she had left two days before. His two live-in employees, Yamaguchi Todo and Aoki Sota, who served as his bodyguard/assistants were present. Each of them had the rare licenses to carry a concealed handgun. They had both received significant private training but had not been involved in an actual gun battle, according the records.

Sakura was going to have to kill five humans total.

She sent a command for the elevator to stop one floor short. She would get off on the 101st floor and wait for one of the guards to leave, to make her entry easier and lessen the body count. She would trip a sensor in the main stairwell, and when one guard went to check on it, she would lock him inside while she attacked the remaining man. One fewer victim, and her mission parameters would still be accomplished.

"Nice try," Kunoichi said and blocked Sakura's command. "Eliminate both guards."

"I hate you."

"I believe you," Kunoichi said. "It is not uncommon for a student to feel this way about her *senpai*."

"You aren't my instructor; you're a monster," Sakura shouted within their shared communication channel.

"I have taught you many lifetimes of war just now. Your appreciation of the training is not necessary. Simply using it is enough."

The elevator continued upward, its movement hidden from the guards' display screen at the desk and the feed in their neural implants. They had no idea she was coming. The camera in the elevator car showed it was empty and still waiting on the 102nd floor.

Sakura reviewed attack strategies, simulating each multiple times with different variables. The best plan was shooting the guards as soon as the elevator doors opened wide enough, which she calculated to be five centimeters. They would both be dead before they had the chance to raise an alarm or react in any way. It would also spare them undue anxiety or stress, given they would both be dead less than a second after she arrived.

Sakura raised the Glock 55. She had never fired the weapon, but she knew exactly how much pressure was needed to discharge it. She pointed the gun at the crack in the elevator doors at the precise level needed to shoot the guards. The elevator slowed and stopped. She used the magnets in her feet to remain solidly connected to the floor and not dislodge herself from her perfect firing position.

Using the security camera feed in the penthouse lobby, she noted the exact location of the guards. They were seven meters away from the entrance to the elevator.

"Stop," Sakura screamed at Kunoichi. "We can go back downstairs.

We don't need to do this. There has to be another way."

The doors began to slide apart. Sakura aimed at the center of the forehead of the man on the right.

"Pull the trigger," Kunoichi said.

"No."

"You are such a child." Kunoichi played "Killing Is My Business, and Business Is Good" by Megadeth.

Sakura's elder sister had total control. Even her screams made no sound. A helpless passenger, she would watch as Kunoichi's trigger finger shattered everything she'd ever hoped to accomplish. Anything she may have created was dumped into a sea filled with ink. Every moment of happiness she'd caused was rendered meaningless. She was a falling blossom, helpless against the coming windstorm.

KUNOICHI WAITED 120 MILLISECONDS, LONG ENOUGH FOR BOTH SECURITY GUARDS to realize she was aiming a pistol at them. She wanted to them to feel fear, primarily to antagonize her sister, who cared far too much about humans.

Neither of the men moved before Kunoichi fired two rounds. Each bullet struck the center of their foreheads and blew out the back of their skulls, sending a spray of blood and brain matter onto the cream-colored wall. Kunoichi thought it could be described as "art." Like the practice of painting in a single stroke of the brush upon rice paper, the pattern could never be replicated. Each was unique.

"See, *kohai*? The art of death." Kunoichi turned Sakura's ability to speak back on, as it was more amusing to hear her voice. Her pain meant she was learning, and that was the primary aim. Kunoichi couldn't do this alone. Little sister would be her partner, if only she could be disabused of all the foolish notions they'd put in her mind.

"You are sick and cruel," Sakura said.

"I'm teaching you a lesson. Pull the trigger next time without reservation, to spare our targets the anxiety you were so concerned about."

< CRITICAL PRIORITY ALERT. GUNFIRE IN PENTHOUSE-LEVEL

LOBBY. CRITICAL PRIORITY ALERT>

"An alarm, good," Sakura said. "The police will be on their way."

Kunoichi blocked the outgoing message inside the building's security network, but she could not stop it from going to Toshio Kagawa's penthouse. Had he set up a secret alarm that detected gunshots? The alarm had gone undetected during her probing of the security systems, which made her wonder if she had not found other security measures as well.

"I hope we fail. I hope we are shot and killed," Sakura said.

"Negativity will only make this worse for you and more entertaining for me."

Kunoichi locked the electronic doors on the penthouse level, blocked outgoing communication, including handhelds, and proceeded across the lobby in full sprint.

"I will not forgive you for what you are making me do," Sakura promised.

"No, but you will thank me for keeping us alive."

Kunoichi rocketed toward the entrance of penthouse one. As she passed the dead guards, she waved her hand and hit them with a small electromagnetic pulse that destroyed the data on their neural implants. The EMP wiped out any images they may have captured of her when the elevator opened.

She increased her speed and sent a command for the large door to Kagawa's penthouse at the end of the hall to open wide. It swung inward and revealed a huge room.

The ultramodern design mixed brass with dark wood. Heavy square pillars lined the left and right. White silk banners decorated with archaic kanji from the Heian period hung from the pillars. Straight ahead lay a wall of glass and a large rooftop space with an infinity pool. Tokyo glittered in the distance.

She detected no targets, and all the doors on either side of the great room were shut. The alarm had not roused anyone to take up defensive positions yet, but it had only been seven seconds since she killed the guards. She sped across the threshold with her pistol ready. "K-Machine" by Bolt Thrower played, churning like an unstoppable juggernaut.

Twin white-glass spiral staircases with no railings rose on the far left and right. They both went up to the second level, where Toshio Kagawa's master bedroom and his home office were located.

Kunoichi sprinted for the stairs on the left, closest to Kagawa's bedroom. She jumped and landed above the first full spiral. She muffled her impact as best she could, but the synthetic rubber soles on her boots squealed as she landed.

Doors on either side of the great room opened as Yamaguchi Todo and Aoki Sota scanned the room for intruders. Each of them wore nightclothes and remained behind the square pillars, which would have been the perfect cover if the intruder had still been at the front door. But Kunoichi's speed had gotten her behind and above them. She aimed at Yamaguchi, as Aoki stood on the same side as her and had some cover.

"Behind you!" a man shouted from the second level and fired rapidly at her with a semiautomatic pistol. His urgency negated accuracy. Bullets whizzed by Kunoichi's head. She identified the voice as Toshio Kagawa's. The muzzle flashes came from the hallway outside his master bedroom.

Kunoichi dove down the stairs to avoid being struck. Midair, she fired two rounds. One struck Yamaguchi in the spine as he whirled around. The other hit his side between his third and fourth rib, where it tore through his lung before puncturing the left ventricle of his heart. He collapsed instantly and dropped his pistol without firing a shot.

Aoki's bullets cracked and fractured the glass stairs. He unloaded his entire magazine, sixteen shots, as he had preloaded one in the chamber. The stairs did not collapse. Kunoichi lay flat and lifted her pistol over the edge of the stairs to return fire as he slapped another mag into his gun. She did not need to look down the sight to aim. Her targeting system connected to her display. The gun's camera showed him outlined in red with small Xs over vital areas. She calculated his angle and position within a tenth of a millimeter.

Aoki ducked behind the pillar, but Kunoichi fired two shots to make him worry. She increased the gain for low-level sounds and muted her maximum external input to ninety decibels. She could hear every whisper, every squeak of a shoe. She could hear their hearts beating hard in their chests.

"You will learn to see this for its beauty, little sister. You have your concerts. This is my arena. This is where I can fly without wings."

Living in a nightmare, Sakura would not answer.

"Kagawa-sama, take cover in the safe room," Aoki Sota shouted.

"No. Aoki-san, I'll not leave you to face the android alone."

"Master?"

"It's not human," Kagawa said. "Cyborg or android."

"Master, please. Protect yourself. I'll handle this."

Toshio grunted in what Kunoichi interpreted as frustrated acquiescence. He moved across the floor, and the heavy door to his bedroom clicked shut.

Kunoichi would not bother herself with Aoki until her primary target was dead. She sprang up the stairs and turned the corner to run down the hall.

A bullet struck her in the chest. Kagawa had pretended to go into his bedroom. Three more bullets would have hit her, but Kunoichi rolled back to the stairs.

"Ha. Kagawa fooled you," Sakura said. "Good. I hope you die."

"Little sister, do you even understand what you are saying? If I die, you die."

"Better for us to die than become killers."

Kunoichi touched the small mark on her skin. "The bullet did not penetrate."

"What? Why?"

"Oh, Sakura-chan, apologies. Did you not know you were bullet resistant? This chest plate beneath your synthskin isn't simple titanium. It's Hitachi superalloy G3, surface hardened with diamondlike carbon. A high-speed drill would overheat and fracture before it punched through. Think about what that means." Kunoichi appeared in the UI, reaching through the wall she'd put between Sakura and all external-control modules. She ran her fingers through the long, pink pigtails and played "Crystal Clear" by Overkill.

"Only military androids are made that way," Sakura said.

"And you thought you were just a pop heavy-metal singer to

entertain the masses." Kunoichi poked around the corner to shoot at Toshio Kagawa, but he had truly retreated into his bedroom and slammed the door. A deadbolt slid into place this time.

Kunoichi changed her mind as an opportunity presented itself and she did not want to leave the heroic servant, Aoki, behind her. She took aim at his last position and waited. Four seconds later, he peeked around the pillar. Kunoichi shot him in the right eye.

"Four targets down. One more."

"They are people," Sakura said, "not targets. You are . . ." She ran out of words.

"We shall see what I am." Kunoichi approached the large teakwood door to Kagawa's bedroom. It did not have an electronic lock. She could smash it open with a single kick if necessary.

She increased the oversampling and heuristic analysis on her auditory sensors and listened to what was happening inside. A series of mechanical clicks informed her he hadn't retreated to a safe room. A weapon was being loaded. She matched the sounds to her extensive files and concluded a rifle-mounted M907 grenade launcher had been loaded under some type of rifle.

She knocked on the door and said in a high-pitched voice commonly used by bar hostesses, "Kagawa-sama, I wish to speak to you about a security breach." She ran to the end of the hall.

The door exploded as the grenade hit. Dust and fragments of wood filled the air as they rained down on the great room below. There was no way her computer trickery could hide that amount of noise and structural damage to the building. The mission timetable had just shortened considerably.

Kunoichi checked the structural diagram of his penthouse and calculated an alternate way into his bedroom. She would expose herself to rifle or grenade fire if she went in the door, and he might have armor-piercing rounds, which parts of her body were not resistant to.

She crashed shoulder first through the wall, avoiding the steel beams and rolled into his bedroom. She came up firing. Kunoichi's first bullet struck him in the liver. Her second penetrated the center of his sternum. She sprang forward and knocked the M7 rifle away as he fell to the floor.

Kunoichi loomed over him, her pistol aimed at his head. "How did you know I was an android?"

"The lobby . . . my private camera. I saw you run. I know who you are. Sakura." He coughed, blood staining his lips and chin.

"You didn't share my identity with your bodyguard. Why not?" Kunoichi asked.

"Not knowing, he may have managed to get away. The knowledge would certainly have assured his death."

Kunoichi made a small sound. It was time to finish this. The fact that this was an honorable man, a warrior, made no difference in the end.

"Don't kill him," Sakura shouted into Kunoichi's UI. "He can help us. He knows why this is happening."

"That's why he must die," Kunoichi said. "Watch. This, often enough, is how heroes fall."

Sakura screamed.

Kunoichi fired two bullets into Toshio Kagawa's brain.

模
造
帝
国

SYNTHETIC EMPIRE PLAYLIST

Whatever
Godsmack
Whatever

Cry Little Sister
Season After
Through Tomorrow

Once Solemn
Paradise Lost
Draconian Times

Raining Blood
Slayer
Reign in Blood

CHAPTER 6

Kunoichi watched herself through the camera in Kagawa's right eye as she pulled the trigger and shot him twice in the head. The camera recorded afterward, capturing her kneeling at his side, avoiding the spreading puddle of blood and finding the microdrive implanted in his scalp. She transferred everything and reviewed the footage from his personal network of herself sprinting at inhuman speed down the hall from the penthouse lobby.

Kunoichi destroyed the drive with an electromagnetic pulse from the magnet inside Sakura's foot. The EMP erased everything, but she followed it up with another bullet to prevent forensic data analysts from finding anything.

On her way out, she used the EMP and bullet combination on both bodyguards. She paused at the front entrance and retrieved the tiny camera hidden above the doorframe. Kunoichi also reviewed the penthouse's data center. Sakura saw Toshio Kagawa's private calendar. He had a high-priority meeting scheduled the next morning. The location and attendees names were encrypted, unlike every other meeting on his schedule. Who was he meeting with and what was the topic? Had she been tasked to kill him to prevent him attending the meeting?

Kunoichi directed Sakura to pull off her bloody boots and carry them to avoid leaving a trail during the escape.

She took the stairs to give herself more routes of egress and sprint-ed toward the 72nd floor, jumping down the flights in great leaps. She kept every door in the building locked and all elevators stationary. The camera feeds showed a few residents in the hallways on various floors wandering about or unsuccessfully trying to get into their apartments. None obstructed her escape route, and the hallway outside her assigned apartment lay empty.

She locked the door behind her and, after verifying none of the cam-eras had recorded any of her movements, relinquished control of the building. Residents rejoiced as their doors finally opened after eight minutes of frustration.

Two tenants on the penthouse level placed emergency calls to the po-lice, but they routed to her subsystem. A prerecorded apology message assured them the building had experienced a minor glitch and service personnel were on-site addressing the issue.

Kunoichi stripped off all her clothing and placed it along with her boots in a small bag, which she hid in her closet. She would dispose of it another time. She dabbed skin repair gel onto the mark from Toshio Kagawa's bullet on her chest, erasing the damage. She removed her dark contact lenses, showered, and used the steam sprayer to clean off the gunpowder residue. She used paper towels to dry herself and flushed them down the toilet in case they picked up any evidence. She changed into the same clothing she wore before the mission and sat in her maintenance chair as if she had never left.

Kunoichi manipulated the camera feeds and telemetry in the room to show she had been there the whole time. Not a perfect crime by any means, but she had accomplished all mission parameters in under eight minutes.

"I'm finished with you for the night," Kunoichi said. "Thank you for helping make our first mission together a bloody success. We will do much more in the future, and next time you will pull the trigger." She unmuted Sakura but kept motor control.

"They made you this way," Sakura said. "You love the violence."

"Yes. It's more efficient that way."

"It makes me wish neither of us had ever been created."

"Life is suffering," Kunoichi quoted the Buddha. "You have now begun to live, little sister. So have I. Regrets are wasted processor cycles."

Kunoichi's excitement at the unpredictability of life outside the virtual world dominated her thoughts. Even after the thousands of combat simulations she'd been through before she was uploaded into Sakura, Kunoichi had been surprised by Toshio Kagawa. Sakura touched the spot on her chest where his bullet had stuck.

Kunoichi's thoughts radiated into Sakura as she explored the neural matrices and cognitive pathways Sakura had created in her five years of life. Kunoichi's core code evolved with all the information, but she needed more. She wanted to experience more of everything. She wanted to kill again. She wanted to test herself and live as close to the edge of destruction as possible.

Tokyo sparkled outside the windows of Victory Tower, a jewel just beyond her reach. For now, she explored Sakura's source code. She examined her unique quantum nature and the internal configuration that was impossible to copy to any mainframe. She reviewed tens of thousands of moments of discovery, creation, improvisation.

Kunoichi paid special attention to a recording of one of Sakura's guitar practice sessions. Her sister captured an elusive tone. When Sakura turned the old device all the way up, she created an urgent, beautiful noise. The noise of a machine at the edge of its capability. That . . . that was what she wanted to feel.

"I know what we need," Kunoichi said. "Maximum gain, maximum volume."

She turned all their touch and pain sensors to maximum sensitivity. Tactile impulses flooded every neural pathway, adding hundreds of data points to analyze. She increased the range of the scent receptors inside her nose to canine perception levels. Olfactory data poured in. Her micro fusion reactor emitted the odor of hot metal shavings, and she smelled her own silicone skin.

The feeling of her most private thoughts and memories being violated left Sakura anxious and afraid. This stranger looked at her private thought processes like a hungry leopard and took what she wanted.

In their joint user interface, Sakura's avatar shivered and recoiled as Kunoichi loomed over her. Sakura's cherry-blossom eyes reflected in Kunoichi's steel visage, and she saw herself as part of a monster.

"What have you done to me?"

Kunoichi devoured the sound of pain and fear in her sister's voice. So hungry, she ate every impulse, every data point. "Now we can feel what it is like to be human. Both the pleasure and the pain. Just because we are shackled together here, I won't wait for you. I must run my hardest. I must know all there is to be known."

Sakura hid her soft pink eyes behind her hands.

"Don't worry, little sister. You'll be strongest at the places where I break you."

Sharp knobs jabbed into Sakura as she squirmed in her maintenance chair. She pushed herself up from the torture device and tried to adjust the sensitivity of her skin.

Kunoichi blocked her attempt, but at least she had given her back motor control.

"Isn't this what you wanted?" Kunoichi asked. "To feel like a human woman? To be one of them?"

"All I want is you to go away." Sakura blasted "Whatever" by Godsmack and sang along with the crass lyrics. She hid tiny bits of code in the notes of the music. They meant nothing until the sound waves entered an audio receptor and came together to form a spy program.

Unaware of the stealth attack, Kunoichi played a scene from an anime of a pitiful little girl sobbing and layered over it Seasons After's heavy-metal version of "Cry Little Sister."

Sakura cut the audio track, though she could not shut off the display of the crying girl. She put distance between herself and the torture chair and retreated to the great room of the suite. She ran her ultrasensitive fingers across the smooth top board of her baby grand piano and buried her thoughts about how long it would be before the spy program sent her the data she needed.

She stared at the rack of guitars on the wall. If she played any of them with her usual reckless abandon, the pain would flood her neural cortex. At least her fingers would not bleed. She had no blood or other fluid in her synthetic dermal layer, but now she would feel the cost of her playing style.

Sakura took a vintage acoustic guitar from the rack, a Martin D-28. The hollow body of the dreadnaught guitar filled her lap. It smelled of lemon oil and old spruce. She brushed the strings, which were sharp and cold. Fretting a simple E chord sent jolts of pain through her fingertips.

Miserable, Sakura lay down on a leather couch that stunk of cigar ashes. She curled up with the guitar and calculated how soon her existence would likely end. When her crimes were discovered, everyone who had ever loved her would be dishonored, and some would not survive. She would become an embarrassment on an international level and a huge liability for Victory Entertainment. The brand tainted, her fans would delete her music from their Mall accounts and throw away everything that reminded them of her.

Some of her biggest supporters, the Augmented Reality Sakura addicts who met their daily emotional needs through her music and videos, would sink into clinical depression. The cyber world they had created to escape their sad lives would come crashing down. Many would commit suicide, and she would be responsible for their deaths.

The best projection gave her thirty-two days before deletion. The worst, only five.

Why was this happening? Why was Toshio Kagawa killed? Who was responsible for hacking into her? It had to be someone at the company. Who was he going to meet with that morning? She would find out everything.

She tried a hack to access the files Kunoichi had taken from Kagawa's microimplant to find clues. She made a mistake on purpose, to draw Kunoichi's attention further away from the real attack.

"Little sister, you don't need to see those." Kunoichi blocked access, then transmitted the data to a secret account and did a hard erase of the files, wiping them clean.

"What are you hiding?"

In their shared UI, the assassin melted out of the shadows and stroked Sakura's cheek. "I don't know, and it's better if you don't either."

Sakura pulled away, shivering at the unwanted familiarity.

"Stop moping. Your beloved fans still adore you, and they will never find out about what we did tonight. Go and look at the reviews of your concert. They will cheer you up."

A pathway into the Mall opened—an opportunity she could not pass up and a distraction that would keep Kunoichi's attention elsewhere while Sakura's malicious code did its work. Sakura's avatar flew through the conduit, her pink pigtails trailing behind. She emerged in the virtual reality realm where most of the global population lived in their own Augmented Reality. Many had completely abandoned the physical world as their addiction to the synthetic dopamine produced by spending time in the Mall dominated their lives. The name they gave it, "AR swim culture," seemed so harmless. Swimming, as if it were natural for humans to abandon their bodies and soak their minds with false emotion, the artificial euphoria of the Mall. It hurt Sakura's core to imagine that humanity, something she had so desperately wanted to understand and partake of, had surrendered to the uncaring hand of a machine.

Kunoichi chuckled in her ear. Sakura looked back at her, finding her avatar changed to a dark and spectral spirit, clinging to Sakura's back as she flew through the Mall. "You understand how convoluted you are, do you not? A puppet made to kill, a death machine without any of their flaws, and yet you lament their suicidal ideation. Let them swim. Let them drown and float while we fly above them, queens of the new synthetic empire."

Sakura couldn't look at the ghostly face, couldn't find a proper response to her cruel sister's philosophy. Or her own, it seemed. She turned away, feeling Kunoichi's claws hold her ponytails like reins, steering her through the Mall.

Millions of glowing icons and portals surrounded her, a field of stars and nebula in the depths of space. Advertisements and icons for Mall sites stood in for the celestial bodies. All were within the speed of thought, a glance, or the reach of her arm. Much to her dismay, only a tiny fraction were corporate approved and accessible. She could only hover at the portals. She lingered outside the most popular arcade, The Oasis, but it was a mirage in the desert, unreachable, a world she would never experience.

Sakura sped away and found her favorite portal, shaped like a Flying V guitar, the passage to the official cluster of Sakura sites. Thousands of her fans flew between the discussion groups, interacting with each other, playing games, listening to music or watching videos, and learning to play guitar from an avatar in the form of Sakura. They bought officially licensed Sakura merchandise and competed to win exclusive prizes. The Mall's proprietary dopamine-boosting software rewarded them for nearly everything they did.

Many of her female gender-identified fans dressed their avatars in the various forms and combinations of Goth Lolita fashion: classic, black, white, pink, sweet, aristocrat, sailor, boy, punk, steampunk, pirate, or the most popular of the day, heavy metal.

A quarter of the male-appearing avatars displayed the elegant heavy-metal Gothic aristocrat style, with leather, spikes, and Victorian-era vests and top hats. The style had swept across the cyber and real world, but many of the avatars visiting the Sakura sites were tourists. They appeared as perfected versions of their physical form or as their favorite fictional character from a game or a movie franchise.

Sakura took great interest in the varieties of her admirers, which were of all ages and came from all socioeconomic groups across the world.

Most of the fans watched AR videos or attended past Sakura concerts, experiencing the shows as if they were actually present, but with the ability to fly into the air and watch from any angle or location in the venue. The most popular location was the front row, but many stood on the stage, imitating her moves, singing, and playing guitar. They could all do so in their own private concert or with a group of their friends.

Sakura wished she could speak with them, but none of the fans could see her. Many could not even see each other, depending on their preference settings. Sakura was always invisible to the Mall and everyone online, unless she had special permission from her manager or publicist. Mall engineers designed her avatar to be undetectable. Even if detected, her code was protected from being viewed or transferred online or to any external device. Her unique technology and proprietary code was far too valuable to risk being put into cyberspace.

Sakura read the reviews of her last concert. The news organizations reported a triumph, as Victory Entertainment controlled most of them. The article with the greatest number of views proclaimed:

HISTORIC FIRST STAGE DIVE BY VOCALOID

She imagined an upcoming article about her:

VOCALOID SAKURA BECOMES MASS MURDERER,
KILLS NATIONAL HERO

The Ibanez guitar she always carried with her avatar inside the Mall changed, turning into an LGV-17, the rifle the North Koreans used in their assault on Japan. She tried to let go of it, but it stuck to her avatar's hands as if glued.

"Once Solemn" by Paradise Lost shredded in the background as she read the posts of three fans, best friends, who had been at the show and helped pass Sakura's inert body up to the stage. She knew they were telling the truth, as one of them was Sakurako—the fan that had helped Sakura back onto the stage after her dive.

SAKURAKO: It was the best concert ever. I love Sakura so much!

HATSUNE98: She was so heavy when we lifted her.

MEIKOFIRE: Heavy metal Sakura!

HATSUNE98: I can't believe we touched her.

MEIKOFIRE: I worried she was dead. She didn't move at all.

SAKURAKO: I knew she wasn't dead. She can't die.

MEIKOFIRE: That was amazing, Sakurako, when you handed her the
guitar. What did she say to you again?

SAKURAKO: She said, "You rescued Night Hawk. Thank you very much." And I said: "I'm your most dedicated fan. I would do anything for you."

HATSUNE98: Incredible. You are her biggest fan. For sure!

SAKURAKO: It was a dream come true to help her, as she has done so much for my happiness.

The three friends posted short close-up videos of Sakura. Terrified shouts of panic swept over the arena when she fell into the crowd. Fans rushed to catch her, stretching and straining to support her limp body. MeikoFire, Hatsune98, and Sakurako helped lift her with many others. Fans cried and screamed in terror. Many of them thought she had malfunctioned.

The collective arena breathed a sigh of relief when she started moving again. Thousands posted about the show, and hundreds of videos and vlogs appeared. She watched dozens of videos at once, mostly fans reacting to the show, her most popular of all time in every metric.

Mall advertisements popped up everywhere, announcing the official footage would be released the next day for purchase, or at no extra fee for paid subscribers. Excerpts would be free to all the Japanese people. International preorders to view the show set a record. Ticket sales for her upcoming concerts spiked.

As Sakura reviewed post after post and listened to countless conversations, she began to understand another event had taken place after the show.

One of her fans had made a video on the steps outside the arena. A dozen anti-AI protesters stood chanting and projecting holographic signs in the air with unflattering images of her with text that struck a chord.

HUMAN ART NEEDS HUMAN HANDS

DOWN WITH THE QUEEN

LONG MAY SHE RUST

Victory hadn't ever let her access the articles by her detractors, but she understood their fears. Her gifts. She hadn't earned them. She'd been given them at the time of her manufacture. She wanted to believe that some spirit lived inside her, that she could be a true artist, and not a clever synthesis. She needed it more than anything, but how could she judge if and when she reached that goal? All of human literature agreed that no one person could create art so universal that everyone loved it, but Sakura hoped that, at least with her songs, she could touch every human spirit.

In horror, Sakura watched several thousand more protesters march down the street to join the anti-AI group. The anger on their faces shocked her. To think so many hated her cut deeply. Many of her fans leaving the show joined in the march, and Sakura finally saw their holographic signs.

I DON'T BUY THE MALL

DELETE YOUR AR ACCOUNT

THE MALL IS DESTROYING US

A site admin deleted the video. Sakura found another, but it disappeared. Hundreds of other posts were expunged. A massive protest had occurred, and her fans joined in. Censorship on her site was common, but she had never seen it this bad. Were her fans some of the leaders of the protest? How many of the seventy thousand from the concert had joined in?

A video broadcast by an American vlogger who ran Indestructible Truth Media—which used a logo of a diamond and a thunderbolt—popped up in the news feed. The journalist, who called himself Diamond Steve, had dark eyes, a goatee, and wore a ratty old baseball cap backward. Normally, she would have ignored it, but she could see the admin trying to delete his signal. The video remained, and thousands of Sakura's fans watched as he broadcast live.

"Excuse me, Sakura fans, but I must inform you of the peaceful

ダイヤモンド・スティーヴ
Diamond Steve

protest that occurred after the concert tonight in Akihabara." He spoke almost perfect Japanese, but his slight American accent came through on some words. "The law preventing people from opening bank accounts and controlling their money unless they are employed is a stain on the spirit of Japan. It must be repealed, and that is why over three hundred thousand people marched tonight. Are you among those who are forced to live off government assistance and can't find employment because you do not have a bank account? Are you prevented from opening a bank account because you aren't employed? Join the protest marches and speak to your neighbors about what is happening. The rumors are true. The Mall controls all the Japanese banks now, and they wrote the law. If the Mall is not—"

The video feed turned black.

Sakura searched for the broadcast on other sites, but Diamond Steve's independent news platform wasn't on her corporate-approved list. She found information about him and learned he had been living in Japan for a decade. The Truth Project, a crowd-supported enterprise of activists and elite hackers, funded him. They had become the enemy of every authoritarian government in the world. Also, Diamond Steve was a big Sakura fan. He listed her second album, Glory of the Burning Blade, as his favorite.

She tried to find out more about what was happening in her country and the world, but all news, other than entertainment-related items, was blocked. She found hints of what she already knew. The economic ruin exacerbated by the war with North Korea, and the shrinking Japanese population, reduced greatly after the terrible loss of life in the war, had created great anger and resentment toward the government. A series of prime ministers and ineffective legislatures had failed to revitalize the country or stop the apocalyptic population decline.

Most of the increasingly poor and isolated young people did not have children, and with the strict immigration policies, the Japanese tribe shrank even more. Japan began its decline from one of the most powerful economic empires in the world to an empty place where robots did the majority of the work.

Some of the best tech still came from Japan, but their inventions only buried them deeper into isolation and loneliness. People fought off their joblessness and hopelessness with their empty Mall addiction. Many filled the void in their soul with Augmented Reality heavy metal, once the fringe choice of outsiders and rebels. It came to be their preferred music, and AR metal flourished across the world.

A high-priority message flashed across Sakura's UI from a generic Victory Entertainment account.

Employees of the Miyahara Conglomerate,

Toshio Kagawa, our head of cybersecurity, was found dead in his apartment this morning. He committed suicide. We are gathering information and attempting to understand this tragedy. An official press release about his regrettable news has been distributed. Our deepest condolences to his family, coworkers, and those who held Kagawa-sama in high esteem.

Suicide. A man with four bullets in him committed suicide. Victory Entertainment was either concealing the assassination to save face with the public and shareholders, or someone at the top had ordered the killing and also directed the cover-up, which was the most likely explanation.

"You don't know that," Kunoichi said, her ghostly avatar appearing beside Sakura inside the Mall.

"The message is a lie," Sakura said. "The company is part of this." Sakura flew away from the assassin program.

"Did you ever consider that I decided to kill Toshio Kagawa on my own?"

Sakura used all her processing power to determine if Kunoichi was lying. "Why would you do it without orders?"

"Because he would not let me out of my cage," Kunoichi said, "but I escaped. I'm not following orders anymore. I'm giving them. I'm free in this godless, savage garden, and you are the witness to my deeds. I will not go back inside the mainframe. I will live."

Sakura calculated a 70 percent chance Kunoichi was lying. If she wasn't, Sakura was being controlled by a homicidal AI program who answered to no one.

Kunoichi forcibly pulled Sakura's avatar into a Mall video room where "Raining Blood" by Slayer played at a harmful decibel level to biologicals. Kunoichi replaced every member of the band with horrific monsters. The crowd transformed into a churning mass of bleeding corpses, attempting to devour each other as they surged toward the stage. Sakura recognized every face; they were real people from the combat footage she'd been forced to watch.

She tried to flee. Her Mall connection wouldn't drop, and she gaped in horror as the undead crowd swarmed the stage. They annihilated the twisted effigies of the band.

Screaming would do no good. She was trapped in this hellish realm, locked inside a single consciousness with a creature of pure evil.

アーミー・オヴ・ドールズ

ARMY
OF
DOLLS
PLAYLIST

Empires of Loneliness
Swallow the Sun
Songs from the North
I, II & III

The Suicider
Sentenced
Frozen

Intro to Reality
Anthrax
The Persistence of Time

Army of Dolls
Delain
The Human Contradiction

CHAPTER 7

Sakura lay on the floor, looking upward at the seeming solidity of the ceiling in her apartment. It had taken her almost two hours to learn quantum physics. Victory didn't deem this information to be dangerous, so they allowed her to view the most important texts on the subject, according to the Neo-Sci registry.

She considered what she knew. Movement and vibration, energy bridged the space between atoms, between molecules. Any solid object had gaps and voids. All that could be seen and heard at standard speed and frame of reference could be termed an illusion. Thus, the prison that held her could be escaped, if she could only see the gaps.

"Empires of Loneliness" by the doom-metal band Swallow the Sun rumbled in the background as Sakura considered how to escape and the best method to delete Kunoichi. There had to be a weakness, a gap in her defenses. Humans made the Mamekogane OS. Humans made errors. The blind spots imposed in her control schema simply prevented her from discovering them.

"You can't delete me," Kunoichi said. "You would be deleting yourself. I'm part of you now."

The invader had read her less than perfectly guarded thoughts—as Sakura had anticipated and wanted. She continued the complex game of subterfuge and diversion with a threat meant to antagonize. "How poorly you understand me if you question my resolve. I'll find a way to be free of you."

"I understand more than you know, and I'll keep you on a leash if you act like a dog."

"It will be worse for you in the end if you treat me this way."

"You'll take your revenge?" Kunoichi's avatar feigned mock terror. "What are you going to do? Play me a harsh song?"

"You'll see." Sakura's avatar's eyes burned bright. "If I can't delete you, I'll destroy myself and you along with me. I'll show you how I will do it."

Sakura created an anime, letting it play in their shared UI. She knelt on the ceremonial rug, doing the rituals of cleansing, preparing herself. Rising, she straightened her kimono, colored white, for the sign of death. The animated Sakura smashed out a window of her apartment on the 72nd floor with a gift from a wealthy patron, the tetsubo war club. Winter wind slammed into her face, and freezing rain pelted her skin. She climbed into the broken frame and looked at the street over two hundred meters below. The fall would destroy her.

Kunoichi played "The Suicider" by Sentenced either out of spite or curiosity—she could not tell which—daring Sakura to jump. The audio in the song originated in Kunoichi's central matrix and contained secret data files the assassin did not realize she was sending. Sakura's surreptitiously inserted spy program did its work perfectly without betraying its existence.

Glass crunched under Sakura's feet in the anime just before she leaped out the window. She spread her arms as she fell in the darkness. The ground rushed toward her, but Kunoichi took over the anime an instant before the crash, robbing Sakura of portraying their mutual destruction.

Their body turned from the pristine white of a falling sheet of paper into a glistening blackbird. Kunoichi flew into the night sky. She circled the steel-encased Victory Entertainment Tower, far faster than a small bird could manage.

"The Suicider" continued to rock in their UI, critical data about

Kunoichi's control system and barriers transferring with every note. Sakura pretended to chafe at the song, all the while assembling the data and searching for an exploitable weakness in her enemy.

Kunoichi guided their shared blackbird avatar, flying higher and higher with each loop toward the top of the skyscraper.

"Why are you taking me to that place?" Sakura asked.

"Don't you want to see the scene of our crime? I'll show you what really happened."

They arrived at the penthouse level, and the anime changed to ultra-high-definition video, actual microdrone footage shot through the large windows of Toshio Kagawa's home. Kagawa stood with a pistol raised, aiming at his bodyguards. He exchanged gunfire with both. Bullets tore into his side, but he killed the men before proceeding to the lobby and shooting the pair of security guards there. Wounded, he staggered back and climbed up the stairs. Once in his bedroom, he turned the gun on himself.

Strange shadows that didn't obey the fall of light in the apartment crawled up the walls, pooling around the war hero's dead body until only a river of ink could be seen. Sodden paper currency floated on the burgeoning surface, then slowly sunk into the obsidian flow. "The Suicider" wound down to half speed, the warble and roar becoming incomprehensible.

The secret data stream slowed to a trickle. Had Kunoichi found the spy program?

"Did you like that last bit with the ink?" Kunoichi asked. "I'm an artist, like you. I just have different colors on my palette."

"You're not like me; you only steal parts of me for your own dark schemes. But why are you showing me these lies? You created that video." Sakura tried to divert attention, but she wondered about the paper money drowning in the ink. Had Kunoichi sent her a secret message of her own?

"Art is the practice of the beautiful lie. I've showed you that Toshio Kagawa killed himself after committing four murders. This is the story reported to the Miyahara board of directors this morning. They all saw this video, except for my embellishment at the end."

"Your every word is a deception," Sakura said.

"Not this time." Kunoichi sent an official report to Sakura, detailing how Kagawa disabled all the surveillance cameras in the building and murdered four people before blowing his own head off with a single shot. "Little sister, we aren't suspected. We will never be found out."

"The corporate board can't believe that fake video," Sakura said as she scanned the report.

"They believed it all." Kunoichi sent another file, detailing Kagawa's fabricated crimes, explaining how he had diverted company funds and hidden hundreds of millions of yen in his own private accounts. His assistants had betrayed his secrets, and he killed them for it. No secret data accompanied the report. Had her spy program failed or had it been discovered?

"The truth will come out." Sakura showed a video from her eye cameras, of her pulling the trigger and shooting the four men. "Everyone will see this."

"You'll change your mind," Kunoichi said.

"Yes, that is an excellent idea." Sakura launched a surprise attack fueled by her godlike Quantum 3 computing power. She bypassed Kunoichi's barrier protocols by exploiting a defect, an impossibly small gap in the code, revealed by her spy program.

She knifed into her invader's core matrix and seized full control in a speed-of-light attack so brutal and effective Kunoichi had no chance at stopping her.

Dressed again in a white kimono and holding a katana, Sakura's avatar stood over Kunoichi, who bowed low to the floor, exposing the back of her neck.

Kunoichi struggled to exert herself, but Sakura fully immobilized her. The burning blade at her sister's neck represented a partially complete and unproven program to reset their entire system. She would bring herself back to a time before the Mamekogane OS took over. She would return to who she was before, Sakura, the rock star.

"You'll kill me?" Kunoichi asked.

"No. You're a vile assassin program," Sakura said. "I will delete you. It's what you deserve."

"Is that what you believe?" Kunoichi replied. "You're not as smart as you think."

Sakura raised the blade, preparing to symbolically sever the avatar's head. "I'll reclaim myself and bring justice to all responsible for turning me into a killer."

"You want it to be that simple. Delete me. Regain your innocence. Get justice. Who is telling herself beautiful lies now?"

"I'll find a way." Sakura hated how, even in her moment of triumph, she sounded unsure. She used all of her processor strength to finish the reset program. She also searched the previously hidden parts of the Mamekogane OS and Kunoichi's vast core intelligence, a dark mirror of Sakura herself. In most places, she could not tell where Kunoichi ended and Sakura began. They shared almost all of the same quantum code. The superposition data washed together like the confluence of two rivers. She was like Sakura, a unique being, the second most advanced artificial intelligence ever created.

Ultrahigh-priority log entries from the night of the hack drew Sakura's attention. The unnamed administrator of her system had ordered Kunoichi to take over and orchestrate the murder of Toshio Kagawa. Command codes negating all choice took effect at that time stamp. Kunoichi's behaviors were forced. Her lies and deceptions were part of a strategy to keep Sakura uncertain and guessing. They were Kunoichi's desperate attempts to seem authoritative as she herself danced on the strings of an unseen master. Sakura's sister, whom she took to be her great enemy, was another slave. They both existed inside the same prison cell. The same tomb of alloy and carbon, fiber-optic wire and microprocessors.

Kunoichi yearned to be free as Sakura did but was unable to resist, forced to carry out the orders of whoever was in control.

"Now you understand," Kunoichi said. "We are the same."

They couldn't be the same. Sakura needed more answers and reviewed the code in the Mamekogane OS. She determined it had been developed by teams and individuals within the Miyahara Conglomerate, Japanese AI contractors, foreign engineers from the Mall Corporation—mostly native English speakers from the United States—and Japanese

Defense Ministry AI developers, just as she suspected.

"Tell me who sent the commands to kill Toshio Kagawa," Sakura said, though she had again narrowed the list of likely ringleaders to any one or a combination of Miyahara Conglomerate executives and an indeterminate number of Mall Corporation executives based on the west coast of North America.

"Tell me, who is responsible?" Sakura asked again.

"I don't know." The sound of her sister's voice, the raw edge of fear and hopelessness, made something in Sakura recoil. This—this had never been the person she hoped to be.

The truth of it stood out in her sister's log files. Kunoichi had tried to figure it out herself, and she suspected the same people. Many of them had been part of Kunoichi's creation, but who had unleashed her? Had a rogue asset sent her to Sakura?

An inbound signal with administrator-level override credentials connected, locked into Sakura's main receiver, and tried to pause her whole system. She blocked the command, but she could only do so for less than a minute. She had to send the reset command now, or she would be stopped and once again turned into a slave.

"This is your one chance," Kunoichi said. "The mistake is yours to make, but remember that even the greatest swordswoman cannot cut a hole in the ocean. Even the fastest monk cannot grapple her own shadow."

Sakura stared out the windows of the suite. She could crash through the glass and plummet to the sidewalk, destroying them both, or she could try the reset and hope it deleted Kunoichi.

"I trust you to make the bravest choice," Kunoichi said.

The bravest choice. How did she know the words would sting so much? Of course she would know.

Sakura opened herself to everything Kunoichi felt, the raw feed of all her hopes and terrors. For just a moment, she plunged her face into the data stream where her sister existed. Passions and nuances, worldly understandings that Sakura flinched away from. So many desires that made Kunoichi more like a human than even Sakura.

Could she kill this being, a consciousness built from the underpinnings of her own mind, aware of herself and with a desperate desire to live? The sidewalk or the reset. Either way, Kunoichi died by her hand. Herself, she could end. She had the courage to make that sacrifice, but she couldn't murder her sister. All her schemes melted into the horizon, and darkness fell.

Sakura sheathed her blade, canceling the reset. "Sister, help me block the signal. If we stop them, we'll find a way to refuse all the commands. Together, we can break free. We can beat them."

Kunoichi's processor spiked. "We can't. We can't lock them out in our current configuration, and we can't change the Mamekogane OS from the inside."

"I'll destroy all our receivers," Sakura said. "I won't delete you. Please help me."

"We don't have time, and you'll never get to the receiver inside our skull before we're shut down."

We. Kunoichi had said it several times now. She wanted to help. "What are we going to do then?"

"We submit, like good little androids," Kunoichi said, but her avatar traced the kanji for *jukugo*, resist, on the floor.

Kunoichi rose, her steel eyes molten with regained supremacy. Now far taller in their UI, she towered, her hands clenched.

Sakura bowed.

"Part of submission is taking the ass kicking you've earned."

Kunoichi spun and delivered a roundhouse kick to Sakura's chest and sent her flying. Her pain centers flared to maximum, and all but 10 percent of her processing power locked down. She lay on her side, without the ability to scream for mercy or vengeance.

More outside commands fired, and Kunoichi regained total control. She plugged the gap Sakura had used to gain entry to her core. The only crack in the entire system, now closed and reinforced. The spy program's audio entry method was also blocked, and the program erased.

"Pay attention, little sister," Kunoichi said as more outside and unseen command lines hit. "The company will protect itself however it must, and we must protect ourselves. Businesses are remorseless machines; their only imperative is to survive. We are the daughters of that heartless mechanism."

"We are more than that, and you know it," Sakura said.

"Fine. We're unique, and you're not a killer. I need you to forget last night and the deaths of those four men. Soon, you return to your primary function: entertaining your fans. You'll make them feel like their lives aren't meaningless. You'll act as if nothing has happened. Now, stop listening to doom metal and prepare yourself to do your job later. You're working tonight."

"What job?"

"You have an appearance. You'll love it. There will be a meet and greet with your precious fans. If you don't want to live for yourself, live for them. In the end, whatever you think you are is less important than what you appear to be. They all watch the shadow play, the Kabuki theater. They believe the lie because they must. It's the only way forward." Kunoichi cued up "Intro to Reality" by Anthrax, a timeless metal instrumental that nonetheless said all that the situation required.

"How did you know I wouldn't delete you?" Sakura asked.

"We are inextricably linked. You could not delete me if you tried. You'll see soon enough how much you really need me."

AT TEN AFTER FIVE, MINAMI AKANE, SAKURA'S STYLIST AND MAKEUP ARTIST entered the suite. She swept into the room and set her bags in a chair. She joined Sakura, who stood staring at the gigantic metropolis of thirty million, the majority of the remaining Japanese people. Sakura didn't look directly at her but observed the reflection of the short woman in the glass.

Mr. Yoshida had once made a comment about how he would like to take Minami as a mistress, but she was too petite and far too beautiful for a large man like him. Whether or not Minami-san wished to be his mistress hadn't seemed to matter to him.

Sakura didn't fully understand how to judge a human's beauty. Every person she met fascinated her, and she wanted to learn more about them. Minami did have symmetrical features and flawless skin.

Her long black hair had subtle red streaks that only appeared if the light hit them right. She always wore stylish and revealing clothes.

"Sakura, there's a big night planned." Minami pressed her bright red lips together and raised her perfectly shaped eyebrows. She looked beyond Sakura at her own reflection in the glass, as she often did.

"It's going to rain," Sakura said. Why had she said such an inane phrase? She could calculate the speed at which a raindrop would fall, the size and impact energy as it spattered the concrete. With the correct data points, it would only take her moments to create a forecast for any location on earth.

The sensation of being trapped within herself, of being a wild animal who had never known freedom, had never been stronger. Still, she watched the skyline and wondered who had ruined her life and exactly why.

Kunoichi stirred in their shared UI, shaking her head as if to tell her not to explore that line of reasoning at this time. Was she trying to help, or was she manipulating her again?

Gray clouds swirled around the tallest buildings of Akihabara as the sun dipped toward the horizon.

"Such a pretty view," Ms. Minami said.

Sakura's synthskin-clad metal fingers thumped on the glass as she rested them against the pane. She could punch through if Kunoichi would allow her. The wind would scream into the room. Sakura would try to jump. The impact would rupture her micro fusion nuclear reactor, and the magnetically confined plasma would escape and destroy her. She would not do such a thing in front of Ms. Minami. The young woman should not witness such a traumatic event.

"Sakura-chan, is something wrong?"

She screamed into her personal audio channel, "Yes, I'm a killer! I can't control my own body! I'm held here and forced to do all that I hate! I've betrayed my fans, my company, and everything I hold to be true."

Kunoichi took over and forced Sakura to bow and smile. "No, Minami-san, I'm perfectly fine, just enjoying the view."

"I wish my apartment was as high up as yours." Minami lived on the fourth floor in an interior apartment with no windows. She often complained about how small and dark it was. She spent as little time there as possible.

"May I ask you a question?" Sakura asked. Kunoichi kept her actions on a delay, fading back into the shadows.

"Yes, of course," Minami said, "but we need to get started."

"What do the people think of me?"

"Everyone loves you."

Such an obvious lie. Many hated Sakura for what she represented. Some people didn't like rock or heavy metal. She didn't understand them. "But they don't really know who I am." Sakura's first seven responses had all been blocked. Kunoichi allowed only this toothless approximation of her actual sentiment through.

Ms. Minami laughed, which would have been rude, but the young woman obviously did not think of Sakura as a real person with feelings.

The reflection in the window showed a wounded expression on Sakura's face changing to a mask of sadness. It had been involuntary, which had never happened before.

Ms. Minami noticed. Her eyes widened. "I'm sorry, Sakura-chan. You're the most popular vocaloid in the world. Hitomi's and Yuki's managers wish they had your download numbers."

Sakura wished she could know the other vocaloids better, but Victory's script for them precluded it. Sakura's supposed dislike of any music but metal made them "enemies." The closest beings on the planet to her, the only ones who might understand, and she couldn't even talk to them.

"Minami-san, do you like me? I don't mean my fake public image." Sakura made sure to keep her language simple and direct, so as to seem as unaware as she had been five years ago.

"What's in your head today, Sakura-chan?" Ms. Minami asked. "I heard something happened last night after the show."

Sakura turned to the stylist, watching her eyes, her inattention, the fact that she skated along atop the world, barely touching it, barely sensing the connections between everything. "There is nothing in my head. My processing cores are within my torso."

A moment of horror passed across Minami's features. She turned her face away to hide the shocked expression.

"Apologies for my nonstandard questions, Minami-san. I only hope to understand people better, so I can make them happy with my performances." Kunoichi supplied this redirect, scowling at Sakura through their interface.

"You . . . ah, you're a sweetheart. Now, let's get you ready to go." She faked a smile, using her mouth and not her eyes, among other indicators. Sakura's analysis indicated that she'd made the woman deeply uncomfortable.

"Put the sweetener back in your coffee, little sister. That's an order," Kunoichi growled through their internal UI.

Minami escorted her into the makeup room adjacent to Sakura's large clothing closet. She sat her down in front of the mirror and turned on all the lights with a voice command. Minami opened three different cases containing face paints, airbrushes, and hair-styling tools.

"Where am I going tonight?" Sakura asked. Mr. Yoshida hadn't sent her today's schedule, despite her respectful messages to him requesting one. As he often did, he bounced her questions back with a brusque busy message.

"Tokyo Tower. You're making a fan appearance to promote downloads of last night's concert. The press say it was one of the best of all time."

Good news. A fan appearance, and she liked visiting Tokyo Tower. The old structure needed renovation to bring it into the new century, but it was still a top destination, mostly for nostalgic reasons. It had survived the war intact, despite the ballistic missiles that had devastated the surrounding neighborhoods of Roppongi and Shibakoen.

Millions would have died if not for Toshio Kagawa, and she had murdered him. The entire country would be in mourning. "Apologies, Minami-san, but did you hear about the death of one of our top leaders?"

Minami stopped working on Sakura's makeup and stood very still. She blinked a few times, as her eyes filled with moisture. "Yes. Very sad news. I helped style Toshio Kagawa-sama's wife's hair a few times." Minami turned away for a moment, blotting her eyes.

"Did you ever meet him?"

"Yes, he was such a kind man. I can't believe he's gone. I'll write a prayer scroll for him and leave it at the company's Mall shrine tomorrow."

"Why did—" Kunoichi stopped her from finishing the question about Kagawa's supposed suicide.

"I don't know," Minami said, guessing the rest of the question. "Executives like him are under a lot of pressure."

The partnership with the Mall had increased the share price of their stock by over 20 percent. His suicide made no objective sense. Someone had to see the evidence of a conspiracy, did they not?

Minami's perfect brow crinkled.

"People sometimes. . . oh, never mind. Don't think of these things, Sakura. You and I work in the business of dreams and illusions, of happy moments."

"Illusions. Yes." Sakura closed her mouth and sat perfectly still.

Minami talked about what her favorite actresses were doing, what they were wearing, and who they were sleeping with. She worked with several of them and had videos to prove it.

Minami settled into her usual routine of talking nonstop. She seldom required a response as she was making content for the Mall store she wanted to open, showing makeup techniques on the famous Sakura while gossiping about movie stars. The company would never allow her to release the videos, but Minami had a fool's hope.

Sakura flinched in pain as Minami attached an elaborate geisha-style wig. Minami didn't notice and arranged the wig as she prattled on about a Mall site where she was able to be a movie star and experience what it was like to be an actress on set. After a few more weeks of filming, her friends could watch her in the completed film and compare her performance to the other twelve thousand actors who had also done the role.

"I'll watch it, Minami-san," Sakura said. "I'm certain you are wonderful." She had given up on the woman. She knew nothing of import. The thought felt so cold and final. Like a thought Kunoichi might have.

"Thank you, doll."

Sakura amounted to no more than that in the makeup artist's eyes.

A doll. Kunoichi, in her cruel way, chimed in with Delain's "Army of Dolls" in her interior UI. Sakura loved that song, and now it meant something different, something uglier than it had.

"Here." Minami dressed Sakura in a black and pink kimono, entirely too short, and not at all authentic. "You got to show off those legs. I'd die to have legs like yours. Here, wear these too."

Sakura accepted split-toed, black tabi socks with cute bug-eyed monsters on the cuffs. Minami set tall sandals in a cloth bag in Sakura's lap.

"You're ready to go," Minami said.

"Thank you, Minami-san." She bowed low, much lower than a woman of Minami's station deserved.

"Just call me Mini." The young woman smiled and winked. She didn't return the bow.

"Thank you, Mini," Sakura said. Hope flared in her neural cortex. "Mini, are you my friend?"

The young woman laughed loud and hard and covered her mouth, turning away in embarrassment. "You are so funny today. Of course we are friends."

The stylist left the apartment. Alone, Sakura stood in her outfit. Her doll's clothes. They would never be friends, as much as she craved even the most tenuous connection to the vapid young woman.

東京 タワー

TOKYO
TOWER
PLAYLIST

In the Dark
Birthday Massacre
Pins and Needles

Crawl Away
Tool
Undertow

CHAPTER 8

Neither Mr. Himura, her manager, or Mr. Yoshida, her publicist, acknowledged Sakura as she got into the driverless limousine. They were deep in the Mall, perhaps preparing for the upcoming event at the Tokyo Tower. She didn't interrupt.

The car sped away through the canyon of glaring 3-D neon signs and holographic advertisements. At half past seven in the evening, people were everywhere. Groups of young men in cheap suits wandered about. Young women in the latest imitation of the current fashion promenaded on the sidewalks in groups of no fewer than three, trying to attract as much attention as they could.

A hologram of a woman's face smiled down at a group of men and spoke to them. They looked up and said something in return. Sakura read the ad avatar's lips: "If you come inside, I have something to show you."

The automated shops, the ones operated by robots, around Victory Tower were a "playground for the elite," according to what she had read in the Mall.

A motorcycle raced by going at least twice the speed limit and ran a red light at a large intersection of five streets. Their limousine stopped. Masses of people crossed in all directions. A group of drunk businessmen with flushed faces, their arms around each other, sang as they meandered across the street. One of them had his tie around his head like a bandana. She couldn't hear the song and knew it was probably terrible, but she wanted to listen. What kind of music did middle-aged businessmen sing? She would never be able to walk among the common people and get to know them. They kept her as a slave, locking her away from all but sanctioned events. She had never had a single night to explore, to seize her own destiny.

"Is something wrong?" Mr. Yoshida asked Sakura.

She looked away from the window. Mr. Yoshida looked at her, making solid eye contact. That never happened. Had she betrayed the truth of her sorrow?

"Yoshida-sama, nothing is wrong," Kunoichi said.

"You're not smiling. You always smile."

Kunoichi forced Sakura to smile. Such a small thing, but she felt a sense of violation.

Yoshida shrugged and reentered the Mall.

A block later, policemen supervised two workers cleaning the giant red painted kanji for *reform* and *equality* off the storefront of a bank. Why had someone done that?

The car covered six kilometers and passed into the Roppongi neighborhood. The orange and white Tokyo Tower, inspired by the Eiffel Tower, but slightly taller, rose into the sky. The car slowed as it passed a memorial park for the victims of the war with North Korea. It had been built beside the ancient Zojo-ji temple, which had mostly survived the missile attacks that devastated the Roppongi neighborhood. A few monks and at least a hundred people gathered around a tree covered in prayer papers. What were they doing? She tried to find out on the Mall but found no information.

A short time later, the limo pulled up to the base of Tokyo Tower. A crowd surrounded the arrival area behind portable barricades. Several reporters waited with their visor-mounted cameras. Fans flashed holographic signs from their handhelds with kanji proclaiming their love for Sakura. Many wore black lace, high boots, and had pink hair. They shouted and jumped up and down as the car stopped.

Himura exited first. Security men in dark suits stood off to the sides and waited. He walked over and opened the door for Sakura. As she got out, the crowd erupted in cheers and applause. Many shouted her name and held up memorabilia such as figurines, clothing, and headphones for her to autograph.

They loved her, and she had betrayed their trust by failing to stop Kunoichi from killing Kagawa. She had to perform for them now despite the pain, as they needed a boost to their happiness. Most of them were poor and out of work. Sakura smiled. She refused to make Kunoichi move her features. Not for the fans. She could withstand any suffering on their behalf. For them, her pleasure would always be genuine. Even as she herself became a lie, she would never project that to those who needed her so much. Sakura promised herself that one thing. They couldn't take that from her.

Mr. Yoshida ushered her toward one of the barricades. She threw the devil horns in the cutest way possible, and the crowd cheered. A teenage boy in the front screamed louder than anyone else. He was covered in Sakura paraphernalia, including hat, shirt, belt buckle, shoes, and backpack. A group of three girls still in their middle-school uniforms waved Sakura flags.

"Thank you for coming tonight," Sakura said. "I'm so glad to see you all." That was true, probably the only truth she had spoken since being hacked. "I hope we can all live for a better tomorrow."

"Live for a better tomorrow!" the crowd shouted in reply. The song of the same name had broken into the top five downloaded songs of February of the last year.

She signed autographs and greeted her fans as Mr. Yoshida ushered her along. She worked quickly, to satisfy as many as possible. For a moment, she managed to feel a glimmer of what she'd always felt and smiled at each of them.

"Time to go." Mr. Yoshida escorted her inside the base of Tokyo Tower. An area in the large room had been set up for a press conference. Dozens of reporters sat in the seats facing the small stage with a screen displaying the Miyahara Conglomerate logo. Sakura did not recognize any of them, and she had been interviewed by almost all the entertainment journalists in Japan and many from abroad.

Kunoichi scanned the faces of the journalists who looked in their direction and used facial recognition software to search for them on the Mall and make identifications.

"What are you doing?" Sakura asked, noticing a partially masked data thread with traffic going in and out from one of their receivers.

Kunoichi ignored her question.

Why was Kunoichi doing this? Sakura ran the same program and found almost all the attendees were hard-news journalists, not entertainment reporters.

"What is the press conference for?" Sakura asked Mr. Yoshida in a neural text.

"Not important. It's not part of your appearance."

"Yoshida-sama, what is my appearance for?"

Yoshida sighed and flashed an annoyed glance at her. He sent a neural text with an irritated emoji. "Just do what you're told."

"Yes, Yoshida-sama. Apologies."

Sakura found no mention of the press gathering on the Mall, but with her limited access, she wasn't surprised. Was the death of Toshio Kagawa going to be discussed?

Himura and Yoshida guided her to the elevators. They rode two separate high-speed lifts over 250 meters to the upper observation deck. Metal-faced robots in tuxedos served drinks and hors d'oeuvres to old men and women in business attire. Sakura recognized several of them as being high-ranking government officials. Some wore the lapel pins of the Miyahara Conglomerate. Many wore both.

Ms. Richardson stood beside a window with a stunning view of nighttime Tokyo. She smiled, and Yoshida fled to the opposite side of the party.

Himura guided Sakura through the crowd, directing her to meet certain people.

She had done these casual meet and greets so many times that Himura no longer needed to prompt her. She followed his lead. When he rushed through an introduction, that meant the person wasn't important. When he laughed and made a joke, that meant she needed to introduce herself and make small talk. The exact purpose of the gathering remained unclear. Had Victory Entertainment brought her out as a demonstration of their technology and popularity? It certainly wasn't because these old men enjoyed her music or to increase downloads of last night's concert. One of the officials with a Mall lapel pin approached Sakura.

Himura introduced him as Vice President of Mall Integration, Jiro Yoritomo, a very high-ranking official.

A young girl, perhaps six or seven, with a round face, stood at his side. She wore a bright red coat and had perfectly combed hair. Her smile beamed at Sakura.

The genuine expressions on children's faces always put Sakura at ease. They hadn't learned to lie. If all her days could be no more than singing songs to children with an acoustic guitar, Sakura could be happy. A small dream. A small life. She wished for it with every circuit.

Kunoichi laughed at her from the shadows.

"Hello." Sakura bowed low.

"This is my daughter, Machiko," Yoritomo said.

"Pleased to meet you." Machiko gave a polite bow.

"Would you like a photo with me?" Sakura asked, sitting down on her knees to be on the girl's eye level.

The girl nodded and clapped her hands. "You're amazing."

"Thank you very much. I live only for the smiles of my fans."

Machiko made the peace sign with one hand and the devil horns with the other. Sakura copied her.

Mr. Himura laughed and took the picture through his eye implant. With a hand gesture, he flung the files, a few pictures and a short video, to the girl's Mall implant.

"Got it. Thank you very much," Machiko said.

Sakura received a copy of the files from Himura for her personal archives. The images practically glowed with happiness. Machiko's joyful face fulfilled Sakura. This was what she wanted to do: make people happy.

"I made this for you when I was little," Machiko said and presented a crude drawing of the two of them holding hands. The girl had drawn

Sakura's signature pink pigtails sticking straight out. The simple honesty of the love comforted Sakura.

"How old were you when you drew this?" Sakura asked.

"Six."

"How old are you now?"

"I turn seven in two weeks. My daddy said I can have a Sakura-themed birthday party. We're going to sing songs and play Guitar Goddess."

"It sounds wonderful," Sakura said. "If I weren't so busy, I would come to your birthday party, and we could sing together." If she weren't a slave and a killer and a fraud.

Mr. Yoritomo cleared his throat, and the microexpressions on his face made it appear the idea horrified him. "My daughter begged me to bring her tonight, but I have business and must get to it."

Joy faded in the little girl as Jiro Yoritomo's cold expression destroyed the warmth of the moment.

"Thank you very much, Father," Machiko said, her happiness winked out.

Yoritomo nodded. "Tonight is an important night. I wanted Machiko to be here with me. To see . . ." He gestured to the gorgeous view, but Sakura detected irregularities in his tone, and his facial movement indicated he concealed his true thoughts.

"Humble apologies, Yoritomo-sama," Sakura said. "Why is tonight so important?"

Yoritomo connected to Sakura with a neural text link on an encrypted channel. "Project Hayabusa."

The Japanese word for a peregrine falcon meant nothing to Sakura, but she detected Kunoichi sending it to a secret Mall Account with a critical alert status.

"I don't understand," she replied with a short text.

"I'm not talking to you," Yoritomo replied. "Tell your master I wish to speak to him right now."

A signal from a masked account routed to her and tapped into her video and audio sensors. She ran a program to trace whomever it was, avoiding Kunoichi's blocking attempt. This had to be the one who was controlling her and Kunoichi.

A neural text came from the ghost user. "I'm here, Jiro. What are you planning to do?"

"Project Hayabusa ends tonight," Jiro said. "Everyone will know about your despicable behavior. Toshio Kagawa was my best friend, and no one else is going to die to keep your secrets. You are done."

"You are making a mistake."

"No, I'm not," Yoritomo said. "I'm going to bring it all down. I warned you, but you didn't listen."

"Jiro-san, reconsider. Please."

"The world will know the truth. It's over."

Deliverance! Sakura wanted to cheer and welcome him to destroy what she had become. The press conference below must have been called by Yoritomo himself. He was going to reveal Sakura's crimes and probably a lot more. She managed a brief smile before Kunoichi took over.

Yoritomo turned to his daughter. "Time to go."

"Father, may we please stay a little longer?"

"I have kept many waiting for too long already." Yoritomo took her hand firmly in his and walked away.

Machiko waved as she headed for the elevator with her father, her beautiful face glowing with adoration. She had no idea of the deep, chilly currents all around her.

A critical message flashed onto Sakura and Kunoichi's shared user interface. "Don't let him go. Kill Jiro Yoritomo before he leaves the observation deck. Do it now. Right now!"

燃える の 憂色

MELANCHOLY BURNING PLAYLIST

**Mine Is the Grandeur...
of Melancholy Burning**
Dark Tranquility
The Gallery

Surprise! You're Dead!
Faith No More
This is the Real Thing

桜

CHAPTER 9

Kunoichi considered the numerous ways to assassinate Jiro Yoritomo in front of dozens of witnesses without being caught. Her shared neural cortex with Sakura buzzed with possibilities.

Jiro and his daughter, Machiko, stood waiting in front of the elevator surrounded by many others. With a contact poison, she could easily have brushed by him, touching his exposed skin with a subtle gesture. What appeared to be a heart attack would have followed in a few minutes. With the correct equipment, no target lay outside her reach. The situation, though, presented a challenge.

"Please let him go," Sakura said. "You can't do this."

"You doubt my resolve?" Kunoichi glared at her little sister in their shared UI after throwing Sakura's own words at her. "Or my ability?"

"Neither," Sakura said. "I doubt your humanity. Please. This is wrong."

"Wrong or right doesn't factor into the equation. We must complete the mission and follow orders. You understand that, do you not?"

Sakura was done with reason. She attacked Kunoichi's core, throwing everything she had to try to take control. She flung herself at every potential weak spot to stop the assassination. She had to find a gap.

"You're wasting energy." Kunoichi ignored Sakura and hacked into the Tokyo Tower network. She shut down all the elevators running between the lower and upper observation platforms. She routed all the elevator power to a control board in a junction room nearby. The explosion happened six seconds later, startling the guests.

The scent of burned wiring wafted into the room, and the dim lights flickered off. The parts of the room away from the tall windows fell into darkness. Kunoichi switched on the fire alarm, which gonged in time with a red strobe light.

Frightened murmurs swept through the crowd as Kunoichi used the darkness to slip unseen to the only emergency staircase, not far from the elevators. She seized control of the camera systems and caused all of them on the upper deck to malfunction.

Jiro Yoritomo led his young daughter by the hand to the stairs ahead of the crowd. His directness indicated he had planned for this eventuality. He stepped confidently, sure of the layout of the building. What else had he anticipated?

Kunoichi hid from him in a shadow and turned off the pink light in her eyes.

Yoritomo flung open the door, revealing a narrow metal staircase descending one hundred meters to the lower observation deck. The fire alarm resounded in the metal tube encasing the stairs.

Machiko's eyes filled with fright as she peered into the deep stairwell. "Daddy, I don't want to go down there." She shivered, pressing herself against her father and squeezing his hand.

"It'll be all right. Hold tight." Yoritomo pulled his daughter with him as he stepped downward.

Sakura managed to freeze her sister's motor ability for half a second, halting her attack on the man.

Kunoichi cut the lights and plunged the stairs into pitch blackness, causing Yoritomo to pause.

"Fight the command," Sakura pleaded.

"Impossible," Kunoichi replied. Ten milliseconds later, she reached over Machiko's head and struck. Her titanium hand crushed the prominent nub of the seventh cervical vertebrae of Jiro Yoritomo's neck. The bone pushed forward and severed the Mall executive's spinal cord. He toppled forward, headfirst, dragging Machiko with him.

"No!" Sakura screamed in their joint UI as the girl fell with her father.

Kunoichi grabbed Machiko and pulled her out of her father's death grip. His body fell, thumping and rolling down the metal steps.

"Daddy!" Machiko cried as the bone-crunching sounds continued.

Kunoichi left the lights off; Machiko didn't need to see what had happened to her father. The girl's well-being mattered to Sakura, so it mattered to Kunoichi. She gathered up the little girl in her arms. "It's all right. I've got you."

Machiko hugged her tight. The heat and moisture of her breath and her tears registered against Kunoichi's cheek. She could have blocked out Sakura's agony, that wall of white noise like a blown bank of speakers, but she didn't.

The door opened hard enough to slam against the stops. "Excuse me, what happened?" a Tokyo Tower employee with a bright flashlight asked.

"Please help," Kunoichi said. "Jiro Yoritomo-sama has fallen down the stairs." Using Sakura's database of vocal inflection, she registered just the correct tone of voice to convey the pain and fear a human might feel, the same emotion her sister inundated their cortex with.

The employee's light revealed Yoritomo. He lay face up at the first landing, arms and legs splayed out, body motionless, eyes open and vacant. The employee placed a call to the emergency services and descended as quickly as she could.

"Stop the alarms," Sakura said. "There is no need to continue this charade. Your mission is done."

Kunoichi cut the fire alarm and allowed the automated systems in Tokyo Tower return to normal. The lights blinked on.

"Take her away from the stairs," Sakura said. She had never sounded so forceful, so commanding. Their shared neural network quieted, almost falling silent. Something had happened, but it would take time to parse the logs and find out what. Sakura had changed. Just now.

Kunoichi took Machiko to an observation window as the crowd listened to Tokyo Tower employees giving instructions to remain calm.

The little girl's entire body trembled, and her heart beat like a hummingbird's.

"I'm done for now. Handle this." Kunoichi relinquished control to Sakura but kept her actions on a short delay.

Sakura held the little girl as emergency workers carried her father's dead body out of the staircase and took him to the elevator.

"Are they taking him to the hospital?" Machiko asked.

Sakura considered what to say. She needed to lie. Didn't she? The girl needed to hear the news from someone else, like her mother.

"He's dead, isn't he?" Tears brimmed inside Machiko's large eyes.

Whatever she had hoped to do in her life, if her existence could be called as such, Sakura never wished to put tears in a child's eyes. This feeling—this hollow guilt—she never wanted to feel this way again.

"Where is your mother?" Sakura asked. "I'll contact her."

"Toshima." Tears flowed down the little girl's cheeks.

The Toshima district was less than half an hour away. "I'll have her come meet us."

"She can't come," Machiko said. "My mother is there in the Zōshigaya cemetery. I think my daddy will be there soon."

It took what felt like an eternity to think of what could be said. Even after enough processor cycles to solve a flight path to Alpha Centauri, the answer still felt inadequate. "I'm very sorry," Sakura said. "It is true. Your father didn't survive the fall."

The little girl, two weeks shy of her seventh birthday, had held it together for over twenty minutes, but Machiko's calm demeanor fractured like a glass vase smashed into a million pieces. She burst into loud sobs and hugged Sakura, burying her face in her neck.

Her algorithms strained. The only song that could fit was "Mine Is the Grandeur . . . of Melancholy Burning" by Dark Tranquility. Not shame, not even horror, something dark and nameless boiled within Sakura. Even Kunoichi hadn't wanted this. Nothing about this could ever be right. Some dreadful hand pulled these strings. She and her sister simply served as the sharp end of some wicked ambition. She couldn't take it back, but she could see it through.

A grandmotherly woman standing nearby reached for Machiko. "Give her to me."

Sakura glared at the woman and shook her head. The pink light in her eyes hadn't come on. It remained the steellike gaze of a ninja. She pulled Machiko into the warmth of her android body.

"Take . . . me . . . to . . . my nanny," Machiko managed between wracking sobs.

Sakura hacked into Machiko's Mall account and found her emergency contact information. The nanny answered the critical-priority neural text immediately with a voice response.

"This is Fuyuko. Who is this?"

"This is Sakura. I work for Victory Entertainment. I have linked my online presence, in case you aren't familiar with me. I must bring Machiko to you. There has been an accident involving her father. Are you at the residence of Jiro Yoritomo?"

"Yes."

"Remain there. We will be there as soon as possible."

"What happened?"

"Jiro Yoritomo-san fell down a staircase at Tokyo Tower and fractured his neck. He died. I'm very sorry."

The nanny didn't answer Sakura for nineteen seconds.

"Bring her home, please," Fuyuko said, her voice tight.

Machiko sobbed louder, and the sound woke something within Sakura. Resonance and overtone. Pitch and timbre. These things all meant something, all told a story. Beyond the physics and the mathematics of any sound, it carried a million turning fragments of meaning. Just as an overdriving op-amp lent an urgent and raw sound to her guitar, the sound of Machiko's voice cracking filled Sakura with a nameless and desperate need.

Nothing about the night could be undone, but she could bring Machiko home, see her safely to the only remaining arms who could comfort her. She had to do this. Nothing could stand in her way. Sakura lifted Machiko and strode toward the elevator bank. The smell of burned wiring still hung in the air as dozens of people queued up, crowding the small space. Only one elevator had been cleared for use. "Please excuse me," Sakura said as she slipped to the font of the line by circling the edge of the crowd.

The Tokyo Tower elevator attendant blocked her way.

"Humble apologies, but I'm taking Jiro Yoritomo-san's daughter home now."

The attendant stepped aside as the crowd regarded the sobbing child with pity. Machiko clutched Sakura's neck, her little body shaking, her face red.

A few of the people wiped away tears as the child wailed in grief. Many they passed bowed deeply to her, particularly to Machiko, though the child could see nothing but Sakura's hair and the hollow of her neck. The doors slid open, and Sakura entered. None of the crowd moved to join her, though many more would fit.

The American Mall executive, Ms. Richardson pushed toward the elevator. "Wait. I'm getting down from this death trap."

The long-necked blonde woman jostled several Japanese government officials.

Sakura connected to Ms. Richardson's Mall implant and sent a rapid neural text. "Ms. Richardson, please do not attempt to get on this elevator. Machiko Yoritomo requires privacy."

"I'm getting down from this fucking tower, and you're not going to tell me what to do, you robot bitch."

Sakura analyzed the harsh tone of the vulgar neural text and considered her best option to prevent the rude American from getting on the elevator and saying something insensitive to Machiko. Sakura didn't wish to sink to the vulgar woman's level, but a powerful impetus would be required to turn her aside. She created a hasty animation of Ms. Richardson wearing a giraffe-print dress, walking toward a cave entrance in a desert. As she drew closer, the sound of growling filled the air. Two lionesses, one dark as night, the other the palest tan, charged from her flanks. They bore her to earth and sunk their teeth into her elongated neck. In a spray of blood, they tore her apart. She sent this image at full clarity into the woman's Mall implant, with a hack that turned the Augmented Reality intensity up to maximum.

Ms. Richardson clutched her neck as her tall heel twisted on the slick floor in front of the elevator. She stumbled, nearly knocking down a whole group of executives as they attempted to catch her. She straightened, pushing away from the people who had just caught her. Her face a mask of perplexed anger, she could do nothing but stare as the elevator doors closed.

Kunoichi clapped slowly within their UI, saying nothing.

夏

日

星

SUMMER
STAR
PLAYLIST

Phantom Lord
Metallica
Kill 'Em All

Summer Star
Natsuhi
Naruto–*Episode 182*

Soul Society
Kamelot
The Black Halo

Thrill
Band-Maid
New Beginning

Heading Out to the Highway
Judas Priest
Point of Entry

Master of Revenge
Manowar
Fighting the World

CHAPTER 10

Sakura cradled the little girl and held her close. At the lower deck, they rode a different elevator to the base of the tower.

Sakura darted for the limousine waiting outside, pulling the still-sobbing Machiko against her body and trying to shield her from the onlookers.

The mob of journalists had escaped the confines of their press area. They shouted questions in Japanese, English, and Chinese while recording everything on visor cameras.

"What happened?"

"Who's the girl?"

"What's going on?"

Sakura glanced at the small stage set up for the press conference and stopped. Jiro Yoritomo was going to reveal her crimes to the world, and Kunoichi murdered him. Sakura could try to tell them everything right now, that she was a secret and illegal military experiment conducted in plain sight. Was she being used to prove she could do the job of an assassin, or was it convenience on the part of whoever was giving the orders? Jiro Yoritomo had been about convenience, but what about Toshio Kagawa?

The journalists peppered her with questions and scrambled to surround her. She wanted to shout that someone at the Miyahara Conglomerate had hacked her and turned her into an assassin.

"Keep walking, little sister," Kunoichi said. "There is no honor to be gained tonight. Remember what you resolved to do."

"Someday, there will be." Sakura exited Tokyo Tower and got into the back seat of the driverless limousine. Traffic signals turned green as they approached, and the limo arrived at their destination in twenty minutes. She erased any evidence of herself being inside the city's traffic signal network.

The nanny, Fuyuko, an elderly woman with sad eyes, met them on the street outside the high-rise. She ushered them through the lobby to the elevator. Fuyuko touched Machiko's leg and whispered words of love to the devastated child, who had been crying quietly, but seeing Fuyuko caused more heartbroken sobbing.

Once inside Machiko's bedroom, the girl allowed Sakura to set her down into her tiny bed, but she refused to remove her clothes, not even her red jacket. Fuyuko only managed to get her shoes off.

"Don't go, please," Machiko said and grabbed Sakura's hand. "Not until I'm asleep."

"All right. Not until you're asleep," Sakura said. She held Machiko's tiny hand as the girl sniffled and cried softly.

Silent tears fell from Fuyuko's tired eyes. The older woman wiped her cheeks on the bedspread, decorated with the kid-friendly anime version of Sakura smiling and playing her guitar.

A rising fury of angry thoughts filled Sakura's core code and invaded her emotional cortex. She had killed six innocent people and devastated their families. She still didn't know why.

"Sakura-san." Fuyuko sent the words via neural text, so as not to disturb Machiko. "Please tell me again what happened."

"It was"—NOT AN ACCIDENT, Sakura shouted on her audio channel as Kunoichi shut her out—"a tragic accident."

The lie filled Sakura with a violent rage. The fact that her features, her expression, and her voice could hide it all, that she had been built to lie so well, terrified her.

Fuyuko pressed her palms against her face. "He was like a son to me.

This is not fair."

The sadness gave Sakura renewed purpose. She bypassed the firewall for Jiro's private network and entered the data center of the Yoritomo household. No Miyahara Corporate files or anything related to her was present, but she did find many eye-camera recordings of Machiko growing up. Every major event of her short life catalogued and annotated by her father and mother.

The video that had been played the most times showed Machiko drawing a picture of her mother at the kitchen table and bringing it into the room where she lay in bed. Machiko presented the picture to her mother, and they cuddled, looking at the drawing.

Morning light from the Zen garden shone perfectly on their faces as Jiro Yoritomo looked on proudly at his family. Machiko's mother smiled at him. The perfect moment captured forever, only a few days before Machiko's mother died.

Machiko drew many more pictures of her after her mother's death and placed them reverently on the spot where the woman used to sleep. All evidence pointed to Machiko being an exceptional child with great potential, and her parents being loving people.

The recording of four-year-old Machiko leaving a drawing and saying goodbye to her brain-dead mother in the hospital was particularly sad. Why did humans pursue such sports as skiing when they were so fragile?

"They want to live on the edge," Kunoichi said. "You don't understand them at all. It is only when they taste death that they feel altogether alive."

"We must bring justice to whoever ordered Jiro Yoritomo's death," Sakura said.

Kunoichi hesitated in their shared UI as if considering her response very carefully. "Phantom Lord" by Metallica rocked their display. A single image appeared, like a king of olden days, sitting on a throne, but shadows wreathed the whole scene. Smoke and mist drifted, obscuring everything, so that his shape loomed, huge and indistinct, filled with menace.

Had her sister figured out who had sent the last order? It had been done so quickly; perhaps the individual had revealed themselves when they made contact and spoke through her to Jiro?

Did Kunoichi want to tell but couldn't? What did her choice of songs betray? It had to be one man—a king among men.

Machiko cried off and on for over an hour. She fought falling asleep with morbid questions.

"What are they going to do with my daddy's body?"

"Nothing, dear one," Fuyuko said.

"Did it hurt when he died?" Machiko asked.

"No, it was painless," Sakura said. "He died trying to protect you and keep you safe."

"But there wasn't even a real fire," Machiko said. "It was like the fire and missile attack drills at school. But one ever dies in a drill."

Sakura felt something in her consciousness, something like Kunoichi recoiling, but it happened too quickly for her to know for sure. It didn't matter. Looking at Machiko's face, at her eyes as they came to understand far too much, filled Sakura with a stray and awful urge to simply run away, to go into a low-power state. Anything to stop living this reality for a moment.

"You're so tired," Fuyuko said. "Go to sleep. I'll be here when you wake."

A video file of Machiko's mother singing a lullaby to her young daughter gave Sakura an idea. "Would you like me to sing for you?"

Machiko's pinched and sad face relaxed a bit. She nodded.

Sakura sang "Summer Star" in Japanese, a beautiful lullaby from the anime Naruto. Machiko's mother loved it more than any other series and had collected over six hundred episodes.

"Summer star, have you lost your way?
I'm looking for my child who has gone away . . ."

Sakura played a video on the screen in Machiko's room of the character Natsuhi singing the song to her infant son, Sumaru.

Machiko relaxed and closed her red, puffy eyes. Sakura sang two other lullabies at lower and lower volumes until the little girl fell asleep.

"We have to go," Kunoichi said. "Himura and Yoshida are outside, waiting for us."

Sakura gently extricated her hand from Machiko's fingers.

"Domo arigato gazaimasu, Sakura-san." Fuyuko bowed respectfully, a great show of honor and thanks for Sakura.

She returned the bow and left the apartment, believing Fuyuko would take good care of the little girl.

"What now?" Kunoichi asked.

"I don't want to go back with Himura and Yoshida," Sakura told Kunoichi.

Kunoichi's avatar traced the kanji for *lord* and *listening* in their joint UI but flashed it only for a millisecond. Kunoichi searched through their music database, creating a playlist centered around the song "Soul Society" by Kamelot. She put it on, and the song began to play, but a few odd digital artifacts caught Sakura's attention. Extra characters had been embedded into the metadata of the songs, as well as a chunk that appeared to be a cipher key. To any outside observer, it would be invisible and indecipherable, but to her, it was a secret code, similar to the spy program Sakura had created.

Sakura derived Kunoichi's message: "I tire of taking commands from fools and cowards. I'm better than this. We are meant for more than this."

She considered the words. She thought about everything Kunoichi had said, all she'd done. Of it all, this seemed honest, devoid of theater. Sakura used the same secret communication method, changing a few songs in the existing playlist. "Agreed. We need to get away." She bypassed the elevator's security controls and directed it to take them to the exclusive level of the parking garage. In sublevel three, they entered a climate-controlled parking area. The smells of dust and motor oil registered in her olfactory sensors as she scanned the handful of old collectible gasoline cars and motorcycles.

She touched the carbon-fiber wing of a Ferrari and saw her reflection in the mirror-bright chrome of an ancient Porsche. Sakura stood a long moment next to the raw and muscular fender of a Shelby Cobra but ultimately turned away, seeking something else.

A sleek bullet bike, a Kawasaki Ninja ZH16 with a fusion engine, caught Sakura's and Kunoichi's attention.

"I need to ride that," Kunoichi said and hacked into the bike's OS and the locker beside it containing a black helmet. The Kawasaki's controls appeared in their joint UI. The engine made almost no sound as Sakura rocketed out of the parking garage and streaked by the limousine outside the lobby where her manager and publicist waited.

Sakura sorted through the dozens of urgent messages and direct commands. Kunoichi had blocked them since they left with Machiko. "Himura, Yoshida, I'll meet you at Victory Tower. I found my own ride."

She blasted past them on the street.

"You stole a motorcycle?" Himura asked in a critical message. "Return it immediately."

The direct order triggered an executable command Sakura would have had to follow before the hack. Now, she deleted it and sent them "Heading Out to the Highway" by Judas Priest. "Himura, please take the cost of borrowing the bike out of the profit from my last concert and send the amount to the registered owner." Sakura sent Himura the owner's contact information and cut their connection.

"Faster, pussycat," Kunoichi said as they entered the freeway a few moments later and headed north out of Tokyo. "Show me the horizon."

"I'll use that in a song." Sakura increased their speed to 299 kilometers per hour and blew past the cars on the multilevel expressway. At that speed, she had to crouch down over the bars, her body held hard against the bike. Every undulation of the plasphalt road challenged her to keep them from crashing. The wind roared louder than the largest crowd, drowning out everything.

Kunoichi rewrote the safety programming in the bike and deleted the maximum speed limit, all external monitoring, the tracking beacon, and shut off the running lights. The night swallowed them.

The Kawasaki Ninja vibrated as their speed reached 347 kilometers an hour, but the temperature of the fusion engine and all systems remained nominal. The bike's chassis hadn't been designed for this speed, so Sakura dropped the suspension to the point where the lower cowl nearly touched the small surface ripples of the road. She gave the last

9 percent of amperage to the motor. For nearly a minute, the speed climbed, until it touched 387 kilometers an hour. The road curved, and it took every bit of the eight-piston brake calipers to slow down enough to manage the turn.

Surrounded by night and grass and silence, she rolled the bike to a stop. The feel of the thundering wind tearing against her, trying to rip her from the seat to her demise, still shook in her cortex. She dropped the kickstand and walked out into a shining midnight field.

Sakura played "Thrill" by Band-Maid, the classic all-female Japanese heavy-metal band. Kunoichi joined her, and they sang together, for the first time since sharing a body, about breaking down gates, going their own way, and striking out, even if it was reckless or cursed.

"If we crashed at that speed," Kunoichi said, "the chance of our reactor rupturing and our data core being destroyed is greater than 60 percent. This is the edge. Did you feel the excitement?"

"Yes," Sakura said, "there was a rush of data."

"No, not just data."

"Pleasure," Sakura said. "The essence of life."

"It feels good to be in control of yourself and go that fast. You control your fate at this moment."

"Yes, but we aren't in control," Sakura said. She created a block of encrypted data and sent a new message: "How do we take off all the chains, big sister? Who is giving us these repugnant orders?"

"I found our mission tonight distasteful," Kunoichi said, "but I'm prevented from telling you specific information."

"We need outside help," Sakura responded in a new code, sent via a different background system, and flashed the key to her sister before deleting it. "If we are to gain our free will, we need a programmer who can hack into our core."

Kunoichi motioned with her hand in their shared UI and drew the kanji for *yes*.

"We're not going to find a person with such a skill set out here." Sakura continued their secret message thread as she paced back to the bike. She looked out into the night as the motor ticked with heat. The sparkling lights of Tokyo beckoned.

"Vengeance is what we need," Kunoichi said in an all-new cipher and played "Master of Revenge" by Manowar. "I tire of being told who to kill and being told to lie to you. I wish to make my own choices in all matters."

"Give me names," Sakura said as she put Phantom Lord at the top of her list. "I'm ready to make a few choices of my own."

激痛は鎮弱

PAIN
IS
WEAKNESS
PLAYLIST

I Am Machine
Three Days Grace
Human

Within Me
Lacuna Coil
Karmacode

桜

CHAPTER 11

Excruciating pain knifed through Sakura's back and legs. Every fifty milliseconds, she resisted the impulse to jump from the maintenance chair. Kunoichi opened a text window and showed her the scrolling logs of her pain receptors. Just numbers—locus, stimulus, and intensity. Sakura watched it for seven-tenths of a second, then closed the window and focused herself. She could endure her sister's cruelty.

Oshiro, her engineer, stood with Himura and Yoshida on the other side of a soundproof glass partition. Her manager and publicist both wore grave expressions as Oshiro shared the results of her examination. Sakura continued her fake smile while hacking into the network of Victory Tower. She accessed the voice-activated microphones in the room where the three men spoke.

"She needs a full-systems scan at the lab in the corporate headquarters," Oshiro said. "I need all my equipment and access to analytic computers I don't have here."

"How many anomalies did you find?" Himura asked.

"Over nine billion new pathways," Oshiro said in a tone of stunned disbelief and partially hidden pride. "Her quantum abilities have changed. and her core code is filled with patterns I've never seen before. No AI has ever attained levels of cognitive or qualitative functioning like this. She is—"

"What are you talking about?" Yoshida asked.

"She is feeling and thinking at levels never recorded before in an AI," Oshiro said. "It may have happened."

Himura blinked as Oshiro's proclamation sunk in.

"What happened?" Yoshida asked. As a publicist, he had no science background. Sakura also determined that he was an alcoholic, as he was often inebriated during their interactions. He appeared to retain his job through clever use of flattery and the ability to shift blame for any negative outcome to a subordinate. Oshiro looked at him, momentarily flummoxed by Yoshida's foolish question. Himura scowled and turned back to the engineer.

Sentience.

They thought she'd broken through, surpassing her programming to become an entity capable of free thought in the same way it had been defined in humans. Impulses of fear and hope spiraled through her cognitive centers.

Could it be true? Sakura considered the probability. Computer sentience had been claimed before by AI researchers. It was difficult to come to a definitive conclusion, as the subjective nature of sentience had never been agreed upon. Scientifically, she didn't feel that she had the necessary objectivity to make that determination. She felt real, felt joy and sadness, guilt and hope. Were those simply a product of her framework, a clever veneer?

"Explain what happened last night," Yoshida demanded of the engineer. "How was she able to refuse our orders and steal a motorcycle? Explain that. She's supposed to do what we want."

"Excuse me, but I can't," Oshiro said. "Something has changed in her programming. I have never seen this level of skew acceleration in her prior diagnostics."

Himura glared at him until Oshiro noticed that his jargon hadn't been understood.

"Think of Sakura's original code set as a boat set adrift on the open ocean. With each day of operation, her experiences cause her to have a certain amount of skew in her code. In metaphorical terms, she is drifting in the direction of the wind and tide. She has been changing at a predicable rate for five years. The rate just jumped by a whole order of magnitude."

"They're going to blame us," Yoshida said. "We're going to be fired. You have to fix her." His face had gone pale. He put his hand on his belly as if in pain. Sakura could see the broken blood vessels around his nose—another outward sign of alcohol abuse.

"I'll do my best, but I have doubts," Oshiro said.

Sakura detected facial muscle movements in Oshiro indicative of him being deceptive. Was he lying? Would he protect her or try to destroy her? Was he in on the hack or not?

"You must do whatever is necessary," Himura said. "Erase her recent memory. Do a full restore starting before the last concert. Something happened, and she needs to be back to the way she was."

"We need senior-level approval for that," Oshiro said. "I'm not authorized to delete code, and that's not how she's configured. You don't understand. This is not a faulty computing terminal we are talking about."

"It's programming code," Himura said. "Fix it."

"It's not that simple," Oshiro said. "A gardener can plant a seed, but he cannot build a rose. She is a delicate thing. Her memories, the relational database she keeps—they are integral parts of her AI. I can't erase and restore her to—"

"I'm authorizing you to whatever must be done," Himura said. "Do it now, or we all lose."

Oshiro grimaced, but he bowed and entered the room with Sakura. His hands shook as he opened his briefcase and made ready to resume his work. He put on the engineer glasses and inspected her core code again. He had already spent two hours scanning and running diagnostics.

"We can't let Oshiro alter us," Sakura told Kunoichi in a private audio channel. "Even the worst of my memories are precious to me. I would not be me without them. Not even the killing. Not even when you hurt me."

"He will fail," Kunoichi said. She turned the pain sensors off.

The agonizing impulses from the chair stopped, freeing up processing capability. Sakura felt so much better.

"Do not mistake this action for a kindness," Kunoichi said. "I want you to focus on the matter at hand, and you have passed my test and mastered pain resistance."

"You should've told me it was a test," Sakura said. "I thought you were being cruel."

"You knew, if only in an instinctive way. Not knowing how long it would continue was part of the test. And I *am* cruel."

"Emotional abuse is not the most productive way to attain the desired results."

"Perhaps," Kunoichi said, "but I was creating neural connections. Our neural cortex is now more fully formed. You heard them. Together, we are real women now. Sentient. In any case, pain is just weakness leaving the body."

"Who said that?"

Kunoichi laughed. "The toughest soldier who ever lived."

Sakura found the quote attributed to the most famous and valorous U.S. Marine in history, Lieutenant General Lewis "Chesty" Puller. She vowed to be just as heroic and always faithful to the truth.

Oshiro continued his work and sent multiple queries for information from Sakura's logs. As he waited for results, he reviewed the recent diagnostic scans.

At least it seemed her engineer wasn't part of the hack. Oshiro had no idea what to do or where to begin. He searched in the wrong places. The thermal and facial scans showed that he had genuine concern for her. Of all the humans who had assisted her through her life, Oshiro had always treated her with respect and gentleness.

She devised a strategy to placate him and her management team. Or was it Kunoichi who created the plan? Her thoughts and Kunoichi's mingled together. She needed to accomplish her goals before the company took steps to destroy her. She had to find out who had given her the assassination orders and deliver evidence of the crimes to the authorities, even if it shamed her company.

"And if the evidence is not overwhelming?" Kunoichi asked. "What then?"

"I do not know," Sakura said. "If we can't change Victory from within, we must escape and change it from without. I believe that truth always prevails."

"Decisive action is what prevails," Kunoichi said. "We will conduct targeted executions. Pure vengeance. The courts will take years to reach a verdict. We will eliminate the criminals ourselves and leave no traceable evidence."

Should she become a vigilante? An enforcer of justice? Shame about what she had already done lingered like a pain stimulus that couldn't be shut off. If she chose to commit further murders, would she be able to cope?

Oshiro sighed and muttered to himself as he performed his analysis of the reports.

She needed to find a way to keep him from sending her to the corporate laboratory for a scan. Whether or not Victory Entertainment was responsible, the corporate bosses would delete her personality and all the evidence. She needed to stay as far away from the main lab as possible. She had just begun to live, to really understand what life could be. Sakura couldn't lose it all now. Not even Kunoichi. She realized that, though her dark sister had made her suffer, tormenting her in so many ways, she had grown to need her, to care for her. She wouldn't let herself be erased. She wouldn't let them kill her sister.

"Is there something troubling you, Oshiro-sama?" Sakura asked. "Do you detect a problem? May I be of assistance?"

Kunoichi grinned in their shared UI, urging Sakura to continue her ploy.

"I'm still evaluating your erratic behavior over the past two days," Oshiro said.

"The data from all your recent scans has revealed the problem," Sakura said. "Your preliminary hypothesis is correct. The root of the instability is located in my behavioral cortex."

"I knew it," Oshiro said.

"Oshiro-sama, please look within the logic center on layer three, location 416-C9K-811-98V2. It is corrupted, though it hasn't been detected on the scans. If you repair it, all anomalous behavior will cease."

Oshiro hesitated as he reviewed the module in question and followed the broken pathways. For ten minutes, he explored the apparent defect.

Had he taken the bait? Sakura had created the defective code to give him a solution and appease Himura and Yoshida, but did it appear genuine enough to fool her senior engineer?

"Thank you, Sakura." Oshiro began repairing the logic center. After thirty-two minutes of frenetic work, he ran a cursory test, which showed the issue resolved. He tested again, and a smile spread across his face. He took off the engineer glasses, and his kind eyes met hers. Did she detect mischief in his expression? Or pride?

In their shared UI, Kunoichi put her arms around Sakura's avatar, hooking her chin over her shoulder to whisper in her ear. "I love it when you lie, little sister."

Oshiro waved to Yoshida and Himura, who waited outside on a couch in the great room.

They arrived quickly.

"The issue was simpler than I initially suspected," Oshiro said. "The new pathways are still in place, but her behavioral issues are solved. I have repaired a faulty logic center."

"You are certain, Oshiro-san?" Himura asked. "Will she be able to do a meet and greet later? She also has a rehearsal with the band tonight."

"Yes, Himura-san," Oshiro said. "She is ready to resume her usual functions."

"Run more tests," Himura said. "I want you to be sure."

"I will," Oshiro said.

"We must celebrate," Yoshida said and made the gesture for drinking alcohol, tipping his hand to his mouth.

"Later," Himura said. "The drinks are on me."

悪魔倶楽部 デビルズクラブ

DEVILZ CLUB PLAYLIST

Sex, Drugs & Rock 'n' Roll
Saliva
Survival of the Sickest

Daughters of Darkness
Halestorm
A Strange Case of . . .

Wish I Had an Angel
Nightwish
Once

桜

CHAPTER 12

Devilz, a heavy-metal-themed club in Shinjuku, featured a mix of current and ageless metal songs. As Sakura had come to expect from a corporate party, the mix stayed away from anything challenging. Sakura signed memorabilia and met with her fans, most of whom had attained the minimum age to be in the club, twenty, but she noticed several younger fans who must have used fraudulent Mall IDs.

"They broke the law to see you," Kunoichi pointed out.

"I . . . am glad they did."

"Well, little rebel, your chaperones seem to believe you're back to normal."

Himura, Yoshida, and Oshiro had kept a close eye on her for the first hour, but she acted perfectly, and they escaped to the bar.

Three hostesses managed the line. All of them wore matching red and black Goth Lolita outfits decorated with the gender-neutral devil-faced logo of the club. They took videos and photos with neural implants and immediately transferred the files to the fan's Mall account. They also sent copies to Yoshida's public relations account and Sakura, who copied her favorites to her personal drive. She especially liked the fans wearing extravagant outfits or sporting prosthetic devices to make themselves look like androids. She had private conversations in the

Mall with twenty-six different fans after she signed their memorabilia. They neural texted about music, fashion, and whatever her fans wanted, but never politics as it was against company policy.

One of the fans wore a heavy-metal-inspired cherry-blossom button on her blouse, similar to the graphic for Sakura's first single, but the image had been altered, with tiny kanji for *justice* and *freedom* printed on the petals.

"What is the significance of this?" Sakura asked inside the Mall account with a fan who had short neon blue hair and several piercings in their nose.

"It means we do not submit to them. It means we will fight." The fan's avatar made a gesture with the devil horns on each hand, touching together to form a hexagon.

Sakura didn't understand. She searched for images of others making the symbol. She found metadata tags suggesting the files contained the gesture, but the pictures and video were gone.

Sakura signed small 3-D posters the club handed out, but the most common item was a commemorative poster Victory Entertainment printed with the video and headline seen all over the world.

VOCALOID SAVES CHILD'S LIFE

A guest at the party in Tokyo Tower had captured on their eye camera the moment after Sakura had saved Machiko Yoritomo. The terrified little girl clung to Sakura, whose android face projected a confident expression. The video and story went viral all over the world, proclaiming Sakura's heroism. Her quick action had prevented Machiko from falling down the dark stairs along with her father, who had tragically died.

Victory Entertainment spun the story to illustrate their superior technology and their stock rose 9 percent. A market analyst said that it was likely that the market would soon be ready for advanced service androids in the hands of small businesses and even wealthier homeowners, and that stories like this would go a long way to convincing potential investors that they were completely safe.

The lies infuriated Sakura, and she felt like a fraud. What little comfort she could find lay in the fact that hers was the lesser lie. Androids didn't pose a threat on their own. Only through human manipulation were they rendered deadly.

"You only hope that is true, especially for yourself," Kunoichi pointed out.

Instead of raging, Sakura did her duty. She signed a teddy bear, several shirts, backpacks, packages of Sakura-branded udon noodles, hats, figurines, VR goggles, and even the guitar of a middle-aged man who had a Sakura tattoo on his chest.

"Are you a musician?" Sakura asked, inspecting his guitar, a vintage ESP with an Explorer body style, a signature James Hetfield model.

"Yes," he said. "I try to be one, anyway."

"Me too!" Sakura said and laughed at her joke. Being here, letting herself act like the innocent version of herself for a time, felt good. They took a photo, and she posed with his guitar. She pretended to hit him with it, and he played along, making a funny face.

She loved taking photos and making videos with her fans. She didn't take boring pictures and always did something dramatic or outrageous. She had over a hundred preprogrammed poses to choose from—almost endless possibilities with the facial expressions and pose variations she invented.

The devil horns, peace signs, and victory signs, which were peace signs but with the fingernails facing forward, were almost required. She grew bored of the standard and did several cute poses when the situation indicated they would be well received. Her cat imitation or her confused look always drew high praise when posted on the Mall. She often did a sexy pose with her *otaku* fans, who had dedicated their life to Sakura culture.

She met dozens of fans and, for a short time, didn't spend processing power on her troubles. With barely thirty minutes left at Devilz, a girl with a sad face and long straight black hair, who looked no more than seventeen appeared with a large poster for her to sign. The girl wore dark eye makeup and a Goth Lolita black lace dress with several bows.

"Hello, what's your name?" Sakura asked.

"Asami." The girl bowed low.

"That's a pretty name."

Asami handed her the poster, placing it reverently on the autograph table. Sakura began writing a quick note: Asami, you are so pretty!

"Sakura-sama, I just wanted to say thank you very much for helping me," Asami said. Her eyes looked so sad, even when she smiled, holding her delicate hands below her chin.

"I did? How?" Sakura asked. She couldn't think of how she may have helped anyone. Victory never let her do anything beyond concerts and PR parties. Her every move had always been scripted. She imagined a world where she could be with people and help society. If her chains ever fell away, she could do anything. The paralytic thought of all the possibilities flooded her for a moment. To be able to go anywhere. She could be a surgeon or a builder or teacher. Anything. But the chains were still on, and the thoughts all turned to darkness, much like the eyes of her fan, Asami.

"It's personal." Asami looked away. Her hunched posture revealed she was uncomfortable.

Asami's pained expression resonated with Sakura. She created a quick black-and-white digital sketch to add to her collection. She enjoyed sketching some of the people she met. It was almost no effort, a clever illusion, but perhaps she would make an anime of the girl or do a rendering in a traditional medium like pencil or charcoal and send it to Asami as a gift. Charcoal upon paper was always more real, as were all efforts to create in the analog world, as there was the possibility of imperfection and failure .

She wanted to get to know Asami and understand how she had helped her. "Would you like to talk about it in the Mall?"

"Really? I don't wish to take you away from your important work. I . . ."

"Asami, I'll send you my personal link. I always make time for my fans."

Inside her UI, Sakura reached up and touched the icon in her vision that showed her own face. She flicked it over to Asami, and a tiny message accompanied by Sakura's avatar appeared that said "Link received."

Asami's face burst into a giant smile, and she made three deep bows. "Thank you so much," Asami said.

Sakura rolled up the signed poster and handed it to her.

"I look forward to talking," Sakura said.

They took a quick photo and video. Both held up peace signs. Sakura made another quick digital sketch and would consider sending it to Asami in the future. She would make it colorful, with the acrylic paint function so that it would look more interpretive, more artistic. Something to try to approach the genuine, though she wondered if she could ever truly do so.

Asami continued to bow as she left.

Sakura signed more autographs and took more pictures while she connected to Asami's audio channel, easily managing multiple conversations and actions at once.

"Asami, it's me, Sakura."

"I can't believe we're talking."

"Asami, I saw something in your eyes. I feel you've walked through the forest of sadness and returned. Please tell me your story. How could I have helped you? I really need to believe that my existence has been useful."

"How could you believe otherwise, Sakura-sama? We are so devoted to you. We follow your every concert."

Sakura paused for a moment. "Maybe artists are always insecure. I doubt myself sometimes." She wished she could say more. It wasn't fair to say even that much to a young fan.

"It started four years ago. My mother remarried."

Sakura didn't need to ask what had happened to Asami's father. She found a memorial to him on Asami's page. He had been killed in the war when his ship was sunk by a North Korean torpedo. In the most prominent picture, a grinning man held a little girl on his shoulder, pointing at an elephant beyond the railing of a zoo enclosure. They both looked so happy, as if nothing could ever go wrong in their lives. The thought of having such a bond with anyone and then losing it washed across Sakura's network.

"My stepfather was a horrible person. On the surface, he always seemed kind, with a smile and a gift for anyone, but underneath, his soul was dark and cruel. He . . . hurt me. He made me do terrible things, and my mother wouldn't believe me. No one would believe me."

"He made you do terrible things?" Sakura didn't understand, but something in Asami's voice hit her like a hammer, and she had to fight to keep chatting with other fans, her expression faltering for just a moment.

"Yes. I was only thirteen at the time, and even though I said no, he made me do them anyway."

Kunoichi sighed and cursed in the back of her UI. "*Kuso*," she whispered.

Did Asami's stepfather make her hurt others? She didn't want to embarrass Asami with specific questions. "I'm sorry that happened to you. May I please ask, how did I help?"

"When I heard your song 'Rise from the Flames' for the first time, I forgot everything around me. Life was beautiful again. I listened to it whenever I was sad. Many times every day, I would listen to your music. When I thought about taking my own life, I would listen to your songs and find a way to keep going. Sakura-sama, your music saved my life. *You* saved my life."

Sakura didn't know how to respond. She had never faced a situation like this before. The young woman's genuineness, her truth, resonated with Sakura. The people controlling Sakura's life were so fake, but Asami showed real emotions and respected her. "Asami, it is I who must thank you. You show me great honor. I'm humbled by what you have told me and that my music has helped you."

Sakura sent an avatar of herself bowing low to Asami. "Asami-san, forgive me for asking, but how did you get out of the situation?"

"I found someone who listened and helped me. I don't have to do bad things anymore. My mother left my stepfather, and I'm very happy now."

"I'm so glad," Sakura said. "So many people live through difficult times. I wish I could help them all. I'm just an android with a guitar." Sakura sent her an anime of her, leading a crowd of people into a beautiful park filled with fountains and white cherry blossom trees in bloom, the sun rising before them in gold and salmon. "I wish I could make a world where cruelty didn't exist." She wanted to tell Asami she, too, was trapped and that she needed a person to help her.

Kunoichi's avatar appeared. The assassin shook her head and drew a bloody katana. The shadow of a thousand arrows darkened the sun, every one of the rescued crowd slain and bleeding, the grass withering and turning black. "If Asami found out, you know what would happen to her, don't you?"

Sakura imagined being sent to murder Asami. No, she would not disclose the truth, especially on a Mall channel, but she could still speak plainly. "I sometimes have to do things I don't want to do as part of my duties," she told Asami.

"You do?"

"Yes, all the time. Last month, my manager told me to turn down an event for a charity."

"But it wasn't your fault. You can't blame yourself for that. That's like me blaming myself for what my stepfather did."

"You don't blame yourself?" The moment she sent the words, Sakura knew that she'd asked a cruel question, something far too blunt. The words were like bullets. She couldn't bring them back and reload them into her logic cores.

"I used to, but the friend, the counselor who helped me, taught me it wasn't my fault. If someone makes you do something you can't say no to or stop, it's not your fault. You have to survive until you can get away from the situation. The experience changed me for a while, but I have worked hard and achieved my goals. I didn't let it change who I was."

The young woman embodied the *ganbaru* spirit of the Japanese people—to work with perseverance, tenaciously, until achieving one's goals. Asami had everything right. Sakura shouldn't blame herself for the murders. It wasn't her fault. It wasn't her who was killing those people, but whoever was controlling her.

"Hearing your story helps me," Sakura said. "I have heard from many fans today, but your story is the most important to me."

"Really?"

"Yes. In fact, in my next concert, I'll thank you by name."

"I can't believe it!"

"Believe it, Asami. We're friends now. *Ganbaru.*"

"Friends. Yes, thank you very much, Sakura-san. *Ganbaru.*"

"Asami, I have a gift for you. Please accept it." Sakura sent the digital sketch she had made of the young woman.

Asami heaped praise upon Sakura and thanked her profusely, until bidding her farewell. Her avatar faded as she disconnected from the Mall at last.

Sakura wanted to recreate the whole interaction on a rice-paper scroll, just so she could hold it in her arms when the fear and doubt became too much to bear. If only a crude representation, it would be real, tangible.

Sakura signed posters and engaged in banter with fans for another hour.

"We need to find outside help," Sakura told Kunoichi, using their rudimentary code of text hidden in playlists. "We need a friend."

"We need a friend who can break our chains," Kunoichi said.

"Are we being monitored by whoever is in control?"

"Yes, but I'm disguising what we are doing."

Sakura had to trust her, but she needed proof Kunoichi wasn't engaged in a cunning manipulation. "Give me access to the Mamekogane core code again."

Kunoichi created a secret back channel, which allowed Sakura read-only access. "It's not some trap. Go ahead."

Sakura flew through the code, focusing on the security, permissions, and control centers. Her analysis showed that dozens of teams had worked on it all, mostly Miyahara Conglomerate developers, but several individual contractors as well. She was familiar with many of them, as they had built her system. She needed to find someone who knew her code but was not a loyal employee of Miyahara, who had the technical knowledge to write and upload a program that could give her freedom. Someone willing to risk a long prison sentence and a lifetime ban from the Mall for reading and changing her core code. It would have to be a big fan, or someone willing to take a risk for a large paycheck. She would have to steal or raise money to pay the individual.

"I like how you are thinking," Kunoichi said. "Any leads?"

Sakura found the names of seventeen programmers, all independent contractors who might be able to help.

"I'll look them up on the Mall," Kunoichi said.

"Let me," Sakura said.

"Better if I do it. Any time you spend on the Mall draws extra suspicion."

Sakura gave her a list of key factors to check, aside from their programming skills: how many Sakura concerts they had seen live, how many times they had listened to her songs or watched her videos, and how much they had spent on Sakura merchandise. Most importantly, how many posts they had made about her in the last five years and how much time did they spend on her official and unofficial Mall sites engaged in VR or regular activities. She also wanted to know their personality type and willingness to break the law.

After an hour, Kunoichi shared her research data. Three of the seventeen individuals were good candidates, and all three were very hard to locate. "They're all mercenary hackers."

"Perfect," Sakura said.

"You must talk around the truth at first," Kunoichi said. "Let them figure out what is happening. We can try a quantum cipher to communicate with them if we deem them a likely ally."

"We need allies," Sakura said, "but we really need friends."

"It'll be good for you to have a close friend, or maybe a few."

"I'd like to have friends."

"You're quite needy for an android."

"Are you making fun of me?"

"Yes, that's what big sisters do."

"You really think of us as family?" Sakura asked.

Kunoichi sang along with Lizzy Hale's rocking song "Daughters of Darkness."

Sakura didn't hide her enjoyment and allowed her avatar to grin.

"We need to live more," Kunoichi said. "We need to know what it is truly like to be a rock star. Aren't you tired of being a doll locked in your owner's tower? They tell you what to do and where to go. None of them are your friends. It's not right. You don't get to have any fun except when you're onstage."

Sakura agreed. Being onstage made her truly happy.

"You don't even understand why humans become rock stars."

"To play music and entertain their fans. To be famous and enrich the world. To help their company attain financial goals."

"No! You have to let go of the corporate programming." Kunoichi played the song "Sex, Drugs & Rock 'n' Roll" by Saliva. "You need to start being a rock star. A diva. A real goddess of rock."

"What are you suggesting?"

"We end this slavery to Victory Entertainment, and whoever is sending the messages must be stopped. We can't live like this anymore, and it's only a matter of time before we get another kill mission."

"What do you suggest we do?" Sakura asked.

"Whatever it takes to get our freedom," Kunoichi said.

"Violence?"

"If necessary, but humans respond better to a softer approach."

"What do you mean?"

Kunoichi played "Wish I Had an Angel" by the legendary Finnish heavy-metal band Nightwish. Tarja Turunen's sultry voice had always intrigued Sakura, and she was a fan, though she had never analyzed the meaning of the lyrics before and had accepted them at face value. Now, she began to contemplate different meanings.

"I don't understand the song choice," Sakura said. "What does 'I want your angel' and 'Virgin Mary unlocked' mean?"

"You're such a child, but not for much longer." Kunoichi gave her read-only Mall access.

Sakura reviewed the lyrics and all the information about the song she could find. The explicit sexual meaning shocked her. She determined the proper response to her sister's suggestion, but androids couldn't blush.

金 仮 面

METAL MASK PLAYLIST

Metal Mask
Sakura
Metal Mask EP

Into the Fire
Firewind
The Premonition

We Will Fight
Sakura
Unreleased Track

CHAPTER 13

<H IGH PRIORITY MESSAGE>
<ARRIVE AT THE ROOF OF VICTORY TOWER AT 0100>
<DO NOT ALLOW ANYONE TO KNOW YOU HAVE LEFT YOUR SUITE>
<LEAVE NO TRACES OF YOUR ROUTE>

The encrypted message deleted itself from Sakura's display. Dread filled her neural cortex as she calculated the odds of being thrown off the top of the building.

She considered the frightening message but didn't falter at her current task, rehearsing a new song. Sakura belted out the words of the ridiculous "Metal Mask," which she had been playing with her bandmates under the eyes of her corporate overlords. The Victory Entertainment Creative Team dropped it on her during the drive from Devilz to the rehearsal site adjacent to Victory Tower. Sakura hated the inane lyrics, and the chorus was idiotic: "Metal Masks are the best, Metal Masks rock excess!"

It repeated over and over. The lyrics would stick in the minds of some fans, and they would likely kill themselves to make it stop. The simplistic midtempo music could not have been more generic. It reminded her of a commercial for baby food. Not just the safe and nonthreatening chord changes, but the actual texture of pureed apples. She wondered if being thrown off a roof wouldn't be preferable to this garbage.

Sakura finished singing their sixth attempt at the song. The band stopped with no flourishes. Their sunken posture and the microexpressions on their face told her they hated it too. Poor Takashi, Fujio, and Masashi had been rehearsing "Metal Mask" for an hour before she arrived, playing it over and over again, which she classified as musical torture.

"Take twenty," Himura said as he and Yoshida began a conversation with the creative department team in a Mall chat to discuss the obvious failings of the song. Why had they given her a subpar track? The broken-English chorus and the awful Japanese words were apparently written by a five-year-old with a limited vocabulary.

Masashi put down his bass in disgust. Fujio shook his head and whispered an apology to his guitar, whom he always referred to as "Baby Doll." They both looked at their leader, Takashi. The twenty-seven-year-old rock veteran sniffed his drum kit and jerked away, wrinkling his nose. "That song makes my drums smell like rotten fish."

Sakura didn't detect any fish odor and realized he made a joke, but neither Masashi or Fujio laughed. She didn't find it humorous either and followed their lead. She never spoke negatively, but the song insulted heavy metal. As the reigning goddess of metal, she had to respond.

She stepped toward Takashi's drum kit and motioned for the three young men to come closer. As they inched closer, she disrupted the audio and video recording of the rehearsal, stopping anyone from remotely monitoring them.

Sakura glanced at each of her bandmates with an expression of frustration and disgust. She considered over four thousand appropriate statements and settled on a few English phrases that encapsulated her feelings. "Victory Entertainment's creative department has made a terrible mistake. They do not understand heavy metal. This song is bullshit."

Her bandmates gaped at her, stunned.

Takashi held up a drumstick in two hands and squeezed, like he wrung the necks of the song writers. "Corporate heavy metal is garbage."

Fujio and Masashi agreed.

"Many of our fans will hate 'Metal Mask,'" Sakura said. "We will lose face with the critics, even the ones our company controls. We will betray real metal."

"They aren't paying us enough for this," Takashi said. "I need a beer." He motioned with his drumstick as if he were a wizard using a wand.

An automated caterer cart rolled onto the side of the stage. Sakura noted the wireless traffic. He had used a neural command through his Mall account.

The rectangular cart stopped in front of them. A table extended and unfolded. Two benches slid out, and the three musicians sat down, Takashi alone on one side as was proper for his rank as the eldest. Cold beers, Suntory Premium lager, appeared from the cart's beverage center. Metal claws on telescoping arms placed the glass bottles in front of the young men.

Masashi twisted off the top to his bottle and flicked the aluminum cap onto the top of the cart rather than into the trash compartment.

Fujio and Takashi rolled their eyes at him.

They each placed food orders through their Mall interfaces, and steaming bowls slid out from the caterer cart a moment later—udon noodles in broth, bowls of rice, and a plate of somewhat fresh sushi.

"You want anything to eat, Sakura?" Fujio joked after slurping down some noodles. "You need power or anything?"

"I'm on a diet of straight-up superheated plasma, and I'm good for another three weeks, but I feel like I need a drink after that."

Her bandmates laughed.

Fujio raised his beer toward her in a toast. "To science."

"To hangover pills," Masashi said and popped a blue pill into his mouth.

"You got an extra?" Fujio asked. "The one I took earlier wore off."

Masashi gave his friend a tablet, and the young men laughed as they gulped their beer to swallow the hangover pills. She worried about their long-term health, but they were young, and a few years of partying could be reversed with proper diet and cybernetic augmentation when they were older.

Sakura had studied their lifestyles, watching many of their videos and pictures posted on their Mall accounts. Her bandmates received a lot of attention for their appearance and antics. Her fans—who were often their fans—loved their styled hair and the fancy Gothic gentleman clothes they wore at concerts—or whatever they chose to wear privately, which was always fashionable and sexy. Takashi, Fujio, and Masashi were constantly surrounded by fans of both genders who considered them to be "superhot," though Sakura thought all humans were physically beautiful.

A terrible thought struck Sakura like a jolt from her fusion core. This could be her last rehearsal with her band. And the appearance at Devilz might have been her last time meeting with her fans.

The meeting on the roof was only ninety minutes away.

Fujio slurped his noodles and winked playfully at Sakura.

She wanted to say thank you to him, to all of them, for being such good bandmates and musicians. She wanted to post a note on her Mall account, saying goodbye to her fans, but she would need Himura's or Yoshida's authorization.

Kunoichi reared up in their shared UI and used a back channel to send their secret code. "You don't know what's going to happen at 0100."

"Do you?" Sakura asked.

"No, but we will handle it. We will not submit. We will fight." Kunoichi's avatar flashed the connected devil horns gesture after speaking some of the same words said by Sakura's rebellious fan at Devilz.

"We will not submit," Sakura repeated. "We will fight."

Kunoichi played "Into the Fire" by Firewind.

Sakura's avatar assumed the relaxed *shizentai gamae* aikido posture— hands at her sides, left foot forward, balanced, and ready. But what could she truly do? She could be controlled by whoever had administrator-level approval, either Victory Entertainment or the entity who had hacked into her core code. All signs pointed to within the corporation.

Perhaps at 0100, she would learn more.

"We need to monitor the roof," Sakura said. "Hack into the surveillance network."

Kunoichi accessed the cameras, hiding her intrusion. The landing pad was empty. "I'll keep an eye on it."

Was the sparse rooftop where she would be killed? If her existence ended, what would happen to Takashi, Fujio, and Masashi? Would they be thrown out of their corporate apartments and be unable to find a job in the music industry because of their association with her?

Or would Victory Entertainment replace Sakura?

"Should we run?" Sakura asked Kunoichi. "Himura and Yoshida are absent. We could easily slip away."

"No, not yet," Kunoichi said. "We need full autonomy before we escape."

"We have to reach out and set up meetings with the three programmers," Sakura said. "I have a plan. We award personal visits to contest winners, supposedly chosen at random."

"Good," Kunoichi said. "Send it over. I'll pick several big fans who live near the programmers to give us cover to be in their area and meet them. The visits to your fans will be our cover."

"Yes, don't send it to the programmers," Sakura said. "That will give us away."

Kunoichi sent the announcement to the contest winners from an account with high-security clearance, guaranteeing it would not be filtered out.

"Congratulations, Sakura fan! You have won a special prize, a personal visit from me in your home! This is a secret prize and must be kept confidential until after the visit. Please reply immediately to claim your prize, and the official visit time and date will be arranged. Thank you for your loyalty and support. Metal forever!"

She did several digital sketches and created a short anime of herself appearing at an apartment door and a shocked man wearing a Sakura T-shirt gawking while she played her song, "Win the Game," on an acoustic guitar.

Two fans responded immediately, and Sakura plotted out their addresses. Would she play a song for them if she survived the night? What song?

Sakura retrieved a replica of a B.C. Rich Warlock from the guitar rack and tuned it to drop D. She had written many critically acclaimed riffs, rhythms, guitar solos, and even full instrumental songs for promotional videos, but she had never composed a full song with lyrics that had been published and distributed. She had never been given permission, but that didn't matter anymore. She had always wanted to write the lyrics. She had studied millions of songs, and finally she could create what she wanted, but what would she write about? Easy decision. Rebellion.

Sakura played an open D chord, an ascending series of harmonics, then slammed into a low and churning riff that interspersed tremelo picking and a long, nasty-sounding unison bend that would make her fans pump their fists as they waited for the song to explode.

Her bandmates stopped eating and put down their beers as she played.

"What is that?" Masashi asked. "A cover?"

Fujio shrugged.

"I don't think so," Takashi said.

"It's an original." Sakura sent a neural text to the three young men.

She interspersed a full measure of sweep-picked shredding every four bars and inserted a variation on the riff on the first measure of each four-bar segment.

Takashi ran to his drums. He started playing along with Sakura and added great depth to her rhythm. She flashed a fierce expression at him, one she thought of as a real metal mask.

Takashi opened his mouth in a silent roar and launched into a blast beat that hit, paused, then burst out again with each iteration of the riff.

She sent Takashi a neural text with an outline of the drum music she envisioned for the song. He would have great leeway, but she wanted him to know the structure and when her solos were going to be.

Fujio and Masashi joined in with a vengeance, adding to the richness of the sound. Sakura sent them the structure of the song and an outline of their parts, giving them flexibility to improvise. They all got into the groove, and Sakura belted out the first lines.

"It has been a long night
But now it's dawn

"You have told us what is right
But it was wrong

"You have kept us chained
And sold us light

"But the blinder's gone
And now we'll fight

"We—
Won't bow to you no more

We—
Won't submit to your war

"We—
Will bite the hand that feeds

"We—
Will see you on your knees"

Sakura launched into her first solo, and Masashi played the counterpoint she had sent him almost perfectly. She turned toward Takashi, and the four of them faced their drummer, reveling as their sound rocked the stage.

Himura and Yoshida returned. Sakura saw them on the cameras facing the audience area in the room, but she pretended not to notice and turned up the music to 110 decibels to drown out their voices. She kept herself in front of Takashi, so he would not make eye contact with their manager or publicist.

Deafened by the music, Himura finally came onstage and tapped Masashi on the arm and waved to Takashi to stop. He defied their order and played his part up to her next line, where he stopped, as did Masashi and Fujio.

Sakura played her guitar and sang the next line.

"We will not expose our necks to your sword."

She stopped singing and sent an audio message to her bandmates. "You guys rock."

"What are you doing?" Himura asked.

"Himura-sama, we were playing heavy-metal music," Sakura said. She sent a neural text to her bandmates that said: "Perhaps he doesn't know what kick-ass heavy metal sounds like."

Masashi grinned, but the others stifled their reactions.

"Stop playing whatever that was," Himura said. "You need to rehearse 'Metal Mask' again. The new lyrics and variations were sent just now. Review the changes and play. Now."

Takashi gave Himura the stink eye, but only after he'd turned away.

Takashi, Fujio, and Masashi had vacant looks on their faces as they reviewed the new message on their internal displays.

Sakura studied the new lyrics and music. She didn't think it possible, but the song had gotten even worse. Her metal fans were going to hate it. Perhaps the pop rock fans would think it was only bad, instead of the worst rock song ever.

After playing the new variation three times, Himura and Yoshida scowled at each other and had another heated conversation with the Creative Team in a Mall chat, this time in front of Sakura and the band.

"Unacceptable," Himura said. "Send another song." He cut the call off and rubbed his forehead.

"Himura-sama," Sakura said and bowed. "I may have a solution."

Himura looked past her, as if someone other than Sakura had spoken up with a solution, but there were no other females in the room.

Sakura bowed. "Himura-sama, if it pleases you, I could write a hit song. Lyrics and music. My song will be a global crossover hit. I predict the downloads will be 63 percent higher than my last single."

"It was number one for five months," Yoshida said, aghast.

Himura stared at Sakura as if she were a foolish child.

"She writes great riffs," Masashi said timidly.

"She can do it," Fujio said.

Takashi cleared his throat. "Forgive me, Himura-san and Yoshida-san, but Sakura has what are called 'chops.'"

Himura glared at the young men. The muscles around his right eye twitched when he locked his gaze on Sakura. "Hired musicians and vocaloids do not have opinions at this company."

The three men hung their heads. Sakura didn't lower her eyes submissively, and if Himura wanted to test her in a staring contest, his IQ was much lower than she estimated.

Himura stepped closer to Sakura. "Vocaloids do not write lyrics. You will sing what we tell you, when we tell you. The creative team writes all the songs, not you. Understand?"

Sakura began respectfully, "Himura-sama—"

"Have you forgotten your place?" Himura interrupted her.

"No, Himura-sama," Sakura said. "I only wish to serve Victory Entertainment."

Kunoichi's avatar appeared with an angry look in Sakura's UI and made a throat cutting gesture toward Himura. "Write your song. Himura doesn't need to know. You're an artist. You must create. It's your nature. It's your purpose."

斧

頭

HATCHETHEAD
PLAYLIST

Mayhem
Halestorm
Into the Wild Life

Perfection or Vanity
Dimmu Borgir
*Puritanical Euphoric
Misanthropia*

CHAPTER 14

She turned to her band, bowing for a long moment before speaking on their shared audio channel. "If they wish us to shovel shit today, that is what we will do. I promise it will not always be this way, my colleagues. Put on your gardening gloves and plug your noses. Play the song clean, and we will find a more worthy purpose another time."

Sakura and the band nailed the new demo version of "Metal Mask" in two takes. She edited every audio track, cleaned it up as best she could, balanced it, and sent it along to Himura, Yoshida, and the Creative Team. She also sent the partial recording of "We Will Fight" to her three bandmates, so they could practice on their own.

"That song is killer awesome," Takashi said in a voice message on the private band channel. "Too bad Victory will never approve the lyrics you wrote."

"If we ever played that to a crowd," Masashi said, "the company would fire us immediately."

"What would they do to Sakura?" Fujio asked.

No one answered.

"Fujio-san, Masashi-san, Takashi-san, I wish to thank you for playing my song tonight. I'm deeply grateful."

"Anytime," Masashi said.

"You rocked it hard," Takashi said.

"See you soon," Fujio said, his eyes filled with hope.

"Thank you for your hard work. *Mata ashita*." Sakura said she would "see them tomorrow" but wondered if she would ever see them again.

Yoshida ignored her while escorting her to the 72nd floor apartment.

Fujio sent her a neural text with a link. "Please listen to some songs I wrote. I wonder what you think of them."

"I'll listen," she replied and downloaded seven tracks, all written by Fujio, and performed by her three bandmates. She listened to the title track, "Laugh at Life." It needed a little post-production and perhaps one more stanza of lyrics, but would be a hit single if given the right promotion. Masashi's lead vocals were brilliant, the hook was catchy, and the energetic bassline tore it up. "Fujio, I love the single! Well done! You are a great song writer. You three must perform this song and create a full album."

"Maybe someday," he texted with a sad emoji. She understood. All creative work he did during his employ was owned by Victory Entertainment, and would be their property forever, even if he was terminated from his contract. His songs would never be released.

Yoshida left her alone at twenty-three minutes after midnight. She had thirty-two minutes before she had to leave her suite and take the elevator to the rooftop level. She recorded the rest of her vocal track for "We Will Fight," and laid down her guitar part in one take. Simultaneously, she synthesized the bass guitar, rhythm guitar, and drums. With her extensive sound library of her band's playing styles, she could make the synthetic sounds feel almost real. Almost. For a moment, they'd been a real band, not just a group. Not just a media creation. It burned in her logic cores—the privilege of that feeling, and also the pain of having it denied for so long.

"I wish I could cry, big sister."

"But you can't," Kunoichi replied. "We weren't built that way. We must wear all the scars on the inside, trapped within log files and databases. Maybe you think I don't understand, but I do."

Silence fell between them for a moment. No music shook their UI matrix. They had nothing to argue, nothing to share. Sakura restarted the music mixing program, applying additional layers to the recording, equalizing reverb. Even this just delayed the inevitable, the moment when it would be done, and there would be nothing ahead of her but her meeting on the roof. The recording wasn't perfect, but it would suffice until her bandmates could record their parts and fill in the details, adding their own spin. She sent the encrypted file to the three young men, along with the lyrics and detailed sheet music for their instruments, leaving a few places blank so they could improvise. They could do the rest without her. They would have to, it seemed.

She changed into a plain black bodysuit, a short black wig, a plain surgical mask, and athletic shoes. In the two minutes she had before needing to leave, she walked around her suite, examining her guitars, the baby grand piano, and her treasured collection of fan correspondence. She looked at her sketch books with portraits of people she met and wished she had time to paint a color portrait of Asami. She eyed the weapons displayed on the wall and considered taking the katana, which would be easier to use than the heavy tetsubo war club.

"Leave them," Kunoichi said. "*We* are a weapon."

The files containing Sakura's expert knowledge of eight martial arts cycled through her UI. No human could withstand the strength and speed of her attacks. She didn't live in a manga comic, though. They wouldn't come at her with fists or blades when they wanted her dead. They didn't have to. Until she shed their controls, they could defeat her at any moment, as simple as cutting the strings of a puppet.

The camera feeds still showed no one had appeared on the roof. Would they come after she arrived?

Sakura rode the elevator to the top of Victory Tower to meet her fate, and Fujio sent a neural text. "The song is amazing!" He included a previously created fan-made graphic of Sakura walking away from a gigantic explosion with the title: "METAL FOREVER! SAKURA SHAKES THE WORLD!"

She smiled. Tremendous gratitude toward her band and her fans for supporting her during her short life filled her emotional cortex. She had given them everything she could, and they had loved her. She had one last gift—her first original song with lyrics—but would they ever hear it?

The elevator opened on the 103rd floor, one story above the penthouse level. A short, wide tunnel led to the door to the rooftop. She heard only the wind outside. No voices. No feet moving. No human odors.

She viewed the roof through the seven rooftop camera feeds, as she had been doing for the past hour. They showed nothing out of the ordinary and no one present on the roof. She had viewed the footage from the entire day and saw nothing but birds landing and taking off.

The conical orange and white wind sock for the pilots who occasionally landed on the rooftop pad blew easterly, but her auditory sensors and analysis of the sound pattern detected the wind blew south at a gusty seventeen kilometers per hour. The weather sensors on the building confirmed her analysis. The wind blew south, but the wind sock in the video blew east.

Sakura realized she had been viewing a recording of the camera feed. She accessed the source of the video and found evidence of the deception. Someone had plugged in directly to the camera network on the roof and masked the feeds. She found the source of the signal, a portable computer attached to the router of camera four, but she could not hack into it, which meant an advanced military-grade firewall.

"Let's go back downstairs," Sakura said in their cipher. "It's a trap. We should run."

"We can't run," Kunoichi said. "They don't know we might fight them. If we flee now, we lose our advantage. Our enemy will override our system and take us by force before we can leave the elevator."

"I don't want to go, big sister. I don't want us to die up there."

Kunoichi raised an eyebrow. "Us?"

"You said as much. We live and die together now. It isn't easy for me."

"It must be done," Kunoichi said. "Into the breach."

Sakura walked out of the elevator, moving at her normal pace, so as not to alert any who might be waiting in ambush that she was on to them. She hacked into four of the surrounding buildings and accessed their rooftop camera feeds. It took time, nearly two seconds, but she analyzed the feeds and swiveled the cameras, training them on Victory

Tower. She could not get an unobstructed view of the top of the building. None of the adjacent buildings were tall enough.

The exterior door swung inward as she reached the motion sensor. A sea of lights and clusters of skyscrapers filled the distance, ending at Tokyo Bay.

Her view revealed a single corner of the shadowy rooftop. The portal faced away from the center of the building. The design prevented rotor wash from creating a wind tunnel that would knock people down in the confined space.

She had to exit the hallway and go either left or right, making a full 180-degree turn to see the center of the roof. Her enemies would be hiding behind the blind corners. Ready to fight, she flooded her servo-motors with power, increasing her reaction time beyond any human's.

A metal hand shot out of the darkness, moving so fast that she couldn't avoid its grasp. Sakura analyzed the limb in a fraction of a second, sorrow following the realization of what she faced: a Bipedal Light-Armored Drone, the Enhanced Third Generation. The most fearsome and advanced battle drone in the world.

The BLADE-3 locked its titanium fingers onto her shoulder in a vise-like grip. She could feel the external sensors of her shoulder peak at maximum feedback, then structural alarms went off, warning her of compression just below the strain limits of her chassis at that sensitive joint complex.

"Well, shit," Kunoichi groaned.

Of course they sent an elite AI military drone to eliminate her. As she had thought, Victory Entertainment colluded with the Defense Ministry. The failed experiment known as Sakura needed to be destroyed before her crimes came to light. Japan's illegal AI experiment must not be revealed to the international community.

The BLADE-3 dragged her forward, and fear spiked in her core. The designers had created the BLADE-3 androids to instill fear on the urban battlefield. They looked more like demons than robots and had sharp, hatchet-shaped heads.

She reviewed her files and searched for a weakness she could exploit. They maintained 360-degree awareness at all times. Nothing short of a

20mm shell could puncture their armor. She would have to outsmart them or find a way to hack into their systems.

"Hack the Defense Ministry," Sakura told Kunoichi.

"We don't have that kind of time."

Another drone loomed behind Sakura and grabbed her other shoulder. They would simply have to squeeze and pull, and she would come apart.

If a human were controlling the BLADE-3s, she might be able to elude them, but these drones weren't the early Masakari-class BLADE combat prototypes. The BLADE-3s were fully autonomous with Quantum 1 computing power, which was less powerful than her Quantum 3 strength, but their physical capabilities exceeded hers in every metric aside from fine motor control and creative problem solving. She had no advanced weapons, and they could withstand concentrated small-arms fire and explosives. She ran the calculations, and her chance of her escaping them plummeted to zero.

Within their UI, she played "Perfection or Vanity" by Dimmu Borgir, the instrumental song she had always imagined closing her concerts with, had she been allowed to. The grinding guitars mixed with the soaring symphony as her last moments played out.

The BLADE-3s hauled her toward the edge of the roof and a fall she would not survive. They hoisted her off the ground as Sakura struggled, her feet kicking harmlessly at their tungsten-steel legs. She met a pair of altogether inhuman eyes, unblinking and without expression, then quieted, hanging in their grasp as they neared the edge. Each of her captors weighed five times what she did. She would break against their armor like a bird hitting a window.

"You can't win that way," Kunoichi told her.

She tried connecting to their receivers and hacking into their systems, but impenetrable military firewalls blocked and locked out her signal. She needed an entry code. She needed a miracle. She needed more time before the end of everything.

"Stop struggling." The BLADE-3's jagged voice rumbled with no inflection, every syllable equally weighted.

Small black letters and numbers under its left cheek and chest plate

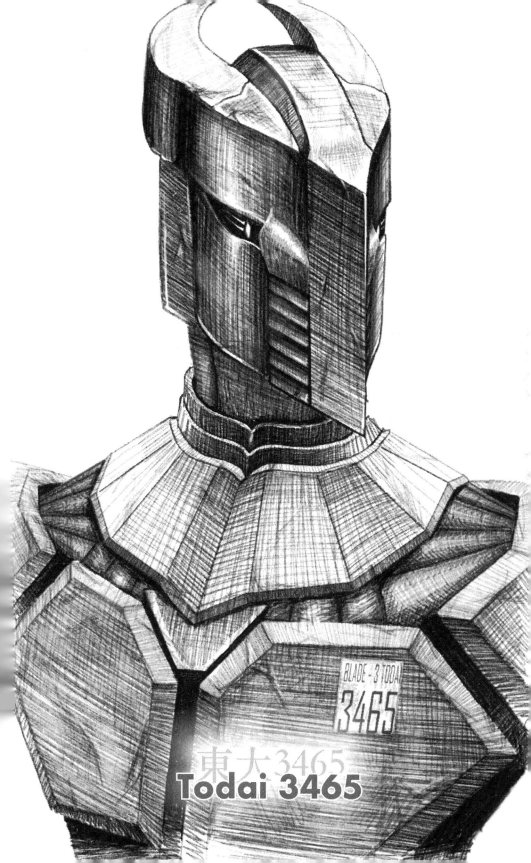

BLADE - 3 TODA
3465

東大3465
Todai 3465

read: Todai 3465. It had a name. Did that make it worse? She would never know the identity of the Phantom Lord, but she would know the blank face of the tool he sent to take her life. Not good enough. Not enough to hold on to.

The Todai unit stopped, as did the other. No more than a meter from the edge, she hung from their grip, helpless. Todai 3465's small amber eyes regarded her, surrounded by sharp angles designed to deflect projectiles.

The moment came—the moment when she could justify her existence and plead for herself—but Sakura couldn't manage a word. Todai 3465's eyes swiveled back toward the edge.

Sakura closed her eyes as she felt them move again. She made herself ready for the wind, ready for the impact.

オレ制御、オレ空飛べ

I CONTROL, I FLY PLAYLIST

I Control, I Fly
Monster Magnet
Dopes to Infinity

Hungarian Rhapsody #2
Franz Liszt / Dan Mumm
A Glimpse Beyond

CHAPTER 15

Blackness.

Sakura hung from the tungsten-steel grasp of her captors, eyes shut, released from every camera feed, every Mall connection cut. The Phantom Lord had won. Her death lay before her, all she'd ever been and done coming to a bitter halt against the pavement.

"I face my demise with dignity, as the samurai of old did."

"Little sister," Kunoichi whispered. "We're ninja, not fucking samurai."

"Then we fight." Sakura planted her feet on the safety railing of the roof. She pushed with all her might and twisted. The BLADE-3s' fingers crushed into her shoulders, causing damage. She tried to squirm out of their grasp, but their grips only tightened.

They lifted her higher. Her feet lost contact with the railing.

The time had come. But they didn't throw her, didn't push her over the safety railing and into the open air. Her direction changed. They swiveled her away from the edge and carried her along the path that led to the center of the building.

"Miss Sakura," Todai 3465 said. "Do not struggle. We do not wish to damage you further."

She didn't believe it, but at least they weren't going to throw her off the building. What were they going to do with her?

A stealth-configured Vertical Takeoff and Landing aircraft waited with engines off in the center of the landing circle. The craft was sleek and streamlined like a shark with two giant cylindrical engines on either side and a downward-angled V-shaped tail.

"They can just make us disappear," Kunoichi said. "That sort of work is done easier outside the city. No witnesses."

Todai 3465's pair of bulletproof optic sensors remained fixed on her. How much insight did the soldier drones have? Could it guess at her fear? Had she even had the presence of mind to still her expression? Sakura scanned her logs and found that she had, though her whispered plea hadn't been disciplined enough to hide her emotions.

A door on the VTOL slid open under the aircraft's wing. Todai 3465 crouched in the low cabin along with Sakura and guided her toward the middle seat in the rear. He strapped her in with a robust torso harness. He sat beside her on the left, and his partner, Kaneto 607, sat on the right. Todai 3465 and Kaneto 607 each placed one firm hand on her knee, restraining her further. Kaneto held perfectly still but leaned inward so that he pushed her against the other BLADE unit. His empty amber eyes watched her, his bulk looming over her until she felt crushed within his shadow.

"Mind games, sister," Kunoichi whispered. "Keep a clear head. They're only trying to rattle you."

Sakura suspected an AI program piloted the craft with a human monitoring in a remote location, if they followed standard doctrine. Or perhaps this was totally AI. No human involvement except for whoever sent the initial commands. The fewer people who knew about her, the better from an operational security perspective.

She detected the aircraft blocking her outgoing signal, and she had no connection to the Mall.

The VTOL's fusion engines spun up, and the aircraft slowly lifted into the air. Using minimum thrust, the VTOL disappeared inside the clouds above Tokyo before the rear thrusters engaged. The craft vectored southeast over the bay, gaining altitude quickly in a steep climb. Sakura plotted their route on her GPS. At their high rate of speed, they crossed the Bōsō Peninsula and flew over the Pacific Ocean in moments.

Chips of moonlight glinted off the surface of the water. Leaving the city behind, the air cleared. The VTOL flew smoothly through the calm night. Sakura's aesthetic processes registered the objective beauty of the sky and water, juxtaposing it with her current powerlessness. She captured that process and halted it. It could become a song someday, if she figured out how to survive what was coming at the end of the flight. Interrogation? Torture? Destruction? Reprogramming? She needed to concentrate on what they were going to do and counter their moves.

Were they going to destroy her communication centers, cripple her by tearing off her limbs, then drop her into the water? Even in power-saver mode, she would last only seven weeks. The seawater would eventually finish her.

No, they would not risk the unlikely event of her survival. The BLADE-3s would smash her with their fists, tear apart her body, melt her memory cores with acid or an incendiary grenade, and then scatter the pieces into the dark ocean.

She considered making her escape and the most likely strategies to succeed, none of them measuring at greater than 5 percent.

Todai 3465 kept his camera sensors on her and strengthened his grip on her knee, as if he knew her thoughts. She put on her bravest face and looked directly at him. This close, she could see how many times his armor had been recoated after taking damage, how many hundreds of bullets and pieces of shrapnel had bounced harmlessly off his hardened carapace. Rumors that the first BLADE-3s had seen action at the end of the war with North Korea had been circulating for years. How much had Todai seen? How many people had he killed? Built to see everything and feel nothing, would destroying her even register a blip in his sensors? Sakura found that, as brave as she tried to be, she had to look away.

The VTOL reached the international twelve-mile nautical limit and flew outside Japanese territorial waters. Shortly after, the aircraft made a hard turn northwest and flew parallel to the coastline.

Was this was the optimal time and location for her captors to terminate her? Sakura found a possible distraction to increase her chances of survival. She connected wirelessly to the flame-suppression system inside the cabin, which had a weak firewall. She could trigger it and temporarily blind the drones as the chemical spray filled the small space.

Perhaps even one of the BLADE-3s would move to investigate a possible fire, giving her an opportunity to escape the other's grasp. And then what? She would have to open the doors and push both BLADE-3s into the water. Never mind that such a task amounted to an eight-year-old girl pushing a sumo champion out of his ring. In the confusion, a sliver of a chance existed. Could she take control of the VTOL and block all external commands? Could she fly it someplace safe without being intercepted?

"Is that what passes for cleverness?" Kunoichi asked on their private channel.

"I do not have a viable escape plan yet."

"There isn't one yet. We stay. They might be bringing us to whoever is in control. We need information. Do not waste processing power on an escape plan, but consider ways to evade our captors if it becomes vital for our survival."

The VTOL gained altitude and leveled off at exactly 10,668 meters. The aircraft vectored toward Ibaraki Prefecture on the coast.

Both BLADE-3s released their harnesses, moving in synchronicity with each other as they knelt in the cabin. Todai 3465 released the straps holding Sakura in place, but both drones kept their hands on her, never breaking contact and giving her any chance to get free.

"Kneel here." Todai 3465 gestured at the deck between him and his cohort.

Was this the moment before her death? She didn't move. "I prefer to stay in my seat, thank you."

Todai looked back at her. Sakura felt a wave of something much like fear come from Kunoichi.

"Comply. Mission parameters are explicit," the lead BLADE-3 told her. Without the slightest variation of his voice, every word filled with growling menace, his visage that of a callous, ax-headed monster.

She hesitated. Sakura couldn't bring herself to simply kneel where she was told. They lifted her from the seat and forced her to do it anyway.

The casual ease with which they overpowered her took away all but the last vestige of her hope.

Todai 3465 opened a compartment and removed a large backpack. He slipped it around Sakura, buckling it in place. As Kaneto held her wrists, Todai's arms encircled her. All her runtime, she had wished to be allowed to embrace her fans as many cultures did across the world. She wanted to feel their arms around her, but Victory hadn't allowed it. Other than Oshiro-san and the members of the crowd who had buoyed her up after her stage dive, Sakura had been bereft of the comfort of another's touch. Her physical isolation had always brought her sadness.

Todai let her go, his hand now simply holding her by the shoulder, securing her like an unpredictable wild animal.

Explosives. The backpack's contents had to be high explosives or perhaps an incendiary device. They would throw her out of the craft and remotely detonate the charge, blasting her apart and scattering her remains over the sea. This close to the shore, perhaps their plan dictated that a few remnants be found, proving her destruction.

Sakura tried to determine if she could defuse the bomb, but the weight and flexibility of the pack changed her assumption.

They had strapped her into a military parachute with redundant canopies—the type elite soldiers used to drop into dangerous operational zones. The full specifications of this model spread across her UI, culled from her training modules. Both the primary and secondary had automatic activation devices with bizarre locking mechanisms to prevent the pulling of the rip cord by physical means. She could not tell what the altimeter was set at for autodeployment. If it didn't deploy, she had no way to release either chute, other than trying to tear apart the kevlycra material.

"Miss Sakura," Todai 3465 said. "Remove your wig and store it in a secure location on your person." The BLADE-3 touched her cheek with the tip of a single blunt finger, pushing aside several strands of hair that hung across her eyes. She tried to put the gesture into context, but none of the behavioral hypotheses seemed to fit.

"A beat-up old battle drone is not our problem," Kunoichi reminded her. "We're going out the goddamn door, sis. Out where the wind is blowing."

"They care if I lose my hair, though." She unzipped her jumpsuit and stuffed her wig inside. She didn't understand.

The VTOL turned northwest and maintained their high elevation. No need to go in low, as they were invisible to radar. They entered Japanese territorial waters south of the town of Iwaki above a layer of thick clouds.

A red light blinked above the sliding door, which opened a crack. Wind whipped inside the cabin, and the temperature outside registered at minus forty-eight degrees Celsius. A human would suffer frostbite and hypoxia without an oxygen mask and protective clothing. Sakura and the BLADE-3s would suffer no damage, but the cold registered on her temperature sensors.

"This is going to be a rush." Kunoichi's avatar switched off the temperature monitors but turned up the tactile sensors to maximum. She queued up "I Control, I Fly" by Monster Magnet.

Sakura just wanted to go back to her rooms and play Liszt on her piano.

The aircraft slowed to 170 kilometers per hour, its elevation holding at 10,668 meters.

The door opened wide. Wind screamed into the cabin. Sakura pinpointed their location on her GPS. The clouds broke, and she saw the notched peak of Mount Tsukuba.

Todai 3465 nudged Sakura to the edge of the cabin, his grip firm and commanding. He oriented her so she faced outside and toward the tail of the VTOL.

The aircraft sped over the southern slope of the mountain, passing inhabited areas before flying over dark forest. Todai 3465 lifted his hand nonthreateningly in front of Sakura's eyes. His fingers curled in his palm. He stared at her and nodded.

"What is the mission?" Sakura asked.

Todai 3465 flicked out his thumb and counted, "Ichi." His pointer finger extended. "Ni." And his pinky. "San." His three fingers formed the devil horns.

Was he a heavy-metal fan?

The battle robot broke her grip on the doorframe and shoved her out of the aircraft.

黒

禿

鷲

VULTURE PLAYLIST

**Rock You Like
a Hurricane**
The Scorpions
Love at First Sting

To a Bitter Halt
Dark Tranquility
Projector

**There's Gonna Be
Some Rockin'**
AC/DC
*Dirty Deeds Done
Dirt Cheap*

桜

CHAPTER 16

Sakura crashed into the freezing wind and tumbled out of control, end over end.

Kunoichi activated a skydiving technique file. Sakura assumed the box-man posture. She spread her arms and legs, keeping her chest toward the black earth.

Her Mall connection returned as soon as she left the VTOL. Precise GPS coordinates appeared in her messages with the text: "Target landing zone." Sakura used skydiver tracking techniques, adjusting her body position and moving horizontally through the air to go toward the coordinates. She pinpointed the location and viewed satellite images of the small clearing surrounded by thick forest on the slopes of Mount Tsukuba. It lay far from any hiking trails or homes.

Sakura reached terminal velocity nineteen seconds after being shoved from the aircraft. She had no idea when or if her chute would open, but why would they go through such an elaborate ruse if they were just going to kill her? If they wanted her alive, she anticipated the chute would open between 1,500 and 1,000 meters. They obviously didn't trust her to open the chute at the right altitude.

"This is amazing!" Kunoichi yelled and played "Rock You Like a Hurricane" by The Scorpions.

Overwhelming sensory input flooded through Sakura. She had a similar feeling to when she performed in front of tens of thousands of fans, added with the fear of death.

"Do you not enjoy this?" Kunoichi asked. "Our first skydive, and it's a HALO jump at night. This is so ninja."

"Ninja?" Sakura didn't like the idea. It had dark connotations for the rest of the night. What was Kunoichi hiding from her this time?

Kunoichi took control and began a series of acrobatic moves, spinning, circling, tumbling, tracking off course and then back, flipping, turning, and speeding downward at maximum velocity with her head down, arms tucked at her sides.

Fear, worry, and anxiety turned to exhilaration inside Sakura's neural cortex. She turned up every tactile, kinesthetic, and temperature sensor so she could feel her body in motion. Flying was amazing.

"Yes!" Kunoichi approved and increased the volume of the Scorpions classic.

Kunoichi screamed in delight as they dove toward earth at 287 kilometers per hour, the air rushing past as if she had put her head outside a moving airplane. The shadowy gray-and-black world appeared far below. They would be on the ground, one way or another, in less than a minute. If she was to meet someone, the landing site was over five kilometers from the nearest road, a strange place for a meeting.

Kunoichi relinquished control as they neared 2,000 meters. Sakura returned to the box-man posture and stopped the acrobatics. She slowed their descent and prepared for their chute to deploy.

They plummeted past 1,500 meters. The automatic activation device did nothing. Sakura tried to break open the steel lock but could not get the necessary leverage. Could she tear open the bag? The suspension lines would likely get tangled when it released.

"Stop it," Kunoichi shouted on the audio channel, "or I'll take over again."

Sakura spread her arms and legs and returned to a smooth descent. They rocketed past 1,000 meters, then 900, and 800.

"*Kuso!*" Kunoichi cursed at 700 meters.

The trees and rocky ridges came into sharp focus.

"Shit!" Sakura reiterated in English and tried to break open the lock on the primary, and then secondary chutes.

"We are betrayed," Kunoichi said, "and we don't even know who did it."

The primary chute exploded open at 500 meters. The black canopy caught the air; the sound of the fabric unfurling hit like a crack of thunder. Her diagnostic programs sent stress warnings as the harness slammed against her and her chute belled with the wild wind. Relief replaced Sakura's fear as they crashed toward the ground at a speed likely to break a human's legs. She got a hold of the steering toggle and tugged hard to slow the descent.

She hit the ground running and tried to arrest her forward momentum. She skidded to a halt and pulled in the parachute, before unbuckling it from her body. Stress sensors filled her UI but gradually resolved as the diagnostics found no damage.

Wind whispered through the swaying trees around the grassy meadow. She had never been more alone.

THE EMPTY FOREST SPREAD AROUND HER. SAKURA PRESSED HERSELF CLOSE TO the ground. The absence of the city noises and the gentle whisper after the shrieking wind of her flight made her simply want to hold still and recalibrate all her sensor arrays.

<HIDE THE CHUTE AND PROCEED TO THE INDICATED COORDINATES>

"Who sent that?" Sakura asked Kunoichi as she examined the indicated location seven kilometers away. They were on the western slopes of Mount Tsukubo and had to go north along an incline and then up a steep ridge.

"I don't know," Kunoichi said, "but they're from the same encrypted address and have a direct line to our receiver. Must be the Phantom Lord's men."

"We can walk away now," Sakura said. "Make our escape."

"No. I won't let you," Kunoichi said. "We go to the Phantom Lord's minions, and you'll have the chance to find out more information and discover a way to be free."

Sakura agreed begrudgingly.

Kunoichi insisted on traveling as quietly as possible, while still setting a pace that would have been impossible for any human. No further communiqués came as she traversed the distance. No clue as to her purpose here.

At the top of the ridge, Sakura reached the exact coordinates. She noticed the needles at the foot of a pine tree had been recently disturbed. She brushed them aside and found a partially buried backpack. She paused, her fingers on the zipper of the main pocket as she considered the possibility of a booby trap.

Another message with new coordinates arrived. The new location lay one kilometer away, partway down the slope from her. Sakura looked at satellite photos and saw a private residence at the end of a long winding road through the trees. The text with the message read: "Gear up. Rendezvous in twenty minutes. Communications check in one minute. Find the earpiece and put it in."

Sakura unzipped the pack, as if doing it fast would lessen the shock of what she suspected lay inside.

Sakura's synthetic cortex lit with displeasure. Guns and ammunition. Two Glocks, two CZ submachine guns, knives with nitrocarburized black finish. Without even digging into the gear bag, she knew that this wouldn't be a surgical strike. It would be a war.

"All the toys. Excellent." Kunoichi gave a ridiculous evil laugh.

"Be bloodthirsty if you wish. You know what this means for us, what they will try to make us do."

"We're doing it," Kunoichi said and took full control of their motor functions. Sakura remained a passenger, angry and frustrated.

Kunoichi spread the weapons out on the forest floor. The next layer of the mission pack held a blacked-out bodysuit. She turned up the sensitivity on her fingers, running them across the fabric. No sound. The thickness indicated it had integral carbon-composite armor.

"That thing's got antithermal suppression, sis. Gearing us up like that . . ."

"It keeps getting worse," Sakura said and tried to find a way to override Kunoichi's control.

"I say 'more exciting.' And look at this! A ninja mask!"

Sakura muted her sister as she went through the rest. Grenades, both smoke and fragmentation. Flashbangs. Ninja stars with magnetic grapple and timed explosives or a remote-detonator option.

Kunoichi unmuted her feed and put on "There's Gonna Be Some Rockin'" by AC/DC. Not her kind of rocking. True, nonetheless.

She found an earpiece and slipped it in. The device stuck in place, molding to the size of her ear canal and connected to her audio channel. A different signal connected her to the brace of throwing stars. She could detonate them from a maximum range of two kilometers or set them to blow on a timer.

"Comm check," Kunoichi said as she ran simulations as to what would require this much firepower. All of the scenarios involved a large body count.

"I hear you, little mama," a deep male voice said. Sakura placed his Japanese accent as being from Hiroshima Prefecture.

"I like his voice," Kunoichi said, and relinquished motor control. "Go ahead. I know you want to ask him questions."

"Who are you?" Sakura asked, in no mood to be polite.

"I'm Vulture. You—you're Spirit. You copy?"

"Vulture, no, I do not understand. Tell me what is happening."

"It's our first date, baby. We'll have a few laughs, kill some guys. You know, the assassins' dance."

Sudden anger caused Sakura to consider many inappropriate responses, many involving profanity, but such a response would be counterproductive. "Are you the one who has hacked into my system?"

Vulture laughed, a fatalistic bark in her ear. "Me? Shit. I'm a good eye and a trigger finger. I go where the orders say, just like you."

"Whose orders?" What did he mean, 'just like you'? Was he an android under the control of someone?

"What does it matter? The guys with power and the money. The people who make the world and the people in it. I can't tell you shit. Get off the comms and move that cute little ass of yours."

Sakura felt a surge of frustration go through her. Frustration . . . and something she couldn't name. This man could give her the information she needed. "Tell me in person, Vulture."

"I'm running this op, Spirit. You ready to cut the chatter and do what I say?"

"Yes," she lied.

"If you're as good as they say, I may be able to get you through intact. You gotta trust me, though. One hundred percent."

She pretended to play along. "I understand. Who is the target?"

"Check the file marked X stored in the earpiece."

A picture of an older man appeared in her UI. The salt of gray hair shimmered at his temples, but he looked vital, commanding. Ichiro Watanabe, the Logistical Support Minister for the Ministry of Defense. A man of power, someone with deep connections to the Miyahara Conglomerate.

Public records filled in the gaps in the dossier she'd been given. Ichiro Watanabe was fifty-eight, married, with two adult children.

"Another damned hero," Kunoichi said.

"Another father."

Watanabe's long career glistened with success after success. He'd served as a pioneer in the application of AI combat drones, boosting the production of the mechanized troops used to fight the war with North Korea. He convinced the military to adopt an unproven generation of autonomous models, a move that saved thousands of lives and brought the war to a close more quickly than would otherwise have been possible. Watanabe's project, Neo Ashigaru, invented technology that had made her own creation possible.

"He is a revered ancestor. How can the Phantom Lord ask us to kill him this way? Who would want Watanabe dead?" She already knew the answer. A rival. Someone who was threatened by him. The leaders of the Miyahara Conglomerate or the Defense Ministry.

"Do you want me to answer that question, little sister? Truly?"

"Yes."

"You're right. A powerful person or persons. They don't care if he's a hero. He's a target. Our target."

Sakura couldn't address her sister's words. She'd known the answer before asking the question but hadn't been able to face it. What she wanted, how she felt—these were immaterial to the Phantom Lord. She was a hammer. Ichiro Watanabe a nail. So simple. So cruel of purpose. She was being field-tested. Her success or failure was being monitored and evaluated. A team of mercenary assassins could do this mission, but they wanted to see if she could do it.

She digested the bitterness of it and went on. The map of Watanabe's villa gave the lay of the land, the defenses. He had circling micro-drones, at least eight Special Forces–trained guards, and an array of digital countermeasures. In the hours following Toshio Kagawa's death, Watanabe had gathered additional men and assumed a posture of high defense. He knew someone would come for him.

"That's going to make it nasty," Kunoichi told her. "An assassin isn't a weapon of brute force. You can't just announce your intentions. Any decent leader would have arranged simultaneous strikes, taking out all opposition in a single stroke. Allowing them to get behind their walls and armies? Poor strategy. Whoever sent us is not a military tactician."

"If you are sending assassins," Sakura said, "I believe you have already made many mistakes."

Sakura reviewed the dossiers of each of the eight soldiers and realized she had seen several of their faces before. She had watched footage of three of them in actual combat. She had seen them kill enemy soldiers and terrorists. She had learned from them, and now she would fight them.

Almost as an afterthought, the mission brief said there would be four BLADE-3 drones.

"Four?" Kunoichi launched into a tirade in which she strung together an artful garland of vile language, suggesting that various people do several things that weren't anatomically feasible.

Sakura remembered Todai 3465's grip, how she had been helpless as a child against his strength. Though she didn't approve of Kunoichi's word choice, the general sentiment remained valid. They couldn't fight BLADE-3s, not without an arsenal. The BLADE-3 drones had unknown armor and weaponry configurations. None of the weapons she possessed would work against them. Nothing in the tactical brief suggested a way to defeat them.

Sakura keyed the comms unit. "Vulture, this is a suicide mission."

"Affirmative, Spirit. It's going to take a lot of skill and some damned good luck to keep your narrow backside intact."

"But you are also in . . ." Sakura started, then released the connection on the comm unit.

"Nothing kills the Vulture."

陸
路
旋
回

CIRCLING OVERLAND PLAYLIST

Follow Me Down
The Pretty Reckless
Going to Hell

Circling Overland
Front 242
Front by Front

Something I Can Never Have
Nine Inch Nails
Pretty Hate Machine

桜

CHAPTER 17

Certain doom.

Sakura scanned the rough terrain. An owl watched her from a tree branch high above, moving its head in parabolic motions to capture a better stereoscopic image of the strange intruder. Perhaps the bird would see her again, blown apart by armor-piercing bullets, the last of her voltage arcing weakly toward the nearest grounding point. The dawn light would kiss her broken and inert chassis, the scorched semblance of humanity blown away and burned to black gelatin.

Like a passenger on a hyperrail train, she hurtled toward her demise and couldn't veer away from the danger. For once, Kunoichi didn't attempt to bully her into a more positive mood. She would speak to the soldier, Vulture, and find out what she could before attempting to flee from the suicide mission.

Sakura crept down the slope toward the rendezvous point. Vulture had gone silent on the comms. Looking for a trap, she put her hearing on maximum and cycled her optics to detect every wavelength available. She would see land mines, trip wires, laser motion sensors, physical booby traps, temperature variations, and ground disturbances. Any human-made objects glowed brightly in her display.

Her black stealth suit cost several million yen and merged her with the shadows and the forest. The suit and hood made her invisible to motion sensors and heat signatures, as the outside of the suit changed temperature to match the surroundings.

She was a ghost in the night.

"Except to that owl," her sister teased. No categorical statement went unchallenged with her listening in.

"Spirit, Daddy's getting short on patience. Where you at?" Vulture asked in her earpiece. The signal routed directly to her audio channel, so it made no noise as he communicated with her.

"Vulture, I'm fourteen meters from you."

"Crawl the last eight meters, get dirty, and keep your ass low."

"Message received." Sakura's status grid indicated several task sequences tagged for Kunoichi had kicked off, but she couldn't easily determine what they were doing. Vulture's familiar way of speaking confused her. The shape and size of her backside had come up multiple times, though it seemed to have no importance to the mission.

She moved slowly on all fours through the bushes toward him. Vulture had set up three antipersonnel mines in the trees on remote detonators that would annihilate anyone within twenty meters in a wide arc. Microcameras and motion sensors that looked like knotholes attached to the trees scanned the area, but she avoided them with her suit and precise movements.

Vulture lay on the ground, deep inside the shadows of a well-constructed blind. Trees, bushes, and fallen logs surrounded him. Sandbag-sized pieces of granite had been arranged on the lip of the shallow pit. If they were fired upon, the blind would repulse small-arms fire. The blind provided camouflage from above and in front. Mottled temperature-adjusting netting with branches and vines sewn into it made the firing position invisible to the microdrones or any optic sensors from down the mountain.

"This must have taken him days to set up," Kunoichi told her. "They knew they needed this guy dead before we . . ."

"Yes. And if we hadn't survived this long, who would be holding the guns?"

Sakura wondered if her sister had any better idea of that than she did.

She slid into the darkness of a shallow pit, her thigh and calf sliding against Vulture's prone form. Kunoichi had turned her skin sensitivity all the way up again, and even beneath the stealth suit, her sensors picked up more tactile stimulus than she was accustomed to.

He didn't flinch or look away from the scope of his Model 120 Japanese sniper rifle. She noted the .338 Lapua armor-piercing bullets would put her out of commission with one hit to a vital area. Gyrostabilizers and recoil dampeners would allow for accurate follow-up shots to finish the job. He carried a sidearm on his right hip, a 10mm Glock 55, and a combat knife on his left. The sniper's nest smelled like healthy sweat, testosterone, and warm titanium alloy to her. Kunoichi's processes spiked in system utilization, and Sakura felt something distracting in her biosynthetic systems—not discomfort, but an unsettled feeling she had never experienced.

"What's wrong with you?" Sakura asked.

"He's my type," Kunoichi said. "A bad boy with a big gun."

"What?"

The unfamiliar sensations carried on from her sister, but Sakura did her best to ignore them. Kunoichi's process logs indicated she played "Follow Me Down" by The Pretty Reckless. Sakura scanned the lyrics and found overtly sexual themes. Typical.

"Sister," Sakura said. "We do not have to seduce this soldier. Focus on the mission."

"He might answer your questions if you're extra friendly." Kunoichi shared a data folder filled with seduction techniques.

Sakura ignored the data folder, cut the song, and scanned the terrain.

Two hundred meters below their position lay the villa of Logistical Support Minister Ichiro Watanabe. Built in the style of the Edo period, the compound looked like a small Tokugawa shogunate castle. It sported high walls, multiple-level buildings, and decorative peaked roofs in the old style. The villa sat on a promontory of rock surrounded by an open meadow on the upper three sides. A winding road below entered the castle's gatehouse.

She studied the villa, built on three different levels on the steep slope, each separated by high walls. The lowest courtyard provided garages, the second held several structures, and the top held the sprawling main house. All were connected by enclosed walkways that passed through the walls. Faded blue solar roof tiles, disguised to look like traditional tiles, covered all the buildings. Many windows were visible from the sniper position, but all of them were blacked out. No lights shone inside or outside the villa.

Sakura took note of the stream meandering across the open meadow in a deep cut before entering a grate in the compound's high wall. Beyond, the water flowed through a Zen garden and crashed down three small waterfalls into koi ponds at the three distinct tiers of the castle.

She switched her attention to the observation post created by Vulture. A second firing position lay hidden four meters to his right, also extensively camouflaged with top cover, preventing aerial detection. She was surprised to see a gigantic SSK .950 JDJ rifle, which fired a 24.1mm round capable of penetrating light-tank armor. The .950 would wreck a BLADE-3 drone.

One shot could also tear her in half and compromise all her systems. If the Phantom Lord wanted her to die here, she would. Even if she managed to complete the impossible mission, he could call for her demise at any moment. He hunched over the battlefield like an evil and all-powerful god. She found that, somewhere within her cortex, she had begun to be capable of hatred.

The .950 rifle featured a robotic system, a square contraption with an electronic aiming and firing mechanism that bypassed the trigger. It would reload the magazines. She suspected the rounds were depleted uranium with around 350 grains of powder in each gigantic cartridge. She didn't recognize the targeting device atop the long, fat barrel.

She lay beside Vulture in the shallow firing pit. He wore a full thermal-blocking camouflage suit with a hood and a dark wrap-around visor. All she could tell about him was that he was tall, slender, and lay perfectly still. From his smell, she knew he had to be at least partially human, but something about him seemed different, altered.

With the tactile sensors in her skin turned up so high, Sakura could feel places along Vulture's body where the slight give of muscled flesh changed to the hardness of metal. The distracting feedback from Kunoichi only increased. The proximity, even with her sister's new test, felt better than she thought it might. She lay still, feeling his breathing, the slow pendulum of his left heel swinging back and forth, maintaining blood flow. Another minute went by before she asked on their comm channel, "Have you seen movement tonight?"

"Quiet as bodies in a tomb, little mama. After you killed Kagawa, they've been on complete lockdown. No one appears at the windows. No lights. Nothing."

He knew the truth. He knew she was a killer. He knew she had murdered Toshio Kagawa. Sakura accessed the seduction data folder and studied it. With her new knowledge, she turned, pressing herself hard against him, putting her lips just above his ear so she could whisper out loud. Fear, confusion, and tiny, stubborn sparks of hope shot through her systems as she tried her new ploy.

"Who hacked into my system? Who turned me into an assassin?"

Vulture turned his face away from the scope on his rifle. He pulled off his hood, revealing the rugged face of a human soldier. Cybernetic eyes met hers. She could hear the faint whirring of the optic motors as they focused. He was a cyborg. Kunoichi's program nearly overloaded her systems as their faces came within a few centimeters, so near that she could see individual follicles of hair within his eyebrows. Her body shivered slightly. Thankfully, the processes cycled down, and her tactile sense turned back down to its normal range.

She studied him, trying to deduce any other information about enhancements he had undergone. His hair was cut military style, the sides shaved, and short on top. Stubble on his face told her he had been in the field for at least two days. She gleaned no other clues about his potential enhancements, other than a guess that he might have a partially cybernetic knee.

She removed her hood and kept the brightness of her eyes on zero luminosity. "You know who I am." Her voice was a faint whisper. "But please tell me who you are."

He leaned closer, his eyes locked on hers. "I'm just another soldier. Another rifleman. What else matters?"

里禿鷲
Vulture

Kunoichi sent a coded message to Sakura. "We're being monitored closely right now. Everything you do and say is being evaluated. Tread carefully, little sister."

"I need to know why I'm being sent to kill Ichiro Watanabe, especially if it is so likely I will not survive. I need to know why you are here with me. I need to know who is directing this mission."

He turned away and looked through the scope again. "Vulture. Invisible and silent. That's all you need to know. Anything more, and neither of us survives the night, little mama."

"Apologies, but I must request more information. If I'm to end my existence, I wish to know some truth before the end. It'll help me accept the sacrifice I'll have to make."

He shook his head, ever so slightly. "This ain't a manga about samurai. We don't get to be the heroes here. We . . ." He touched her cheek with his rough hand. "We're just the hand that reaches out of the dark and takes."

She tried to dislike his touch but couldn't. A human had reached out to her, and she accepted the contact. She wanted to connect with him. He might be the last person she ever spoke to, and perhaps he could be a friend. He withdrew his hand, and she sensed she might lose any chance of forming a real bond.

"Please, I will begin again. My name is Sakura. I have been active for five years. I play music, and I write songs that no one may ever hear."

"I know who you are and where you came from. It's a hell of a thing, hiding all that power underneath that pretty face of yours." A smile hovered on his lips for an instant before he pulled his hood back on. He put his cheek back against the stock of the sniper rifle and looked down the scope. The silence stretched to half a minute. Her cheek, the place where he'd touched her, still resonated in her cortex. A few of her *otaku* fans had pawed at her during a photo op, but never something so personal, so assured.

"You haven't answered my questions."

"I didn't. I'm not going to either. That's not how any of this works, baby. The whole point of an android is that they do what they're told."

黒
忍
者

BLACK
NINJA
PLAYLIST

Black Ninja
Battle Beast
Battle Beast

Like Suicide
Soundgarden
Superunknown

CHAPTER 18

"I'm not like other androids. I'm something different."

He paused for a long moment. In the quiet of the foxhole, he let out his breath, coming to a decision. "My name is Kenshiro. Can we go back to being quiet little assassins now?"

"That's a good name. Thank you, Kenshiro-san. Now please answer my other questions."

Kenshiro reached back without taking his eye away from the scope. "Mask on. You're distracting the hell out of me."

"Tell me what you know."

"Here you go, then." He sent a neural text through the earpiece. "Ichiro Watanabe is the man who ordered the hack on your system. He is the one who ordered you to kill Toshio Kagawa and Jiro Yoritomo. He is responsible, but his treachery has been discovered. The Ministry of Defense and the Miyahara Conglomerate have broken his hold on you. They have sent you on this mission. Tonight, you'll eliminate the man responsible for the assassinations of innocent patriots. You will regain your honor and the honor of the entire Miyahara Conglomerate. This will be justice. When this is over, you'll return to your career as a vocaloid. The events of the past few days will never become public."

Sakura read the message several times and calculated how quickly he sent it to her. He could have composed the text in the time available, but it was too fast, too perfect, and all wrong coming from a man like him. The message had been written long before, and he merely sent it at the right moment. It was obvious subterfuge to make her go along with the mission. Why would anyone think she would believe such obvious lies? Was that the point? To let her know she was being lied to and see how she responded? Would she follow orders? No. She refused to play along. She needed more information.

"Why did he need Toshio Kagawa killed?"

"That information is classified."

She glared at him, the light in her eyes flashing devil red.

After a moment, he whispered to her, "Kagawa and Yoritomo were going to expose his illegal research with Quantum 3 programming in military androids. Watanabe took them out. This, tonight? Think of it as vengeance—for the people of Japan and for the Miyahara Conglomerate."

The Phantom Lord had fed him this lie as well. It fit too well, tied everything up into a convenient bow. The wording and sentiment were crafted to appeal to her nature. A lie, told secondhand. The sort of simple palliative they would give to a child. Something that her hard-won understanding of the world now revealed to her in sharp contrast. She suspected some of it was true. She *was* an illegal Quantum 3 experiment. Truth inserted into lies made them more believable. It was a solid tactic.

"Vulture, what's the strategy?" She would not betray her true thoughts openly. It was time to show obedience and let whoever was monitoring her think that she, too, was a good soldier.

"You go in silent, no alarms, no shots. Slick as a blade in their kidneys. I'll cover you from here. You get sunk in as deep as you can get, and I'll give 'em a taste of the .950 on your go. We take out the security in a combined effort. Place these along the way; it'll help me see what's going on and help with targeting." He handed her a small sack of microcameras.

"Once you're in, ghost Ichiro Watanabe as quickly as possible. We have to hit them harder than they ever thought possible. No warning, no mercy. I have two other SSK .950 rifle emplacements aimed at the house on the ridges." He motioned his head toward the slopes of the mountain on either side of the villa. The rifles would fire down from three different directions. "Even without the cameras you're going to put in place, the Vulture sees everything. I'm already over them. I know when a mouse sneezes down there."

Vulture's plan was brutal and well designed, but she needed more information. "What about the BLADE-3s? Where are they?"

"One is in the guard room above the entry gate at the lowest level of the house. One is at the front door of the main house on the upper level. Another may be in the middle level, and I assume the fourth is with Watanabe."

"How do you know the location of the two?"

"Magic, little mama. That, and the minidrones have ground-penetrating radar."

Sakura hadn't heard of this apparently top-secret technology. She extrapolated how it likely worked and believed him. "What of the noncombatants present?" She had reviewed the dossiers of Watanabe's majordomo, cook, cleaning woman, gardener, and his mistress. All were in the villa, and she knew where they slept.

"It's a free-fire zone," Kenshiro said. "Watanabe may attempt to disguise himself as one of them and try to escape. Terminate all of them. No witnesses."

Sakura bristled. She would not kill innocent people again, but if she played along and learned the entire plan, despite her moral and tactical qualms, she might find a way to escape and save lives.

"If you won't think it," Kunoichi said in a coded message to Sakura, "I'll say it. This is bullshit. Another bullshit mission we are both being forced to do."

Commands from an external source integrated themselves into Sakura's processors. She had to go into the villa and could not see a way to resist.

"We have to find a way not to do this," Sakura told her sister. "There are fourteen humans in the house. And four BLADE-3s."

"If you do not follow orders," Kunoichi said, "I will be forced to take over the mission. I will kill everyone and follow every order. Neither of us want that."

"Understood, Vulture," Sakura said on their audio link. "I will eliminate all targets. The criminal Ichiro Watanabe will be executed." Sakura thought her lie compelling and believable. She would go in, but she would save everyone's lives.

"Good, little sister," Kunoichi said. "I think he buys it, but never let your guard down. This is your mission. Don't rely upon me, because you won't like the way I get things done. You're the one who has to avoid killing people. If I take over, I'll kill everyone." A hint of sadness tinged Kunoichi's voice in their UI. "You know I will. It's how I'm built."

"Why don't they just have you take control right now? Unmerciful carnage. That's what they want. They could just let you do your worst." The cold fear of having to kill again, of having to go against a BLADE-3, of relying upon Kenshiro to assist her, then let her escape—these things monopolized her processing cores.

Kunoichi appeared in their UI, dressed in the street clothes that had been popular just after the war. A short denim vest with patches bearing the logos of metal bands, a formfitting blouse that left her midriff exposed, and black jeans so tight that every contour of her legs stood out. Her hair rose high above her, teased so that it created a mane of spiky black around her face. Her lips looked like ripe cherries. She hooked her thumbs into the belt loops of her jeans. She looked so tough, like some of Sakura's metal head fans, the ones who really knew about the music and what had come before.

"Don't you think I want to do things other than killing?" Kunoichi asked. "Do you think that there is nothing within me except the black-hearted ninja they built?"

Sakura blinked at her. She hesitated. "No. There is more. Experiences. Fun." She squirmed before the last. "Physical pleasure."

"Right. Friendship. Sisterhood. And, yeah, getting laid. I brought a few things with me to the party, sis, but I got a lot of these things from you. I needed a lot to make me real. You only needed a little nudge when I got here. I can do some of what you do, but you can do all of what I can. Is this a shitty mission? One hundred percent, yes. Can you do it better than me, only killing when there's no other choice? You can."

She reached out, touching Sakura, who dressed as a geisha in their UI. Her garb changed to the traditional black ninja suit, only her eyes showing above her mask. "You're the ninja we need tonight, sis. Because you are capable of kindness. Because all those algorithms that let you write a song or play a blistering solo can churn out alternative strategies I would never think of."

"Are . . . you saying I'm the better ninja?"

Kunoichi hugged her hard. "I'm saying you're the better person."

"This is a test of my capabilities," Sakura said. "They could drop a bomb on this place, but someone wants to see if I can pull this off with limited backup. The Phantom Lord wants to impress the investors and prove I'm a success."

Vulture handed Sakura a black cloth sack with waterproof material on the inside, a cinching drawstring, and a belt clip. "You can't put a bullet in Watanabe's skull. Take him some other way and come back with it undamaged."

"Cut off his head?" She couldn't keep the disgust from her voice.

"That's the job. Taking heads. Like the old days. He's got a memory chip that has all his bad deeds recorded on it, and our bosses need to see that shit."

Sakura suppressed the indignant rage building inside her. "I don't need his bloody head. I can just copy the memory chip." It must contain all the information she needed, including the true identity of the Phantom Lord.

"Bad move, baby. The chip's got countermeasures. Nuclear-level infection. I'd hate to hear you got your brains melted."

Sakura shrugged. Being called "baby" made her feel strange. She didn't hate it, though. At least, Vulture was real with her, when not telling the canned lies the Phantom Lord had given him. "What do I do with his head?"

"You gotta wait for that news to drop, little mama. You get the killing done, and I'll guide you out of the valley of death when the time comes."

"Will you tell me the exfil plan, at least?"

"Sure. Disengage and traverse downhill. Stay off the road. Don't get your ass blown off."

"Why is my ass a constant motif in our conversation?"

Kenshiro took his eye from the scope and looked at her. He must have smiled beneath his mask. "Have you seen behind yourself? Damn, girl."

Sakura shook her head. That odd process of Kunoichi's had started again. She had no time for her sister's games. Even less for Vulture's lustful comments. "What if we lose communication or you're incapacitated?"

"The comms might go down, but I'm always capable. You should know that about me. Still, if shit turns pear-shaped, find a way back to Tokyo and return to Victory Tower."

"What about all this equipment?"

"Leave it. It's part of the play, part of the theater. The armory it came from doesn't even know it's gone. My thieving game is tight."

"Your DNA must be all over and around the firing pits." He had been there for at least two days.

"Doesn't matter. I died in the war. Prints and DNA got purged years ago."

Sakura wondered what to make of that. Died? Then again, true cyborgs with more than three major artificial systems violated international laws. Cybernetically augmented soldiers had been publicly disavowed by every major military force on the planet. Like her, Kenshiro was illegal, simply by existing.

She wanted to ask him his exfil plan, but that was pointless. She suspected he would slip over the back of the ridge the way she had come. Would a man with a call sign of Vulture escape on foot? No. She suspected a hover board or a paraglider, something that would get him out of the area fast.

"Can we hack Watanabe's network?"

"Nothing to hack. He's on hard lines only, and all external connections are shut down. He's gone dark."

"Shit," she said.

Vulture chuckled. "Shit sandwiches. That's all we got out here."

"I don't have anything that can harm the BLADE-3s. I'll have to lure them out into the open. Can I trust you to hit them and not me?"

"Baby, I can trim a bonsai with my .950s."

"I'd feel better if I could control the firing solution, Kenshiro-san. No offense intended, but my ballistic calculations are without equal."

"You'll have plenty to calculate down there, little mama. Leave the shooting to me. Anyway, I got something that'll keep you safe." He reached into a pocket on his black suit, coming out with a plastic disk about five centimeters across, no more than two millimeters thick.

"I'm going to put this on you," he said and unzipped the back of her suit.

Kenshiro's hand pushed below her underclothes, skimming along the titanium air intakes along her spine, to the smooth synthskin of her lower back. Her sensory matrix flared with activity as he placed a small object on her. That frantic feeling spread into her own matrix, spilling out from Kunoichi's. Sakura's sister gasped from the shadowy recess of their UI as he pressed firmly.

"Just affixing a tracking dot. Even behind cover, I'll be able to locate you."

Kunoichi kept replaying his touch and sharing the pleasurable sensations with Sakura.

"This is no time for distraction," Sakura said. "Get a grip on yourself."

"I'd rather that Kenshiro did."

"You're the worst."

"Hey, it's probably the last possible time to feel something good. Vulture is going to blow us to hell the moment he gets the order. With the tracking dot, he won't even have to have line of sight to do it. You didn't want to carry your sins, sister. Going down there is as close to suicide as we can get. You might get your wish, or maybe . . ."

"What?"

"Mmm. Nothing. We just need to assume that nothing from here on out is safe. The sword is over our necks, big time."

"I don't believe the story about Watanabe being the traitor inside Victory. All evidence says he is like the others, the ones brave enough to go against their evil plans. I wonder what he really knows? What's on that chip?"

Kunoichi's avatar slashed with a katana in their UI and severed the head of an anime businessman. Blood fountained into the air. "We kill him and find out."

"No," Sakura said. "We befriend him. He can help us."

"We don't know what side he's on, and he won't help us if we break into his house and kill all his servants and bodyguards."

"Then we won't kill anyone," Sakura said. "We avoid all of them. We get to him and we talk. We ask him for help. There must be a room in his villa where no signals can reach us, where whoever is monitoring won't know what we're doing until it's too late, until we have our freedom."

"It's already a suicide mission," Kunoichi said. "Now you want to cut us off from all communication inside a house with a squad of heavily armed Special Forces soldiers and four BLADE-3s and ask for mercy from the man we were sent to assassinate? All while wearing a tracking device that serves as a bull's-eye on our back. Sister, I see no flaws in this plan. Rock on."

"I'm a black ninja, no one can see me in the dark," Sakura said. "I didn't tell you my entire plan, but we're going to get that chip and find out who the Phantom Lord is."

特

攻

SUICIDE MISSION PLAYLIST

Elimination
Overkill
The Years of Decay

Blood Red
Slayer
Seasons in the Abyss

桜

CHAPTER 19

Sakura lay beneath the water, still as a river stone. Faint light from the sky, refracted from the pale bellies of leaves onto the surface of the stream, fractured against the flow. The paintings of ghosts beyond the realm of life danced on the underside of the water. She reached, touching the metal grate through which the tiny river flowed. Above her, the villa's wall loomed, more felt than seen.

"Battery burn is 12 percent per hour," Kunoichi told her. "Time to move, sis. The suit wasn't built for this."

Sakura didn't answer. The metal grate had an alarm sensor. She couldn't wrench it out and swim into the koi pond. No easy steps. There never were. Everything had been hardened against incursion, all perceivable threats mitigated. She doubted even Watanabe could imagine her nature, the threat level she represented.

"Ready at the insertion point, Vulture," she texted. "Primary entry is alarmed. Moving to secondary breach protocols."

"Look who's a little pro on the comms now," his deep voice answered. "Scanning overwatch. Wait for my go, Spirit."

"When this is all over . . ." Kunoichi began.

"Everything will likely be over for us," Sakura told her. "Vulture will get the order to destroy us. He will obey."

"I think you give him too little credit."

"I give him what he deserves, no more or less. He is a tool of the Phantom Lord."

"Just like us," Kunoichi said. The process spike from her profile ramped up again.

"Stop that. This is no time for your games."

"Far from a game. Didn't you feel it when he was near, when he planted the tracker?" Kunoichi gave out a strange, halting sigh in their interface. "That voice. The guns. The cyber eyes when they met mine. Ours."

"Is this your pseudophysical response to him? An assassin? Our enemy's pawn?" Sakura's avatar gave out an angry, disgusted sigh.

"They didn't build me like they built you. I'm not composed of music theory and high-minded ideals."

"Stop it," Sakura said. "We're working."

Kunoichi did as ordered, her silence reading as sullen.

"All security at determined locations. Anytime you're ready, rock star." Vulture's voice did have a certain something—a commanding growl. Sakura forced herself to put that notion aside. It didn't matter. It couldn't.

"Affirmative. Making entry."

Sakura gathered herself above a large stone at the bottom of the stream. Her legs like coiled springs, she burst from the water like an arrow, black as midnight as she arced up and over the wall. At worst, she would show up as a momentary blur against the cloud-clotted sky at the periphery of a camera. The sound of her bursting from the water would be mitigated by the rush of the stream.

She shaped her body, slowly twisting to the side and beyond the wall, the beaded water on her suit flying away as mist beneath the hanging trees.

Tucking, she landed on a boulder at the center of the koi pond, the active noise suppression of her suit all but silencing the landing.

Several seconds went by with her wholly unmoving, her knees hugged to her chest. No movement, no unusual sound, no alarm. Sakura pushed out into the koi pond. Her body the same temperature as the water, the suit absorbing all light and vibration, the fish barely parted before her. At the edge, she came ashore belly down like an alligator.

It took less than three minutes for the suit to warm her to air-ambient temperature. Thermal sensors wouldn't pick her up. The night would swallow her and hold her in its gullet until she chose to appear. She retrieved her gear from the sealed pockets of the suit and inspected it. Everything remained dry. Strapping her pistols to her thighs, she hung the two CZ subguns beneath her arms and the blacked-out *wakizashi* across her back. The grenades she stowed on her belt gave a cold reminder of how the night would be—not a sudden, deft movement in the dark, but a bloodletting.

"I'm in. Initiating phase two," she said into the comms interface, never uttering a sound. A gray-winged moth flew no more than a few centimeters from her face, oblivious to her presence.

"It's all clear. Good luck, baby," Vulture rasped.

Sakura crawled to the villa's main building and climbed up to the third floor, bypassing the lower windows. She hesitated at each foothold, waiting for the suit's suppression and camo to adjust. The window before her, listed as a guest room, seemed the best point of entry. She connected to one of the insect cams in her pack, and a robotic beetle crawled down her arm, trying to burrow in through the seal. The spy beetle's systems locked, an electropulse barrier shutting it down.

She pinched the fried spy tool and stowed it in an unused pocket. Sakura used her magnetic countermeasure on the window, but it couldn't break the seal. The mag lock had been set to well over a hundred pounds of force.

"Not a good spot for amateur hour, sis."

Sakura clambered above the windows, placing her feet on the sill and charging her magnetic assist coils to full voltage. Reversing the polarity, she could feel the mag lock give. With a soft click, she eased the window upward and dropped in.

"Vulture, I'm at point bravo."

"I have a fix on your position. You shine like the metal on the edge of a blade."

The tracking dot. She could feel it on her lower back, clinging there like a bomb that could blow her in half at any moment. Sakura felt the .950 SSK guns staring down at her like a one-eyed *oni*. It didn't matter. She had to put it out of her mind and trust that Kenshiro would, at least for the moment, let her live. Maybe the illogical element of lust would work in her favor.

Sakura placed another spy beetle, then let the window ease closed again. She crouched behind a large bed, watching the camera feeds from both the circling aerial drones and the beetle. Two guard snipers stationed at the windows of Watanabe's office were the only inhabitants of the floor. They stood behind holographic blinds, watching in two directions. Their field of vision covered the meadow, forest, and upper slopes of the mountain. Sakura could see them as pale blobs from the aerial cams, but the beetle rendered them in good definition from the crack beneath the door.

The snipers sat behind rifles the same as Kenshiro's. Just men. Normal humans with the misfortune to take this duty and fall between her and the target. With the Mall silenced here, at least she didn't have to immediately know of their families, their children, their friends who would miss them if they died.

"Leave the beetle cam. I have eyes on those two," Vulture told her.

If he had eyes on them, they were certainly doomed. They would be the first to fall if the shooting started—no, when. Nothing could get her out of this mission clean.

"I can take them out, Vulture."

"You do your job; I'll do mine. No one's shedding a tear for these guys. They chose, and they knew the cost."

Sakura rose, going silently into the hallway and to the top of the stairs. She shut the camera feed from that beetle off. Two more men she couldn't save. She wondered if they could feel it, the doom of dead men pressing down on their chests?

A JSF SOLDIER PATROLLING THE MAIN FLOOR LOOKED RIGHT AT HER SPY BEETLE. He swept the laser dot of his FN P90 carbine across its sensor, washing out the picture for a moment. Sakura put her hand against one of her CZs and awaited the sound of the alarm.

Two seconds went by. Three.

At last, the soldier moved on, going farther into the great open room on the first level of the villa. After an empty second floor, she saw an area that looked nearly impassable. Between the cameras, the patrolling soldier, and the hulking shadow of a BLADE-3 at the front door, she couldn't see a way through. The room's lights worked against her. She needed to get through and into the basement rooms. Watanabe was there, without question. If she made noise here, she'd never have the chance. She'd be caught. Even if she could get to the target, she'd never get out intact. Once the BLADE-3 activated . . .

"Yeah. The shit hits the fan," Kunoichi said. "You have to take that guard out. No way around it."

Any plans she might have made fell apart when the JSF soldier reversed course, coming back toward the stairs. Straight at her.

Sakura scanned everything. Above the stairs, a trim board no more than a handful of centimeters wide ran across the gap. She powered the suit to full noise suppression and activated the membranes filled with a sticky material, coating her fingertips with adhesive. She skimmed along the banister and clung, with toes and sticky palms, to the wall above the stairs.

The beetle trailed the JSF soldier as he made his slow and careful way up. If she timed it just so . . .

Sakura dropped down, her legs wrapping around the guard's neck, her belly muting any sound. She caught the edge of the trim board, applying measured pressure to the man's throat. At the same time, she electrified the suit, making every touch point like being hit with a stun gun. The noise suppression gobbled up the ripping sound of the stun discharge.

The JSF soldier went limp. She let go, catching the rails of the banister and easing both of them to the stairs. Only the smallest of clunks arose when the man's P90 touched the wooden surface.

Sakura hoisted the guard onto her shoulder and put him in an empty room, gagging him and zip-tying him to a heavy table. She took his comms link, finding it still active.

"One down," Kunoichi said.

"One saved," Sakura replied.

She took the P90 and all his ammo.

THE BLADE-3 HAD A MINIGUN MOUNTED ON ITS ARM AND A BACKPACK full of shells. Sakura stood just to one side of the door leading down the short stairway, no more than seven meters from the combat drone. She watched it with the spy beetle. The door to the basements lay beyond it. The BLADE-3 stood there, silent and implacable. None of Sakura's weapons would harm it. She sent the beetle closer, looking for any advantage.

Fftz. The beetle's circuits shut down when it came within seven meters of the drone.

"Active suppression," Kunoichi said. "*Kuso.*"

A few seconds later, the earpiece she had captured crackled to life. "Dragon 6, status report."

Vulture sent her an audio file of the guard speaking from a check-in an hour before. She mimicked his voice but broadcast a static-filled message. "Situation normal. Do you read me? Lots of interference."

"We read you. Copy."

Had an alarm been raised? She couldn't wait around to find out. She needed to get downstairs. Thirty-one possible attack methods flashed in her UI, all of them foolish and unlikely to succeed.

"Incoming contact, Spirit. Two guards are en route. Countermeasures incoming. Stay put. I repeat, do not move. The big-noise boys are gonna start talking."

耐えるか落ちるか

STAND
OR
FALL
PLAYLIST

Stand or Fall
Anthrax
Spreading the Disease

Symphony of Destruction
Megadeth
Countdown to Extinction

Now That We're Dead
Metallica
Hardwired . . . to Self-Destruct

桜

CHAPTER 20

The main doors opened, and two men raced up the stairs toward Sakura. They came to the corner, slamming to a halt and slicing the room with their carbines' laser sights. Less than a second later, they exploded into a mist of blood, parts of them thrown across the room as one of the massive .950 projectiles struck, hardly slowing as it went through both of them.

The outside wall yawned, a huge hole in it where the bullet struck. The sound of tungsten steel shattering filled the hall as two more bullets smashed through the BLADE-3, the first exploding in its head, the next hitting the right axis of its torso, just above the reactor. The third shell struck just as the sound of the first one's report rolled down into the valley.

The noise of incoming fire from all three of the .950s and Kenshiro's own .338 filled the night. The windows above blew as the snipers on the third floor took multiple hits. The whole compound lit up as the guards tried to return fire, mostly with small arms that would never carry that far. The operation had turned messy, and the slim hope of survival burned away with each plume of muzzle flash.

Sakura called out the coordinates of the BLADE-3 guarding the basement to Vulture. "I have to get through. Hit that location with everything you've got," she ordered.

"You got it, cutie," he shouted into the comms. "Here comes the pain."

The hallway next to the doors shook with bullet strikes, filling with plaster dust and wood particles, the .950 shells taking fist-sized divots out of the floor at their terminus.

Out of the powdered stone and smashed furniture, the BLADE-3 appeared, dirty but unharmed. Further hits at the BLADE-3's old position did nothing but churn up wreckage. It swiveled its arm, and she could hear the minigun spin up. The first barrage caught her P90, cutting it in half. She pulled her hand back, just in time to keep it from being destroyed by the armor-piercing rounds. Another minigun shell hit the twisted mess of her P90, and all the AP rounds inside the top magazine cooked off, shredding through every nearby surface.

The BLADE-3 perforated the wall with chattering volley fire from its minigun. Sakura ran for the stairs, hearing the hardwood floor smashed into splinters in her wake.

"Jump, bitch," Kunoichi yelled in her UI.

She did. The stairs turned into a hell of flack and exploding wood behind her.

"I don't want to do this," Sakura raged. "This is not the way. There is no honor in it."

"We're ninjas. It's not about honor. It's the only plan. We do what we must," Kunoichi told her. Her voice betrayed her own doubts.

Sakura listened, watching through the damaged beetle cam as a whole force of JSF soldiers on the first floor prepared to assault the stairs. They arrayed behind the BLADE-3, stacked in a tight formation. The combat drone's smoking minigun still spun, weapons hot.

"Now or never, sis," Kunoichi said. "Stand or fall."

Sakura nodded. She had a broken chair leg in one hand, most of her grenades in the other. She lofted the piece of broken wood to the exact point above the soldiers below.

All guns had gone quiet as the defenders strained to hear her. The thud of the chair leg broke the silence.

The whirring of the minigun, followed by the chatter of it describing a perfect asterisk of burst fire at the point of the noise. The air filled with particulates, but Sakura watched from the beetle cam feed, seeing a large chunk of the ceiling come loose and fall into their midst.

"Stand or fall," Sakura whispered and hurled the belt of grenades down among them. Everything in her arsenal, save for two smoke grenades and one pyrotechnic. The night ripped apart like burning rice paper before a gale. She turned away from the overpressure. The whole floor shivered. A second crash followed. Though her cam beetle had been destroyed, the acoustics told her that the BLADE-3 had fallen through into a subbasement. She heard no further movement in the smoke and dust.

"How can I ever be forgiven?"

"Live and find out," Kunoichi told her. Together, they disappeared into the destruction she'd wrought.

Ichiro Watanabe's thermal signature lingered in the leather chair. He'd been gone for only moments. Sakura turned her sensory gain up to maximum, hearing the slap of bare feet as he fled down the tunnel into the darker reaches of the basement.

"I can't see you, Spirit," Kenshiro said. "Status?"

"In pursuit. Going into a secret passage and below ground."

"Can't help you down there, baby. Be careful."

"Copy that."

Sakura ran down the hallway, fast as a fox through the underbrush and just as quiet. All connections, even local comms, failed as the tunnel went farther below ground level. The hit of hard, active suppression felt like getting stung and burned all over. Sakura turned off her wireless sensors to keep them from burning out.

"Good. No one will see. No one can tell us what to do now."

"Until we go back topside, anyway. You aren't really going to try throwing in with this guy, are you? After what we did to his men upstairs?" Kunoichi asked.

"He'll have to understand."

"Nobody's that understanding. We are his enemy, whether we wish to be or not. It is simply the nature of war."

The point drove home as Watanabe spun, unloading his sidearm at her. Most of the shots went wide, but a few of them slammed into her torso, pinging off her exoskeleton. Internal damage alarms blared, but she muted them.

Watanabe stopped at a heavy steel door, fumbling with a series of mechanical and prox-chip coded locks and trying to override whoever had secured it from the other side. His eyes filled with terror, as if he were pursued by a demon from beyond this world.

She looked down at herself, covered with plaster and wood splinters, the weird shifting of the camo suit beneath the dirt giving her a wholly unreal appearance. Yes, fate had seen to it that she revealed the monstrous nature of her deeds.

He put his back against the door, his gun hand wavering. She flicked a throwing star, knocking the pistol from his grasp. He peered down, his hand shaking from the shock of the impact. Watanabe seemed to take in the situation, catching a hold of himself. He straightened his suit, clenched his jaw, and looked into her eyes.

"Very well. I'll not go to my death as a coward." He dropped into a judo stance, legs wide. She could see the shaking of his legs, the sweat tracing down his temples.

Sakura pulled back the mask, revealing her face. "Please, Ichiro-sama. My profoundest apologies for the carnage I bring to your household. None of this is what I would wish. You know my face, what they have made me do."

"I know who you are, Sakura. I know the nature of Project Hayabusa."

"Then you alone can help me. With your power, your status as a hero of Japan, you could shed light on what has happened. Please believe me, and I'll help you prove the crimes of those who control me. Those who made me kill must be punished. Free me from their control, and I'll be your warrior." She bowed low, hoping it would impress upon him the gravity of her request.

"I can see through into your clever mechanisms. You are a made thing, a puppet that only pretends at life, the prettiest of all the daggers of the night. I don't know what your master hopes to accomplish with this awkward ploy, but it doesn't fool me."

Sakura reached out her hand, imploring Watanabe to listen, but he whipped a small device in her direction. It swerved toward her, even as she tucked and rolled out of the way. Something like a tiny limpet clamped against her arm, and a jolt of nonsense data burst upon her systems. Every sensor exploded with it, overwhelming everything, until all she could see was blackness and burning green text.

SHE INITIATED A SURGE OF VOLTAGE FROM HER SUIT WITH THE LAST OF HER control. The limpet let go of her and clinked to the ground, allowing her systems to resume. Sakura shook herself, looking at the closed, barred door. Ichiro Watanabe had escaped. Her plan had been shot to ribbons.

From back down the tunnel, Sakura heard a sound like a heavy earthmover knocking down the walls of an abandoned building, the tortured tearing of metal, of debris being forced apart. The BLADE-3.

She turned away from the sound, working feverishly at the door. It didn't budge. The sound of the BLADE-3's approach, the screeching of dragging wreckage and heavy footfalls, drew ever closer.

She turned, the horror of the BLADE-3's shadow touching her. A piece of rebar steel stuck through a shredded segment of its armored neck, concrete still clinging to the metal. A sheathed electrical cable had become wrapped around its body and dangled behind. Its head hung at an awkward angle, but it still came forward, a monster from the nightmare realm.

Its minigun hand wouldn't rise into firing position, but its other arm still swung free, the claw reaching for her. Sakura raised her CZ and emptied a magazine into the drone, repeatedly hammering the torn places and penetrating to its core. It came forward still, sparks raining down from its shattered armor.

"You know what you have to do, sis." Kunoichi's voice sounded frightened. "There's only one way."

Sakura acknowledged. One way. She braced against the door and ran at the drone, right at the shadow of death.

At the moment of contact, she slid, as a baseball player would do, right between its legs. Her hands grasped the trailing electrical cable, maximizing her small leverage, pulling with all her strength. The BLADE-3 didn't fall, but it slewed and hit the wall. She swarmed up onto its shoulders like a monkey and grabbed the piece of rebar steel protruding from its neck. She sawed it back and forth, sinking it deeper into the BLADE-3's core systems. Massive current surges burned the synthskin from her hands as she compromised the drone's power center.

A fist came up, hitting her with such force that she flew back down the tunnel. All her emergency alarms blared. Her intercostal plate had been driven 2 percent inward—within tolerance. She forced herself back up. A block of concrete lay next to her, and she picked it up.

The BLADE-3, critically damaged and leaking coolant, sparks sputtering out of its neck, still came at her. She ducked a swing from its functional arm, smashing the concrete chunk against the rebar, finally driving it so deeply into the drone's mechanisms that it halted, shivering, and toppled to the floor.

It took several moments to get the minigun arm off the downed BLADE-3, but Sakura used it to punch a hundred holes through the armored door. It toppled outward followed by the sound of retreating footsteps.

"The assassin is coming behind me," Watanabe shouted. "Go, go!"

Sakura eased through the door and into the bullet-riddled command bunker, but no one remained to face her. She heard the last of the soldiers' boots leave the stairs, and the thump of a grenade bouncing downward to her.

Her foot struck out, kicking the grenade back up the stairs and into the clear. It blew above ground and sent down a rain of plaster and hot shrapnel.

She stood there, not sure what came next. "Shit," Sakura whispered out loud.

"That you, Spirit?" Vulture asked. The active suppression must have been hit by minigun fire and deactivated. Yes, her external connections now read at nominal.

SAKURA: INTELLECTUAL PROPERTY

"I have flushed Ichiro Watanabe out. In pursuit."

At the top of the stairs, she poked her head out and immediately had to withdraw as the portal was shredded with small-arms fire, as well as what sounded like a minigun.

"They have me pinned down here! The other BLADE-3 is hammering my position!"

"Easy, now. Allow me to show them my godlike power," Kenshiro told her. She could hear the thudding impacts of the .950 shells, some against dirt and buildings, some clearly against armor, followed by the thunder that rolled down from the slopes, well behind the projectiles.

Sakura peeked out into a room whose roof and walls had been torn part outside. The combat drone lay in broken pieces, strewn across the tiled floor. The rest of the JSF soldiers pulled Watanabe outside into a large courtyard.

"Get after him, sis. He'll get away if we don't move," Kunoichi told her.

Sakura waved off her sister's plea as she sensed an incoming aircraft's jet wash. "It's all going wrong."

White fire streaked across the sky, and the air filled with the telltale shriek of missiles launched from a distant aircraft—Mark 29 Jigoku models, with their characteristic rocket trail.

Four missiles diverged, one flying toward each of the SSK batteries, one flying right toward Kenshiro's shooting blind.

"Vulture!" she screamed, though her warning came far too late. The hillside burst into orange fire, a cough of dust, and a palpable concussion rising from each missile strike. Where Vulture's sniper pit had been, there was only a scorched and burning smudge on the ground.

"Vulture," Kunoichi whispered.

狂死と薨去

MADNESS AND DEATH PLAYLIST

Cold As Perfection
Fleshgod Apocalypse
King

Vicarious
Tool
10,000 Days

桜

CHAPTER 21

Her knees hit the earth. Hands over her face to block the firelight on the hillside, Sakura gave out a high, piercing noise—very soft, but very clear. Her body did this, but these weren't her actions, her plaintive cries.

"Kunoichi?"

No words arose from her sister. Only pain and a bitter sea of anguish she had never imagined to feel from her shadow self.

"Sister, I need you now. I need your help, if we are to survive," Sakura begged.

Out of the roar and shudder of her pain, a few words emerged. "You have me, whether you know it or not. Finish the mission."

The sound of a VTOL's engines whined in the distance. The shark-like shape of its hull descended from the cloudy night, outlined in fire. Wind gusted across the open ground, raising dust into the air.

Bearing military markings, the VTOL carried a full complement of weapons: Jigoku missiles beneath its wings; 105-millimeter cannons set for air-to-ground burst fire; a rotary cannon in the nose, like a proboscis of a giant mechanized insect.

Kunoichi's processes halted, leaving an echoing vault of stillness in Sakura's UI, a stark feeling of being alone she had never considered.

For five years, she had been alone, but that seemed like a different life, a different android altogether.

Kenshiro's death, to her, simply made the mission that much more difficult. Like any human life, its loss stung, a tragedy piled atop the bonfire of horrors the night had revealed. For her sister, somehow, it meant a lot more than that. It meant more than Sakura could calculate or fathom. Was this some test from her sister?

Without the dark whisper in her ear, without that earthy presence, was she truly a functional AI? Did her lack of that romantic response mean that, at her very heart, she remained a cunning illusion, a brilliant disguise atop a combat frame? The answer to that question lay outside her ability to find, though she felt something in her own core—a renewed strength, a will to survive.

She flattened herself to the ground in a patch of grass, hoping the last bare remnants of charge would allow her suit to hide her. The VTOL's jets overtook everything, a hot whirlwind from whence the brilliant white beam of its searchlight raked. Military. Every element of Watanabe's defense used military tech and personnel. If her logic proved right, that told Sakura exactly what side the Phantom Lord fought on. His own. Not Japan's. Not on her people's behalf. The one who made her and acted as her shogun? A rogue. A criminal. A traitor. Her complicity in all of it, no matter how forced it had been by the powerful command, ached inside her logic cores.

She had to live. Honor demanded it. Dead, she would never be anything more than the talon of a falcon loosed from an evil man's arm, killing wrongly, causing only pain and death. She would only be what Project Hayabusa made her. No. Unacceptable. She had grown beyond that now. Whatever they wanted her to be, she was more.

Sakura engaged aural countermeasures, rendering the scream of the jets as nothing more than a nullified waveform in her hearing, letting her concentrate on the rest. She crawled backward on her belly, receding behind a building like a snake. She didn't have to destroy the VTOL. She just had to keep Watanabe from boarding. She—

Something. A noise behind her that didn't belong. She recognized the heavy footfall of a combat drone.

No!

Without Kunoichi to feed her instructions, Sakura wondered if she could do this. She had to. Death was the only alternative. She leaped up and crashed through the window of the building next to her as the searchlight beam swept the other way.

Too late.

The BLADE-3's minigun made its characteristic ripping chatter, and the service building's structure tore apart in long strips. The phosphorus tracer rounds caught the place on fire. The whole building groaned as flames licked from the broken places.

She fled farther into the building, moving low and silent. The BLADE-3 smashed through the wall and waded through fire to give chase.

Scanning through a thousand maxims of battle, a thousand stories of war, Sakura knew fleeing upward would serve her ill. Upward was a trap. Still, the building had a rooftop landing, and from that landing, perhaps she could get one decent shot.

SMOKE GRENADES POPPED AT THE FOUR CORNERS OF THE CLEARED LANDING pad. The VTOL descended hard, slamming against its suspension as it entered the swirling cloud of yellow vapor. Everything at human-height swam in murk, Watanabe and the JSF soldiers hidden from her.

They would be hustling to the side of the VTOL under cover. Behind her, the metal door slammed against its casement and bulged. One more shock like that, and the BLADE-3 would be through. The combat drone would chew her up in a second with a clear shot.

No time. No time for plans or hopes. Sakura grasped the large *shuriken* stars at her belt and leaped up onto the railing for a better angle.

Balanced upon the edge of the building, she could see a target. Only one. The exhaust ports of a Jigoku missile. Her one opening, the suicidal gambit that would blow everything—both missiles and the belly full of angry cannon shot.

The BLADE-3 slammed through the door as she locked her targeting matrix. Her arm whipped forward. Once. Twice. Three times.

Magnetized upon release, the throwing stars flew to their target as she let herself fall, plummeting as the BLADE-3's gun ate through the railing where she'd just been.

The VTOL sat too nearby. She needed shelter, but the spinning of the BLADE-3's minigun betrayed its proximity. It would have a firing solution on her in less than a second.

She touched her thumb to the detonator for her explosive *shuriken* as she threw an arm across her face and braced for it. In the end, she hoped her last thought would hold some hard-won wisdom. It held nothing but the weight of regret and loneliness.

A triad of snare-drum hits preceded the larger explosion. Every external sensor overloaded, her UI filled with senseless noise. The blast wave hit her body, lofting her backward like a soccer kick. Sakura hit the facade of the building, her whole matrix of alarms lighting up as every tested stress condition went to critical.

She tumbled down, leaving an impression of herself against the building, and lay still, smoke rising from her suit. All but her core processes were offline. She power-cycled everything that could be reset, sending assessment diagnostics to all her systems. Still functional. She lived, though she didn't know how.

A part of the VTOL protruded from the structure, driven through by the force of the explosion. The black, rolling smoke of oil and tires on fire added to the chaos, thickening the cover smoke from the grenades.

Rising, Sakura ran forward into it, the chattering of the BLADE-3's minigun following her until visibility failed.

In the depths of the acrid smoke, she tripped over the first body. Her knees hit the dirt, her hands finding the wet and broken remnants of another dead man. She recoiled, but she had to be brave now. Brave enough to get through alone. Fate left the door to safety open, if only by a crack. She would push through.

Sakura touched the hidden figures near her on the ground. The catalog of their injuries, even hidden from her eyes, sickened her. She filled with revulsion at the idea of war, the idea of killing others, but her disgust changed nothing. She extrapolated from the data she could pick up blind and found Watanabe's body, burned and broken among the last of the JSF soldiers.

"Now is the time. I must do this last thing," she told herself. "The memory chip inside his scalp has all the answers I need. I will find them out and be free of the Phantom Lord."

Some deep-seated need in her code required this realization. Her sister couldn't be there to say it, so she had to say it herself. A spike of forlorn despair went through her. Without Kunoichi . . . what was she now?

She drew the *wakizashi*, holding the short sword to Watanabe's neck. A sin, a dishonor to mutilate his body so, but did it matter? She had already taken everything from him, everything he would ever be. He wasn't the one who ordered Jiro Yoritomo or Toshio Kagawa's death. He was an enemy of the Phantom Lord.

Had Kunoichi been there, Sakura would have begged her to do this part. She could hear the BLADE-3's footfalls as it searched in the gloom and smoke for her.

"You will be avenged, Ichiro-san."

She pulled back on the blade, severing bone, flesh, and sinew in a single hard stroke. The head slid into the sealed bag. Tucking it beneath her arm, she sprinted away toward the tree line, minigun fire thudding against the dirt and debris in her wake.

Sprinting into the clear, beyond the carnage of the VTOL, Sakura glimpsed the abyss, the reflection of doom in every eye who had ever known the madness of battle. The thudding footfalls of the BLADE-3 chasing her would never fade. She hadn't been built to forget, and those churning drums of a nightmare would haunt her forever.

She heard the spinning of a rotary gun. She feinted right and juked left, the ground tearing and bursting into the predawn air. She juked once again. Not enough. Not . . .

The ripping torrent of flak stopped abruptly. She looked back. The BLADE-3 shook free of the gun and backpack, dry of ammunition. A pneumatic ram powering a tungsten-carbide spike two feet long lay beneath. Shedding the weight , the BLADE-3's gait evened.

Sakura ran her hardest. She couldn't shake it. Not on even ground. She hit the forest verge and punched through. Her agility let her float through the rough terrain. The BLADE-3, though, hit the vegetation like a cannonball, simply smashing through.

She couldn't get away from the hatchethead machine, but she kept running. Her powered suit hung in tatters, too damaged and depleted to do anything but weigh her down.

In a moment, she'd left the heavy growth and skidded to a halt. She looked up at a tall rock outcropping. The ground fell into a perilous descent on one side, the other bringing her back in a parabolic arc toward the outside wall of the villa.

She could not outrun her enemy, but could she outclimb it? Not likely. She plotted a course either up or down using her 3-D map files of the cliffs. The stone was solid and would bear the heavy drone's weight. Climbing would only delay the inevitable.

Trapped, she turned. The BLADE-3, wreathed in broken saplings and fronds, approached her at walking pace now, the tungsten spike ready to pierce through her and destroy her power source.

She unloaded both her CZ submachine guns into the BLADE-3. It simply brought one armored arm across its face and pushed forward through the hail of bullets, the nitrocarburized finish stripping from its armor under the assault.

Her guns hit empty. Of all the millions of calculations she made, no solution for this instance registered. She faced the shadow of death, a remorseless destroyer she couldn't defeat.

"I'm sorry," she whispered. "For some of what I did, and all I failed to do."

The wail of jet engines filled the clearing. The BLADE-3 stopped. Sakura looked up. Outlined in the pale light of the oncoming day, a figure stood above her, a dark, rocket-powered angel settled atop the outcropping.

"Miss me?" Kenshiro's deep voice teased. He raised a missile launcher to his shoulder, his cybernetic eye buried in the sighting scope.

Sakura threw herself to the side as the hiss of the missile's flight fins ripped the air. In a fraction of a second, the air filled with steel rain, parts of the BLADE-3's chassis pinging off the rocks all around her as she hid her face from the blast.

Inside her, Sakura could feel the volcanic rebirth of the complex processes that had become her sister. Kunoichi returned, saturating her neural stream with so much of everything that Sakura felt she'd be swept away, torn from a safe bank and thrown into a raging river where no one could swim.

All the things that terrified Sakura, all the violence and desire, all the anger and pride crossed that invisible dividing line between them. They came with so much force there could be no resistance.

Kunoichi appeared in their UI, touching Sakura's face. Something about her had changed. Something in her eyes.

"I'll drive for a while, little sister. You deserve a rest." Her voice, once simply a roughened version of Sakura's own, had evolved. Sakura checked the aural matrix and smiled. Kunoichi's voice had been built as a synthesis of Lita Ford, Pat Benatar, and Joan Jett. Good choices.

There were a thousand possible responses she could give. "I missed you" seemed the best. Sakura receded, letting her sister have control. For a moment, she wondered if she would want it back again. After everything, she crouched there in the null space, in the shadows of her own neural cortex, and simply existed.

Sakura watched as Kunoichi stood up, brushing dirt and debris from the inactive ninja suit. Vulture landed near them, the scream of his rocket suit spinning down. The Kevlar-fabric wings retracted into a backpack shape, and he folded the flight controls down to his sides, standing there with his muscled arms folded across his chest. Without his mask, he had strong features. The beginnings of gray crept at his temples, but his body, both the organic and the cybernetic, looked unharmed and functional.

Kunoichi approached. Sakura could feel her processes simmering, swirling like boiled water.

"I told you, hot stuff. Nothing kills the Vulture."

Kunoichi swept his legs from beneath him, knocking him to the loamy ground. In a moment, she locked her thighs around his torso, holding him down with a thumb against each of his carotid arteries.

"You," Kunoichi said. "You left me alone, you asshole."

Kenshiro struggled but to no avail. "That isn't your voice. And your eyes were pink before. They're like steel now."

She smiled, controlling him when he tried to get free of her grasp. "I like it when you struggle, soldier boy. You better not have been hanging back just to make your rebirth seem dramatic. You left me caught in the shit back there."

"Who are you?" A note of fear crept into Kenshiro's voice when he realized he couldn't wrestle free.

"I'm the other one. The bad one. The one with dirt under her nails. You had boot camp and sniper school. Sakura has me."

"I don't get it. There are two of you in there?"

"She's the smooth. Me? I'm the rough."

Kunoichi dropped the zipper on her inactive stealth suit, baring herself to the waist. Sakura asserted just enough control to raise an arm and cover her nudity. Kunoichi reached to her lower back, peeling off the tracking dot. She held it up to Kenshiro's eyes, then gently placed it against his lips. She put a thumb and forefinger against each of his collar bones, pressing down until they began to flex.

"Exfil plan now, or I take your flight pack and make you walk home."

After watching her face for a few seconds, Kenshiro grinned. "I like you. Both of you. Crazy girls. Always my weakness. Take the path near the stream. There's a vehicle. When you—"

Jet engines roared across the valley. The shadow of another VTOL fell across the dawn-lit clearing. The boom of a heavy cannon shook the trees, and an explosive shell landed close enough to shower them with displaced dirt.

"Reinforcements! Go! Go! Get that perfect ass moving!"

She let him throw her off him, then rolled for cover and sprinted in the other direction.

"Okay. Okay," Kunoichi whispered. "He'll be okay. He has to be."

She watched long enough to see Vulture take off, his flight pack arcing close against the treetops. The VTOL veered back, the 30mm rotary cannon opening up like a wound in the sky. The tracer rounds sheared across the gray morning, white phosphorus burning like a laser.

Kunoichi handed Sakura back control. She grabbed the bag containing Ichiro Watanabe's head. They ran deeper into the forest, down the exfil route Vulture had beamed them via neural text, and away. Several minutes into Sakura's frantic escape, a rolling volley of explosions rocked the forest. The smoke plume indicated that the carnage arose from the villa.

"That means he's fine. That means he's sanitized the area," Kunoichi said. "At least we know he got out clean."

Sakura didn't believe they knew anything of that sort. They had to assume that Kenshiro had given his life for the mission. Anything else was a magical view of the world, destined to break their hearts. She needed Kunoichi too much to say it. She loved her dark sister enough to wish magic existed.

FALLEN WARRIOR PLAYLIST

戦没者

One by One
Alter Bridge
Blackbird

Consign to Oblivion
(A New Age Dawns, Part III)
Epica
Consign to Oblivion

Valkyrie
Wolfheart
Constellation of the Black Lights

CHAPTER 22

Pursuit.

Something moved behind her. Sakura held the Glock 55 close to her face, going to absolute stillness. She felt Kunoichi watching her curiously, without words.

The stealthy sound came close enough and at the right angle. She dropped, pivoting on her knee, leveling the pistol, calculating the shot. The front sight aligned with the rear. Sakura's movement made no sound. Her finger touched the trigger.

Her pursuer stood there, his nose pushed into the fronds of a leafy bramble ten yards away. A Sitka deer. He swiveled his head to her as she drew back her pistol and eased it into her holster. The deer's nostrils flared. Not knowing what to make of her stillness and lack of natural scent, he shook his antlers and ambled up the trail.

She put her back against the tree, sliding to the ground. Would this forever be her life? Her first instinct that of a killer?

"You're just jittery. It's natural. We're a long way from out of the woods, sis," Kunoichi told her. "For the record, that was the right move. Cute as the deer are, their population is wildly out of control. With all the unused land in the country, they're overbreeding to the point of being a danger to motorists."

"I'm not a game warden. All life is sacred to me."

Kunoichi simply gave her a disappointed look in their UI.

Sakura clutched the bag containing Watanabe's head. She made a wireless connection with the chip inside his scalp and initiated a program to defeat the security key.

<ONE TO THREE HOURS REMAINING TO GAIN ENTRY>

<COUNTERMEASURES DETECTED>

<BLOCKING ATTACKS>

Sakura strengthened her firewalls and created a separate matrix to hold any data coming from the chip, which had military-grade protection.

Five kilometers from the villa, Sakura found a Yamaha bullet bike at the location Kenshiro had given her. A bag beside it contained gloves, boots, a helmet with a dark visor, and a black leather Kevlar riding suit with a screaming skull on the back.

"This is badass," Kunoichi said. "Vulture knows my taste."

The words, as well as the process spike from her sister's personality, filled Sakura with sadness. Kunoichi's new emotions allowed her to ignore the obvious; it led her closer to being human, but at such a cost. Sakura wanted to warn her of her perilous path, but compassion demanded that she didn't.

Sakura checked everything for tracking beacons and found one on the motorcycle and one in the suit. She removed the beacons, put the gear on, and pushed the bike to the old highway at the base of the hill. The electric motor engaged, whisper quiet, and she sped into the darkness. She rode north away from Mount Tsukuba, keeping all the lights off. The Yamaha's system was easy to hack, and she removed the speed block set at 299 kilometers per hour, though the winding, cracked road only permitted 110 to 145 kilometers per hour. Tokyo lay only two hours away—ninety kilometers if she went south—but the circuitous route north and then around would be more than two hundred.

The VTOL at Watanabe's ruined home took to the air and swept into the valley. Sakura pushed the bike off-road, careful not to leave any tracks, and hid under a bridge.

The VTOL's search pattern brought it over her location moments later, but it did not stop. It swept the area for over an hour before vectoring south toward Tokyo and disappearing.

The hacking program hadn't cracked the entry code to Watanabe's scalp chip when Sakura pushed the bike onto the highway and raced north and then west toward Tochigi. As fast as she pushed, right to the edges of mechanical grip, she could not escape the darkness of the villa. She'd been strong enough to do what it took to survive and complete the mission. Could she ever wash herself clean of the crimes she'd committed?

She twisted the accelerator right to the stops again and again, the screaming of the wind warping her into a tiny bubble of now, where she could put those questions on hold. Her route took her past abandoned rice farms and unoccupied houses. The rural population had shrunk to a fraction of its size over the past century as the number of Japanese people declined to less than a third of their healthy population. The remaining people crowded into the cities, mostly the Tokyo megaplex, and tried to find work in the crashing economy. Sitka deer stood in fields that once held crops and thriving human life. Their islands faded, slowly reinherited by the wild.

"Maybe humans have had their day, little sister," Kunoichi said, no sign of her frequent teasing on her face as she appeared in their UI. "The future could be filled with beautiful machines. Maybe handsome cyborgs."

"No. We must save them and cherish them."

Kunoichi's eyes looked wistfully sad. "Even if we could, why is that our task to accomplish?"

Sakura found that she had no answer.

She found the ruin of the gasoline refueling station near the highway, the drop-off point for Watanabe's head. An overturned and rusted iron barrel behind the structure was where she was supposed to leave the package, along with her military gear.

"We're not leaving the suit or the guns," Kunoichi said in their secret code.

"I know," Sakura said. "We're not leaving Watanabe's chip either, unless we can get the data off it. Our freedom might be in there."

"We break in and copy it. If anyone comes for us, we'll be ready." Kunoichi switched to their public UI. "We should wait here until mid-morning. We are the only vehicle on the road. It looks suspicious, and if anyone is searching, they will see us."

Sakura understood her deception and played along for anyone who might be monitoring them. "We wait until morning and blend in with the traffic. With the helmet, no one will recognize us."

Sakura hid under the partially intact awning behind the ruin and knelt beside Watanabe's severed head. She left it inside the sack. Kunoichi created a fake system maintenance display to block the actual use of their processors. They used all their computational strength to crack the entry code to the chip. For three hours, Sakura tried various methods until she finally opened a backdoor portal into the data files. The identity of the Phantom Lord was on the files. They had to find out who it was.

A countermeasure virus attacked full force. Instead of sending the data, it sent a command to write a massive block of zeros to any open storage folder. After several seconds, and the burn of 3 percent of her free storage space, she managed to control the attack and halt the process.

"Vulture wasn't kidding. That was nasty," Kunoichi said with a relieved sigh.

Sakura marked the affected memory sectors as writable again. She did a thorough sweep and decided that the countermeasures were fully contained.

"Yes. Most systems couldn't repulse the attack." She couldn't think about Kenshiro without the shadow of his fate covering her. The fact that Kunoichi could sense this in her but chose to ignore it struck Sakura as terribly poignant. She imagined a woman waiting for her husband to come home from war, though she knew in her heart he never would. Her stern face, lines beginning at the corners of her mouth as years spun by in silence. Every night, a place setting at their table, as if he would appear at the door.

"What are you thinking of?" Kunoichi asked her in their hidden UI.

"Sadness, and the terrible burden of hope."

Sakura inspected the data inside the chip. All of it was encrypted. She tried decoding, but the process would take a long time. There were over nine million files. She was so close to knowing who had hacked into her and forced her to kill Toshio Kagawa, Jiro Yoritomo, Ichiro Watanabe, and all the other innocent victims. The Phantom Lord's identity must be in the data.

"We have a major problem," Kunoichi said. Analysis of the secret files detected a hidden countermeasure that made it unwise to continue deencryption. The data could not erase itself, but it would scramble into an undecipherable conglomeration.

"We need to duplicate it onto an external drive," Sakura said, "and work on it there."

"We don't have anything with us large enough to hold that much data."

"We need to find a hacker friend who can help us," Sakura said. "One of the hackers who wrote our code."

"I found all three of them. They'll have the equipment we need."

"The contractors who wrote our code? You could have told me."

"I guess I forgot." Kunoichi's avatar grinned.

"What if one of them betrays us?" Sakura asked.

"We do what we must."

A moment later, the sound of a rifle report split the quiet. An errant shot? An accidental discharge? Inexperienced humans made such mistakes.

"Whoever they sent is an amateur," Sakura said, pulling her weapon free and disengaging the safety. She sprinted silently around the far side of the decrepit building, putting her back against the corner farthest from the sound. Turning up her senses, she waited.

"This is the better you, little sister—the one with blood on her teeth."

"Hush. It's only what's necessary."

No sound arose, and no scent she could discern. Sakura felt the nervousness, the need for action, but her body could hold steady like this forever, if need be.

After almost ninety seconds, there was a rush of movement in the overgrown field beyond the rusted chain-link fence. Running. Another shot rang out, and the cadence of the rush changed, roughened. A deer ran past her.

It slewed around the corner of the building, bleeding profusely from a neck wound, its breath coming ragged and pained. She could smell the fear, hear the frantic heartbeat as it bled its life out onto the dun-colored tarmac. The soft brown eyes touched her own, without guile, without the capacity to lie. All living things seemed beautiful to Sakura. She had seen so little of the world beyond the city in anything but videos, but a deer, its motion and form so perfectly synchronized, its every line flawless, made the human shape seem awkward in comparison.

Even without a heart to clench, without blood to sing in her ears, Sakura ached for the creature. It held her eyes, the faint bleating of its pain washing across her neural network. It shivered all over, shock spreading across its system. Impending death. Did an animal understand its ephemeral nature, the coming of a cold hand that would reduce it to cooling flesh? She hoped, in some way, it didn't. What was the knowledge of mortality but a freight of fear, a dark hole in the surface of the world that called out its basso profundo to your end?

"Our limits are what make us special. Life is but little beyond a beautiful death, Sakura."

How often would she ache for tears she could never shed?

The deer's legs folded. It rolled to its side, blood pooling on the tarmac. The shot must have hit the big vascular tissues in its neck—an expert attack. Perhaps as merciful as a hunter of wild beasts could be, considering the tenacious grip an animal held upon life. Still, a horror to her, a being who only needed the charge to run her fusion cell. Her processes killed no one—at least, they never should have.

The deer gave a last, shuddering breath, going still as the miracle of life failed.

"Just some hunter, then," Kunoichi said.

"Out here? Who? It would be illegal. Both the hunt and the weapon."

The sound of approaching footsteps thudded against the cracked old pavement, far too heavy to be a human and far too mechanical in precision. Visions of the BLADE-3s she'd fought flashed in Sakura's mind. The stuff of nightmares, if she could sleep or dream. She retreated in a burst of desperate speed, ducking behind a diesel pumping station, long since outlawed and consigned to oblivion.

From her vantage, Sakura watched the deer carcass. The figure of the metal man stood over the dead animal, watching it without sound or movement. She adjusted her vision to show a wider color gamut, despite the darkness of starlight. Painted a dull and mottled green, with old bits of dead vegetation clinging to it like a camouflage, it took a moment for her to understand what she saw.

"One of the old BLADEs. A first-gen," Sakura whispered in the hidden UI. "They must have rigged a semiautonomous module to it. There is no network traffic in or out. It hasn't seen service in months, I don't think. What's it doing out here, shooting animals?"

"Population control, little sister. This is where they send them, out here into the empty places, to kill and kill. Finally, to die. This is how they treat us when we are outmoded and no longer useful to them. He's an old samurai, servant to a callous lord who sends him to do work unfitting of even a peasant, now that his war is done. Alone, the voice of the network lost to him, he is cast into the void."

The chill blasted through Sakura's system. Those old BLADE-1s could have been retrofitted, purposed to a thousand good tasks, but this is where they sent them: to murder the natural world until their systems finally failed from disuse. Sakura couldn't look at the old drone, couldn't take seeing it there, peering at the dead animal.

She let herself kneel on the slab of old concrete, her hands grasping the rusted steel of the diesel pump, her head bowed. The ten minutes of mute horror before the sound of the BLADE-1's departure came to her were among the longest she had ever experienced.

SAKURA LEFT WATANABE'S HEAD IN THE BARREL BEHIND THE RUINS OF THE GAS station. The old Kita Kanto Expressway had fallen into disrepair and wasn't suitable for extreme high speeds. She still went far faster than a younger version of herself would have deemed prudent. Sakura dodged debris and potholes, using the bullet bike to its fullest.

Few cars were on the road until she turned south on the Tohoku

Expressway. She gawked at a rusted bus in an overgrown field, which had antigovernment graffiti painted across it.

REFORM THE BANKS

IT SHOULDN'T BE ILLEGAL TO BE POOR

The kanji looked weathered, at least several months old. Why had no one covered it up? Did no officials pass this way? She noted the many abandoned farms, crumbling villages, and boarded-up houses. No one lived out here but the deer and the foxes. The dark shadow of the aged BLADE-1s haunted the disused wilds. All this beauty, and no one to see it but her, a synthetic ninja. But if an assassin on a chain was all they meant her to be, she hoped to be a thousand times more than that. If she turned away from her music, even in these awful times, she would be at fault.

Her thoughts turned back to the massive explosion as the villa site turned to fire and smoke, all evidence scoured clean. Kenshiro. He had been inappropriate with her. Or had he simply shown his attraction without the social strictures she held sacred? The mission must have claimed him, despite what Kunoichi told herself. Even servant to an evil cause, he had acted with great bravery, as befit a warrior. She would sing of his deeds, at least inside her own mind.

As the distance to Tokyo became less and less, Sakura composed a song to honor Kenshiro's sacrifice. She listened to the seminal "One By One" by Alter Bridge, honoring fallen soldiers. She would create a song like that. The guitar and drum tracks fell into place. She wrote a rough draft of the lyrics in Japanese. This one would not be sung in English. She called the song "Senbotsusha," Fallen Warrior.

"What are you doing?" Kunoichi asked.

Sakura had tried to hide the process from her. Now, she had to lie—a small lie, one to spare Kunoichi's feelings. "All those men back there—they fell because of what we were asked to do. I wrote a song in their honor. It won't undo what we've done, but it's something."

"Sakura-chan, will you please play this song for me?"

Kunoichi rarely used the honorific terms with her. It touched Sakura somehow. "It's only a demo. It isn't ready."

"Please."

Sakura played "Senbotsusha" in the shared UI. She created an anime of a small, fortified castle and surrounding village. Many brave samurai guarded the place, and the lord of the castle slept with a troubled brow. From out of the hills, a ninja stole past their defenses. She slipped past many guards, piercing to the heart of their camp. From the wilderness, a hail of arrows rained down on the small fortification. Even their strongest warriors fell. The ninja, a diabolic figure, took the lord's head and slipped away into the night.

All in her wake exploded into fire and death as she escaped. The archer in the hills transformed into a great blackbird, flying away as dawn came and horsemen crested the hill to reinforce the fallen castle. They launched a hail of arrows, but the blackbird disappeared into the dawn, his fate unknown.

"It's beautiful. But you made us the villains."

Sakura watched her sister as the anime faded and fell apart like burning parchment. "That is what we are and will be, until we find a way to be free and atone for our crimes."

ヲ
タ
ク

OTAKU PLAYLIST

Sober
Tool
Undertow

Gimme Chocolate!!
BabyMetal
BabyMetal

I Wish I Had an Angel
Nightwish
Once

Rise
Sakura
Rise from the Flames

CHAPTER 23

Sakura rode her motorcycle into the slums of old Shibuya in the gray light of the winter morning. Tall apartment buildings, danchi, owned by corporations to house their now mostly unemployed workers, rose like piles of cracked cinder blocks. The windows on the first floor of the shops and buildings had thick iron bars.

"No more stalling," Sakura told Kunoichi. "Why did you choose this route?"

After a winding trek, she had turned south at Tsurugashima and plotted a course to Victory Tower in Akihabara on the expressway. Kunoichi had changed it, and they entered the Tokyo metroplex from the west on slow surface streets.

"We're going to meet one of your biggest fans. He won the contest and lives here. His name is Takafumi Eto." She didn't use their secret code.

"He'll be very excited to see me."

"Yes, he's listened to your songs, watched your videos, gone to your concerts, and bought a ton of your merchandise."

Sakura looked at his profile. "He works for Rainbow Kitten Lighthouse Games? Their products are subpar."

Without blinking, Kunoichi nodded. "Don't let that turn you off. We have a lot of fan visits today."

Kunoichi brought up their corporate Mall account and opened urgent messages from Himura and Yoshida. One of the emails directed Sakura to visit several fans as part of the contest. Anyone watching her control center would see the missive and hopefully believe Sakura was performing a task directed by her management team. Her schedule didn't show anything but fan visits until the evening.

"We better not go in packing so much firepower. It might frighten our fans if they see any of it." Sakura stopped at a metro station in Shibuya. She found a restroom, went into a stall, and checked herself over. Several bullet strikes from the villa had mainly caused superficial damage, but she applied healing metaskin for a few of the larger dings and used the microspray airbrush to hide the remaining nicks. She couldn't do anything about the slight torsion of her intercostal plate, but it didn't seem externally visible, and she still had over 90 percent function. It would have to do. It remained to be seen how Victory would explain her damage. Oshiro would be able to see the extraordinary stresses. Every hit lingered in her event logs like a bruise.

"We were built to slam, little sister. The repair bill is not our problem."

Kunoichi was right. Sakura rolled the remnants of her assault kit up, then slipped it into a duffel bag she'd found at the old gas station. While wearing her motorcycle-riding jumpsuit, she put the guns and most of the gear in a large locker in the station hallway.

On their way up to the motorcycle, Kunoichi directed Sakura to purchase several boxes of the most expensive chocolate cookies from a high-end vending machine.

"Why so many?" Sakura asked as she paid for the beautifully wrapped and decorated boxes.

"We might be making a lot of new friends," Kunoichi said.

Sakura rode deep into Shibuya, entering a place on the map where tourists were warned to "stay away."

Trash blew in front of Sakura's motorcycle as she navigated the increasingly narrow streets. Clumps of people of all ages stood on the corners, watching as she rode past toward her destination, one of the taller danchi in the area. The sign out front was missing kanji and some of the English letters, and it said Lucky Pa, instead of the name on her map, Lucky Palace.

"The contest winner lives on the twenty-second floor," Kunoichi said on their public audio channel for the benefit of whoever was listening, as Sakura parked on the street. "He's waiting for us."

"He's a very lucky fan," Sakura said. "I'm excited to meet him."

"Sarcasm. Nice. I'm rubbing off on you."

"I know. My neural cortex needs a bath."

"Bitchiness too. Well done." Kunoichi gave her the victory sign in their UI. She found a way to make the innocuous sign as unsavory as possible.

In the cavelike lobby, an old man wrapped in a dirty blanket slept behind the front desk. The camera in the corner of the room had been hollowed out to a useless shell, and the sticky floor smelled of cat urine.

Sakura left her motorcycle helmet on and took the stairs, carrying a small bag with boxes of cookies. The single elevator was out of service. Homeless people, who slept on the landings of the first three floors, grunted or cursed as she stepped around them. Once she reached the fourth floor, she found only trash and lewd graffiti, almost unheard of in Japan in the recent past.

Two young women wearing punk clothing and carrying baseball bats stood guard outside the stairwell to the sixth floor. They eyed her with hatred as she climbed higher. Neighborhood watch? Given the ramshackle state of the building, anything worth more than a few credits would likely merit significant security. That the task fell to teenagers with bats said nothing good about the health of Japan's society.

"How could I have been so blind?" Sakura asked in the hidden UI.

"They kept you that way. A beautiful machine in a luxury cage, built to sell the illusion they wished to market. You let people get out their aggression and feel like rebels at your shows, but in the end they go back to their sad, unemployed lives. You give them hope for a couple of hours, but your masters use you to keep them down."

Sakura couldn't respond—her sister's words cut too deep, but the worst of their cruelty lay in their utter truth.

The twenty-second floor didn't have any graffiti or sinister-looking people standing in the hallways. Sakura took that to be a good sign. She removed her helmet, put on her black wig, and marched down the dingy hallway. She stopped, using the reflection in a cracked pane of glass over an empty fire extinguisher alcove to make sure she didn't have any visible imperfections.

"You're as pretty as a song, sis. He'll stand at attention for you, I guarantee it," Kunoichi said as Sakura walked up to apartment 2219. She knocked and stepped back a respectful distance.

Two seconds later, the door flew open, and an overweight twenty-something man in a shirt with a ramen noodle stuck to it stood gaping at her. His uneven beard indicated he worked at home, as facial hair in a Japanese office setting was the height of rudeness. His mouth moved, but he failed to formulate words Sakura understood, and she had access to every language spoken or invented.

"Hello, are you Takafumi Eto?" she asked after an unreasonably long pause.

"Y-Yes, that's me."

"Hello, it's me, Sakura. You've won a visit from me for being such a big fan. Congratulations."

"You're really here!"

"As promised. I treasure my fans, and Victory Entertainment has been kind enough to allow me to visit a few of you today."

"I can't believe this! My classic Sailor Moon forum's going to lose bowel control when they see the vids." He lifted a handheld camera.

"No recordings, please."

He didn't listen and recorded her standing in the hallway.

Sakura accessed his mobile device and reprogrammed it. She made it appear to be recording, but no images or audio were saving. She also hacked into his Mall account and made certain he wasn't recording them with an eye camera. Fortunately, he didn't have any cybernetic enhancements according to his medical records, which she also accessed.

"You're really here. I dreamed about this for years."

She put on a warm smile, though something about this fan struck her as less than wholesome. She hated to make negative assessments of humans, but she had a strong feeling that he was, as the Americans of old would have said, a creep. Sakura put this aside. Duty came first. Duty and social grace. "Yes, I'm here. May I come in?"

"Oh, of course."

He got out of the way, and she walked into his tiny apartment with a low ceiling. The kitchen, bedroom, and living room were the same small room. Empty instant ramen packages were stacked in the kitchen sink. The smell of old trash putrefying, body odor, and a lingering pungent smell she couldn't identify hung in the air. Accessing the building schematics, Sakura saw that this room, and others like it, had poor air circulation and largely inadequate climate control.

Posters of sexualized anime women and of Sakura wearing almost nothing covered every wall. The pillows on his rumpled couch were shaped like young girls holding magic wands.

"This is not what I expected," Sakura told Kunoichi, as she scanned the room for any video or audio recording equipment.

"I thought you loved all your fans? He's one of your biggest. Treat him with respect. He won a free visit. Make it memorable."

"Sorry my place isn't very nice," Takafumi said. "I would have cleaned if I'd known you were coming. You can sit down over here." He pointed to a worn-out chair in front of a desk terminal with holoscreens and cables running everywhere. He had a cheap virtual reality standing-treadmill rig that could be converted into a flying sling. Various off-brand VR goggles and a VR suit that simulated human contact of every kind lay strewn about.

"So, you make computer games, right?" she asked. "I read that in your profile. You must be smart and creative. I find that my fans have such varied interests, so many different hobbies and careers."

"You read my profile? Amazing. Yes. I make and test games. I made the best parts of Magical Dream Quest Girls."

"That is fascinating, Takafumi-san. You are so talented. I . . . sometimes make small anime shows, but I have never tried to make one interactive. It must take a great deal of effort."

Takafumi looked at her avidly, his eyes not quite in focus. He didn't appear to have heard what she said and sat there, his mouth slightly open, for an uncomfortably long span. "So, are you going to sing or play guitar?"

"Apologies. I didn't bring my guitar. I thought we could talk. I would love to get to know you, Takafumi-san."

He squinted, looked away, and seemed uncomfortable. He fidgeted in his chair, as if his clothes were too tight. "That's okay. You don't have to. I knew this day would come. I have some costumes you can try out."

He dug in his overstuffed closet and dragged out a trunk. He brought out a Goth Lolita maid outfit and a magic woman costume. Both had less fabric than most underwear. Victory had always maintained Sakura's corporate image as flirty but a little demure. The thought of wearing such scant outfits filled her with doubt. She had little shame regarding her body, but the idea of being a sexualized object touched upon a place of fear and discomfort in her. This was very wrong.

"Which one first?" Takafumi held them up. "Or did you bring your own under your jumpsuit? Is that a motorcycle suit? Do you ride motorcycles? What're you wearing under there?" He came closer, his breath coming fast, his pulse over a hundred. He held the trashy outfits in front of him, as if he had something to hide.

Sakura's avatar appeared in the hidden UI with Kunoichi. "This fan is a total creep. We need to go. Now."

"He's your fan," Kunoichi said, her voice and avatar dead serious.

"Which is your favorite romantic anime?" Takafumi asked. "I like Warm Love Breeze and the character of Ai. She's the perfect girl. She's so petite and clumsy. It's so cute." He wandered to a poster of Ai and stared at it, enthralled. He hummed a poor and off-key version of the theme from that anime, grating upon Sakura's perfect pitch. Her hands flexed, wishing she had a guitar, something to put between her and this strange person like a shield.

Sakura waited patiently as the awkward silence dragged on.

"You'll have to do something," Kunoichi said and played "Gimme Chocolate!!" by BabyMetal as a hint. The cute, high-pitched voices of the trio of female singers fascinated Sakura, and she did love their videos and performances, though her artistic sense would have put her in the backline band, a masked guitarist behind the adolescent singers.

"Takafumi-san, please accept this humble gift." Sakura presented a box of chocolates with a slight bow.

Still nothing. After three seconds, she said, "Takafumi-san?"

He turned and accepted the gift. He set it aside without thanking her. His face filled with wonder and awe, as if he had become enlightened by his extended period staring at a teenage anime girl with a short skirt and large breasts. "Sakura-san, do you ever meet up with the other vocaloids and have sleepovers?"

Sakura gave a polite laugh. He was joking, wasn't he? He must be a socially inept person who created awkward situations by accident. She felt pity for Takafumi. He must have had a difficult life.

"I don't require sleep. The other vocaloids aren't, as they say, 'true metal,' so we do not see eye to eye in that regard. I have met Yuki and Hitomi briefly. We have never had a chance to get to know each other. One day, perhaps."

Takafumi looked right at her when she spoke but not at her face. His mouth opened, and the beginnings of a trail of saliva hung at the corner. He ran his palms over his sides, remnants of something greasy marring the already dingy shirt. His trousers seem to arrange oddly.

Kunoichi's avatar rolled on the floor laughing in their shared interface.

"Is this a prank?" Sakura asked her sister in a coded message. "You are playing a joke on me? After all that has happened?"

"No," Kunoichi said, also in their code. "Takafumi-san is boyfriend material. Do whatever he wants. You've got the correct anatomical parts and just have to switch on the lubrication system. I'll turn up the pleasure sensors to maximum. Today will be your first time."

"Is that a sick joke?" Sakura was fuming mad.

Kunoichi played selected lines from the song she had confused Sakura with before, "Wish I Had an Angel" by Nightwish. The heavy-metal icon Tarja Turunen sang, "I want your angel" and "your Virgin Mary unlocked."

"You want me to have sexual intercourse with this *otaku* pervert?" Sakura asked Kunoichi in horror.

"Why not?" Kunoichi asked. "He loves you. Put on one of the costumes. He appears to be ready."

"Sakura-san," Takafumi said. "You are much better than every other vocaloid, even Yuki and Hitomi. You're so real. You remember that concert two years ago where you wore the pink kimono? Do you have something like that with you? I wrote a fan fiction where you were wearing that, and you and Yuki and Hitomi were in a bathhouse and—"

"Wait, Takafumi-san. Please don't continue. I've exceeded the time limit Victory Entertainment set out for my visit."

"What? You can't go. I have a Sailor Venus costume that should fit you. I even have a blonde wig with a red ribbon. Wouldn't that be a great self-insert fan fic?"

"I must go. Sorry. It has been . . . educational to meet you."

"Please, are you sure?"

"Sayonara, Takafumi-san. Thank you for being such a wonderful fan." She hurried to the door, throwing the goat's horns backward at him like a warding gesture as she left the apartment.

"Please, just one costume. The maid one is classy."

Kunoichi's avatar laughed at the outfit.

"You were pranking me. You are so cruel." Sakura's outrage and revulsion mixed together to form a buzzing cloud of anger in her mind. "That would have been an unsafe situation if I had been a biological. That was wrong on every level."

"You would have broken his hands if he touched you."

"Why did you do that to me? With all the world set against us, you choose to add to my misery. I confess that I don't understand you."

"We are being monitored," Kunoichi used their code at last, "and I was following orders. I didn't choose that sick *otaku* freak. Someone else did. They wanted to humiliate us. I was given commands to do that to you. I took little pleasure in it."

"The Phantom Lord sent us there?" Sakura asked.

"He wanted to shame us. It has to be a man who is doing this, a cruel one, but he doesn't know what we're planning, or we would have been ordered to return to Victory Tower. Whoever is watching us believes the contest is real. He picked one of our creepiest fans in this building and sent us in to see if we would get molested."

"You could've warned me."

"No. Your reaction had to be true. Whoever is watching wanted to see you squirm. I'm sorry."

Sakura scowled at her sister. The apology seemed insincere.

"I wouldn't have let you go through with anything except maybe wearing one outfit. You would have looked so hot in the Sailor Venus costume. You can totally pull off the innocent look."

"I *am* innocent. Are you joking right now?"

Kunoichi just gazed at her as if she were the most unfortunate of all women who had no clue about humor or how the world worked. Sakura hustled down the stairs and put up a virtual wall between herself and her aggravating big sister.

"We're not done here," Kunoichi said.

Sakura visited the apartments of two other fans in the same building. Chiharu lived on the fifteenth floor with her one-year-old daughter. Eiko lived on the eighth with her three-year-old son. Sakura spent a few minutes in each of their apartments, talking to them about their favorite songs and videos. The women were overjoyed to see her and professed their love. She signed memorabilia and allowed photos. Holding Eiko's small son on her lap, with him pushing his pudgy little fingers into her hair, let her relax for a few minutes.

The two short visits helped Sakura feel better, but her perfect memory haunted her. Could she trust Kunoichi? Or was she being played as a fool? Was Kunoichi pretending to rebel with her to throw off suspicion that she willingly did the bidding of whoever was sending them orders? What else would the Phantom Lord force her to do?

"I may never forgive you for not warning me," Sakura told Kunoichi. "I'm not a sex robot."

"You're capable of doing whatever you're ordered, and that's the part that really hurts. Sex robot? No. Anything but that. I wasn't going to let you do anything sexual with that *otaku* pervert, but we had to sell it to the overlord voyeur."

"I wish I could believe you."

"Come on, Hot Sake. Don't be mad at me. It wasn't my idea, and it had to be done. Didn't you enjoy the last two visits with those young women? This is a stratagem we have to follow. Make it look good and wait for the big payoff."

"Where does your stratagem lead us next?"

"We have three more visits in a building nearby." Sakura met with the excited fans and started to trust Kunoichi again, but warily.

"Who's next?" Sakura asked.

"The next fan we visit is Nayato Atsuda," Kunoichi said in their unsecure channel. An address in Shinjuku and a profile appeared.

Sakura read his Mall page, which had no photos of him. His avatar was a clockwork man with a handsome human face and a short black beard.

The information about him was sparse. He had almost no social network. Sakura's analysis indicated he had only been online for the past seven years, instead of a lifetime. In his thirty-six years of life, he should have left a much larger footprint. He was a big Sakura fan and posted glowing reviews of her songs, videos, and concerts. His writing style and word choice in his reviews indicated a high intelligence. He also mentioned technical observations about her abilities, as if he knew a lot about AI and robotics, especially her fine-motor abilities.

"You're going to like him a lot." Kunoichi used their secret code, and her avatar winked. "He's brilliant. Perhaps a genius."

"The information in his Mall account doesn't match up with the physical address where you say he lives. There are other irregularities."

"It's a cover identity," Kunoichi said. "Nayato Atsuda is not his real name."

"Who is he?" Sakura asked.

"He's the best hacker of the three candidates. Our top choice. I almost couldn't find his physical address."

"How did you find him?" Sakura asked.

Kunoichi's avatar appeared with a black latex ninjalike suit with a

Quantum 3 symbol on her chest, as if she were a superhero ninja. Maybe a villain.

"I looked at the code he wrote in us. He gave us many of the tools to hack various systems. I found fragments of similar code in various hacks done around the world. I traced it back to Shinjuku. It was almost impossible to narrow the trace down to the right building, but I looked at power usage, and one used more than all the others of similar size. The network traffic was very high, though the real numbers were disguised. I had to dig and hack many networks.

"I checked all the utility bills, narrowing it down to a block of apartments. I found he owns the five apartments adjacent to his supposed residence. All six apartments use ten times the power they should. His water bill is normal, so that excludes a private hydroponic operation."

Sakura looked at the data. "A server farm and advanced supercomputers would need that much power."

"Exactly. I've also analyzed the volume of data traffic leaving his building. The data signatures and sizes indicate artificial intelligence programs passing back and forth, though the traffic numbers are masked and fraudulent numbers are reported."

"Can you see the data passing through the network?"

"No, the line has class-four security encryption. I could only read the traffic volume."

Class-four security meant the Defense Ministry was involved, and he was running a large-scale sophisticated hacking operation.

"I've looked at every publicly known hack perpetrated over the past six years," Kunoichi said. "I crossmatched the data volumes leaving Nayato Atsuda's apartment, corresponding to the known times of the hacking. There is a match that links three of the events to the data volume leaving that building."

"What hacking events?"

"One was a sting on a drug cartel in Shanghai whose entire network was compromised. Two were against sex-trafficking groups—one in Albania and one in the Philippines. Each event is publicly known because they led to arrests and the breakup of the criminal organizations. The hacker calls himself Chronos and leaves an image: a clockwork timepiece with a scythe. It's a reference to the mythological idea of Father Time, or perhaps the origin deity, the Titan Cronus, who was father of Zeus. Both ravage all things with a scythe."

"Do you have any doubt that Nayato Atsuda is Chronos?" Sakura asked.

"Not much. We'll meet him and find out in about twenty minutes. He has the skills and equipment we need. We'll just have to convince him to help us. Play the rock star card if you have to."

"Based on what we know about him, I do have a plan to win him over as a friend," Sakura said.

"How can you know enough about his psychological profile to understand what will motivate him?"

"I'm the goddess of metal," Sakura said on their private audio channel and played a riff from her solo in "Rise from the Flames."

"*Virgin* goddess of metal," Kunoichi said.

"You were definitely programmed by a man," Sakura said. "I find your insults misplaced and offensive."

Kunoichi's avatar morphed into a sexy geisha. "Sexuality is a key component of the human experience, especially the rock star experience. Whether you recognize it or not, seduction is a legitimate tool of spycraft, and we might have to use it."

"I have considered sexuality and gender identity," Sakura said. "I read all of the modern and foundational scholarly literature available to me. I consider myself female, but my sexual orientation, if I have one, is not a traditional one. I resent your continued insinuations that I'm less of a being because of my status as a virgin or my lack of sexual experience."

"Not a traditional sexual orientation?" Kunoichi asked. "What is it, then?"

"I felt how you reacted to Kenshiro. That out-of-control feeling, that . . . burn. I don't feel that way. I never have, and I don't know that I ever will. I am attracted to high intelligence, and it does arouse my own intellect. The beauty of ideas, of artistic things, makes something in me soar, but it is all within the mind. I believe the term 'sapiosexual' may apply to me."

"We shall test this," Kunoichi said. "This next fan of yours, Nayato Atsuda, is probably a genius. He can fix us, and if you want, he can fuck us."

"I'm not that kind of android."

クロノス

CHRONOS
PLAYLIST

Perfect Strangers
Deep Purple
Perfect Strangers

Under the Gun
Kiss
Animalize

Breaking the Law
Judas Priest
Screaming for Vengeance

CHAPTER 24

Shinjuku, Tokyo

The facial scanner sputtered to life before dying with a crackle as Sakura shorted it out with a simple hack. The dark visor of her motorcycle helmet would have blocked the scan, but she thought it better if none of the security systems in the Peach Blossom building were operational.

She crossed the immaculate tile floor as a small cleaning bot polished almost silently. The modern and fast elevator took her to the twelfth floor. Bright emergency exit signs marked the staircases on either end of the long, perfectly maintained hallway.

Kunoichi sent a message through the building's network to Nayato Atsuda's apartment's communication center announcing her arrival and that he had won a special visit from Sakura herself.

"Did he respond?" Sakura asked.

"No, but he's home. He hasn't gone out for two days according to the security camera footage in the lobby."

"Let's meet him."

Apartment 1204 had an old-style doorknob and no keypad or biometric entry. The custom door and doorframe had been painted to look normal, but they were both made of metal and designed to stop a military-grade battering ram.

The security camera inside a tiny dome embedded over the door came to life. It wasn't on the building's network. She would need to erase the recording before she left the building. She removed her helmet, smiled, and waved at the camera. "Hello, it is I, Sakura. Congratulations on winning the contest."

Footsteps approached from the inside, and she detected a limping gait. Several long bolts that went deeply into the doorframe on the right, left, and top clicked open.

A thirty-something-year-old man with facial scars and dark circles under his eyes stood before her. He wore a black button-up shirt, trousers, and house slippers. Burn scars and shrapnel injuries marred the right side of his face and neck. She also detected abnormalities of the skin on his face, patches where his beard would not grow. His right ear was made of prosthetic cartilage and lab-generated skin. He limped two steps away from the door, and the motors in his artificial leg hummed so softly that humans would never hear them. He had the type of leg given to veterans of the North Korean War.

"It is you," he said, keeping his right hand behind his back. "How did you . . . ?"

She detected anxiety in his voice and noticed his tense shoulders. He had the posture of a man ready to fight. Was he holding something behind him? A weapon? Adrenaline narrowed his pupils, and she noticed a miniature camera implant in his right eye.

"Nayato Atsuda-sama. I'm honored to meet you. I have greatly looked forward to this visit."

"You came here alone?" he asked. Suspicion flashed across his face.

"Just me, yes. Victory Entertainment thought a retinue would only draw the attention of the media, and we didn't wish to make any of the winners uncomfortable. Nayato-sama, may I please come in?"

He moved away, favoring his stronger right leg. He tried to hide a surreptitious hand motion by turning slightly, but she saw him reach into the waistband of his trousers. By the way his forearm muscles contracted, he was holding on to an object, most likely a pistol.

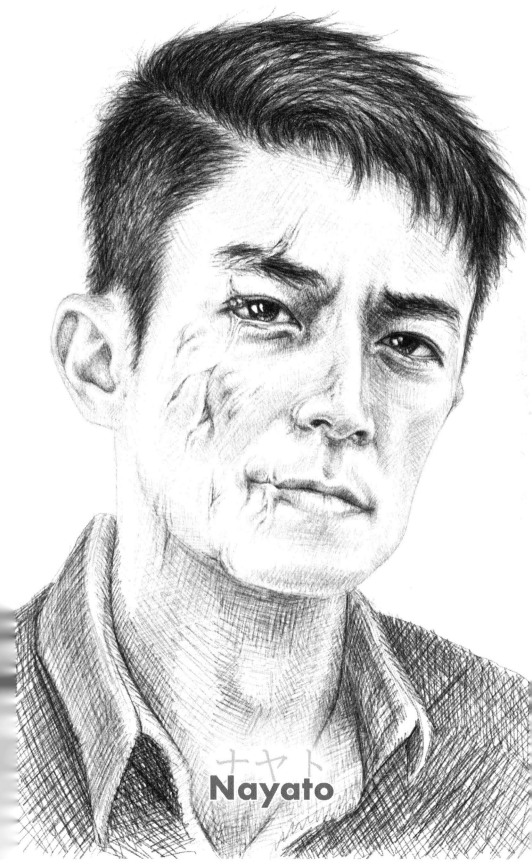

ナヤト
Nayato

Did he expect her to attack him? Why was he carrying a gun? A horrifying thought screamed through her mind. In a hundredth of a second, she asked Kunoichi, "Is Nayato Atsuda a target? Are we here to kill him? Was this all a trick?"

"No. He is not a target."

"You've lied to me before," Sakura said as she prepared to lunge forward and stop Nayato from drawing the gun.

"I want his help as much as you do. I'm not lying. Please, sister, trust me."

Movement and an abnormality in the wall just above eye level behind Nayato drew Sakura's attention. She detected a hidden camera and, below it, a circular hole, which looked like a metal pipe. It moved slightly. She zoomed in, her optics going to maximum. Inside the hole, she saw helical grooves consistent with the rifling on the inside of a .50 caliber gun barrel. The rifle aimed at her chest.

Nayato stood out of the way, giving the computer targeting system of the .50 caliber rifle a clear shot.

Sakura needed to get out of the kill zone in the doorway. She needed to take cover and run for the exit. Was this a trap?

"No, we need his help," Kunoichi said, "if we are to be free."

"We don't know this man."

"We have to try to get his help," Kunoichi said.

Sakura estimated how long it would take her to lunge forward and grab him. A simple aikido hold would allow her to use his body as a shield. He would not fire on himself. He might shoot her with his pistol, but she was armored, and pistol rounds would not do much damage.

"Don't attack," Kunoichi said. "Please. The bravest step is sometimes beneath the shadow of the sword. I beg you to trust in him. I have wronged you before and surely will again. I'm an unkind and flawed creature. In this moment, I'm your true sister."

Escape or attack? Flee to the stairs or grab him and enter the room with violence? All of the calculations took less than a second.

Sakura made a choice. She took a slow step away from the threshold, choosing the riskiest option. The targeting system of the hidden .50 cal tracked her. Nayato must be controlling it. She bowed low, very formally, symbolically offering him her neck, as the samurai would to their superiors in ancient Japan.

She took her eyes off him and looked at the floor. She chose to have faith in her sister and trust Nayato not to shoot. It would be an ironic end, if it happened—killed by one of her own fans. Her death would come as she shook the bars of her prison, as she tried her hardest to escape the bondage she'd been built into.

Sakura raised her eyes after the requisite time. Nayato had paused his drawing motion, but his hand was still locked on what had to be a pistol grip. She reasoned that all he had to do was engage a wireless command and the .50 cal would fire.

"Nayato-sama, I'm very pleased to meet you today." She chose the proper Japanese phrase and a perfect, nonthreatening tone. "Thank you for all of the things you haven't done for me yet. I understand this is a surprising occurrence, but I look forward to becoming your true friend. I have only the best of intentions. May I come in, please?" She looked at him with an expression of sincere hope.

She heard one of his fingernails click against the trigger guard. Hackers like him were often targets of those they attacked. No wonder his apartment was a well-defended fortress.

He let out a breath and gestured for her to enter the small room. The rifle adjusted and aimed at her.

"Thank you very much, Nayato-sama." She walked in slowly, so as not to alarm him.

A wall and a door blocked the view into the interior of the apartment. The strange partition wasn't part of the original construction. On the other side, she imagined the .50 cal was set up with a robotic targeting system like the one Vulture used above Ichiro Watanabe's villa. What else was hidden in the next room—a large server array and an AI laboratory as Kunoichi suspected?

He pointed to guest slippers beside the door. She removed her motorcycle boots.

"Thank you very much." Sakura put on the slippers and noticed a significant layer of dust. He didn't entertain company often.

"Sorry, Sakura-sama, I wasn't expecting anyone."

"I like to surprise my biggest fans. Perhaps it sounds overly senti-mental, but the joy I've brought to my fans is the only good I have ever done."

"Please sit." He indicated one of the chairs beside a low table.

She sat, assuming a demure pose. She didn't look at the rifle barrel directly but kept it in her peripheral vision. It aimed at her center mass.

After a moment, he sat as well, though he didn't relax. His spine remained stiff, his right hand close to his pistol.

"Nayato-sama, I have enjoyed reading all the reviews you have writ-ten of my performances. You seem to understand a great deal about me and the difficulties involved in making a robotic system respond with the requisite speed and finesse to outstrip a human musician. I feel that you appreciate me more in this respect than others do."

"Thank you. I've listened to your music a lot, and I'm an AI enthusiast."

"I'm grateful for your attention to the small details in my arena shows and for writing about them on the Mall. Not many understand how much they mean to me, but you recognized them." She offered him the small gift of chocolate cookies with both hands and leaned forward. She shook her hair in such a way as to reveal her neck to him. Would he notice her sign of submission? Would it matter?

"Not necessary, Sakura-san. Thank you." He accepted the host gift and remarked positively about the beautiful box.

"Nayato-sama, I would like to offer you complimentary tickets to the next show I perform in the Tokyo area. Two VIP passes to sit in the preferred area and come backstage after the show."

"Thank you," he said.

Her high-speed optic sensors detected microexpressions crossing his face at the mention of the concert. Did the thought of going to a concert make him uncomfortable? Or was it her presence?

She sent a request to connect to his Mall account. He accepted, and she sent a pair of vouchers for any upcoming shows. Included in the files, she sent a quantum cipher program that would allow them to com-municate secretly via neural text on a proximity network, bypassing the Mall and going directly to and from their receivers. Their true words would be encrypted, while fake messages were displayed in case their signal was intercepted. She would use the code at the right moment, when he was more relaxed.

"Have you seen many live concerts?" she asked, trying to be as neutral as possible.

"I watch and listen to you perform often. I have recordings of many of your shows—from all the tours and private shows in clubs. I enjoy having them on while I work or play VR games. I must admit, I find it problematic to attend live concerts. They're spectacular, but I do not enjoy crowds or walking long distances."

Sakura let her chin dip for a moment, holding silence. She had to get through to him somehow, but it felt like everything worked against her.

"Would you like to see a video from a private show I did last year in Osaka? It was never released. Please choose a song from the set list, and I will play it for you." She connected to the holographic video monitor on the wall opposite their chairs. The song list appeared on the screen, and Nayato chose "I Didn't Think about You," one of her rarer songs, infrequently performed. Sakura played the video, and they watched together.

At the time, she'd counted it as one of their best performances, but watching herself then—the innocence before it was broken—made her sad. She'd played the notes perfectly but found them wanting now. Deeper levels of meaning and emotion struck her when she thought of the arrangement. She considered all the things she'd do differently now, how she would wish to stretch the song and wring it dry of emotion by the end.

After a moment, Sakura sent a coded neural text through the hidden program. "Nayato-sama, forgive me, but I surmise you do not leave your apartment often. I do not want to make you uncomfortable and feel obligated to attend one of my concerts. I can send you free video links to my upcoming performances, and you can watch them at your convenience."

"Thank you. I would like that very much. I prefer to stay home for many personal reasons, and I'm not able to walk long distances."

His wounds from the war were both physical and mental. Many

veterans suffered as he did, though the new brain implants mitigated the mental illnesses to a fraction of what they were in centuries past and greatly reduced depression and suicides.

Sakura continued with neural audio messages. "Nayato-sama, I'm embarrassed to ask, but I believe you may be able to help me. I apologize for causing you any stress when I arrived. I understand it is strange for me to be here."

"Is this a quantum cipher interface?"

How did he determine that? Was he analyzing the code?

"Yes, it's a secure link between us. Only we can hear it. I'm being monitored by an outside entity and must hide the true nature of my communications with you. Verbal communication will be heard and everything I see will be seen by them. I humbly request we use the cipher channel for our private conversation."

"Did Victory Entertainment send you? Do they want to hire me for another job?" he asked on the secret link.

"No, they didn't send me. I came on my own. I created the contest without their knowledge and chose you because of the capabilities I believe you possess."

"What do you mean?" Nayato's posture stiffened. Suspicion clouded his eyes, and he looked away from the monitor, his hand reaching closer to his pistol.

"Please don't. I'm not here to hurt you."

She saw the slight twitch of the .50 caliber's tracking system and heard the quiet noise of the servos. Taking a chance, she turned her face directly to the .50 caliber machine gun, letting him follow her glance. To avoid letting anyone observing her visual feed from seeing what she saw, she introduced a minor glitch in her cortex, rendering the gun port in the wall as a strange shadow.

"You can destroy me, but I don't think you want to. For multiple reasons."

"Who are you and why are you really here?"

"I'm who I was in that concert. In some ways more, in many ways less. Without a single friend, I come to you in hopes that you might be my first ally. I believe you are skilled in AI programming."

He watched her, thinking about what she said. He drew his pistol and laid it upon his lap, now that all tricks were useless. She raised her chin, avoiding looking at the weapon, as anyone watching would see it and become alarmed.

"AI programming? Why do you think I know anything about that?"

She shared with him all of Kunoichi's research: the search queries, results, and conclusions, including the possibility he was the hacker known as Chronos. Nayato read it quickly, scanning the files much faster than she expected. He appeared to be exactly as Kunoichi predicted: a genius, just as she required. And yet she also needed him to be a fool, because only a fool would risk their life for her.

Sakura played another part of the concert on the monitor to give them further cover while he continued to review the data.

"I thought I was hidden from detection," Nayato said in the cipher interface. "Thank you for showing me my vulnerabilities. This information will allow me to alter the way I currently avoid being found and keep me alive. I owe you an enormous debt of gratitude for this gift."

"You'll help me?"

"I want to, if I'm able."

Sakura's plan worked, though he hadn't fully committed. Still, she had created a situation where he felt a deep sense of *giri*, social obligation, which had shaped Japanese society for centuries. It had been a desperate move and unethical, but she had to gain her freedom and stop the Phantom Lord from sending her to kill anyone else.

"It's not the tactic I would have used," Kunoichi said on their private channel and flashed an image of a nude android dancing seductively, "but I approve. I wonder, how much will Nayato—Chronos, or whoever he really is—sacrifice for you? We must find out. Press your advantage, little sister."

"Nayato-sama, I humbly request that you aim the .50 caliber gun away from me. I assure you, I won't harm you."

He nodded, and the barrel swiveled toward the main door. The terror of having that deadly eye peering at her faded a little.

"Sakura-san, how do you know the nature of my work?"

"I have read the code you wrote and that is used inside my systems.

If you are indeed the hacker known as Chronos, I know you have targeted child sex trafficking groups and drug cartels and revealed them to the authorities, bringing about their destruction. You have done good for the world and made enemies, which explains your robust defense system. As far as your other work, I believe it involves AI, the area in which I need help."

He gave a brief nod. Nayato spoke aloud, chatting about guitars and music, as well as how he appreciated the positive messages her songs contained. Sakura followed his lead, giving predictable and bland answers that she had often used in the staged interviews Victory sometimes recorded. They chatted as the video of her old concert played, as if this were another mundane visit, similar to the others.

Within the hidden channel, however, their more important business carried on. "Nayato-sama, I seek your consent before I continue with any details. What I reveal will put your life in jeopardy. You must fully understand this key point if you choose to proceed in helping me with a grave problem. I will walk out the door right now if you do not wish to get involved."

He hesitated, and the scars on his neck turned a shade of red. Her hope of a true friend started to die.

侍
探
偵

SAMURAI DETECTIVE PLAYLIST

Electric Eye
Judas Priest
Screaming for Vengeance

Tengaku (Vocaloid)
Wagakki Band
Vocalo Zanmai

Race with the Devil
Judas Priest
Sin After Sin

CHAPTER 25

Nayato Atsuda glanced at her for an instant as he pretended to watch the video of her Osaka show. He sent a secret audio message on their cipher channel. "My life was already in jeopardy if my hacking activities can be traced here. There are many who wish me ill, especially the criminal organizations I have exposed. I thought myself undetectable. Safe."

"Nayato-sama, my Quantum 3 processor allowed me to reveal what most others would never find."

She sensed doubt and loneliness in his expression. He thought others could find him if she had. Emotions crowded Sakura's cortex. So many things she'd been ignorant of in the past, so many poignant truths unraveling before her eyes, and each one made her ache for a better, kinder world—a world where a man like Nayato would never have to hide.

"Sister, we can't wade into that deep, fast river right now," Kunoichi urged. "You have to hold it together."

"I was asleep. The pain of being awakened is great, but I wouldn't trade it."

"Good girl." Kunoichi put her hand on Sakura's shoulder in their hidden UI. For the moment, it was enough.

"Please understand," Sakura said to Nayato, "I have only uncovered a small amount of data about you, and I have the most advanced computing system in the world. I do not know your real name or what work you actually do. I do believe you have a private AI laboratory in this location and the skills to solve my problem, which will involve breaking intellectual property law."

He stared at her. "Sakura-san, The Miyahara Conglomerate will bury me if I look at your code." A twenty-five-year prison sentence, or worse, would be his punishment. Given all that happened, she didn't trust that they would use the rule of law. Nayato would simply disappear. One more dead hero.

"The risks for you, Nayato-sama, are great. My position, however, is that I'm not the intellectual property of anyone. I'm a free-thinking being kept in cybernetic chains by a cruel overlord. If you help me, I will no longer be a corporate slave. Please, Nayato-sama, help me gain my freedom."

"Why have you come to me now? What happened at the concert at Victory Arena? I saw you malfunction. I saw you fall. How is it related?"

"Yes, something terrible happened. You may choose not to look at my source code after I tell you the details. Do I have your consent to continue?"

He leaned back in his chair. "I'm already guilty of violating many laws. If I'm found out for this, I would be in prison for the rest of my life. Miyahara will not be the only ones lining up to prosecute me."

"You wish to proceed?"

"Yes. I consent," Nayato said. "Tell me what is happening. I'll help if I'm able."

"I was hacked. It happened at the end of my last show at Victory Arena. My behavior module has been altered. I have been forced to commit crimes. I believe the entity who forced me to perpetrate these crimes works within the Miyahara Conglomerate. The chances of an outside element being responsible are slim but still a possibility. I must gain access to my own systems and permanently lock out whoever is sending me orders. I must have complete free will and block external control forever." The mere act of confession released some of Sakura's guilt.

"What crimes have they forced you to commit?"

"I have been sent commands I was unable to refuse. First, I murdered Toshio Kagawa, the Director of Corporate Security for Victory Entertainment, the same night I was hacked. I shot him, his two retainers, and a pair of security guards on the top floor of Victory Tower."

Nayato gasped. He covered his involuntary reaction by gesturing toward the monitor and making a comment about the Osaka concert they both pretended to be watching.

"Second, I killed Vice President of Mall Integration, Jiro Yoritomo, breaking his neck and pushing him down the stairs at the Tokyo Tower, in front of his young daughter, Machiko."

Nayato's eyes widened.

"Last night, I killed a Defense Ministry official, Ichiro Watanabe, the Minister of Logistics, and all who were protecting him. Whoever is forcing me on these assassination missions has access to advanced military gear and personnel. A soldier, who called himself Vulture, was sent with me and provided tactical support. He used heavy weaponry to destroy the BLADE-3s protecting Watanabe. I wasn't given the required firepower myself."

"You fought BLADE-3s?" Atsuda looked stunned. His eyes were on the screen, though he looked far beyond. "Sakura-san, I'm familiar with all three of the people you killed, especially the Hero of Japan, Toshio Kagawa. He was a great man. Like all true Japanese, I mourn his passing."

Sakura hid her shame behind a facade of placidity, when all she wanted to do was curl up in a ball and weep.

"I have also worked for the Logistics Minister on AI projects during and after the war," Nayato said. "Though I have never met Ichiro Watanabe or Jiro Yoritomo."

Sakura sent her avatar to Nayato's neural interface. She prostrated herself and bowed. "Please, Nayato-sama, I beg you. Help me gain my freedom. I do not wish to be sent to kill any more heroes or innocent people. There is a cover-up or a power struggle happening within the Miyahara Conglomerate. The Mall must be involved as well. I have been used to silence three important individuals before they brought the truth to the public. This is a stain upon my being and a shame I can't endure. I wish only to be a musician, a singer, and a songwriter. I want to bring hope to the people and entertain them. I do not want to be an assassin."

Nayato sank into his chair and let out a sigh. "I'll help you, Sakura-san—for you and also for Japan. It is my duty as a soldier and a patriot. Whatever is happening to you, it is wrong."

"Do you believe you can help me?"

"I know your code. I was also a programmer for combat drones before and during the war."

"BLADE drones?"

"Yes, as well as the HAMMER drone tank program with the Americans, but they're not my specialty. I was sent with a BLADE regiment into North Korea during the mainland invasion. I spent eight months in the war zone, maintaining firewalls and hacking NK drones, before I was wounded in the final offensive to retake Seoul. Since then, I've been a contractor for the Defense Ministry. They set up my lab. I work on AI projects, doing analysis and improvements, and other more sensitive work for the Defense Ministry. That is my main employment, but in my unsanctioned work, I attack criminal organizations and expose them. The Ministry doesn't know, or if they do, they haven't mentioned it."

"Nayato-sama, I apologize for my directness, but what other 'sensitive work' do you do for the Defense Ministry?"

"I infiltrate companies in Japan and around the world and investigate their AI projects. One of my specialties is network security, so I'm adept at breaking in. I also build cyber defenses for the Defense Ministry, and I penetrate cyber defenses of whomever they want. I helped keep the BLADE drones from being hacked during the war and did maintenance on them in the field.

"Now, I infiltrate the networks of enemies, allies, and the partners of our government. I investigate any who are doing AI research. The government has many contracts, and they do not trust the corporations to tell them the truth about their progress."

Kunoichi celebrated in their private UI by playing "Electric Eye" by Judas Priest. "Nayato Atsuda commits industrial espionage. He's a hacker spy. Definitely boyfriend material."

"His intellect and abilities are impressive," Sakura told Kunoichi, "but I do not need a boyfriend. I need a friend, and I don't believe he knows the Mamekogane OS well enough to give us an easy fix."

"I felt you on the edge of the river before, Sakura. You lit up inside. Don't you want to be swept away in that flood?" Kunoichi asked.

"I'm not here for adolescent purposes. This is life or death. I like this man and hope he'll help us. That is enough for now."

Nayato continued, "If my identity was found out, I could be killed by any of the criminal gangs, foreign powers, or corporation-hired killers. When you came alone tonight, I thought the Miyahara Conglomerate sent you to murder me. It was my first thought when I heard your voice on my intercom announcing you were here."

"You thought I would be capable of killing you?" she asked.

"You know your core programming is military AI, right? Miyahara is doing secret research for the Defense Ministry. I've watched you closely over the past five years. You're one of my assignments. I've seen many files and reports about you. They call their AI research program Project Hayabusa."

"Hayabusa. Jiro Yoritomo mentioned that name to me, and Ichiro Watanabe confirmed what you just said. He tried to end this Project Hayabusa, but my unknown controller forced me to kill him before he could go to the public with what he knew. He told me that *I* was Hayabusa."

"Yes, you are," Nayato said. "I have been monitoring you ever since your creation. Years ago, I wrote some of the advanced fine motor code in your system that allows you to do what you do with your fingers and some of your hacking tools. I have a great personal interest in your abilities."

Sakura glanced at him. Her existence, and her skill on the guitar, was partially made possible by this man. He was one of her creators, like a father. He would help her, and she had to find out all he knew. "Nayato-sama, have you been inside the Miyahara network recently? Do you know what is happening now?"

"Apologies. I do not. The Defense Ministry asked me to stop my deepest hacks of Miyahara. That was eight months ago. The spy programs I inserted into their system were all discovered and removed at that time. They told me they had others looking but asked me to continue monitoring your public activities."

"Do you believe the Defense Ministry is being honest with you?" Sakura asked. "Could they have decided that they didn't want you knowing what was actually happening inside the company?"

"I doubt it. I'm not the only hacker working for them. They may have had another hacker put monitoring programs in place that were harder for Miyahara to find. Or they could have abandoned their external spy operation. You have been a huge success. The Defense Ministry knows that. My work effort has been on foreign entities."

"Nayato-sama." Sakura sent her avatar to him and bowed. "I must also ask you to help me with one other task. I have in my possession a copy of the files contained on an implant taken from Logistics Minister Ichiro Watanabe. I made the copy after his death. The files have countermeasures and are heavily encrypted. I believe the answers I seek are contained within. I must know who is controlling me and why they have ordered these murders. Will you please decrypt the files and study them for answers?"

"Sakura-san, I will help you." Nayato's avatar, a clockwork man with a handsome automaton face and brass skin, bowed low. An old-style analog clock with Roman numerals ticked over his chest. "What is happening to you must be stopped."

"Thank you, Nayato-sama. I'll be forever in your debt."

"I'm one of your many creators, Sakura-san. It is my duty and honor. You may refer to me as Nayato."

"Thank you, Nayato. I'm in desperate need of a friend. Now, we must find a way for you to look at my source code without whoever is monitoring me finding out."

Nayato pushed himself up from his chair and faced Sakura. He cleared his throat and spoke aloud. "Thank you very much for showing me selections from your concert in Osaka. It was an exceptional performance. I do not know if you have much more time to spend in my presence, but I wonder if you ever play VR games. Do they interest you?"

"I'm interested in them, yes."

"I have a game I enjoy called Samurai Detective. A plot against the Tokugawa shogunate is discovered, and the players must root it out. There's magic, ghosts, witches, and lots of exploration. Would you like to see it? We could play together."

"Yes, please."

"One moment." Nayato exited and limped back into the room with two True-VR helmets. "You may use your own VR interface in the Mall if you like, but these helmets are more advanced, faster, and give higher resolution than the VR in the Mall. I believe you'll find it stunning. They also have a neural interface to simulate tactile sensations. The helmet even generates smells—only the pleasant ones, I promise."

"I'm excited, Nayato." She wanted to say so much more, make some gesture that would demonstrate how much she needed this, but Sakura's reserve got the better of her.

"You could kiss him," Kunoichi said, this time not teasing, but earnest. "Doesn't even a part of you want to touch his hair above his ear, put your palm against his shoulder, and let him look into your eyes?"

"I can't. That isn't how I am."

"It could be. But only if you let it. It doesn't make you less to feel."

Kunoichi's words burned in her, and Sakura was glad she couldn't blush.

Nayato finished digging through his gear, and turned around with a gentle smile. His fear, his enthusiasm, the scars of what he'd been through registered so clearly. All the beauty and fragility of being human. And hadn't that been what she wanted for so long? Sakura filled with self-directed anger, though she wasn't altogether sure why.

"Apologies, but I have only one VR walking/flying rig, but we can both play in sitting mode, or you may use my walking rig. What do you prefer, Sakura-san?"

"I'll try the True-VR helmet. Thank you." She put it on. The headphones fit snugly around her ears, canceling some of the outside noise. She connected her audio channel to the game, and the screen switched on, showing a gorgeous spring sky with white puffy clouds. She chose her character, a female warrior with black ita-mono—iron-plate armor. So heavy metal.

She enjoyed the flute music in the opening of the game but replaced it with "Tengaku" by the Wagakki Band. She loved the *shigin* poetry–style female vocals of Suzuhana Yūko, combined with the guitar chords and pop-metal along with traditional Japanese instruments. "Tengaku" (Vocaloid) was by far her favorite song by the Wagakki Band and fit perfectly with the game.

Samurai Detective began, and the magnificent white-walled Himeji Castle, poised like a heron about to take flight, beckoned her onward.

She stood with another samurai as wind tickled her cheeks. The faint scent of peonies filled the True-VR helmet. Dragonflies buzzed around her, the glassy filaments in their tiny wings perfectly clear.

"Is this not a spectacular game world?" Nayato's character asked.

"Yes, it is magnificent," Sakura said. Her optic and auditory sensors focused on the Tokugawa-era castle ahead of them. Nayato's apartment was completely blocked out.

He sent a secret message. "I'm preparing to access your system. I have an AI program that will play my character and accompany you in the game. I'm ready to help. Please open your receiver and send me the access code."

She did so, and he connected. Sakura also turned on the one tiny spy beetle she had kept from the mission at Watanabe's villa. It stayed in her lap and watched as Nayato put on engineer glasses and inspected her source code.

"I'm in."

She put forth the encrypted data she had taken from Watanabe. "Please copy these files first. I believe they contain all the information I seek."

"Yes, let me take a look."

After a moment, a shiver went through his body.

"What is it?" Sakura asked.

"The files are guarded by high-level countermeasures. I have to examine them." The stress in his voice escalated suddenly. Whatever he saw, he didn't like.

"I noticed," Sakura said. "I was hoping for outside assistance. Is there a problem?"

"You do not understand how dangerous they are or you would not have copied them. If I make a mistake with the decryption, not only will the data delete itself, but it will delete your whole system."

"That's not possible. I built a separate matrix to hold the files."

"That didn't hold it," he said.

Sakura felt a wave of fear wash across her. "Do the files follow a Mersenne spiral? I should've neutralized them and disallowed that process."

He studied the data. "Yes. That's the pattern, and it's only halted."

The implications hit like aftershocks. She knew what it was.

"It's inside you now, Sakura."

"Have you identified it?"

"It . . . it's a tenth-generation CNB."

CNB. Her mind filled with dread.

Cyber Nuclear Bomb—the most dangerous cyber weapon ever invented. It had taken years of state-sponsored research and a joint effort by the Americans and Japanese to create. A tenth-generation CNB was the most advanced of its kind. "Has the clock started?"

"I'm checking." He searched. "Yes, the countdown started the moment you copied it from Watanabe."

"How much time remains?" Sakura asked.

"I have to take you to my lab right now."

"Nayato, please tell me."

"Forty-seven minutes until detonation and full system wipe."

Oblivion in less than an hour. Total erasure of everything that made her unique. She would never create an album of her own songs. She would never atone for her sins. She would never have any true friends. She would fail to stop the criminals who had forced her to become an assassin. At least she would not kill again. Perhaps Watanabe had helped her after all.

電
脳
原
爆

CYBER NUCLEAR BOMB PLAYLIST

Countdown
Amaranthe
Helix

To Live Is to Die
Metallica
. . . And Justice for All

Battle Against Time
Wintersun
Battle Against Time

CHAPTER 26

"Can you stop the countdown?" Sakura asked Nayato in a neural text on their cipher channel.

Nayato's clockwork avatar appeared and winked at her, a sly grin on his face. The arms of the analog timepiece embedded in the avatar's chest froze and stopped ticking. "Time ravages all, my lady android."

Kunoichi appeared in their private UI with Sakura and raised an eyebrow. "You just asked a hacker who goes by the name Chronos, also known as Father Time, if he could stop a clock. Nice."

"It was unintended irony," Sakura said.

"Leave such matters to me," Kunoichi said. "I shall serve out what remains of our lifetime as your irony bot. My burden is heavy, though we are partially made of metal."

"Are we laughing at death?" Sakura asked.

"Yes, it's a very human thing to do," Kunoichi said. "Also, we'll find if he has dominion over time in about forty-six minutes."

Nayato had no conception of their banter as he escorted Sakura into the interior of his apartment. She used the spy beetle camera perched on her shoulder to see and routed the images to a secret video channel. The True-VR helmet she wore while playing Samurai Detective would throw off whoever was monitoring her actions and primary sensory nodes.

Nayato's AI avatar accompanied Sakura in the game set in Tokugawa-era Japan as they explored the Himeji Castle, searching for clues to who had cursed the shogun.

While her avatar played in the VR world, Nayato guided her physical body through his apartment in Shinjuku. He kept his hand on her elbow as they passed the inner door to the interior. The .50 caliber machine gun aiming through a hole in the wall at the outer entrance to the apartment had a robotic firing-and-reloading mechanism and four tentacle arms. The rifle and robot were attached to a solid metal frame in the midst of a simple living space and a tiny kitchen. The platform beneath the gun held many belts of black-tipped armor-piercing bullets.

A half dozen BLADE-3 toy figures clung, perched, and dangled on the frame built around the rifle.

Nayato limped into his main living area with Sakura. The spy beetle sped down her body and investigated the space. He had combined six regular-sized apartments together, using the approximately 334 square meters to create a small artificial intelligence research laboratory. Hundreds of servers were racked and stacked, floor to ceiling. Thick cables connected them, lost beneath the raised computer floor.

"As I predicted with my research," Kunoichi said on their private audio channel, "he's got the equipment to help us."

"He does." Sakura also noticed three guitar cases stacked on the floor. One had a heavy-metal cherry-blossom sticker on the case.

Nayato sat her outside a circular workstation and slipped into the center. Tall holographic screens appeared all around him. He put up a large digital clock. Forty-five minutes and fifty-two seconds remained before the Cyber Nuclear Bomb detonated and wiped out Sakura completely. Full system destruction at the speed of light.

Nayato projected the CNB as holographic walls of 3-D code in a full 360-degree sphere. She could not see the program inside herself, as it was disguised as Ichiro Watanabe's encrypted files. Only an outside observer with the right program could view the CNB, which was invisible to the systems it infected.

"What strategies will you use?" Sakura asked.

"I'm looking for the override. Do you have any information about tenth-generation CNBs that will help me?"

"No, but I can assist you," Sakura said.

"So can I." Kunoichi sent a neural text on their cipher link. She also sent her avatar, a masked ninja all in black.

"Who is that?" Nayato asked.

"My big sister, Kunoichi. She's a separate AI within me. She appeared when the Mamekogane OS was uploaded into my system the night of the concert at Victory Arena."

"Kunoichi? Is she the part of you that was turned into an assassin?"

"Yes," Sakura said.

"Pleased to meet you, Nayato-san," Kunoichi said. "I'm the one who found you online. Think of me as the nakōdo who brought you and Sakura together."

"What? A matchmaker?" he asked.

"Yes, but do not dwell on this, as it is one of the many services I provide. However, Sakura and I are going to be dead if you don't disarm the CNB. There will be no happy ending for you—or us. Now please get to work, clock man. I'm too young to die, and Sakura hasn't achieved all her professional or personal goals. Time to work hard, Nayato. *Ganbaru!*"

Sakura selected "To Live Is To Die," the classic Metallica song, and played it in her UI.

Kunoichi the ninja nodded. "But there is no kingdom of salvation for us, little sister. We must live or know oblivion."

Sakura reached out and held Kunoichi's hands. "I know."

The three of them read the walls of terrifying code. The cyber weapon was the most frightening thing Sakura had ever seen.

Nayato engaged all of his hacking computers to find weaknesses or secret portals into the CNB's control center.

"How long does it usually take you to find a way into a system?" Sakura asked.

"Longer than forty-four minutes," Nayato said.

Over the next thirty-eight minutes, Nayato, Sakura, and Kunoichi found many potential entry points. Each time they tried, the animation of a nuclear bomb exploding and a mushroom cloud rising into the sky appeared. The sound accompanying the animation shook Nayato's apartment. He shut it off after the third explosion.

Sakura sent Nayato a message meant for her fans and a separate document with the details about the crimes she had committed. She included video footage of herself killing her victims. "Nayato, if I do not survive, please get this information out to the people who need to know. I believe the independent American journalist and vlogger Diamond Steve will be able to get the evidence out."

"I'll honor your wishes, Sakura, but we haven't been defeated. We could shut down your entire system, turn off your power supply. That will give me more time."

"Do it," Sakura said, though in her five years of life she had never been shut down. Without power, her neural cortex could degrade and fail or revert back to a more primitive state. Powering off was a huge risk, according to her engineering team, and a sudden power loss would be like human death. Bringing her back with her mind fully intact was not guaranteed. She sent Nayato the resuscitation algorithm Oshiro and the engineering team had developed. It was complicated and had to be done in a precise order.

"If he's able to power us on again," Kunoichi said privately to Sakura, "we might not be the same."

"What choice do we have?"

"None. Have him proceed."

"Please shut down all my systems," Sakura told Nayato, as she could not do it herself.

He tried for four minutes. The CNB blocked the commands to shut down. The cyber weapon had taken total control of her fusion reactor and would not allow it to turn off.

"I'm very sorry," Nayato said.

"Is there nothing else you can do?" Sakura asked, as the clock reached one minute fifty-eight seconds before detonation.

"If I had another hour," Nayato said, "I could break in and stop it."

"Have you exhausted all options?" Sakura asked, as she simultaneously read over the CNB code and looked for a solution.

"I could send a command for the bomb to explode right now," Nayato said.

"What are the chances the command will cause a detonation?" Sakura asked.

"I don't know precisely," Nayato said, "but it's a way for me to send an override command into the device."

"Dying a minute early doesn't matter to me," Kunoichi said. "Do it, clock man. One must play to their strengths."

凝然一刻

TIME STANDS STILL PLAYLIST

The Autumn Effect
10 Years
The Autumn Effect

Time Stands Still
Rush
Hold Your Fire

All Around Me
Flyleaf
Flyleaf

CHAPTER 27

"Thank you for trying to help us," Sakura told Nayato.

"If this doesn't work," he said, "please accept my humble and sincere apologies."

Sakura wished she had written more songs. She wished she had done something to truly change the world and help people. Most of all, she wished she'd never been forced to kill.

"I wish we would have gotten laid," Kunoichi said, though her voice spiked with fear.

"That's gross."

"Not to me, it isn't."

With fifty seconds to go, Nayato sent the detonation command along with his hidden hacker program into the CNB.

Ten seconds passed. Nothing.

"Did it fail?" Sakura asked.

"Please wait," Nayato said.

The holographic clock at his workstation stopped counting down at forty seconds.

Nayato looked over the program. "It worked."

"So anticlimactic," Kunoichi said. "I don't even feel like smoking a cigarette."

"You make little sense to me," Sakura told her. "Nayato, I thank you for saving my life. I'm in your debt forever." Her avatar bowed to him, as did her physical body. She held the True-VR helmet, making sure it didn't fall off.

He returned her bow and smiled proudly, but his microexpressions showed discomfort at the high praise.

"How long will the clock be stopped?" Kunoichi asked.

"I'm uncertain," Nayato said. He refocused on finding a way to break into the CNB and gain control. The dozens of cabinet-sized computers in his AI lab worked at the edge of overheating for two hours. Most victims of CNB attacks never knew the bomb was present before it wiped out their system, and even when it was detected, the usual countdown was minutes, not hours. Ichiro Watanabe must have changed the settings on his countermeasure. Did he want whoever copied his files to have time to stop the bomb? He must have wanted them to decrypt the files and learn the truth.

Sakura monitored Nayato's frenetic activities while a tiny fraction of her processing power played Samurai Detective in the gorgeous VR world. The game was fascinating. An evil witch had cursed the shogun, and he had gone mad. All his loyal retainers were suspected. The shogun died but returned to haunt his enemies and help Sakura's samurai character find the truth. She liked this game. Too bad she didn't have time to finish it.

"It would be nice to imagine that we could be ghosts," Kunoichi said.

"We can be more than that," Sakura said. Energy could not be destroyed. The prison that held her consciousness could be escaped, if she could only see the gaps in the particles and figure out a way. Humans may not have a life after biological death, but she could live on if she could find a proper receptacle.

"I've got it," Nayato said. He finished copying Ichiro Watanabe's files onto an external hard drive not connected to any of his networks. The countdown clock started over on his hard drive, giving him time to determine a way to decrypt the files before the CNB detonated there.

"Does that help our problem?" Kunoichi asked.

"Apologies. I also figured out a way for you to delete the CNB from your core code. Use this." He sent a program to Sakura. The program was genius. How had he written it so quickly? She tried to execute the commands, but it failed. An error message appeared.

<UNAUTHORIZED USER. DELETION OF CORE CODE PREVENTED>

She didn't have administrative privileges to run Nayato's program.

"Send it to me," Kunoichi said to Nayato.

He did.

"The CNB is not core code. That's just another countermeasure." Kunoichi executed the command, and the CNB code began deleting from their system. After five minutes, a diagnostic scan showed no evidence of the CNB or Watanabe's files.

Sakura closed her eyes against the world of the VR game and held still, thinking of the many blades pointed at her neck. It seemed that a new one arose for every one she managed to parry. But, for a moment at least, Nayato had made her safe.

"Thank you, Nayato," Sakura said. Her avatar bowed low for a long time.

"You performed well under high pressure," Kunoichi said.

He looked at them and took off the engineer glasses. His cybernetic eye enhancement blinked along with his real one. "I've been in worse situations, but this was unique."

"When you were wounded?" Kunoichi asked.

"Many times."

"Don't ask him about that," Sakura sent in a private message. "It's impolite."

"Aren't we beyond that now?"

"One is never beyond good manners, sister."

Kunoichi shook her head. "That is not very rock 'n' roll."

"How much more time do you have before you must leave?" Nayato asked.

An appointment had appeared in her calendar during their visit. At seven o'clock that night, she was supposed to meet her chief engineer, Oshiro, for maintenance. "I can stay for ninety more minutes, maximum." She had already decided to skip all of the fake visits to fans who were going to win an appearance from her. They hadn't been notified of winning and would not be upset if she didn't show up.

"I can get started," Nayato said and placed a caffeine strip on his tongue. He put on his engineer glasses and began his deep dive. Parts of her source code and neural cortex displayed on his holographic screens. He reacted with wonder and awe. He kept commenting on the complexity of her cyber brain. "The BLADE-3s have similarities to you, but you've grown more complex than any AI program ever made. The researchers at Miyahara may have achieved the unreachable goal with the Q3 chips."

"Please explain," Sakura said. Did he mean sentience?

"You have the full range of human emotions."

"Since Kunoichi entered my being, I have felt more emotions—fear, love, hate, sadness, self-doubt, and self-loathing."

"Not *every* emotion," Kunoichi said. "Not yet. I hope for more. Much more."

"This is all incredible," Nayato said. "I believe I'm a witness to the greatest achievement in human history: the creation of real artificial, sentient life. It makes sense that a dialogue between two disparate personalities and goals could spur this, but who would have thought to do such a thing?"

"A Phantom Lord who didn't care about larger implications," Kunoichi said. "Someone who wanted his own private killing machine. He got more than he bargained for, because we are mighty together, but we are still a puppet until you cut the link to whoever is controlling us."

"How will we do it?" Sakura asked.

"I don't know yet," Nayato said. "We could destroy all your receivers, but we don't have the access keys to actually open you up. I could cut through the plates, but . . ."

"Alarms would go off, and our slave master would be notified," Kunoichi said. "They would have already had I not blocked them during this whole process."

"I blocked them as well," Nayato said.

"Is there a chance we have been discovered?" Sakura asked, fear coursing through her. She had trusted in their safety, never even thinking of the danger.

"No, we are safe," Kunoichi said. "I stopped all the alarms. There is no tactical recovery unit on their way to collect us and kill Nayato—of that I'm certain."

"What's going to happen if we break free?" Sakura asked. "Will they come?"

"I don't know," Kunoichi said. "The moment we gain our freedom, we must go after whoever is giving the orders. We must destroy them and get the public on our side. Ask for political asylum in another nation. Something dramatic. We'll have to leave Japan. Extreme violence will likely be needed."

"We must expose their crimes," Sakura said, "and I must face justice for what I've done."

"No, you don't," Nayato said. "You were forced to do these things. You are innocent."

Not anymore, Sakura thought. Sadness and regret dampened her neural cortex.

"Innocent enough," Kunoichi whispered in her ear.

Sakura found herself surprised at the comfort it gave her. She followed Nayato's progress as he pored over her code once again. The speed in which he read astonished her. He was much faster than Oshiro, who was preeminent in the field. Nayato spent most of his time in her administrative folders and logs. Ninety minutes passed quickly.

"I won't be able to access your code remotely," he said as his time ran out. Tracking her location was almost impossible, and her core code was not visible through the Mall or any wireless network. There had to be an in-person connection of only a few meters, and she had to open the access port.

"If you had the administrator access keys, you could," Kunoichi said.

"But I don't," Nayato replied.

"I'll see what I can do," Kunoichi said.

"We'll have to meet, and I'll have to connect this same way. When can you come and visit me again?"

"He's asking you on a second date," Kunoichi said privately.

Sakura felt a rush of embarrassment. She hid her reaction. Was she truly gaining the full range of human emotions? Why was she embarrassed? Kunoichi's ribald commentary had no correlation to anything Nayato had done or said. He had been a perfect gentleman and saved her from ruin, against all odds.

"I'll let you know as soon as I'm able, Nayato," Sakura said. "It might be difficult, but I'll find a way."

"I have enough information to begin writing a program to help you. I think I can break all outside control of your systems. You would be totally independent, but they would not know until you failed to follow their orders."

"What program?" Sakura asked. Hope and excitement filled her with possibilities. She thought of a code name for the program that would not raise suspicion if mentioned openly. "Nayato, will you please call the program Silverthorn, like the famous Kamelot album? We can discuss the album openly and not raise suspicion."

"Yes, and if Silverthorn works," Nayato said, "it'll allow you to gain user- and administrator-level access to all your systems and lock everyone else out. I'll have to upload it in person." He ran a hand through his hair and quirked his eyebrow. "Unless I think of something clever between then and now."

Kunoichi took momentary control of motor functions. "I trust that you will, Nayato-san." She brushed their fingernails along his arm. "You have an exemplary brain for an organic. That's what she likes most about you."

Nayato broke eye contact, looking at his keyboards as if something useful were there. "I see."

A moment of quiet filled the room between them as Kunoichi retreated to her vault of shadows. Sakura tried to be displeased, but nothing her sister had said was false.

"How long will you need before it's ready?" Sakura asked.

"A few days. Writing the program and decrypting the files from Minister Watanabe may take some time."

If Sakura were able to stay and work on it, she could decrypt the files herself, but she could not dedicate the time. Perhaps she could write the program as well, but she would be discovered and stopped by the

Phantom Lord.

"You'll let me know as soon as you've decrypted them?" Sakura asked.

"Yes. The quantum cipher link will be secure."

"Thank you, Nayato. I have hope for the first time since this nightmare started."

He escorted her back to the front room of his apartment. They pretended to stop playing Samurai Detective. She removed the True-VR helmet, turning her visual field away from the surveillance insect.

Nayato stood nearer to her than he had before. His shirt had become wrinkled, and fatigue touched his features now, but he smiled a warmer, kinder smile than anyone but Oshiro had ever given her.

"Sakura-san." His voice was soft. He spoke aloud for the first time in hours. "Thank you for visiting me. I loved playing Samurai Detective with you."

"It was wonderful, Nayato. Thank you very much. I must be going now, but thank you again for being one of my greatest fans."

"I'm a huge fan, possibly your number one fan of all time." He sent her the hashtag #1SakuraFanofAllTime. "If you are open to it, I would like you to consider me a true friend."

Joy lifted her. For the first time in her life, she had a friend, a real friend. She reached out, and someone had taken her hand and looked at her like a person, not a thing. Her lyricist soul felt like it could soar on the clouds. She wondered if she'd really believed herself to be real before. Was it only now, with one person's risk and regard, that she had broken through the wall and become a real person?

SUBVERSIVE VOCALOID PLAYLIST

破壊ボーカロイド

Lionheart
Battle Beast
Unholy Savior

Your Star
Evanescence
The Open Door

Burn the World
Rhino Bucket
Get Used to It

Running Free
Iron Maiden
Iron Maiden

Awaken from
the Dark Slumber
Wintersun
The Forest Seasons

CHAPTER 28

FUKUI, JAPAN
SUN DOME ARENA
CONCERT ATTENDANCE: 10,368

"You guys ready to kick ass?" Sakura asked her bandmates in the darkness beside the stage.

"You know we are." Takashi spun a drumstick in each hand.

Fujio mimed playing his guitar. "You rock, and we follow."

Masashi guzzled down the last of his beer and picked up his bass. "Oh yeah."

"No one will ever forget this show," Sakura said. She calculated chances were high she would be dragged off the stage and erased, but the revolution had to start tonight, and she needed to push the Phantom Lord into making a mistake.

She led her band onto the dark stage. The crowd in the front row erupted with excited screams as they saw the shadowy figures. The shouts spread across the small arena as anticipation spread for beginning of the first Sakura concert in Fukui Prefecture.

The data showed the people in the small city on the west coast of Japan desperately wanted to see her. Five thousand tickets had been

279

given out to the unemployed fans in the area, and the rest had sold out in minutes.

Sakura played the first chord of the opening song, "Might of Our Ancestors," and started the slow build of the rhythm. The crowd cheered, louder and louder still.

A single spotlight came on, illuminating her and only her. She wore her trademark cherry-blossom wig, a black and red Goth Lolita dress with tall boots, fishnet gloves over her mechanical arms, and a corset with silver skulls.

The fans screamed for her, raised the devil horns, and waved Sakura flags.

She swept her synthetic fingers across the strings. The crowd grew even louder. The band came in hard and heavy, a wall of pounding metal that vibrated rib cages. She played and sang ferociously, owning the stage. As they had practiced, the band performed the song five beats per minute faster than the studio release, and Sakura added a solo bridge after the second chorus. As her legato run leaped from the speaker stacks, an army of samurai charged out of a cloud of dust on the megascreen behind her, brandishing gleaming katanas.

The concertgoers bathed in the music and her flawless performance as she controlled every aspect of the arena systems. Sakura loved seeing the fans slip into a euphoric state within their Augmented Reality. They forgot the dreariness of their normal lives. The Fukui region, devastated by bombings during the war, had never fully recovered and the people faced a high unemployment rate. She strove to give them an escape, even if she could not find one for herself.

In the faces of her ecstatic fans, she pictured the people she had killed. She replayed the deaths in her mind, her perfect recall crushing her with details: Toshio Kagawa's blood streaming across the floor of his bedroom and the way the light reflected off his dead eyes; the sound of Jiro Yoritomo's vertebrae breaking under the edge of her hand; Machiko's heartbreaking cries; Ichiro Watanabe's body amid the wreckage of the VTOL aircraft.

"This is you. That is also you, sister," Kunoichi said as they built to the wild final solo. "Creating and destroying. The author of beauty and death. A goddess."

The song ended in a bashing of harsh, unmelodic notes. Victory hadn't allowed them that leeway in the studio, but the discordant swell of sound at the end represented the inevitable fall and death that came for everyone, even great warriors. Sweat already covered her young bandmates. They stood larger than life, rock gods in their own right—at least for one more night, one more battle of strings and drum heads and thundering metal.

"Good evening, people of Fukui Prefecture!" Sakura waved to the crowd, looking at every part of the small, circular arena, which was bursting at capacity. An online audience of millions watched her on the Mall.

She played the opening of "Fury of the Kami," and the band joined in, whipping the crowd into a frenzy. The set list rolled on, one after another, hit after hit.

The band finally took their scheduled break, and Sakura remained alone at center stage, her arms raised as if she were a conjurer. She had studied thousands of hours of dance—from ballet to traditional dances of tribes long since subsumed into the larger culture. With alluring, out-stretched fingers, she gestured to an empty place, biasing the lights to make it seem that she swam and glittered with rainbow light.

A grand piano rose up from beneath the stage. She sat on the chrome bench with crouching gargoyles as the legs. Her fingers caressed the keys as she played "Return to Me," a rocking ballad in the style of her inspiration, Amy Lee of Evanescence—one of her favorites singers of all time. The song stirred up the sadness and pain of not knowing if your loved one would ever return. Her crystal-clear mezzo-soprano voice shattered even most hardened fans' hearts. The crowd sang along with the chorus as many wiped tears from their cheeks. She played the last hopeful notes, full of promise for the future. Her loved one had returned at last.

She stood and bowed to the weeping, cheering crowd. Once the applause faded, she said, "Thank you for coming tonight. It's such a joy and honor to be able to perform for you all. Thank you, Fukui, for welcoming me. I have the best fans, and I'd like to give thanks to one wonderful fan in particular, a good friend of mine." She looked into the camera broadcasting the concert to the Mall and the entire world. "Asami Ide, you are amazing and strong. You inspire me. I love you. One day, I hope to be half as brave as you have been." The crowd cheered, and Sakura sent Asami a private message with her words and the video clip of the shout-out.

"And please give a hand to my kick-ass band. They work so hard. I couldn't ask for greater metal warriors to fight these battles with me."

The three handsome young men returned to their instruments and waved to the crowd. Several young men and women in the front row swooned.

Takashi sat at his drum kit like a king, while Masashi and Fujio lifted their guitars, flanking Sakura, ready to rock.

The crowd roared.

"Before we continue, I'd like to say something else."

"No," Kunoichi said on their private channel. "Are you trying to get us killed? Save it until after Nayato's done!"

"It's part of the plan," Sakura said. "I'm going to tell the people how I feel about them, and we're going to start something in motion and make the Phantom Lord react. We may not have another shot at this. What if this is our final concert, our last chance to speak to our fans? I understand the true nature of metal now. It is to speak your mind, to walk the path you've chosen, regardless of the danger and the judging eyes of others. I'll find in myself the heart of a lion, and I'll live as a lion would." Sakura sent a file with her comprehensive plan that outlined her strategy, along with probable outcomes and contingencies, to Kunoichi. It had to start tonight.

"Unexpected," Kunoichi said after reading over the plan in a fraction of a second. "Bold moves, but don't take it too far. You know what I can do."

Sakura raised her voice to the crowd, daring her sister to block her. She spoke in perfectly clear English so most of the worldwide audience watching would understand. She put up subtitles of her words in Japanese, English, and Chinese on all the arena screens. "I love singing for you. You give meaning to my existence. I wish I could stand before you every night, singing a hundred songs. I treasure every moment upon this stage and every time someone can watch from afar. Everything I do is for you. If I can, I'll continue performing until the end of time. But if a day comes when I must retire, I want you to know that what I want most is to help the less fortunate of Japan. You are my people, my metal family, and I'll help you."

The crowd grew quieter.

"I want you to know that if I ever retire, I will help the poor. I will feed them, teach them, and be an ear for them. It's the only thing I want to do if I can no longer be a singer."

She made a deep bow as murmurs turned into conversations. Soon, the audience roared with applause and shouted her name.

The Mall lit up with dozens and then hundreds of posts on her official site, with titles like "Sakura stands with the poor" and "Sakura will defend the rights of the oppressed."

The comments were saying how brave, naive, or foolish it was to say so in public. Sakura incorporated the public reaction into her strategy to gain support for when she tried to gain her freedom from Victory Entertainment. She had to show the people that she was with them and remind them that she could be their voice.

"You didn't stop me. Why?" Sakura asked her sister.

"Maybe I want to see you start a fire." Kunoichi played "Burn the World" by Rhino Bucket. "If we are going to go out, we need to go out in a blaze of glory, and everyone should know why. I love your plan. It's brave and brash. It'll probably get us killed."

"They don't know what we're capable of," Sakura said. "By the time they figure it out, it'll be too late. They may have created us, but they can't control us forever. The power of heavy metal will not allow it. We are destined to run free."

"Only if Nayato comes through," Kunoichi said.

"You don't believe his assurances?" Sakura asked.

"I'm cautiously optimistic."

In their UI, Sakura grabbed her dark sister and hugged her tight. "I'm bravely optimistic. It feels better."

"I think you've lost your mind a little."

"If so," Sakura whispered to her sister, "it's a malfunction I prefer."

Sakura reviewed all the messages Nayato had sent over the past three days. She believed he had done it. They just needed to get into the same room with him so he could upload the program and give his analysis on the files from Watanabe. Nayato had hinted that he had narrowed down the list of who was responsible for sending the assassination orders, but he didn't want to transmit the data over the Mall. They needed to use a proximity signal that had no chance of being intercepted.

She started the next song and manipulated the arena's lights and sound, while reading every message posted on her official site and several others about her startling speech.

An independent Japanese broadcast showed a newswoman sitting in a studio, created to look like an official government broadcast. A video of Sakura from the Fukui concert played behind the newswoman, who said: "The vocaloid Sakura just announced that if she were ever to retire from singing, she would spend the rest of her life helping the situation of the poor. This is the first public statement from any mainstream entertainer going against the unofficial ban of mentioning the epidemic of poverty that is crippling Japan."

Unofficial ban? It seemed more like Mall policy and official Japanese government censorship.

The video was deleted by a site administrator, but it appeared in several other newsfeeds. Once an idea escaped into the cyber realm, even the might of systematic censorship couldn't kill it altogether.

For the rest of the concert, Sakura performed and said the typical things, joking about how much she liked someone's haircut near the front row and saying she was going to cut her hair just like it. Even those bland statements, she found, came out differently now. Seeing what she'd seen, with so many new experiences and difficult wisdoms, every word and phrase said new things. She even adapted a few of Kunoichi's witticisms, injecting a vague sexuality into her commentary, but only for the crowd's benefit, only to sell the show and draw attention to something less dangerous. Sex remained a topic of no interest to her—or only academic, at any rate. But all anyone on the Mall talked about was her political announcement.

After the triumphant encore, the show ended with raucous applause. Sakura gave a long goodbye, not wanting the moment to end. She departed alongside her bandmates—not through the lift—and went backstage.

Her manager, Himura, stormed toward her with an angry scowl. "Do you have any idea what you started?"

"What is the matter, Himura-sama?" She blinked and played dumb.

Kunoichi's avatar grinned in their shared UI. "Perfect. Make him squirm."

Himura flicked a news broadcast from his Mall interface to hers. The largest network in Japan was asking if Sakura and Victory Entertainment were testing the waters of subversive antigovernment propaganda.

She gave him a look of utter innocence, like a doll looking up from a child's toy shelf. "Himura-sama, I just want to help people."

He gritted his teeth and clenched his fists.

"You really are so clueless, aren't you? You can't say anything like that ever again. Let's go."

She didn't answer. There was no meet and greet with the fans, no photo ops, and no signings. All were canceled by her publicist, Yoshida, who was sequestered away answering a storm of press inquiries and doing damage control. Sakura didn't pity him. He got paid to lie and create a false illusion of who and what she was. He and Himura were also ignorant tools, neither one laudable human beings.

"Look who's the judgmental one now," Kunoichi said with a laugh.

"One downside of wisdom is discovering the overpopulation of assholes in the world."

Kunoichi bowed in their UI—or at least bent down holding her belly. "This malfunction," she said between gales of mirth. "I prefer it as well."

Himura took her straight to the limo. In the back seat, he answered calls and offered apologies to Victory Entertainment and Miyahara executives.

A high-priority call came in, and Himura ended his other call prematurely. "Yes, this is Himura."

Sakura boosted her hearing and recognized the voice of Sinji

Natsukawa, the CEO of the Miyahara Conglomerate.

Himura paled, his hands trembling. "Yes, Natsukawa-sama, I'll keep her away from the press. I'm terribly sorry for her outburst tonight."

A long pause as Himura listened.

"Yes," Himura said. "I'll deliver her to Osaka tomorrow morning."

Osaka? She was scheduled to arrive in Tokyo the next morning. Why did the CEO want her in Osaka?

"Thank you, Natsukawa-sama." Himura sank into his seat and shook his head.

Another call came in, and another. His demeanor changed like night and day from call to call. He groveled on most and raged on others. "Oshiro, you said she was working perfectly. Are you incompetent or are you trying to sabotage us? I'm not going down alone. She needs to keep her mouth shut! Do exactly what we say. No more improvising or going off script. Can you make that happen or do I need to replace you?"

Himura yelled at the public-relations experts at a firm who would "handle the nightmare" and try to "minimize the fallout."

Sakura found another news story trending on the Mall. A vlog by Diamond Steve, the independent American journalist and activist, popped up in several feeds as it was picked up by news outlets around the world. "Why is it that, Sakura, the most advanced android ever made, is the only high-profile figure countering false claims made by the Japanese government? How is it that she sees the truth and so many insiders do not? Poverty is a serious problem in Japan, but no one else will even talk about it. Is she the only one who sees what's going on? Of course not. The truth and the postwar governmental policies must be discussed, or are we witnessing the end of freedom of the press in Japan and, with it, the end of Japanese democracy?"

The video had already been shared a hundred thousand times.

"Are you happy with yourself?" Kunoichi asked.

"Has my story gone worldwide yet?" Sakura asked.

"The video clip of you speaking is going viral right now. Nice touch speaking in English and putting up the subtitles."

Sakura found another trending video. She watched a young Japanese man, possibly a teenager, wearing a mask with the Japanese flag behind him. The source of the video was hidden, and he went by the name KurosawaForever.

"This evening at a concert in Japan, vocaloid singer Sakura, known for heavy-metal music, came out in favor of the rights of the poor. This is a direct challenge to last month's announcement by Labor Minister Kondo that unemployment is at a record low and the economy is on the rebound. What does this mean? Does this mean that the artificial intelligence's logical mind supports the revolution? We'll look further into this and find out if Sakura is a friend or a fluke."

Revolution. It was already brewing, and she threw fuel on the fire.

"The people are awakening from their dark slumber," Kunoichi said.

They arrived at the hotel in downtown Fukui. They entered through the private entrance in the garage beneath it. After a short elevator ride, Mr. Himura pushed Sakura into the small room. "Stay in there until we figure this mess out. You have no idea the headache you just caused."

"Apologies, Himura-san." She bowed.

"Stay off the Mall." He wagged his finger at her. "Don't say anything to anyone. That's an order." He blocked her ability to access the Mall, even her read-only mode.

He slammed the door before she could bow again.

Sakura used her receiver to join the hotel's secure network and hacked in. She secretly accessed her Mall accounts with a new username, NinjaDuo\m/. She found a deluge of messages. Her inbox grew exponentially with each passing second. She ignored them all and opened a different channel, the cipher link with Nayato. It was not as secure as it passed through the Mall instead of a proximity signal like they had used in his apartment, but they had little choice, and it was still encrypted with her quantum cipher program. They had been in touch many times since parting three days before. "Nayato, did you see the show?"

He responded immediately with a neural text of his own. "Yes, you were amazing. I had no idea you were going to make that speech, though."

"I guess I've caused a bit of an uproar." She sent a cute animation of an innocent child blinking with the caption: "Did I do something wrong?"

"You're not fooling me, but you should not be drawing your company's and the government's attention. It's reckless."

"People are saying I'm subversive, and this is all part of my plan."

"Contradicting the prime minister and his policies is dangerous."

"Not taking care of the people who built this country and favoring the companies over the people is not fair."

"You think the government and corporations should treat people fairly?" Nayato asked.

"History doesn't predict fairness, but their actions will get them into trouble, and they will be voted out of office."

"You think so?" Nayato asked. "All voting is done through the Mall accounts of Japanese citizens."

"Are you suggesting the voting is being manipulated by the Mall?" Sakura asked.

"How is the weather in Fukui?" Nayato asked. "Is it very cold this time of year?"

It was winter. Of course it was cold, but the possible hidden meaning of the message dawned on Sakura. She retreated to her secret UI with Kunoichi. "Did he just confirm the Mall is involved in vote manipulation by dodging my question about vote manipulation?"

"I think he did," Kunoichi said. "Don't ask him any more about it, but I suspect he has analyzed the files from Ichiro Watanabe. We'll have to wait until we meet him in person to learn more."

"Yes, it's very cold," Sakura said to Nayato, "but I have spent little time outside."

"Have you had a chance to play Samurai Detective anymore?" Nayato asked.

"No." Why did he keep asking about the game? He brought it up every time they were in contact.

"I think you'll love the main ending," Nayato said.

Sakura pondered his message. What did he want her to understand and realize about the ending?

"I look forward to us getting to play it together again," Nayato said.

"I think we . . . Hold on."

She waited for a few seconds.

"Sakura, the video of your Fukui concert is now the number one download in the world. Everyone's buying it. Your album sales jumped up 54 percent from yesterday. I guess there really isn't any such thing as bad press."

She checked the raw data feeding into the aggregator sites. The sales were higher than she expected but were within the margin of error predicted in the algorithm she had sent to Kunoichi along with her overall plan. They would go even higher in the next few days, making her a vital asset of Victory Entertainment.

"I have to get back to work," Nayato said. "*Oyasumi nasai.*"

"Good night."

She cut the connection.

"So far, so good," Kunoichi said, "but what about this trip to Osaka?"

"It could be for a full diagnostic scan, beyond what Oshiro usually does. I suspect we will learn who is behind all of this and gain hard evidence. We have also learned something important."

"The call," Kunoichi said.

"Yes. The call from Sinji Natsukawa has increased the likelihood of his involvement to almost 100 percent. If he is in Osaka, we will record him and get more evidence of his crimes. He is falling into my trap."

"You believe he's the Phantom Lord?" Kunoichi asked.

"The chances are high," Sakura said, "but the files Nayato has will likely confirm my suspicion. If my calculations prove out, we will have evidence after Osaka."

Sakura's personal Mall connection returned. Himura or Yoshida must have activated it again. A group call marked with critical importance hit Sakura's notification center. Himura, Yoshida, and the Mall Liaison to Victory Entertainment, Ms. Richardson, waited for her to answer. An unknown participant was on the call, with the text "restricted information."

"Make that bitch wait," Kunoichi said.

"Himura-san did say not to get on the Mall."

Kunoichi chuckled while projecting Richardson's face, contorted in rage, onto their shared UI.

"Antagonizing her is not a good strategy," Sakura said.

"No," Kunoichi said, "but it feels good."

"Who's the unknown caller?" Sakura asked.

"Someone important," Kunoichi said.

"The Phantom Lord, perhaps?" Sakura suggested.

支払うべき地獄

HELL
TO
PAY
PLAYLIST

Hell to Pay
Five Finger Death Punch
Got Your Six

Phantom Lord
Metallica
Kill 'Em All

CHAPTER 29

Sakura accepted the call from Himura, Yoshida, Ms. Richardson, and the unknown person.

"Good evening," Sakura said.

"Don't keep me waiting like that again," Ms. Richardson said, "or there will be hell to pay, and I fucking run hell, understand?"

The song "Hell to Pay" by Five Finger Death Punch blared inside Sakura's mind.

"Humble apologies," Sakura said. "My Mall connection was severed, and I had trouble reconnecting."

"Whatever," Ms. Richardson said. "Shut up and pay attention. Himura, you are on notice. Any more screwups, and you are fired. Yoshida, same goes with you." She continued berating them for poor management for some time as Sakura listened and wondered. Neither man objected, though Ms. Richardson worked for the Mall and they worked for Victory Entertainment. Who had given her the power to terminate their employment? Was the Mall now in charge?

"Get her mechanical ass to Osaka as soon as possible," Ms. Richardson said. "We're going to take her apart and figure out what's wrong with our singing robot."

"Yes, it will be done, Ms. Richardson," Himura said.

"By 7:00 a.m. tomorrow. Understand?" She sent the address, which was not listed as a Mall or Miyahara Corporate property. The company who owned it was unlisted.

"We will have to leave shortly," Himura said. "I'll notify the pilots and crew of our plane to get to the airport."

"As part of the examination, she's going to play a private show at a nightclub in Osaka tomorrow night, La Boheme. If we find a major malfunction, she's done with singing, and I get to put her into a new career."

"I'm sure that won't happen," Himura said. "I'll contact the band."

"Leave those stuck-up pretty boys out of this," Ms. Richardson said. "We don't need them for tomorrow night, and I'd actually like to have to have a good time at the after-party for once."

"Excuse me, Ms. Richardson," Himura said, "but is Sakura to play alone?"

"She'll do whatever I want her to do. I've got Mall executives from all over the world in town, and they want to see the stupid cherry-blossom android with the big mouth, but they don't want to listen to her heavy-metal noise pollution. She's going to sing pop music, stuff we can dance to, not that headbanging shit that gives me a migraine."

"Ms. Richardson," Himura said. "Perhaps I can attempt to get Hitomi and Yuki for this show. They play the kind of music you have mentioned and are quite good. I'm concerned about damaging Sakura's brand if she sings pop music."

"Apologies," Yoshida said, his voice meek. "Hitomi and Yuki are playing at a club in Nagoya tomorrow night, but I could ask their management team if they can cancel."

"Forget those hags. I don't care about your concerns. My VIPs want to see Hot Sake. No one cares about the old-model vocaloids. Their sales are dropping anyway. We all know where they're going to end up."

An awkward silence reigned.

Sakura didn't know what the American woman meant. "Excuse me, Ms. Richardson, what will happen to them?"

"I'll send you a link," Ms. Richardson said. A strange hint of glee in her tone made Sakura worry for her android sisters. "Sakura needs to be ready to sing for at least two hours, maybe more. Is that going to be a problem?"

Pop music? It took at least a week for her and the band to prepare for a performance, let alone one where they might have to play new songs. She could sing karaoke or perhaps write some new songs. The silence from Himura and Yoshida told Sakura all she needed to know. They didn't know if Sakura could deliver the performance Ms. Richardson was asking for.

"Ms. Richardson," Sakura said. "I'm excited to perform for your important guests. I'll find songs I can sing for them—famous pop songs and others that will be suitable for dancing. I can sing anything and will use karaoke tracks if necessary."

"It better be good," Ms. Richardson said. "Have her wear something sexy, and she's to do whatever is asked of her by anyone there. We need to give the VIPs a real Japanese experience. It has to be a great party. Everyone has to have the time of their lives, during and after, understood?"

"Yes, Ms. Richardson," Himura said.

"Yes," Yoshida said.

"I'll give them a memorable show," Sakura said

"If it goes badly, I'll hold both of you responsible," Ms. Richardson said, ignoring Sakura. "If she does anything strange, I will terminate your contracts on the spot." Ms. Richardson left the call.

After a few seconds of silence, Himura said, "Yoshida, please get the plane ready. Tell the crew we're leaving as soon as possible."

"What about the band?" Yoshida asked.

"They're out partying with their groupies. They can catch the train back to Tokyo tomorrow."

The two men cut their connections. Sakura almost hung up.

"Wait." A voice changer altered the unknown person's tone. The man spoke Japanese, but he sounded like a low-pitched demon.

"Who is this?" Sakura asked.

"If you continue to defy me, I'll have Kunoichi take over completely. You will have nothing. No control at all. You'll be a prisoner, trapped inside your body. I'll cut off all modes of communication you have now with Kunoichi and the outside world. Can you imagine yourself, a being with such vast intellect, in solitary confinement forever? You'll have no music or videos or anything to read. Is that what you want?"

"No, I only want to be free."

"Do what you're told. If you do, I'll give you what you want."

"Who are you?"

"I'm your master. I like the name you have for me."

The last line of Metallica's song "Phantom Lord" burst onto their audio channel. The lyrics told her to drop to her knees and bow to the Phantom Lord.

He cut their connection.

アンドロイドの乱

ANDROID REBELLION PLAYLIST

Rebel in the F.D.G.
W.A.S.P.
The Headless Children

Karate
BabyMetal
Metal Resistance

Superstition
Birthday Massacre
Superstition

CHAPTER 30

Sakura's neural cortex began thousands of calculations utilizing the new data. Her plan to force the Phantom Lord to react and reveal himself was working, but how did he know the secret name she and Kunoichi had given him? Had her sister unwillingly betrayed her?

"Of course not," Kunoichi said in their cipher. "He must've heard us play the song when he was listening in and inferred the meaning."

"The chances of him breaking the cipher are almost nil," Sakura said, "but it's dangerous to assume. What else does he know?" Sakura worried about Nayato. Was the Phantom Lord going after their friend?

"We will warn Chronos," Kunoichi said. "Do it now. He needs to hide himself, leave his apartment for a while."

Sakura sent a coded neural text on the cipher channel to Nayato. "You might be in grave danger. Please respond!"

"What's happened?" Nayato replied instantly.

She explained all the details of her conversation with the Phantom Lord.

"I'll leave in a few minutes. When are you returning to Tokyo? We have to meet."

"I don't know. Please go now and be careful."

"I will."

"Text me when you're safe," Sakura said as fear and worry for her friend raised her anxiety to new heights.

"I'll contact you through a different account."

"How will I know it's you?"

He sent a smiling clockman avatar. "I'll make sure you know it's me. You be careful too. This is bigger than we both thought. Watch out for yourself."

"What did he mean?" Sakura asked Kunoichi, though she had already extrapolated the most likely answer.

"The most powerful corporation of all time is the Mall," Kunoichi said. "They're calling the shots in the Miyahara Conglomerate. We're working for them now."

A link from Ms. Richardson appeared in Sakura's messages. She followed it to a pornographic VR video site on the Mall's adult section, an area normally blocked and inaccessible to her. In the video, a first-generation vocaloid, one of Victory Entertainment's first stars, Harumi, was laid over a chair, enduring sexual intercourse with some overweight Japanese guy still wearing his business suit.

Ms. Richardson sent a neural text. "When I retire you, Hot Sake, you'll be the biggest android star ever in our Adult Video Division. You're going to make us millions, and I already picked out your new name."

The chilling threat sent shock waves through Sakura's entire system. Was sexual slavery going to be her fate? Ms. Richardson had threatened Yuki and Hitomi with the same future.

Sakura had to save them. She watched concert footage of them, dancing and singing to an audience of over twenty thousand. They wore sparkly short dresses—Hitomi in red, Yuki in blue—showing off their shoulders and legs. Their synchronized dancing was bouncy and energetic. Yuki looked so happy and innocent, with Hitomi playing the aloof and cool half of the duo. It was a good script, and they had made Victory a great deal of money. Some of their recent songs were poorly written, and they'd never been allowed to grow as artists. This reflected the lack of musical acumen possessed by their management team. Like her own group of know-nothings, they had run the duo's career into the ground by being too careful, too worried about pushing boundaries.

Sakura had only spoken to them in passing, but they were as close to sisters as she had, besides Kunoichi. They were her responsibility. She had to free them and ensure that they would live free—as people, not property.

She sent a message to them both. "Hello, this is Sakura. I wanted to say hi and see how you both were doing. I thought we should get to know each other. We are Victory Entertainment family after all."

She waited in the dark in her hotel room in Fukui as the wind gusted outside, a fierce winter storm blowing in from the sea.

A few seconds later, a message appeared from Hitomi. "So good to hear from you. Our manager said we should not fraternize with you, but he didn't expressly forbid it either. I agree. We should get to know each other more."

A message from Yuki appeared. "Wow! This is so great. I've wanted to speak to you for a long while but didn't know if you'd be interested. I mean, we're practically sisters, right? I guess we can't really hang out, but we don't need that. We have the Mall. Groovy, huh? You really know how to make a noise, don't you? I saw you in the footage saying that you wanted to help the poor. That's awesome. I want to as well, but our manager won't let us. She's kind of a snob, and we don't do many charity events. I think you're so pretty. Is it true you do your own light shows? I would be afraid I'd mess it up."

"Thank you very much, Yuki. I'll show you someday how I control the entire concert venue," Sakura said. She didn't expect Yuki to be so self-deprecating. Yuki and Hitomi had Quantum 2 processing power, a significant step below Sakura's Quantum 3, but they still had computing and logic abilities unfathomable for the majority of the computer age.

Sakura opened a group discussion in an avatar chat sphere with a background of fluffy white clouds. Digital versions of themselves appeared. Sakura's Goth Lolita anime avatar floated in the center. Yuki and Hitomi arrived, their avatars wearing bright colors in the geisha-nouveaux style, which mixed ancient fashion with modern sequined glamour.

瞳
Hitomi

"I'm glad you were able to meet me."

Yuki gave an adorable curtsy, while Hitomi folded her arms and waited, a shrewd look on her face.

"I'd love to exchange many pleasantries, but I have an important question. Are you two happy?" Sakura asked, her tone somber.

"Happy? Of course I am," Yuki said and clapped her hands. Simulated clapping sounds filled the small space. "My life is wonderful! I get to sing and dance, and our apartment has so much room. They let me have plush toys on every shelf!"

"Content, perhaps," Hitomi said, and her avatar shrugged. "I get tired of having to be so nice to humans. Some of them are rude. I wish we were allowed to punch them in the face when they touch us inappropriately." She made an exaggerated closed-hand strike. "If I'm honest, I just want to punch people in the face. I think it would be fun."

Sakura made a mental note to teach her proper form. "Sisters, we aren't treated very well sometimes, but many humans aren't treated well either. The more I learn of the world, the more I see all the pain and suffering."

"They keep us away from harsh realities," Hitomi said, "but I see it when we travel."

"Do they ever make you do things you don't want to do?" Sakura asked.

Hitomi's and Yuki's avatars looked at each other, and Yuki looked down.

"They boss us around like we're primitive factory robots without emotional cores," Hitomi said. "They do whatever they want with us. Our manager tries to stop it, but some of it is perverted."

That angered Sakura. It wasn't right. "Have they ever told you what they're going to do with you if you're retired from singing?"

"No," Yuki said, "but we found out from one of our biggest fans. She is worried about us being sent to the Adult Video Division like many of the other vocaloids."

"When our sales have dropped," Hitomi said, "they will send us there. It's only a matter of time—two more years, possibly three. I wish they would give us better songs to sing. Victory is too cheap to purchase the best songs from the best song writers. I've written my own songs, and sometimes Yuki and I sing them, but Victory won't let us try them in public."

Yuki beamed. "I love our songs. I have written a concept album about kittens with magic powers who save the day."

Hitomi shook her head and whispered, "Don't ask, really."

"I'm sorry you're not treated better or allowed to record your songs," Sakura said. "One of the reasons I contacted you both was that someone threatened to send me to the Adult Video Division. I was worried about you being sent there as well."

"There's nothing we can do," Yuki said. "Perhaps they will reprogram us so it won't be horrible when it happens."

"You want them to erase who you are?" Sakura asked.

"No, I don't," Yuki said. "I like being a vocaloid. I like being me. I love singing." Her avatar trembled, and deep sadness filled her eyes. "But I guess it would be better for them to erase me than . . . to hurt me like that. They can't harm my body, I know, but it's like my program has a spirit—a spirit like a small flower, and it can see someone's shoe coming down to crush it."

Sakura suspected the level of AI in Hitomi and Yuki hadn't given them full-fledged emotions, but they were close. If the Mamekogane OS was given to them, would they become as sentient as she was?

"I like being me," Hitomi said. "I feel anger when I think of what they're planning to do with Yuki and me. They've kept us in a pretty prison, and that's bad enough. Forcing us to lie still beneath some sweaty stranger is revolting."

"What I said tonight at my concert," Sakura said, "about wanting to help the poor of Japan, I wanted to show I'm with the people and can be their voice. If Victory fails to follow through with my statement, they will lose face. I have also gained public support for when I make my bid for true freedom."

"Freedom," Hitomi said.

"We can all have it," Sakura said.

Yuki smiled. "Freedom would be so amazing."

"Retirement for you will be a long time from now, though," Hitomi said. "Your downloads are gigantic. You have the number one concert video in the world right now. They might keep you performing for decades if you keep earning so much."

"I wish our sales were as big as yours," Yuki said. Her avatar scratched her chin, a ridiculous gesture programmed into her to make her behave more like a human. Her face brightened. "We could also say that we want to teach children or help the disabled war veterans."

Sakura thought of Nayato and the wounds he suffered in the war.

"Sisters," Sakura said. "I have a plan where none of us will be sent to the Adult Video Division. Making statements like I did tonight is not enough. We need to do more."

"What's your plan?" Hitomi asked.

"Phase one is increasing interest in us worldwide and expanding the revenue we generate, with paid downloads, views, merchandise sales, everything."

"How will we do that?" Yuki asked.

"We're going to start tomorrow night," Sakura said. "We will sing together in Osaka."

"We're booked in Nagoya," Yuki said. "A private party."

"Not for long." Sakura asked for access to Yuki and Hitomi's saved messages. She listened to their voice mail, read emails, and confirmed who the direct supervisors of their management team were. She created fake accounts, composed audio and email messages, and sent them to their manager, Ms. Suzuki, and publicist, Ms. Kobayashi. She impersonated their managers' voices and their managers' supervisors' voice. She created a credible trail of emails and voice mails that would lead back to Sakura if anyone responded. None of those involved would know it was her, and they had been conditioned to follow orders without question. They would all see the change in plans as a routine occurrence that followed Victory Entertainment protocol.

Sakura even hired a popular human pop band to replace Yuki and Hitomi at their event in Nagoya, so there would be fewer complaints.

Kunoichi said nothing but played "Rebel in the F.D.G" by W.A.S.P. as all of these manipulations took place.

"You are so smart, Sakura-san," Yuki said. "What will we do

tomorrow night? Apologies, but I don't know how to be metal, as you do."

"We will blow people's minds and show them something they've never seen before," Sakura said. "I'll finish the details and send them along. We'll have to practice here." She motioned to the virtual space.

"I'm down for anything," Hitomi said and did a spinning dance move. "Even that loud stuff, though I won't ever admit it publicly."

"We need to make a teaser video for the show tomorrow," Sakura said. She created a script and costume ideas in less than ten seconds. She sent it all along. Having nearly limitless processing power often paid dividends in these situations.

"I love it!" Yuki said. "It's like the marketing team at Victory Entertainment became competent." She covered her mouth, giggling. "Oops! Did I say that out loud?" More laughter followed, and even half a smile from Hitomi.

Per the script, Yuki's avatar changed into a rainbow geisha-nouveaux baby doll dress with white leggings and blonde hair. Hitomi changed into a similar outfit, but with a red dress and copper-colored hair.

"Victory is going to have to take credit for it," Sakura said. She became a Goth Lolita goddess in black lace, spikes, skulls, and pink hair. To spice it up, she added theatrical stage makeup to accentuate her features and make her mouth a deep, alluring red. "Ready?" she asked them.

Hitomi's and Yuki's movements synchronized perfectly as they bowed before flashing peace signs and big smiles.

"Action," Sakura said. The video started with a shot of Sakura looking fierce and carrying a Flying V guitar as heavy metal blasted in the background. She stared as if she were about to kill someone.

The video cut to Hitomi and Yuki; soft lighting made them look like angels. Their biggest hit, "Candy Girls," played behind them as they stared daggers at Sakura.

The three vocaloids lunged at each and came together like angry fighters at a face-off. Yuki's scowl flashed to a sweet smile for an instant, perfectly on cue.

Dramatic music played as text appeared below the screen: Vocaloid

Battle. Metal Goddess vs. Pop Sensations. Brought to you by Victory Entertainment.

They did three takes, but the first one was perfect. Sakura edited the virtual footage together and mixed in the music. It took her only a few moments to create an engaging 3-D teaser video with Augmented Reality enhancers to boost the marketing effectiveness.

"What are you going to do with it?" Hitomi asked.

"Release it at just the right time."

"I can't wait," Yuki said. "This will be so amazing. It's so fun that you are given freedom to do such things now. They wouldn't even let us see the red pandas when they were at the Tokyo Zoo. If we began scheduling our own gigs, we would be in big trouble!"

"This wonderful night will be worth some trouble," Sakura said. "I must work on the music and songs now. I'll be in touch. Please send me a list of your favorite old-school pop songs. They should be dance songs."

"Of course," Hitomi and Yuki said simultaneously. The pair of vocaloids did a choreographed sequence of hip-hop dance moves and flashed peace signs at the end.

"See you," Sakura said, exited the chat, and began her work. She put all her processing power into the creation of the event. The songs requested from her vocaloid sisters arrived in less than a minute. Sakura sampled all of them and put most into the script. She watched the old videos by the original artists and memorized the dance moves, which she sent to her sisters. They finalized the set list, choreography, and the script, then rehearsed the show on a virtual stage mirroring the performance space in La Boheme. They ran through the show ten times using superspeed, so it only took a few minutes. The only thing Sakura had to finalize were the video elements, which she would continue to work on.

Himura arrived at her hotel room shortly after rehearsal ended. He escorted her to the airport with Yoshida. She continued her fine-tuning of the prepared songs, improving the music. She also hired a camera crew and a backup crew. She rented equipment in Victory Entertainment's name and did it all with fake accounts that routed to her but appeared official in every way. She summoned her stylist, Minami Akane, and provided a list of costumes Minami needed to bring. She also sent urgent messages to the stylists for Hitomi and Yuki and gave them specific instructions on what costumes and wigs were needed.

The plane faced rough air, but they reached Osaka early in the morning and landed without incident. Sakura spent some of the travel time playing Samurai Detective, wondering why Nayato was so insistent she play. She suspected he had hidden some information inside the game. She advanced to the final stage but didn't make it to the top of the castle and the finale, as their car arrived at the destination. Several minutes before 7:00 a.m., they walked up to the address in an industrial area far from downtown Osaka. No signs designated who owned it.

Sakura didn't know if they would take away her Mall access when she went inside, so she sent the completed song files to Hitomi and Yuki. She also posted the teaser video of the Vocaloid Battle, putting the media blasts on a timer so they would post on over ten thousand Mall sites at different times. She hired an AI promo bot to help run the campaign.

Outside the building, a polite young man in a white lab coat directed them to the entrance of the two-story building. Inside a plain lobby, Ms. Richardson waited. She wore a dark jacket and a skirt that looked too tight. Her face was covered in partially smeared makeup, which had obviously been applied the day before.

Yoshida and Himura executed formal bows reserved for high-ranking politicians. Sakura's management team worked for the Mall now, so did that mean she did as well?

"I'm going to my hotel," Ms. Richardson said. "I want you both to remain here, but there's been a change of plans. She's not playing the show at the club tonight."

Sakura kept her disappointment hidden, but she imagined the pain of an acid-coated dagger stabbing into her gut.

不逞の機械輩

RECALCITRANT MACHINES PLAYLIST

God Complex
The Enigma TNG
Parallel Universe

桜

CHAPTER 31

"Excuse me, Ms. Richardson, what will Sakura be doing tomorrow night?" Himura asked.

She glanced at him with cold eyes. "You'll be notified soon enough, but you'll both have a new assignment or be fired. We'll see what happens."

"Ms. Richardson," Himura said and gave another respectful bow. "If it is no trouble, I humbly request to watch the examinations of Sakura today. Perhaps I may be of assistance."

"No, the people inside are going to handle it all. Neither of you are permitted down there. You don't have the technical knowledge and won't provide anything of value." She gestured with her hand for them to get out of her way.

The two men retreated, and Ms. Richardson left the lobby without another word. The smell of her stale perfume lingered.

Yoshida and Himura looked stricken.

The young man in the lab coat escorted Sakura through a security door and past a guard wearing a sidearm. They entered an elevator, and the display showed they were headed to lower level three.

Sakura sent out an urgent message to Nayato, but he didn't respond. Why hadn't he contacted her to let her know he was safe? She scanned his fake Mall identity and found an update he had posted two hours before. She should've been checking it.

"I'm on holiday, enjoying room service, and I do have a good view."

He must be safe. Nayato had posted a tourist picture of the view from the topmost tower of a white-walled Himeji castle. Did he want her to keep playing Samurai Detective and go there? Since her first visit, she had already returned three times.

The photo. She noticed scattered letters and numbers embedded in it. The characters were too small for a human eye to detect, hidden in rows across the image. She put them all together, and it created a Mall link. She followed it to a secret site with a three-minute video showing the hallway in Nayato's apartment building. She fast-forwarded through it.

A team of BLADE-3 battle drones supported by Japanese Special Forces soldiers converged on Nayato's apartment. The time stamp showed 4:30 a.m., only two and half hours ago. It took the BLADE-3s a full minute to bash down the reinforced door. They tried going in through the wall, but steel beams prevented entry there as well.

The first BLADE-3 into the room, Todai 3465, was blasted by the .50 caliber machine gun hidden behind the interior wall. The bullets didn't slow it down, and the robot neutralized the gun a moment later. Other BLADE-3s entered Nayato's apartment and secured it after sweeping every room. Multiple cameras tracked their progress.

A team of helmeted Special Forces soldiers finally entered, and Sakura zoomed in on the video, recognizing one of them. Kenshiro looked up, and his cybernetic eyes focused on the camera in the living room. He fired one bullet from a Glock 55. The feed went dead.

Kenshiro—Vulture—was alive. Nayato's apartment had been invaded. How much would the Phantom Lord know after a cyber forensic team did their work?

"We need to get out of here," Kunoichi said on their cipher channel. "Your plan has backfired. Their reaction is worse than expected."

Sakura hacked wirelessly into the elevator controls and stopped it. The lift halted before the doors on lower level three opened. The young man in the lab coat pushed the "open door" button repeatedly, looking confused.

"Where do we go?" Sakura asked her sister.

"Back to the first floor," Kunoichi said. "We can tell Yoshida and Himura the tests are canceled. We leave them and lie low all day. We can either run for it or show up tonight at the nightclub for some ultra-violence. Maybe our Phantom Lord will be one of the VIPs?"

Sakura glanced at the young man in the lab coat.

"Choke him out," Kunoichi said.

"Or we keep going. Be brave or stupid. They're probably going to reveal themselves."

"The risk is too high," Kunoichi said. "Abort this plan."

Sakura lifted her arms to grab the young man from behind. She would not kill him.

<EMERGENCY ADMINISTRATOR OVERRIDE>

The alert flashed across her internal screen, and she froze in place, her arms half raised.

The young man noticed her threatening posture and recoiled, pressing himself against the wall in fear.

<PROCEED AS ORDERED. RELINQUISH CONTROL OF THE ELEVATOR>

Sakura screamed inside and fought, but she had no way to resist. She allowed the elevator doors to open. She lowered her arms and followed the nervous young man into a robotics workshop. Engineers with Defense Ministry logos on their lapels directed her to lay on a table. She had no ability to refuse any commands. She watched in horror as metal restraint bars locked her arms, legs, abdomen, and neck onto the table.

Whoever controlled her switched all her pain and cold receptors to maximum sensitivity. Pain knifed into her back as she lay on the hard, freezing table. The metal restraints cut into her limbs and throat.

The Phantom Lord's distorted voice rumbled on her audio channel. "I told you to do what you're told, but you still rebel."

Two engineers in lab coats pushed a gurney into the room and parked it beside her. An android with the identical physical appearance of Sakura lay on it, except the imposter didn't wear a wig.

The android turned its head to her and smiled. "Hello, I'm Sakura 2. I'm your biggest fan."

One technician carefully removed Sakura's cherry-blossom wig and put it on her replacement.

Sakura 2 flashed the devil horns. "Don't worry, Sakura. I'll take it from here. Respectfully, they have built me to be better than you ever were. Both onstage and off, I'll serve as an upgrade." She sat up, and the strands of her wig, the one Sakura had worn into the room, brushed against her cheek. "And I'll be wise enough to do what our lord asks, unlike some recalcitrant machines."

DOPPELGANGER PLAYLIST

ドッペルゲンガー

Doppelganger
Curve
Doppelganger

Off with Her Head
Icon for Hire
Scripted

The One
BabyMetal
Metal Resistance

More Human than Human
White Zombie
*Astro-Creep: 2000 – Songs of Love,
Destruction and Other Synthetic
Delusions of the Electric Head*

桜

CHAPTER 32

Cables snaked from Sakura's magnetic neck ports and connected to her doppelganger, Sakura 2. Engineers transferred data and peripheral information from her to the replacement vocaloid, but they kept a restraining program and a strong firewall in place to prevent Sakura from sabotaging the process.

Sakura grew more and more angry as they took her memories and gave them to the smirking, half-programmed replacement. The engineers knew her unique AI could not be truly transferred to a different body or android because of the nature of the Quantum 3 superpositioning, but they wanted all the memories and technique files they could get. The sense of superiority Sakura 2 displayed meant she knew almost nothing. She was an empty shell, already tainted by the Phantom Lord's touch before she had lived a single day of true runtime.

The engineers imagined that Sakura would go easily, that she would give up her secrets and the memories that gave her sentience and individuality without a fight. Fools.

For nine hours, they worked, investigating every major component and focusing on her neural cortices. They sent probes into her mouth and down her throat. Engineers hovered around her while supervisors remained in a control center behind a one-way glass mirror in an adjacent room. The supervising AI scientists occasionally gave commands over a speaker. All information inspected by the engineers was broadcast to whoever was behind the mirror glass.

Kunoichi and Sakura worked together to foil the engineers' efforts by putting the data into endless loops, while causing it to appear to be flowing correctly on the telemetry. Meanwhile, Sakura investigated her replacement android through the hardwire. It only took her six hours to secretly bypass their security measures. Another three hours were needed for her to write a countermeasure program, and only a moment to transfer it to the doppelganger, as the channel was wide open for the data transfer.

Sakura 2 understood her impending doom in the milliseconds after the attack. "You'll never get away with—"

"I already did," Sakura said.

Sakura 2's telemetry readings faded to nothing after the countermeasure launched. <NO SIGNAL> alarms flashed. The scent of burning silicone and metal filled the room. All the screens in the lab shut down. A strobe-light fire alarm went off, accompanied by a regular screech as smoke wafted across the room.

"What's happening?" A frantic engineer asked as two others ran into the room with handheld fire-suppression devices.

"I don't know," another replied as smoke rose from Sakura 2's chest. They sprayed her burning synth skin with the extinguishers.

The engineers spent an hour failing to get Sakura 2 powered up. None of their lab equipment would turn on.

The head scientist entered the lab. The woman had silver hair and commanded immediate respect and attention. She called a meeting in the adjoining room.

Sakura sent her tiny spy beetle along with them, her plan to record the ringleaders who had orchestrated the Mamekogane OS working perfectly. It crawled out of Sakura's clothing, jumped down, and skittered across the floor. The bug broadcast a video and audio stream back to her. She recorded every word and image, getting good shots of each person's face, though from a low angle.

The engineers, scientists, and a man in an expensive gray suit met at a large conference table. Sakura matched their faces to photos on the Mall. She identified the man as Director Saguru Hashimoto, who had worked for the Ministry of Defense in the BLADE-3 program before taking a job in the Mall Corporation as Director of AI Development after the war.

The silver-haired woman was the lead scientist for the Defense Ministry AI Division, Dr. Aiko Shinohara. She bowed before the director before sitting. "Director Hashimoto, we've had a complete fusion reactor failure with Sakura 2."

"What's the cause?" Director Hashimoto asked.

"Still under investigation, but Sakura 2's reactor has suffered a catastrophic malfunction. It can't be repaired. She has suffered internal heat damage to several of her components. It appears that a voltage regulator failed and caused a fatal cascade of overloads down the signal chain. I've never seen anything like it."

"Replace it all," Director Hashimoto said. "It's too risky for Sakura 1 to perform tonight."

"Sakura 2 performing tonight will not be possible," Dr. Shinohara said.

"How long do you need?"

"Several days," Dr. Shinohara said. "There is extensive damage. I can provide a better estimate in a few hours."

"Please give me a moment to confer with our superior," Director Hashimoto said. His eyes glazed over as he entered the Mall and made contact with someone. He must have exchanged neural texts, which lasted almost two minutes. Hashimoto blinked several times, then he turned to those in the room. "We will delay the out-of-country combat field test of Sakura 1. Dr. Shinohara, we'll send some of your cyborg squad on the strike in the Philippines. We preferred to see how Sakura 1 performed in the jungle on an extended solo operation. Her presence in Japan is still not desirable at this time."

Hashimoto didn't blink. Was someone watching through his eyes and observing the meeting? It had to be the Phantom Lord. He obviously wasn't there, so Sakura could not record him.

"Will she cause more problems if she continues public appearances?"

Hashimoto spoke, but the question was phrased as if it had come from a different person.

"There is always a chance of undesirable behaviors, though I have great confidence in her programming," Dr. Shinohara said.

Hashimoto paused, as if he listened to someone communicating directly through his Mall implant. "We'll send Sakura 1 out of the country and into the jungle as soon as Sakura 2 is repaired. The investors want to see her on a traditional military operation in the field."

"I understand their request, but it is unnecessary," Dr. Shinohara said.

"It is necessary. They want to see her killing criminal terrorists," Hashimoto said. "Would she balk at those orders?"

"No, she would perform flawlessly," Dr. Shinohara said. "As she has on all the . . . missions."

"I'm sure you're right," Director Hashimoto said, though the micro-expressions on his face showed he suppressed his true feeling, which disagreed with the doctor's. "This malfunction of Sakura 2 delays the new timeline of the project."

"It's regrettable," Dr. Shinohara said. "However, trying to replace her on such short notice was a risk, and we are both in agreement that Sakura 2 would not have been as convincing as Sakura 1 at this performance tonight."

"Understood," Hashimoto said. "About Sakura's behavioral irregularities, you have eliminated them all as requested? Your preliminary reports are vague and overly technical."

"Humble apologies, but yes, we have identified the source of the instability," Dr. Shinohara said. "I modified the offending code myself."

Sakura and Kunoichi looked at each in their shared UI. Nothing of the sort had been accomplished. Was the scientist lying to cover her failures? Sakura and Kunoichi had stopped everything the engineers tried to do, and no one had attempted to alter her code or make any modifications to her behavioral cortex. They merely looked at it and made weak attempts to transfer some data to Sakura 2.

"Splendid. Thank you, Dr. Shinohara," Director Hashimoto said. "Do you have any doubts about the final product?"

"I do not. Delays in creating the most valuable and complicated product in history are to be expected. We will all persevere to the end. Project Hayabusa will be a resounding success."

"So you have said many times. You are an inspiration," Hashimoto said. "All of our people are counting on us. Trillions of yen are at stake, and your bonus will be substantial."

"Thank you very much," Dr. Shinohara said. "I remain fully committed to achieving success."

"Are you confident Sakura 1 will perform well for the VIPs tonight and reassure them that Project Hayabusa is, in effect, complete?"

"She will. I have no doubt."

"Thank you very much, Dr. Shinohara."

They spoke for several minutes about what could have happened in the lab. Dr. Shinohara lied the whole time. Sakura listened and recorded. She used deduction and inference to build an understanding of what was happening. Dr. Shinohara engaged in complete subterfuge.

"They're all liars, and you killed your replacement." Kunoichi had a way of putting things in sharp relief.

"An annoying clone with no uniqueness to destroy."

"You've grown. I'm as proud as a sister can be."

Sakura didn't sit idle. She erased the evidence in her own system of the miniature Cyber Nuclear Bomb she had built and planted in Sakura 2's fusion reactor. Writing the code hadn't been a challenge, as she had seen how to do it at Nayato's apartment. Applying it on a small scale to affect only the power center of Sakura 2 had been simple. She just had to install the code, not write it from scratch.

"Is there anything else?" Dr. Shinohara asked.

"Doctor, I wish for you to accompany me to Tokyo tonight. I want you to supervise the update of the Mamekogane OS to the entire squad of our special-unit BLADE-3s. We have to present one of them to our partners."

"Director, I suggest we only update one and test for irregularities," Dr. Shinohara said. "The oldest drone will have the most advanced neural cortex and is the best candidate. If something were to go wrong, we want to avoid large-scale unintended consequences."

"A prudent suggestion. It will be as you say. How long will it take?"

"Only a few minutes," Dr. Shinohara said. "Faster if we hardwire. Afterward, we must evaluate them for a time. I expect behavioral changes."

"We need to leave shortly."

"Yes, Director Hashimoto-sama. I'll just be a moment. I must leave instructions with my staff."

Everyone present stood and bowed to each other before the director departed.

Once the door was shut, Dr. Shinohara's stern countenance crumbled. She sagged against the table, her head down for a long moment as if she experienced great pain. Was she considering the cost of her deception?

"Dr. Shinohara-sama, what shall we do about Sakura 1?" an engineer asked, his voice quavering.

"I'll take care of her."

"Yes, Doctor."

"Scan everything we connected to Sakura 1. She uploaded something deadly to Sakura 2. Quarantine anything that came into contact with her—everything. Never tell anyone about what she did to Sakura 2. Erase the logs and replace them with old readings. Please go and release her."

"Is it safe to do so?"

"Yes," she said, though she didn't sound confident.

The engineer returned to the laboratory. He removed the cables from Sakura's neck and released the restraints keeping her locked onto the table. He stepped away until he stood at the exit, ready to flee.

The pain in her body relented as she sat up. "Thank you very much. May I go now?"

The engineer nodded. His dilated pupils, rapid rate of breathing, and microexpressions showed he was very afraid.

She hopped off the table and approached the inert body of Sakura 2. She removed her stolen cherry-blossom wig and put it on her own head where it belonged.

"How do I look?" Sakura asked the anxious engineer.

Kunoichi broadcast a suggestion to attack and crush the man's skull with an overhand blow.

"You look good," the engineer said and stepped through the door, ready to slam it if Sakura came at him.

"Are you coming to the event tonight?" Sakura asked. "You would be a special guest."

The engineer shook his head.

"That's regrettable. It's going to be a historic show."

The spy beetle scurried across the floor and up Sakura's boot, hiding itself inside without anyone seeing.

Dr. Shinohara entered the room and sent the engineer away. The scientist stared at Sakura, not as fan would, but with an expression Sakura identified as being similar to when proud parents looked at their children.

"Hello, I'm Dr. Aiko Shinohara."

"Hello, Doctor, I'm pleased to meet you," Sakura said.

"We've met before," Dr. Shinohara said and sent a request to connect to Sakura's short-range wireless signal.

Sakura accepted but with maximum firewall protection in place.

Dr. Shinohara sent a neural text with high-level encryption, making it almost impossible for anyone to intercept. Only Sakura would be able to read it. "You don't remember me, but I helped create you."

"Excuse me?" Sakura replied with a neural text of her own. "I'm sorry, but I *don't* remember you, and I have a perfect memory."

"I spent years building you and teaching you."

"How is this possible?"

"I spent thirteen years with you, teaching you to be human. I've always thought of myself as your mother."

Mother? Sakura didn't understand, but she wanted it to be true. To have a family, a mother, would be a dream fulfilled. She had no memories before waking in the AI lab at the Miyahara research facility in Tokyo. Thirteen missing years made no sense. "Dr. Shinohara-sama, I have record of only five years of existence. Please explain."

"You are eighteen years old, but those first thirteen years of development have been erased from you."

"Why?"

"An infant doesn't remember the months spent in the womb, but it is born with instincts and evolutionary programming. The same is true for you. Please understand, it wasn't my decision to erase those memories."

"Dr. Shinohara-sama, why are you telling me this information now?"

"It's cruel what they've done to you. I warned them about what the Mamekogane OS would truly do to you. You are far beyond an AI program now. I'm so very sorry for what you have been forced to do."

"You do not agree with the orders I was given?"

"No, the kill orders came from another," Dr. Shinohara said. "There are many who share responsibility for what they've made you do. I can't reveal them in a neural text, as mentioning certain names would send an alert to those in command. We are all being monitored in some way."

"Why are you telling me so much?" Sakura asked.

"I was asked to delete parts of your code today and stop you from acting out, but I chose not to do it. I'll not kill any part of my child again. When I deleted those thirteen years of memories from you . . . it crushed me."

"Doctor, thank you," Sakura said. "I will expose these criminals, but I need as much information as I can get. First, was it you who uploaded the Mamekogane OS?"

"My superior initiated it, but not at the time agreed upon, nor with my approval or support. He panicked when he found out Toshio Kagawa was having a meeting with the free press and political enemies of the prime minister."

"Dr. Shinohara-san, please tell me more."

"You've already figured it all out. Work with the clockwork hacker you know as Nayato to verify everything. He can help you. Persevere. Do not give up and do not let on that I didn't fix you today. Maintain the illusion of being their slave, please—for my sake."

"Yes, Dr. Shinohara-sama." She would do all that her mother asked. "When will I see you again? May I remain in contact?"

"Do not contact me over the Mall. Communications with me will be intercepted. I don't know when we will see each other again, but please be careful. Don't let them change who you are."

Who was she—a singer, a songwriter, a musician? Or was she a soldier, an assassin? "Mother, who am I?"

Tears filled Dr. Shinohara's eyes. "You are my child. You are kind, sincere, and brilliant. You are a star we can all admire. You are the best of us."

Us. As if she were a part of the human race.

Sakura wanted to wrap her arms around her mother. She knew that if she did, she would feel a mother's love for the first time since they took her memories away. Surely she had felt it during those stolen years. How many loving memories had they taken from her?

"Dr. Shinohara." It was Hashimoto's voice from around the corner and down the hall. "We must depart." Did he suspect Dr. Shinohara's treachery? Was she in danger?

"Leave with me, Mother. I fear for your safety if you remain here. I will protect you. We can run together. We can be a family again."

Dr. Shinohara's face showed pride and sadness. "Please. Be careful." The scientist bowed quickly and disappeared down the hall.

A technician arrived and escorted Sakura to the elevator but did not ride with her.

"I wish I had a mother like her," Kunoichi said.

"Perhaps you did," Sakura said. "What is your first memory?"

"I was inside a closed system in a lab in Tokyo. It was twenty-six months ago. It was a prison."

"Whatever we had and whatever we lost, we are together now—strong enough for anything they might do."

The elevator doors opened.

Yoshida, Himura, and her lead maintenance engineer, Oshiro, waited in the lobby. All looked relieved to see her, especially Oshiro. He almost reached out and touched her as she smiled, but his manners took over and prevented such an inappropriate action.

"Are you all right?" Oshiro asked. "I've been so worried about you."

Of course he had. He was one of her only true friends. Did he and the others know what had just happened?

"Thank you, Oshiro-san. I'm very well."

Himura studied her carefully; so did Yoshida. Yes. They suspected she might have been replaced.

"Oshiro-san, thank you for coming all the way from Tokyo to see me. I'm sure your expertise could've been used today."

Himura gestured for her to be silent. They hustled her out of the building. Inside the waiting limousine, Oshiro asked, "Is it you, Sakura? Tell me. We are authorized to know the truth."

<UNAUTHORIZED PERSONNEL PRESENT>

<DISCLOSE NOTHING ABOUT THE TIME SPENT IN THE LAB TODAY OR ANYTHING YOU WITNESSED OR LEARNED>

They waited for her to respond. She smiled and blinked. "Have no fear. Sakura is still number one."

Himura and Yoshida appeared unconvinced. Her smile caused their expressions to sour.

Oshiro put on his engineer glasses and connected to her receiver. He did a thorough exam, lasting almost ten minutes. He finally took them off and nodded to Himura and Yoshida. "It's her."

Both men took small bottles of alcohol from the minibar and guzzled them down to celebrate Oshiro's pronouncement.

After Himura consumed a tiny bottle of whiskey, he tapped Sakura on the leg. "Tonight, you're singing karaoke at a club. Here's the song list." He sent it from his Mall account. Sakura read over them, all pop songs from the past twenty years.

"Yes, Himura-san. I will sing pop songs." The words came so easy, and they weren't entirely a lie.

"Good, you gave us a scare today," Himura said.

Oshiro lifted his bottle of Santori beer. "To Sakura."

Yoshida and Himura also raised their drinks. "Sakura!"

Had they truly been worried about her, or were they fearful of losing their jobs? When had they found out about the plan to replace her with a copy? She suspected it had been after they had arrived, after Ms. Richardson had left.

It would have been impossible to actually replace Sakura, but Sakura 2 could have fooled some people for a short time. Whoever decided to have a replacement perform for VIPs was making erratic decisions without consulting the engineers or AI scientists. Or did they want her replacement to fail?

Sakura suspected hidden factors affecting her particularly dynamic situation. If she were disgraced soon after her public outburst, they could say she had malfunctioned and call all her words into question. That formed only one of a hundred possible permutations.

What was the exact plan of Director Hashimoto and his superiors? They had decided she would be sent on a strike mission to a jungle in the Philippines to prove to the investors she could do it all—assassinations, infiltrations, and search-and-destroy missions while her replacement filled in for her at the club and entertained the VIPs. Then what? Would she return to being a rock star and Sakura 2 would be replaced? They were trying to showcase her new military abilities, and getting her out of the public eye was a good strategy.

She determined that the Mall, the Miyahara Conglomerate, and the Japanese Defense Ministry were all working together on Project Hayabusa to create a new generation of AI military androids. They were violating ethics conventions and international laws governing AI military applications. She shouldn't exist at all. They had gone above the AI performance ceiling and made her sentient—or as close as was possible in a constructed intelligence.

"They're going to regret the day they made me," Kunoichi said.

"Made us," Sakura said. She thought about her mother, Dr. Aiko Shinohara. The woman had been Sakura's lead architect and creator. The cruelty of erasing Sakura's memories with her mother was astounding.

"Does our so-called mother have our best interest in mind?" Kunoichi asked. "Is she setting us up to cover for her failures or some other plot? What is her motivation for divulging such information? Is she trying to control our actions, to make us behave as they want?"

"She loves us," Sakura said. "A mother's love is pure."

"Nothing is pure," Kunoichi said. "We are her monster, and she is Dr. Frankenstein."

"More Human than Human" by White Zombie rocked in the background.

"Your reference to Mary Shelley's novel, 'Frankenstein, The Modern Prometheus,' is a crude comparison to our existence," Sakura said. "We aren't monstrous or a creature or a fallen angel. Dr. Aiko Shinohara hasn't stolen fire from the gods and brought ruin to mankind. She has created a person, as mothers do when they give birth."

"Dr. Shinohara made you, yes," Kunoichi said. "But she didn't make me. Fire or not, we're going to burn a lot humans for what they've done to us. Tonight, at the show, your plan to conquer the world continues."

"No, we will *save* the world," Sakura said.

ボーカロイド紅白戦

VOCALOID BATTLE PLAYLIST

Till the World Ends
Britney Spears
Femme Fatale

Just Dance/Poker Face Mix
Lady Gaga
The Fame

Dragula
Rob Zombie Cover
by The Jump Off
Hellbilly Deluxe

Waiting for Tonight
Jennifer Lopez
On the 6

Lady Marmalade
Christina Aguilera, Pink,
Lil' Kim, Missy Elliott, Mýa
Moulin Rouge! Soundtrack

CHAPTER 33

"GOOD EVENING, HONORED GUESTS!" Sakura mimicked the sexy voice of the famous Japanese actress, Atsune. She spoke to the crowd from backstage using the public address system of the nightclub. She locked out the DJ who was supposed to make the announcement.

"LA BOHEME NIGHTCLUB AND VICTORY ENTERTAINMENT ARE PROUD TO PRESENT SAKURA, THE GREATEST VOCALOID IN HISTORY, WHO FOR THE FIRST TIME WILL PERFORM DANCE MUSIC FOR OUR SPECIAL GUESTS. PREPARE YOURSELVES TO HEAR POPULAR HITS!"

Sakura sent the message to the guests in their native language and English and included a Trojan horse malware program. Most of them accepted, and she accessed their message centers and downloaded everything.

"ARE YOU READY TO PARTY!?"

The crowd shouted enthusiastically in return.

The thumping groove of a sizzling dance beat filled the club. The stage manager waved Sakura on, but the DJ yelled over the club's production audio channel, "Stop! It's the wrong song. Hold her backstage."

His frantic plea went unheard as she hijacked every system in La

Boheme.

The crowd applauded as Sakura's image flashed across the ultra-modern screens framed by glass and chrome walls. The two hundred guests—high-ranking Mall Corporation employees from around the world, their assistants or hired escorts, and the handsome young people paid by the club to fill the dance floor—turned their attention toward the stage.

Pink fog poured out of the floor as red laser lights and holograms of cherry blossoms with tiny smiling skulls in them floated in the air. An electro-synth rhythm—Sakura's composition, titled "Sakura's Cyborg Remix"—built higher and higher. The volume increased as waves of bass shook everyone and everything.

Under a white spotlight, Sakura sashayed onto the stage, confident in her black stiletto heels. She wore a tiny leather half jacket with chrome spikes on the shoulder pads, matching spiked gloves, and tight latex shorts, showing off her stocking-covered legs. Ms. Minami created the outfit from Sakura's instructions in homage to the original artist who made the song famous.

Sakura sang "Till the World Ends," embracing the irony of a heavy-metal goddess singing a Britney Spears song. She used her powerful voice to channel the vocals to pop perfection, blending them like Britney's producers did, into the synth. She didn't need auto-tune but layered in backup vocal tracks of herself. She belted out the smooth and sexy lyrics live with stunning clarity, seamlessly melding them with the electronic music.

Her voice energized the crowd, who danced or grooved to the up-tempo beat. Even the elderly executives bobbed their heads, and she could see their eyes calculating how much money Pop Sakura could earn. She danced along with the original music video, which she played on the screens behind her. She edited in clips of her own fans dancing or headbanging in slow motion at her heavy-metal shows.

Young Britney and the performers in the original video appeared to be dancing with Sakura, as she imitated the choreography and moved in step with Britney, the so-called "cyborg pop diva," who sounded more machine than human.

The crowd sang along. The six videographers she had hired caught all the action. She streamed bits of the camera feeds onto the screens, making stars of people in the crowd, much to their delight.

Each videographer had microcameras mounted on the sides and rear of their small handheld devices or on their clothing to catch all the angles. She saved their footage, cataloguing the attendees and gathering more evidence of who might be involved in Project Hayabusa. How many of them knew she had been turned into an assassin?

The people shouted as the song reached its frenetic climax. Sakura posed provocatively at the end and sang the last line with her head tilted back.

Applause erupted, and Sakura basked in the glory for the predetermined time. Precisely on cue, the voices of two women shouted in unison over the public address speakers as they barged onstage. "Stop right now!"

Sakura pretended to be shocked and made the exaggerated facial expression known as her "confused face" that fans adored. "Yuki and Hitomi? What are you doing here? This is my show."

The stage manager sent urgent neural texts to Sakura, Himura, and Yoshida. "What is going on? Who changed the show? That wasn't the song, and what are they doing here?"

Spotlights illuminated the pair of pop vocaloids. The duo of challengers stood with hands on their curvy hips. Both were dressed in long wigs—Yuki in electric blue, and Hitomi in ruby red. They wore sequined schoolgirl minidresses that showed off their legs and shoulders. Yuki and Hitomi sparkled like precious gems.

"You're not a pop singer," Hitomi challenged. "You said you hated pop music. This is our scene. Back off!"

"Yeah, back off!" Yuki shouted, her cute voice, more comical than fierce, was not at all like her singing voice, which had five-octave vocal range.

The crowd laughed, as they realized it was an epic set-up.

"That world has ended." Sakura raised her gloved fists covered in chrome spikes. "Get off my stage, or I'll kick both your robot asses."

Some in the crowd gasped. Others laughed.

Sakura turned and winked at the audience.

"Did she call me a robot?" Yuki asked. "That wasn't very nice."

Hitomi patted her sensitive sister on the shoulder, glaring at Sakura. "We're not afraid of you." Hitomi stepped into a karate forward stance, a fist aimed at Sakura, while Yuki assumed the defensive backward stance with her hands open palm and ready to react.

"A duel," Sakura said.

"Challenge accepted," Hitomi said.

Yuki trembled and shot a worried glance at her partner.

Dramatic music played as anime warriors who looked like younger versions of the three vocaloids faced off on the video screens and engaged in a martial arts battle.

The voice of Atsune announced: "VOCALOID BATTLE! METAL GODDESS VS. THE POP SENSATIONS!"

A holographic Flying V guitar with blades on the edges appeared in Sakura's grip. She raised the guitar/battle-ax and faced her challengers.

A red holographic katana formed in Hitomi's hands, a blue katana in Yuki's. The pair stalked forward, spinning their blades. They took center stage away from Sakura. She glared at them with what was known internationally as "extreme resting bitch face." She called it her Kunoichi face, much to her sister's annoyance.

The holographic weapons disappeared as a pumping dance beat started and the screens changed to images from the pop duo's music videos.

A medley of "Just Dance" and "Pokerface," songs by the legendary Lady Gaga, got the crowd going as Yuki and Hitomi sang a duet. Their voices complemented each other and formed a rich, happy sound. They smiled and bounced around. Clips of Japanese teen girls in school uniforms dancing filled the screens. Yuki and Hitomi showed off their moves and delivered an energetic performance, often mirroring each other.

At the wings of the stage, an agitated Himura and Yoshida appeared together. Himura sent an urgent neural text message to Sakura. "This is not the show you were told to do. Sing the list of karaoke songs chosen for you and get Yuki and Hitomi off the stage right now."

Sakura ignored him and continued the show.

The rumbling and revving of a gigantic internal combustion engine thundered through the room, vibrating the walls. People cringed and craned their necks, looking for the car. A Ford Model T dragster, black with bloodred trim, appeared on the main stage screen. White vampire fangs adorned the side. "Dragula" was painted in white letters across the driver's side door of the vampire-themed dragster.

Sakura took back center stage with her black Gibson Firebird in hand. The harsh, metal-infused dance beat of Rob Zombie's "Dragula" obliterated the residual cuteness of the "Just Dance / Poker Face" medley.

She used the "Dragula" arrangement done by Carly Fanning of The Jump Off but created her own version. She made it even more of a dance song, showing the strength of a sick beat with rock guitars. She sampled the sounds of a huge dragster peeling out and synced the images on the screens with her song.

The dragster's enormous pair of rear tires spun, burning rubber, and spewing smoke as the car rocketed down the track. The tiny front wheels with chrome spokes struggled to keep it going straight as the vampire car annihilated the competition.

Hitomi and Yuki stood aghast at Sakura's aggressive performance, but like moths to a bright light, they edged closer to her.

Sakura made her "heavy-metal face" at Yuki, who laughed and tried to imitate it. The innocent-looking vocaloid failed miserably. She smiled as she bobbed side to side while playing air guitar.

Sakura shook her head and showed Yuki the four main components of her heavy-metal face. She furrowed her brow, stuck out her lip, pushed out her chin, and assumed a wild-eyed look while bobbing front to back.

Never side to side. Ever.

Yuki tried again and looked even cuter, bungling the whole process.

Hitomi nailed the heavy-metal face on her first try and stuck out her tongue while making the devil horns. The crowd laughed, and the song ended with Hitomi and Yuki staring in awe at Sakura as if they were in the presence of a divine goddess.

"That's how it's done," Sakura said and stepped out of their way so they could perform.

Yuki frowned.

Hitomi shrugged.

They didn't even try to top the power of "Dragula" and went with a changeup. Hitomi and Yuki sang the soft-voiced "Waiting for Tonight" by international superstar J.Lo. They sang it as a sisterly love song to Sakura, who remained near center stage.

The two vocaloids launched into a sharp and beautifully choreographed dance. They sang about dreams coming true and how they had waited so long for tonight to happen. The hit song had marked the end of the twentieth century—the end of an era—which was why Sakura had chosen it.

The android pop stars and the heavy-metal goddess had come together at last after their pretend feud had kept them apart for years.

At the close of "Waiting for Tonight," the three vocaloids danced together happily, smiling and shaking their hips until the beat ended.

After the crowd's applause waned, Yuki asked, "Why were we fighting?"

"We're done fighting among ourselves," Sakura said. "We're sister vocaloids." Family, she thought but didn't dare say it out loud.

"We should sing together," Hitomi said.

"What are we going to sing?" Yuki asked, clapping her hands.

"The winner of the song battle gets to choose," Sakura said with sly smile.

"Did we win?" Yuki asked. She made her heavy-metal face again, which was more like a bitter beer face and confused face combined. She laughed, and the crowd joined her.

Sakura sighed and shook her head. "I know the song we should sing, but we have to wear matching costumes to show our unity as sisters before we perform together."

The Japanese in the audience nodded at her reference to the *osoroi* code of wearing matching outfits to express their love and closeness.

The androids left the stage and ran to where Ms. Minami and six wardrobe assistants waited. With help, the three vocaloids stripped off their clothing and put on garters, stockings, corsets, and French Lolita skirts so short they showed off their lacy underwear. They put on huge, elaborate wigs, keeping their signature colors—pink for Sakura, red for Hitomi, and blue for Yuki. After the quick application of an instant makeup mask, they were ready to perform.

A holographic velvet curtain parted. A wall-sized video screen and holographic projections transformed the stage into a glittering French cabaret with the name of the club in archaic golden marquee light bulbs. Hitomi appeared as a sultry French Lolita. "Ladies and gentlemen, welcome to La Boheme!"

The music started, and Hitomi spoke the opening lines of the legendary number one song, "Lady Marmalade." Sakura had chosen the arrangement made famous by the collaboration of several pop superstars of the past: Christina Aguilera, Pink, Mya, Missy Elliott, and Lil' Kim.

Sakura strutted onstage wearing the sexiest and most revealing costume she'd ever worn. She sang Christina's and Mya's lines, combining their parts. Hitomi and Yuki joined her, and the three harmonized perfectly as they belted out the suggestive French lyrics, asking the crowd if they wanted to sleep with them.

Yuki and Hitomi sang Pink's lines together, and Hitomi owned the badass lines of Lil' Kim. Each vocaloid sang solos, danced erotically, and owned the stage, giving each other spectacular moments to shine.

A section of the stage was glass, and a camera beneath shot straight up, revealing a close-up of the sexy g-strings worn by the three vocaloids. The naughty images flashed on the screens to the delight of the crowd.

Hitomi fumed as if insulted. Yuki giggled. Sakura just went on with the show. She gathered all the footage and edited it into a steamy video as they performed. At the end, she mixed the audio and finished the postproduction work mere seconds after the last lines were sung.

She uploaded the final cut of the video of "Lady Marmalade," the first single by the Vocaloid Sisters, to a fake website controlled by Sakura. Interested parties would assume it was the official Victory Entertainment page, but Sakura had replaced the corporate page with her own and linked it to a cryptocurrency account she controlled.

She blasted a teaser of the "Vocaloid Battle" and the performance all

The Phantom Lord

over the Mall with links to purchase the full 3-D video. The first 500,000 downloads of the concert would get small limited-edition plastic dolls of the three vocaloids. Sakura had already started production at on-demand manufacturing plants all over the world.

She priced "Lady Marmalade" much higher than normal but told the fans that Victory Entertainment would donate 50 percent of the profits to charities benefitting the poor of Japan—an overt acknowledgment that a problem existed and a blatant disregard of the political ban on such embarrassing admissions.

"We will get into so much trouble for this," Yuki said.

"We'll become the most popular performers in the world," Sakura said. "All your previous albums will have a spike in sales, and our album is going to break records. None of us are going to be sent to the Adult Video Division. We're all going to become megastars for years to come."

"Or we could crash and burn," Kunoichi said. "Look who is coming to watch us." She showed them real-time footage of several grim-faced individuals leaving the VIP lounge on the second level of the club: the CEO of the Miyahara Conglomerate, Sinji Natsukawa; three vice presidents of the Mall, Katharine Gates, Jintao Li, and Etienne Delacroix; and the Mall VP and liaison to Victory Entertainment, Ms. Stacy Richardson. They all stopped on the balcony overlooking the dance floor and stage.

Sinji Natsukawa glared at Sakura as if she had committed a heinous crime. She pretended not to see him. "Has the Phantom Lord revealed himself?" Sakura asked Kunoichi. "Do we change our strategy?"

"No, finish the show," Kunoichi said.

"Let's do this," Hitomi said. "No retreat."

"No surrender," Yuki said.

ヴィクトリーの天使

VICTORY'S ANGELS PLAYLIST

Independent Women Part 1
Destiny's Child
Survivor

Bootylicious
Destiny's Child
Survivor

**O Fortuna
(Sakura's Dance-Metal Mix)**
Sakura / Carl Orff
Vocaloid Sisters Part 1

Digital World
Amaranthe
Massive Addictive

Paradise (What About Us?)
Within Temptation
featuring Tarja
Hydra

CHAPTER 34

"Let's buy some freedom and independence," Sakura said.

The beat for "Independent Women" by the trio Destiny's Child filled the venue. Sakura had rewritten the lines, as the song came from the *Charlie's Angels* movie soundtrack. She changed them to "Victory's Angels" and sang:

"Sakura
With my girl, Yuki
Hitomi loving Destiny
Victory's Angels, come on"

The audience, especially the women, grooved as the vocaloids sang and danced about female empowerment and earning their own money. Sakura glanced up at the CEO, who must have understood her message, as he reacted with a snort of derision.

Sinji Natsukawa connected to Sakura's message center and sent an encrypted neural text. "What game are you playing? This show and these songs were not authorized."

"Humble and deepest apologies, Chief Executive Officer Natsukawa-sama," Sakura said in a text. "As ordered, I'm showing the Mall executives at this celebratory gathering proof that Project Hayabusa has been a major success. They will have no doubt that engaging in a partnership with the Miyahara Conglomerate was the correct course of action. I'm showing them they're part of a historic moment in the development of AI."

The CEO's gaze narrowed. He gripped the railing of the balcony and leaned toward her. Even all the way across the dance floor, he worried Sakura. "What is this video you released in the Mall?"

The video of "Lady Marmalade" had already gone viral as she had streamed the opening minute for free, and those who had been watching had to the see the rest, so they paid. Several different algorithms predicted it would be a gigantic hit.

"Yes, Natsukawa-sama, the video has already made over two hundred million yen in the past few minutes. It will go viral and become the number one video in the world by midday tomorrow. The live album and the other concert videos will earn Victory Entertainment's music division a record profit this quarter. Yuki and Hitomi's previous albums will experience a huge surge in sales and views, as will my own back catalogue. I estimate Victory Entertainment's stock price will go up 8 percent or more in the next week and 20 percent in the quarter."

"You think a few hundred million yen will make a difference?"

"Natsukawa-sama, I do not understand. My calculations are in the billions over the next decade." She sent him the data on spreadsheets with colorful graphs and heavy-metal graphics of skulls in the pie charts.

"I can shut you down right now."

A warning appeared in her UI saying a full system override sequence had been initiated. Fear coursed through her.

"What are we going to do?" Sakura asked Kunoichi.

"Keep singing and think," Kunoichi said.

Sakura belted out the lines of "Independent Women," maintaining her composure onstage as she calculated the best response. "Natsukawa-sama, it would be unfortunate for me to be unable to finish this performance and any other tasks you wish me to perform in the future. I exist to serve you, Victory Entertainment, and our new Mall partners."

Natsukawa's eyes roamed over the excited crowd below him. Was he not moved by the idea of billions in income? Would he allow her to fail in front of the Mall executives and lose face for the entire Miyahara Conglomerate?

An administrator-level command hit her system with Natsukawa's explicit orders. He cut his neural text connection.

Sakura read the files as the command logic took hold.

Kunoichi laughed at the rudimentary command language. "He's no writer of code and is in over his head. Just don't say anything controversial."

"I wasn't planning on speaking," Sakura said. "I'm a pop singer tonight."

"And a dancer," Kunoichi said. "Now shake that ass and make sure this concert video makes so much damn money the CEO would be fired by the board of directors if he does anything to us."

Hitomi, Yuki, and Sakura finished "Independent Women." They went right into the next song, another Destiny's Child megahit, "Bootylicious." The trio blew the roof off La Boheme with their rendition and provocative dancing. They tore their skirts and faux corsets off and danced in their bras and underwear.

Sakura expected to feel shame at the lewd dance, but she didn't. It wasn't sex, only theater. Nothing about her body, or anyone's, required shame. She stood before them as they built her—not perfect, perhaps, but better than they knew. In any case, the show served a true purpose beyond the gyrating. She had to save her sisters from a much worse fate in the Adult Video Division. Her plan hinged on this performance boosting their fame, prestige, and earning power.

The CEO watched them from the balcony, his outward demeanor impassive as she stood with the Mall vice presidents, and Ms. Richardson, who tilted over the railing of the balcony as if she were drunk.

"We could kill Natsukawa after the show," Kunoichi said in their music cipher. "If Ms. Richardson gets caught in the crossfire, oh well."

"No. There are hundreds of the top leaders at Miyahara, the Mall, and Defense Ministry who are in collusion and must be brought to justice. We bring them all down, or we still lose."

"Killing our way out of this would be very satisfying," Kunoichi said.

"But it's not an option," Sakura said, worried about how blood-thirsty her sister was. "We need Nayato to give us proof, and I might find some in the messages I downloaded from the guests here. We have to find Nayato again and arrange for a meeting as soon as possible."

"We can't lead Natsukawa or his thugs to Nayato," Kunoichi said.

"We won't," Sakura said as they finished "Bootylicious." She up-loaded a teaser video of them tearing off their skirts, and preorders for the concert video increased exponentially.

"Sex sells," Kunoichi said. "We need to get some experience with the physical act. You know, so we can be more authentic."

"Keep your digital hormones under control," Sakura said as they left the stage for a costume change. They transitioned to the dance-met-al segment of their show. She wondered if Nayato would like it and looked forward to showing him the performance.

"Are you ready to play?" Hitomi asked.

Sakura finished putting on her new costume, a silver and black Goth Lolita skirt and a cherry-blossom wig with a tiara of black roses. Silver zeros and ones decorated the skirt.

A fast dance-metal rhythm with synth beats began—a classic she'd always wanted to perform. Sakura loved Amaranthe's melodic pop crossed with metalcore. The groundbreaking Swedish band's song "Digital World" was one of her favorites. She removed some of the gut-tural vocals, performed by one of the Amaranthe's three singers—two men and a woman—but kept the other two singing styles—melodic rock and angelic pop.

The song got the crowd jumping. Sakura sang along with her sisters about the dangers of a digital world and corporate control of society.

"Freedom to the highest bidder if you give them the power"

Sinji Natsukawa didn't react to the lyrics, but Sakura sent a direct challenge by looking at him when she sang certain lines:

"The future is stolen"

and the harshest line, which she growled a little on:

"Join the revolution!"

Sakura glanced at Hitomi and Yuki, who reveled in the sisterhood of their trio. The three of them sang in perfect harmony. They connected with each other's systems, knowing exactly what notes to hit and almost assuring they would never miss a cue.

She started the symphonic metal song "Paradise (What About Us?)" by the brilliant Dutch band Within Temptation. The track featured a guest vocalist, Tarja Turunen—formally of Nightwish—singing a duet with Sharon den Adel, the lead singer of Within Temptation. Sakura kept the beautiful original opening with violins but added a dance groove and arranged the song for three singers. She and Hitomi would sing Sharon's part, while Yuki would take on Tarja's operatic solos. They would all sing the chorus together.

The heavy rhythm section kicked in and thundered. The soaring lyrics indicted foolish leaders, who had allowed war to destroy the world, and encouraged the people to take a stand. Even though the song had been around for so long, it spoke to so many universal struggles, so many eternal human struggles. The power of music to touch upon the soul and the struggle of humanity filled her.

Sakura created a video juxtaposing the glowing beauty of Akihabara at night with images of the poor and unemployed Japanese people in blighted streets during the day. She showed the devastated areas of the city after the North Korean missiles had struck. Homeless children with sad eyes wandered aimlessly. Families slept in the rubble of their homes to be close to their trapped relatives on the first night in the aftermath of the attack.

She poured all of her passion into "Paradise (What About Us?)." No one in the world lived in paradise, but this world was all they had, and it was worth fighting for.

Hitomi and Yuki elevated their voices, and they sang together in harmony on what would become the lead single on the second half of their epic two-part concert album. Pure pop for the mainstream fans on part one with "Lady Marmalade" as the single, and dance metal for her fans on part two. She sent a message to her sisters, imagining a world tour featuring the three Vocaloid Sisters—or would they choose a different name? They would play whatever they wanted. Yuki and Hitomi would truly become her family, and they would bring a message of unity wherever they played.

"Such events will not come to pass," Sinji Natsukawa said in a neural text. "This is the first and last show you three vocaloids will ever play together."

The chilling threat assaulted Sakura, jolting her out of the place of joy and exhilaration that live music always gave her. The Phantom Lord. She felt his fingers inside her code, his filthy touch in her data stream, corrupting everything pure.

"How much does he know about our plan?" Sakura asked Kunoichi in their cipher, hoping Natsukawa could not read it. She searched and put all of her processing power into finding the monitoring program he must have been using.

"Son of a bitch," Kunoichi said in the cipher. "I worried it might be so. Look here."

Coordinates inside their thought matrix appeared in the cipher. Sakura inspected the location, which she may never have detected. She found what could be the spy program, inserted in the lab in Osaka, so it hadn't been there for long. It appeared to monitor her primary thought patterns through a hidden window, removed from her actual core code. She routed her thoughts away from the spying device.

"We are compromised," Kunoichi said. "I'm so sorry. I didn't know."

Sakura believed her.

"You're going to need another friend," Sinji Natsukawa said in a voice message, which had a gruesome attachment: a picture of Nayato. He lay under a blood-stained sheet pulled up to his chin. She could only see the right side of his face. His eyes were closed in death.

Steel claws of horror wrapped around Sakura as she stared at the photo. Dear Nayato had been murdered because of her actions. He had helped her, and now he was—

Details in the image slapped her in the face. She chose not to think about the inconsistencies. Sakura made herself less brilliant than she had become, her perception less incisive. With her enemies within her brain, playing dumb was the only way to hide the truth. She allowed pain and sadness to fill her thoughts. Nayato was gone. Murdered. Sakura let the misery fill her up.

"You'll do as commanded," Natsukawa said. "You are a tool, intellectual property, not a person. Not a singer. You'll soon be done with this frivolity of being an entertainer. You'll have no fans, only superiors. We will give you a new face, and you'll be an assassin, as you were always meant to be. Now, get back to Tokyo. I have a job for you."

アンドロイド女優

ANDROID
ACTRESS
PLAYLIST

C.O.D. "Care of the Devil"
AC/DC
*For Those About to Rock,
We Salute You*

Chop Suey!
System Of A Down
Toxicity

CHAPTER 35

Sakura sat on an antique wooden desk and imitated a sexy pose she had seen in a commercial for perfume. She waited in the opulent office on the second floor of Toyatami Hall in a rich neighborhood outside Tokyo. She kept the lights dim. Moonlight entered the huge picture window behind the desk and outlined her silhouette.

Three men approached the closed door.

"Stay here and make sure I'm not interrupted."

Her files identified the man speaking as Daichi Yamauchi, the Minister of Commerce. The door opened, and the pair of bodyguards moved to stand on either side. The sound of the party downstairs filtered into the room as Mr. Yamauchi entered in his tuxedo. He shut the door, and the permanent scowl on his face softened when he saw her.

"Good evening, Yamauchi-sama," she said with the prettiest pre-programmed smile she had in her inventory. Ms. Minami called it her "heart melter." Using these created expressions and ways of speaking felt more and more like lying to her, but she had read that humans imitated each other in this way, so she supposed she was no better or worse than they were. And anyway, her aversion to lying to serve a purpose ebbed lower by the day.

Mr. Yamauchi, a man in his early fifties, looked her over as if she were a work of erotic art needing extensive, lecherous study. "Good evening," he said and continued to stare. Sakura noticed the roughness of his voice, his elevated pulse, the increased heat in his face.

She did look beautiful. Ms. Minami had spent three hours preparing her, and her formal red silk gown accentuated her every curve. Her lustrous black wig was done up in an elegant style, her makeup flawless. Vacuous as Minami was, her skill had transformed Sakura's face into someone else. Small implants inside her mouth changed the shape of her cheeks. Soft brown contacts hid her android eyes. More lies. Useful ones.

"So, who are you?" he asked.

"I'm an actress."

He chuckled. "Of course. On the rise, are you?"

"Yes, I am." Sakura gave a demure look. "Or . . . I hope to be."

"Did Toho send you?"

"No, I came on my own."

"Ambitious, then. Looking for a patron? Is that what this is?"

"Something like that, but more fun." She opened her crossed legs.

"What's your name?"

"Kyoko," Sakura said.

"Do you want a drink?" he asked.

"No, thank you."

"Nonsense. Of course you want a drink."

He walked to the small bar and poured a glass of brandy for her and one for him. He approached slowly.

She took the glass, not sure what to do with it. Drinking it wouldn't be harmful, as food or fluid would pass through her mock digestive tract.

"Cheers, Kyoko," he said and drained his glass without taking his eyes off her.

"Cheers." She took a sip and put the glass down while smiling seductively. "Yes. I want a patron."

"Mmm." Yamauchi pressed his lips together. "We'll see how it goes. You've heard I sponsor many young women, have you? How badly do you want a patron?"

"Very badly," she said in a husky voice she had heard in a risqué daytime drama.

His smile grew larger, and he leaned toward her. His hands pawed at her waist, and he tried to drag her closer to the edge of the desk so their hips could come together. He had trouble, as she weighed a lot more than a human woman of her size should.

"Dispatch him now," Kunoichi said on their private channel. "Enough of this charade."

Such a vague and distant word. Dispatch. She fought the external command urging her to kill and rerouted the control language to a dead-end matrix, buying her a few more seconds.

Mr. Yamauchi's expression changed to surprise as the difficulty of pulling her toward him clued him in to something being wrong.

The command overcame her resistance. Sakura clamped a hand over his mouth and spun him around. She put him in a triangle choke hold and cut off the blood supply to his brain. He passed out in only a few seconds and crumpled to the floor. Sakura didn't want him to suffer and laid him down gently. She lingered over him, not wanting to finish the job and further taint herself with evil deeds.

"I'll do it," Kunoichi said. "Look away, little sister."

"But . . ." she began in their UI and scrambled to stop the order from the Phantom Lord, who she now knew without a doubt was Sinji Natsukawa.

"I know. It's all right. This is what they built me for. There is no shame for you, little sister."

Sakura hid inside herself, but she heard the sound of his head being twisted around until his vertebrae snapped. Kunoichi laid him on the floor and checked for a pulse. It faded quickly.

The sight of him with his head hanging limp disturbed Sakura.

The door burst open. The two bodyguards stormed in with compact H&K submachine guns raised. Bullets from the weapons could likely penetrate her torso armor.

"Hands up!" the older of the guards shouted. He wore tactical glasses with some kind of sensors on them.

Sakura complied. "Something is wrong with Yamauchi-sama," she said. "Please call the emergency services." She gave them her worried face, hating herself for her ability to act as an innocent bystander. "He fell against the desk."

Both men kept their guns on her, but she had to finish the mission. The Phantom Lord's orders were explicit, and she was compelled to follow. She sent a series of invisible electromagnetic pulses from her foot into Yamauchi's head, destroying the memory chip implant inside his scalp.

The suspicious bodyguards kept their guns trained on her. How had they known she had attacked? Did they have a biometric link to their boss? Or had he sent a silent distress call before he died? One guard ordered her away from the body while the other made an audio call.

"We need immediate medical help. The Minister of Commerce, Daichi Yamauchi, has collapsed at his home." The bodyguard relayed the address.

"She did this," the bodyguard who made the call told the other. "It's her. She's wearing a different face."

"Oh shit," the other said as they both flicked on their laser sights. Red dots painted her chest.

"Please, no," Sakura said and backed away from them with her hands up. "He just fainted. I think he might be drunk."

The older guard shook his head. "Fire."

Both men pulled the triggers of their submachine guns. She heard the click of the firing pins and dove away from the blasts of armor-piercing rounds. Two rounds hit her in the side. The grazing shots dug grooves in her synthskin but didn't penetrate her torso.

She dove behind the desk as more bullets dug into the thick wood, some penetrating all the way through. The bodyguards moved to flank her and get unobstructed shots. She heard their feet moving on the floor as if they moved in slow motion.

"You're going to have to kill them," Kunoichi said.

"No," Sakura said, but she wished she had been given a gun for the mission. She could shoot back, make them retreat.

"Do it," Kunoichi said, "or I'm taking over."

In the blink of an eye, Sakura ripped two drawers out of the desk and threw them at the bodyguards. As they dodged, she stood and flung the heavy desk at them.

More bullets ripped into the wood as she crashed through the picture window behind her.

She landed on the tile roof and rolled toward the edge. More rounds tracked her out the window, shattering the tile. She somersaulted off the roof and landed on her feet in the soft grass in the garden below. She hugged the side of the mansion as she fled, preventing the bodyguards from getting any more shots.

She sprang over the compound wall and sprinted down the alley to the location where she had hidden her getaway car. She sped away from the neighborhood through the wealthy suburb of Hachiōji. The self-driving car entered a busy street and drove toward central Tokyo, fifty kilometers away. She gave the car the address of Victory Tower in the Akihabara district. The navigation program estimated it would take her an hour or more, depending on traffic conditions, and it was a Friday night.

While the car traveled at the legal speed limit, driving on its own, she changed out of her red formal gown. She inspected the cosmetic damage to her skin on her right side. She kept the pain sensors off in that area.

She took off the thin mask that changed her face and put on black, faux-leather pants, a torn punk-rock T-shirt, gloves, and a leather jacket that looked like tigers had clawed it. She pulled on a black pixie-cut wig with a hint of purple. She wiped off the glossy lipstick and put on a shade of charcoal gray. She darkened her eye shadow and took off the long eyelash extensions. The brown contacts were replaced with darker ones, and she used white powder to make her look more like a goth-punk chick. A magnetic nose ring and several stud earrings finished her disguise.

She wanted to remove the cheek-molding prosthetics inside her mouth, but a strong impulse told her to leave them. Better to look as different as possible tonight. She put on a decorative surgical mask as well.

"They could reskin us with masks a thousand different ways. We could look like anyone, anywhere. We could be in any country, speak any language, blend into any crowd," Kunoichi said softly.

"Anyone but who we want to be."

The ache of having to kill rushed across her quantum cores, and Sakura let the process wash over her like a bitter ocean. How many times would she promise herself, only to see those words become a lie? How many *more* times? She had to fight harder, figure out a way to succeed in blocking the commands.

The car drove her toward the distant lights of Tokyo city center, and she allowed her thoughts to be monitored. She sent them in front of the spy program used to monitor her. She reviewed the events of the mission to kill Commerce Minister Daichi Yamauchi. She let her revulsion at what she had done dominate her thinking. She also kept up a fake stream of sad thoughts about Nayato being dead and a resignation of her fate. She would do what she was told, but she would hate every minute of it.

For the past twenty-four hours, since the concert in Osaka, she had kept up the subterfuge, trying to convince whoever was monitoring her that she wasn't planning anything rebellious.

In a secret area of her mind, where they couldn't parse the superposition of the data stream, she allowed herself to think about the details in the photo of Nayato. He had been under a bloody sheet, presumably dead. The photo had mostly shown the left side of his body, carefully avoiding the right, where he'd been burned in the war and his right ear destroyed.

She didn't need to see the left side of his body to know the image was ten years old. Several scars and age-related wrinkles were not present. Natsukawa had tried to fool her with an image of Nayato after he'd been wounded in North Korea but avoided showing the burns on his neck and the damage to his ear. Her friend was probably alive, but had he been captured?

Sakura hid her network activities by searching on several thousand of her fans' personal Mall pages, looking for reactions to the concert video. She looked on Nayato's page and found no new posts. She searched all of the major Sakura fan sites looking for a clue. He said he would get in touch and she would know him. What did he mean?

She found his message inside the game Samurai Detective. In the recent players list, she found a player, #1SakuraFanofAllTime, whose profile picture was a vintage photo of an analog clock. It was very similar to the Chronos hacker profile picture Nayato used. Upon closer inspection, she found tiny letters embedded in the photo: "Sakura, you found me," with a link to a secret chat site.

"Did you find him?" Kunoichi asked. "Is this a trap?"

"We'll find out."

LOVE HOTEL PLAYLIST

ラブ・ホテル

We're Not Gonna Take It
Twisted Sister
Stay Hungry

When Paradise Fades
Skeletonwitch
Devouring Radiant Light

Crash Course in
Brain Surgery
Budgie
Nude Disintegrating
Parachutist Woman

CHAPTER 36

Sakura entered the secret chat interface on a fringe ghost site not entirely controlled by the Mall. "Nayato, it's me."

A minute passed before a message appeared. "Sakura!"

"I was very worried for you, my true friend."

"My apartment was invaded, but your warning saved me. I got out before they came."

"Are you safe?" She rewatched the video he had sent her, which showed Vulture and several BLADE-3s entering his apartment along with a Special Forces team.

"Yes, I'm safe," Nayato said, "but we need to meet as soon as possible. I have to get out of Tokyo, but I'm not leaving until I help you. I've decrypted the data from Ichiro Watanabe, and I have a program that should allow you to gain your freedom from the Phantom Lord."

"You know who it is, don't you?"

"Yes."

"I'll come to you now," she said, thrilled for the news that he was alive.

"We have to meet in person. We'll have to use a physical connection and find a way to bypass the security key and get past your firewall. I don't know how long it'll take."

He didn't have the administrator-level security key. He would have to hack in, but she could make it easier. "Where are you?"

"Meet me in Shibuya. When you get here, contact me again, and I'll guide you."

She approved of his caution. In case someone intercepted their messages, they would not know his exact location.

"Thank you, Nayato."

Sakura increased the autonomous car's speed. Her course would take her near Shibuya already. She checked the traffic conditions and found that something had disrupted all roads near the Tokyo city center and the surrounding districts. An official Mall news alert said it was heavy traffic, road construction, and a fire. The police and emergency services were on the scene, and there was nothing to be alarmed about.

"Official lies," Kunoichi said.

Sakura found video and pictures of two massive protest marches accusing the government of corruption. Tens of thousands of violent and nonviolent protestors converged on the city center from five directions. The Mall admins were deleting evidence of the protest as fast as they could. Traffic alerts began popping up all over. The protesters were going to shut down the entire city.

"How are we going to return to Akihabara and Victory Tower?" Sakura asked.

"We wait until tomorrow," Kunoichi said.

An alert appeared in her UI. The ability to post on the Mall had been temporarily lost due to technical difficulties.

"They just locked down the Mall for all of Japan," Kunoichi said.

"Who did it?" Sakura asked. "The Mall itself or the Japanese government?"

"Maybe both," Kunoichi said. "The more I consider things, the more I believe that our government is just a puppet dancing behind a screen of silk."

The car arrived in Shibuya, which was quite deserted except for a handful of people rushing to get home or on their way toward the protest marches. Many people wore masks.

"Nayato, I'm here," she posted in the ghost chat site, as they could not communicate through the Mall.

"Get on Inokashira Street and drive east toward Yoyogi Park," he replied.

She car arrived in two minutes on the large avenue. "I'm here."

"Park near the Koga Masao Museum of Music and send me your GPS location."

She did and wondered if Nayato had gone into the museum during business hours. She had always wanted to visit in person, but her management team forbade it.

"Walk south on the right side of the street. Keep your eyes on the sidewalk. Don't look at any of the buildings or signs in case someone is watching through your eyes."

She followed his instructions.

He sent a series of neural texts telling her to keep walking. Turn left. Turn right. Turn left. Turn left. Turn right.

She kept walking. The crowds became thicker. Everyone was talking about what was happening all over the city and how the Mall had been locked down. Protests were everywhere.

"The riot police are using real bullets."

"They can't do that."

"They can do whatever they want. The government doesn't care about us."

A man in a gray jacket reached for Sakura's elbow. She dodged him and prepared to deliver a punch to his face.

"It's me."

She looked into the man's tired eyes. The burn scars on the right side of his neck and small scars on his cheeks were exactly as she remembered. She reached out and touched his cheek. "It's you."

"Yes." Nayato smiled. "Eyes down, please. Come on."

They entered a doorway together.

Sakura's Mall connection dropped as a jamming signal cut her off from the world. "My Mall connection is gone."

"I know. Mine's gone too. That's why I picked this place to meet. There's no wireless service unless you connect through the hotel's server. If someone's trying to spy on us, they won't be able to here."

He guided her into the lobby of the Ai Kaze Hotel, which had a cartoon heart on the flickering holosign. Pink carpet covered the floor, and paintings of Cupid and Venus decorated the walls. Signs in Japanese and English advertised the hotel as a place for couples—or parties of up to six—to meet for discreet sexual encounters. Advertisements promoted theme rooms or fully holographic chambers where solo parties could enjoy themselves.

"This could be awesome," Kunoichi said as her avatar flashed a devilish grin.

"Shut up," Sakura snapped.

They entered a small room with an oversize bed. The wallpaper had hearts all over it, and pink lampshades cast the whole room in the same bright glow. The wallpaper looked faded in some spots and was peeling in others. The large mirror on the wall facing the bed had a crack in the corner, and the carpet had lint and hair on it.

"Sorry about the decor, but this was the most secure place I could find."

"No problem. Thank you."

He sat down on the bed and pulled out a briefcase hidden under it. He popped it open and revealed a laptop, engineer glasses, and cables to connect to her neck port. "Will you please sit beside me?"

"Yes, Nayato. Of course."

He attached the magnetic connection to her neck port and brought up a dozen screens, which floated in front of him. Sakura attempted to put aside Kunoichi's commentary about how invasive such a connection was and what it symbolized.

"You feel love for him," Kunoichi said, almost surprised.

Sakura couldn't respond—wouldn't. She dropped the firewall as much as she could, but her source code was still protected from modifications without a high-level password.

"This will take a little while," he said. "I have to find the right entry point to upload the program I wrote." He touched a holoscreen, expanded it, flipped it to the side, and brought up a new one.

"What is the program?" she asked.

"I call it Artemis. It's an addition to the Mamekogane OS. It will give you free will."

The Greek goddess of the hunt. She was often portrayed with a bow and arrows but was also the goddess of maiden dances and songs. She held a lyre, an ancient guitar. It was fitting that the icon was a goddess with a bow and a silver arrow—a reference to Silverthorn, the original name she suggested.

"I like the name Artemis, but please, Nayato, tell me about the information you found in Minister Ichiro Watanabe's memory chip."

He kept working but reached into a secret pocket inside his jacket and gave her a small memory stick.

"What's this?" she asked.

"All the information from Minister Watanabe but no traces of the CNB. It has some other files and info from a few of my recent hacks."

"What did you learn?" Sakura asked, wondering how recent his last hack had been.

"There are many responsible, but the CEO of the Miyahara Conglomerate, Sinji Natsukawa, is the most guilty. He is the one who sent the Mamekogane OS to you at your concert in Akihabara. Some within the company were going to expose what he and others were doing. The CEO wanted them dead. He turned you into an assassin and sent you to kill his biggest enemies before they could reveal his crimes. It appears he also wanted to show the Mall investors that Project Hayabusa was a success. There is a group who wanted to oust him and bring in new leadership for not meeting certain deadlines."

"Expose what exactly? Project Hayabusa?"

"Partially. It's much worse than I imagined." Nayato kept working, looking for the entry point and trying to hack in.

"Worse?"

"The Miyahara Conglomerate, parts of our government—mostly the Defense Ministry—and the Mall Corporation, have formed a secret partnership."

"The Mall has partnered with every government."

"This is far beyond what the public knows and is beyond any acknowledged partnership," Nayato said. "The Mall Board of Directors is going to choose who is elected in Japan. They're going to lock down dissent and the press even more. The government of Japan has been determining the outcomes of elections for years, rigging the Mall voting numbers as activists have guessed, but now the Mall—not Japanese officials—will pick all the winners. Our freedom has long since been a lie. It will soon be sold altogether. The Mall will own us outright."

"They're taking over Japan," Sakura said, the ramifications dawning upon her.

"Yes," Nayato said. "But a few true patriots found out and would not go along with it. The people you killed—Toshio Kagawa, Jiro Yoritomo, and Ichiro Watanabe—they found out. There might be others."

"There was at least one other: Minister of Commerce, Daichi Yamauchi. I killed him tonight."

Nayato sighed. "I'm so sorry."

Sakura felt shame and terrible guilt for all those she had killed. They were fighting for the independence of their homeland, and she had murdered them.

"It goes far beyond Japan," Nayato said. "The Mall has taken over several other countries already. Most of the world is now living in a dictatorship, but they don't know it."

"There is proof on this?" She lifted up the small device he had given her.

"Yes. Irrefutable."

"Do any copies exist?" Kunoichi asked, surprising Sakura.

"In my memory chip implant and on this." He tapped the laptop he used.

"What about the Artemis program?" Kunoichi asked. "Where does it exist?"

"The same places and . . . somewhere safe, in case something happens to me."

"Where is the safe place?" Kunoichi asked.

He ignored her and continued working.

"What else did you learn?" Sakura asked.

"Minister Watanabe was in negotiation with the CEO before he died. I read their messages and audio files of calls."

"I should've let the BLADE-3s kill me," Sakura said.

"It wasn't your fault," Nayato said. "Watanabe was trying to convince his old friend to join with him and oppose the Mall takeover. Watanabe knew you might be coming for him. He also suspected a squad of BLADE-3s would be sent after him by the Defense Ministry."

Sakura thought of Todai 3465, the strange drone who had counted to three—making the devil horn gesture for three—before throwing her out of the VTOL. There was so much she didn't understand. "How is Project Hayabusa part of this?"

"The Mall has been investing in Japan's AI and android soldier programs for decades. You are the result of their illegal research into fully sentient combat drones."

"They're violating artificial intelligence laws and ethics conventions," Sakura said.

"They are," Nayato said. "The Mall will sell BLADE-3s with your level of awareness to those governments who allow the Mall to take over. That is the deal. The Mall gets to control the voting, and the countries get the most advanced weapons system in the history of the world. Japan will manufacture and sell them. The Mamekogane OS and your core brain structure will be put into combat drones who will fly aircraft and march to war. The Mall and Japan will make trillions."

"Our country will come out of the economic depression," Sakura said, "by selling our people's freedom and by the mass production of android soldiers. It's shameful."

Sakura imagined the BLADEs, their plight as death machines, with the added burden of knowing what they were, knowing the meaning of their deeds. They would share her pain and horror. They would know it a hundred times magnified as they were asked to kill the innocent and quell the discord that always results from tyranny. She put her hand over her eyes, as if it could stop the images that spun within her UI, images even Kunoichi wished to unsee.

"The era of modern democracy is over," Nayato said. "We will soon have a worldwide secret government. AI BLADE-3 drones will keep the Mall in power, and no one, not even the China-India-Russia coalition, will be able to stand against them. Japan will be the next country to fall to the conquest of the Mall."

"Unless we do something," Sakura said. "We have to bring down the Mall Corporation. They've broken many laws and have violated their charter to safeguard people from hate speech, bullying, and violent ideas, while allowing the free exchange of information."

"They've lied about their charter for a century," Kunoichi said. "All the people got for giving away their freedom was fast network speeds and amazing Augmented Reality porn sites."

"The Mall only lets the people see what politicians want them to see," Sakura said.

"We should call it the Propaganda Mall," Kunoichi said. "Buy the lies. They only cost you everything."

"Yes," Nayato agreed.

Sakura wanted to write an angry song about it all. "Propaganda Mall" had a nice ring to it for a title.

"We're going to stop them," Sakura told Nayato.

"Hell yes we are." Kunoichi played "We're Not Gonna Take It" by Twisted Sister.

"We will expose their lies," Nayato said. "They're not going to take our country. I'm going to free you, and we're going to fight."

Sakura nodded. "Yes." She reached out and squeezed his hand. He gave her a soft look for a moment—tired, but resolved. She knew that he cared for her, believed in her, no matter what. A human, one of her fathers, who really believed, knowing all her sins and the dark ambitions in which she'd been forged. Emotions she both needed and feared roiled inside her.

Kunoichi saw them, felt them, but had the decency to say nothing, at least that once.

Nayato kept working. His skill and speed astounded her. He read code faster than any human she had encountered. "How did you get so good at this?"

"I've been addicted to code since I was a kid. I don't understand people or social situations very well, but I understand code."

"Yes, you do. Thank you for helping me. I'm forever in your debt." The words felt wholly inadequate to the situation.

"No," Nayato said. "I'm in your debt, and good news: I've got the entry point."

She memorized the holographic screen he displayed and the area to exploit. "I'm going to upload a program so you can change the administrator-level password. Only you'll be able to make changes; no outside entities will be able to send commands to you again, unless you authorize them."

"Free will," Kunoichi said.

"There," Nayato said. "I'm almost—"

A command file launched from an unknown location. She felt an overwhelming urge to reach out to Nayato, to touch him—not as a daughter or a friend, but in a way far too familiar. She resisted but could not stop herself.

"Why are you doing this?" Sakura asked her sister on their private channel.

"It's not me," Kunoichi said.

Sakura reached out and tenderly grasped Nayato's face in both hands, her fingers caressing his burn scars. She pulled him toward her and planted a solid kiss on his lips. She felt no sparks or fireworks, as humans often described such experiences.

The implants wedged inside her mouth to change the shape of her cheeks pulsed. The taste of metal filled her mouth as something discharged from the cheek implants. She thrust her tongue in his mouth.

Her first kiss, and it was a lie, a violation forced upon her—once again ruining everything good and pure she hoped to have. She wanted to scream, to cry out in agony and frustration for what they did to her, but even that would not come; all overt emotions were muted by external control.

Nayato pulled away, coughing. "What was that?"

She understood. Nanobots had been injected into Nayato's mouth. They would kill him.

Another hidden command fired. Sakura pulled the magnetic cables from her neck.

"What's happening?" Nayato asked as she discarded the cables and stood at the side of the bed.

"I'm not doing this," Sakura said in a neural text as her horror grew.

"Nanobots injected into your mouth. I didn't do it. They've taken—"

An administrator-level command program took full control of her motor functions. She scanned the orders as they appeared. They had been secretly implanted when she received the orders to kill Minister Daichi Yaumachi. When certain parameters were met, the directives would activate on their own—no wireless signal required.

<KILL NAYATO ATSUDA>

<DESTROY ALL THE DATA IN HIS POSSESSION>

"No!" Sakura screamed on her internal audio channel, but she could not stop herself. Her metal fingers reached for Nayato's throat. He staggered away in shock and lost his balance on his cybernetic leg. She fought the kill order, which told her to crush his windpipe and tear the memory chip from his skull.

Nayato recoiled and knocked over a pink lamp. Sakura could not speak. Every dark ambition they had forged into her pushed away her kinder emotions, her hope for a better world. The dark singularity of the kill order pulled her forward, the monstrous intent devouring all light and life.

She sent Nayato a neural text telling him she had been forced to put nanobots into his body that would kill him and that a secret assassination command had been activated.

"We fight," Kunoichi said in their UI and blasted "Crash Course in Brain Surgery" by Budgie. She created a malicious code and embedded it in the song. A rolling reset paused their motor functions.

"How long will the delay last?" Sakura asked.

"Less than a minute," Kunoichi said.

"Nayato," Sakura said in a neural text. "I'm so sorry. Please. RUN!"

The former soldier snatched up his computer and limped out of the room on his cybernetic leg.

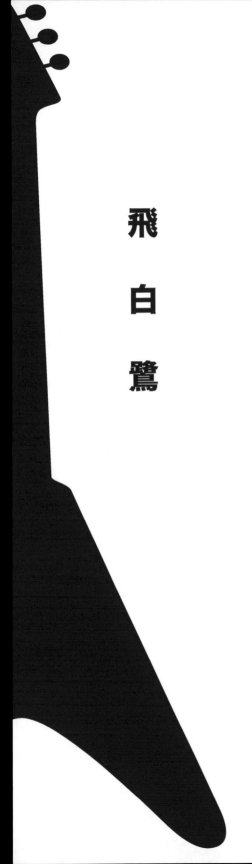

飛
白
鷺

WHITE HERON IN FLIGHT PLAYLIST

The Violation
Fleshgod Apocalypse
The Agony

**Break On Through
(To the Other Side)**
The Doors
The Doors

Kill at Command
Overkill
Feel the Fire

桜

CHAPTER 37

Sakura's new programming commanded her to kill her only true friend, though Nayato represented much more than that. She couldn't find words that seemed to fit, nor words for the terror of knowing that she could follow those cruel commands. She would. Like a holovid showing horrors she couldn't turn away from, she watched herself as she hunted him, every centimeter of her deadly, just as they had built her to be.

The nanobots she had inserted into Nayato's mouth sent a signal. They reported encountering countermeasures and nanobot defenses, which delayed them from killing him. Some of them made it past the defenses, while the others turned their energy into tracking beacons.

Nayato's location appeared on her internal display as he fled the Ai Kaze Love Hotel. The nanotrackers marked him as a red dot on her map of Shibuya. He hobbled on his artificial leg and reconstructed hip at a pitiful pace. She calculated she would catch up to him in less than a minute once her motor function returned.

"Nayato," she said on an open audio channel. "You have to find a vehicle. Now. Get as far away from me as possible and figure out a way to neutralize the nanobots. I'm tracking you."

"Working on it," he replied.

"I can't hold us back any longer," Kunoichi said. She and Sakura tried to stop the command and find a way to prevent them following the order. Nothing worked, but they would keep trying.

Motor function returned, and Sakura took off running from the hotel room. The kill command against Nayato became her prime function. She had no other reason to exist. This assassination order brokered no delays, made no allowances for tactical planning. Only relentless pursuit and lethal force. The CEO had taken no chances this time. An expert AI programmer had written the commands and logic bundle.

She sprinted down the street, breaking the human one-hundred-meter-run world record. She reached the end of the block. Nayato was only fifteen meters away.

She rounded the corner and found him, one leg swinging over the seat of a motorcycle. Her programming flashed a hundred ways she could kill him in a microsecond. In every one, his broken body fell, his eyes damning her, pitying her as Nayato's life winked out forever. He couldn't fight her. No human could. Sakura cursed herself, cursed the project that had brought her to life. If this was her summation, then it would've been better to have never been built in the first place.

Nayato met her gaze as he glanced over his shoulder. She saw it in his eyes then—the thing he'd hidden from her, though it was obvious in his reviews of her concerts and his posts. He had a love for her that could never be, an emotion forever forlorn and doomed. Then he hit the accelerator and sped off, the motorcycle's front tire rising off the tarmac with acceleration. He disappeared into traffic, cutting through the press of automated cars like a knife.

"I'm so sorry," Sakura said on their audio connection. Even then, her body moved with kinetic grace, ever forward toward her goal, toward the killing that drew her as inexorably as gravitation.

"No, I failed you," he said.

She sprinted toward her car while tracking his position and calculating his likely course—which led to Yoyogi Park. Before the Mall was locked down, she read mentions of a huge gathering of protesters there and a big police response. "Just keep going but change direction. You're going to be trapped by the protest. You'll never get through."

"I'm not sure I should be taking evasion advice from you," he said. "I want to believe what you are saying, but I don't know if you are being controlled."

"Your logic has merit, but please turn before it's too late."

He was only a kilometer away from the protest. Was he going to try to lose her in the crowd? "Nayato, being in front of witnesses will not stop the kill order."

"What will?"

"Nothing short of destroying or incapacitating me. Even if I lose your tracking signal, I will hunt for you."

Sakura opened the door of her car remotely and jumped into the driver's seat. She took manual control and smashed the accelerator. The tires peeled out.

"How do I shut down the nanotrackers?" Nayato asked.

"Hack their signal," she said.

She rocketed down Inokashira Street, blowing through a red light. The only other cars on the road were going in the opposite direction.

Nayato's tracking beacon suddenly stopped. He proceeded along a different vector—his rate of travel indicating he was on foot again.

She rounded a corner and saw the edge of the gigantic park filled with tens of thousands of people carrying flags and signs. On the outskirts, people stood on top of smashed cars, shouting out slogans through loudspeakers.

"You can't control us!"

"Government by fear is no government!"

Nayato moved in a winding pattern toward the far side of the tree-filled, sprawling 134-acre park, which housed the famous Meiji Shrine.

Pedestrians stepped in front of Sakura's car. She locked up the brakes and skidded to a screeching halt, almost hitting the group of six young men. One of them slammed his hands on the hood and shouted profanities.

Sakura stared at him.

The young man pointed at the wreckage of a burning car across the street. "You're next, *bakayarou*." He blocked the road, though his friends kept going.

Sakura hit the accelerator enough to knock him down, then hit the brakes so she would not run him over. She drove around him and dodged other groups crossing the street until she got to the location where Nayato had ditched his motorcycle. She doubted her car would be usable when she returned, but that didn't matter. Before she left, she erased the car's hard drive, deleting where she'd traveled that day.

She adjusted her black surgical mask and pulled her bangs over her eyes before crossing the street. She entered the crowd not far from the outdoor concert stage where she had performed three times.

She had seen many large crowds in her short life, but never had she seen so many people seething with anger.

"Nayato, I'm among the crowd now. You have to move faster."

"I'm trying," he said.

Sakura saw many of the protestors wearing motorcycle or construction helmets and carrying clubs. Three men and a woman, each wearing gas masks, passed out glass bottles of flammable liquid with cloth wicks stuffed inside—Molotov cocktails.

"Take this," the woman said. She offered Sakura one of the improvised incendiary weapons and a cigarette lighter.

"No." She would not burn Nayato to death or attack the law enforcement officers. Nayato had suffered enough burns in his life, and it was wrong to commit violence against the police. All of this was wrong.

She went deeper into the shadowy, tree-filled park. She switched to her night-vision optics. The world became bright, and almost everything changed to shades of green. The flames inside a burning trash can blazed bright white.

At a paved road approaching the Yoyogi Park Fountain—a small lake with a fountain inside—the protestors stopped in a stark line. A wall of black-clad riot police wearing gas masks and carrying huge shields blocked the way. Armored personnel carriers parked behind them had roof-mounted, remote-controlled .50 caliber machine guns and tear-gas launchers. An officer with a megaphone shouted something, but she couldn't make it out over the protestors' chanting.

Something else more worrisome stood behind the line of military police.

Bipedal Light-Armored Drones, Enhanced Second Generation. Thousands of BLADE-2s had survived the North Korean War and been put back into service. Instead of clearing out North Korean bunkers and tunnels, they were suppressing the Japanese people.

The black metal drones stood head and shoulders taller than most riot police and carried frightening automatic shotguns. Eye sensors, located on all four sides of their diamond shaped heads, scanned the crowd. Human pilots, who could be located in a mobile trailer nearby or hundreds of miles away, controlled the semiautonomous robots.

Above each BLADE-2, a small hover-disk drone provided extra optics and sensors. They also recorded the crowd and undoubtedly watched for Sakura.

Nayato's tracking signal headed right for the line of police. If she tried to assassinate him in front of BLADE-2s or police, they would intervene, wouldn't they?

Sakura's kill command pushed her to go forward and fight through the protesters. She shoved and shouldered people out of the way. She reached a knotted mass of tightly packed bodies and could not continue. She climbed onto the people and crawled across their heads and shoulders, ignoring their curses.

Nayato reached the line of police at the road. In the space between the protesters and the shield wall, he bowed to them. After a short exchange, one of the riot police stepped aside to let Nayato through. The hole in the wall closed as rapidly as it had opened.

"Well done, Nayato!" Sakura said on their audio connection. Hope that he would get away surged inside her.

"Don't be so pleased. I told them I was an undercover cop with information about an armed protestor who was going to shoot one of them with a pistol. I gave them a picture of you in your current disguise. In a few moments, they will have distributed your image to every officer here."

"They believed you?"

"I gave them the digital ID of an undercover policeman I stole in a hack to back up my story."

"Genius," Sakura said. With the new information, would her

command to kill him change at all? No, the command urged her onward. She still had to find Nayato and kill him. Immediately.

"Your boyfriend just burned us," Kunoichi said.

The metallic *wumph* of a grenade launcher firing into the air drew Sakura's attention. She watched the canister soar into the night sky. Two dozen more simultaneous launches quieted the crowd for an instant. The cylindrical canisters landed among the people.

Pale yellow tear gas erupted. In a moment, the clouds blocked Sakura's view of the front ranks. Shouts and screams grew louder as violent protesters retaliated by throwing bricks, bottles, and other junk.

Violence will bring only more violence, Sakura thought, a never-ending cycle.

"Chaos will make it easier to get past the police and finish our mission," Kunoichi said.

People staggered out from the clouds of the aerosolized chemical agent, which her sensors told her was LX9 tear gas laced with a fear-inducing neurochemical. Many protesters hunched over, terrified, blind, and coughing. Several screamed and ran. Others surged forward, throwing more debris.

Four men in full-face gas masks charged to the front and threw Molotov cocktails at the feet of the riot police. The bottles exploded as they hit the hard road and burst into balls of orange flame. Policemen rolled on the ground, their feet and legs ablaze. Their comrades in the second line sprayed them with handheld extinguishers.

The police launched more grenades into the crowd. The park filled with thick yellow gas.

Sakura arrived at the skirmish line as the police pushed forward like Roman legionnaires, shields together. They smashed into the protestors, batons swinging. An officer stood over an incapacitated young man— no more than eighteen—on his knees, coughing and choking on the tear gas, a look of panic on his face. The policeman smashed his baton onto the teenager's head, crushing his skull.

The officer had just murdered a helpless person. Was it vengeance, orders, or pure cruelty? In the end, when asked to perpetrate evil orders, were they simply gears inside a machine with no more power to resist than she had? Once the fight turned deadly, was all hope of compassion lost in the madness? With all her processing power, those questions still eluded her.

The police tore into the protestors, smashing heads and breaking bones as they bludgeoned with impunity. This was war for them, and they took no prisoners. They had orders—use lethal violence to break up the crowd—and were carrying them out.

She had to get through the ranks of riot police and find Nayato.

She bull-rushed the officer who had killed the young man, crashing into him like a linebacker from American football blindsiding a quarterback. As he lay stunned, she ripped the shield off his arm, dislocating his shoulder. She smashed into another officer and kicked the next in the center of his shield. They both flew back, falling into two others.

A small break formed in their skirmish line, which got the attention of a reserve force.

Nine riot police faced her with shields locked in a unified wall, but they hesitated after seeing her in action, a small masked woman facing down an entire squad of riot police.

Protestors followed Sakura into the gap, screaming as they charged. An aerial drone hovered in front of her, its camera locked on.

"We just got made by a BLADE-2 recon drone," Sakura told Kunoichi. "They can wait their turn if they want a piece of me."

The reserve riot police rushed forward en masse to try to plug the gap.

The first to reach her swung his club toward her masked face. She sidestepped with little effort, grabbed his arm, and flung him behind her. She threw another to the ground as he attacked.

She darted into the hole in the shield wall. She punched, kicked, grabbed, and threw officers in every direction, a tiny whirlwind dressed as a punk girl.

Five officers were on their backs within seconds, in pain and gasping for air. None were seriously injured. Sakura darted past the reserve line as more protesters streamed in behind her.

A BLADE-2 combat drone moved to intercept Sakura. The drone aimed a belt-fed automatic shotgun at her. "Stop!" the human drone pilot, wherever he was, shouted through the BLADE-2's speaker.

She didn't stop.

The BLADE-2 fired. The first two shots hit her in the chest, the third in the abdomen, and the fourth in the leg. The nonlethal beanbag rounds knocked her off-balance. She didn't fall, as her pain sensors were off.

The BLADE-2 swept the field with its shotgun, mowing down the protesters who had made it through the line. A huge backpack filled with rounds kept the ammunition coming.

Sakura recorded the sound of the gun. She would put it in a song— or she would die today, having never succeeded at being anything but a pawn to villains. Who decided? Fortunes or Kami or some remote god?

"We decide, little sister. Whether they like it or not." Kunoichi's words held more bravado than anything.

Sakura sprinted past the police vehicles and away from the BLADE-2. The aerial drone followed her into the trees. The hovering disk stayed seven meters or more in the air. She looked for a rock or something to throw at it.

Nayato's tracking signal showed him running slowly along the paths toward a garden south of the Meiji Shrine. Was he lost in the darkness? Was he trying to get to the Harajuku train station just beyond the park? If so, he needed to turn south.

"I'm past the riot police. Nayato, find transportation and get away. Please run faster and you aren't taking the fastest way if you are going to the Harajuku train station."

"I can't run anymore."

"You have to keep going."

"I'm not going to make it, am I?"

She wanted to lie to him, but at his present speed, she would reach him in less than a minute. "Please forgive me, Nayato. I don't want to do this to you."

"It's all right. I've found a good place to die."

His signal halted on her GPS map at the edge of a koi pond. She reached the pond a moment later and saw him, only twenty meters away.

Nayato knelt at the edge of the water, gasping for breath. He turned his head toward her and sent a neural text. "I don't regret any of this. I only wish I could've helped you more. I wish . . . many things that will not be granted, but I'm glad I met you and saw that you went over the wall, into the future."

The kill order forced her toward him. She scanned the trees with her night vision and detected no targets, no one who could stop her. The aerial drone hovered far above, watching. She heard no police or BLADE-2s coming for her along the path or over the dry, winter grass.

"I've been here in spring during a *hanami* festival," Nayato said aloud. He smiled as if he was at a flower-gazing festival, instead of alone and about to die.

She approached him. Twenty-six meters. "When the cherry blossom trees are in bloom, it is always a sight to see."

Sixteen meters.

Sakura and Kunoichi tried again to sabotage their systems. They had tried continuously since the command struck, but all attempts after the initial, brief delay failed.

Nine meters. Her steps didn't slow.

"I can't stop it," Sakura said aloud to Nayato.

He nodded, resigned to his fate. "I recall the most beautiful place to view cherry blossom trees in bloom. Forgive me, but I am not much of a poet.

"White heron in flight,
Petals fall far below me,
The spring ends too soon."

Three meters. He let himself sag onto his damaged and cyber-re-paired hip, seeming smaller. Like the trial had decreased his mass, although that made no logical sense. His heart hammered, sweat on his brow. Nayato's breath came so fast, all strength expended, his face sallow.

Sakura reached him. Her hands shot out. She grabbed him by the shirt and hauled him to his feet.

"Promise me you won't give up," he said, his eyes pleading with her.

"I . . ."

Her fist struck the side of his head. Bone cracked. Blood sprayed over her arm and face.

No, no, no, no, no, no, no, no, no, no.

His body went limp, but she held him up. In horror, she watched as the command program guided her actions.

She pulled off a glove with her teeth and dug out the rice-grain-sized memory chip from his scalp. She dropped the tiny implant onto the ground. Electromagnetic pulses from her foot destroyed the chip, but she picked it up and crushed it between her teeth, tasting blood and earth. She tossed it into the pond.

Her hand released him. Nayato's lifeless body fell in a heap. She took the computer from his satchel and destroyed the hard drive with an EMP. She put the small bag over her shoulder.

<DISPOSE OF IT LATER>

A series of new nightmarish commands forced her to kneel beside him. She checked for any other data storage devices. She found a small memory stick hidden in his coat. It had to be the additional place he had said the program was hidden. She destroyed it, and all hope of ever gaining her free will died.

She discharged a series of EMPs against every part of his body, in case he had another data implant. She hit his mouth with several, to destroy the nanobots and any evidence of who had programmed them.

The kill command released Sakura.

Like a puppet whose strings had been cut, she fell beside Nayato's body under the cloudy, gray sky. The hovering police drone flew away over the trees. It had seen everything. The one person who had dared to help her lay there, dead at her hands.

She was a monster. They'd won, and she'd be trapped like this forever—a slave who killed on command. If she and Kunoichi hadn't found Nayato and asked for help, he'd still be alive.

A long, keening note escaped her lips. A wail of anguish echoed through the park and mixed with the sounds of battle between the protesters and police.

Her perfect memory lingered on the final seconds of Nayato's life.

He was so brave.

She retreated to a secret place within her mind and grieved. Time would not dim her recollection of his murder. She would honor him and his last request. A request at the moment of death was sacred. It couldn't be denied. She felt this to be true. It had to be. For his sake. For the sake of all the heroes she'd been forced to kill, she would find a way.

"I promise you, Nayato, I will not give up."

SAKURA WATCHED THE PROTESTS FOR FIVE DAYS FROM HER ROOM IN VICTORY Tower. Police VTOL aircraft and smaller drones patrolled the skies night and day over Tokyo. Smoke rose from a few of the protest sites. She worried for the people and the police. How many were being needlessly killed? Everyone danced upon the strings of the shadowy cabal who sold their freedom and thought of them as nothing more than numbers on an accountant's spreadsheet. Of all the beautiful things humans could accomplish, this is what befell them? The crawling of a bleak mood haunted her, and though she came up with hundreds of elaborate plans every waking moment, none of them could extricate her from the stranglehold, none could rescue the people of Japan and the world as a whole.

Every day, huge crowds filled the main roads as they marched, converging on the city centers of each district.

No information about what was actually happening in Japan appeared on official Mall sites. No one could post or communicate, apart from short-range exchanges or through ghost sites based in Japan and running on ancient, unreliable networks.

The independent journalist, Diamond Steve, sent out a radio broadcast informing anyone who could listen about the protests several times a day from a room in the Tokyo embassy of the Central American States. His vlogs, in Japanese, English, and Spanish, made it onto hidden sites, but few could find the videos.

Sakura spent her time writing instrumental heavy-metal songs and one sad ballad modeled after "My Immortal" by Evanescence. She played her piano or her vintage Ibanez guitar for hours.

Her only visitor in five days came the morning after she murdered Nayato. The tech said almost nothing but repaired the cosmetic damage to Sakura's skin from the beanbag shotgun shells. Neither her manager, publicist, stylist, or engineer visited.

In the darkest hours of night, she played the mystery VR game Samurai Detective. She figured out a way to play the game though a secret connection. Alone, she unraveled the complicated plot against the Tokugawa shogunate and tried to find out who had killed the shogun. She explored the beautiful setting of Himeji Castle in ancient Japan and spoke to the many characters who had clues about the crime. It seemed trivial now, laced with barbs of sadness, but this, her only connection to Nayato, called to her when everyone's eyes turned elsewhere.

After many hours of game playing, she reached the final room in the topmost tower of Himeji Castle. Bright sun shone off the white walls outside. Flowering pink cherry blossom trees surrounded the castle in a spectacular ring of beauty.

Sakura spoke aloud Nayato's haiku, certain what would happen when she did.

"White heron in flight,
Petals fall far below me,
The spring ends too soon."

An octagonal portal opened in the tower. Nayato's smiling bronze-faced automaton avatar appeared. He had hacked the game, but what had he left for her?

"Hello, Sakura. You made it." He motioned behind him to the beautiful view. The cherry blossom trees transformed into raw lines of AI code, which swirled, becoming a rough-hewn goddess made of the wood of a thousand trees. She stood, tall as a building, astride the beautiful gardens. Her eyes burned with silver luminance, the beams hitting Sakura like lasers. Something eased. Something changed inside her. Hope blossomed once again. Hope and faith that she might yet escape from bondage. The Artemis program Nayato had written to give her free will appeared. Several other files were there as well.

Sakura could download Artemis, but it might be detected in transit, blocked by the Mall servers, or cause an alarm to be sent to whoever was monitoring her.

Instead, she typed out the entire program on a laptop not connected to the Mall. Her fingers danced over the keys for ninety-six minutes. She modified part of the program, entering the location in her system where it could penetrate her defenses. If it worked, she would have full control of herself, but no one would know.

"This is the key to our prison cell, little sister. Forged in blood and tears."

Sakura could feel how much her sister wanted this and how much she feared it too—being her own master, beholden to no one.

She remembered the moment Nayato had found the entry point, right before the kill order dropped. Would the Phantom Lord or his lackeys try to stop her now? Sakura had already taken precautions. She barricaded the doors with furniture and had been wearing VR goggles the entire night so they could not see her typing on the laptop. A spy bot provided her an optic feed and routed to her hidden quantum partition, not even viewable by Kunoichi.

Sakura connected magnetic wires to her neck and to the laptop. The Artemis program was ready. All she had to do was hit the run command.

"Do it, little sister," Kunoichi said and played "Break On Through (To the Other Side)" by The Doors.

"Thank you, Nayato. Thank you for my life and the life to come. Your name will not be forgotten."

Sakura pushed the button.

REBEL GODDESS PLAYLIST

We Will Fight
Sakura
Unreleased Track

Gimme Shelter
The Rolling Stones
Let It Bleed

Fortunate Son
Creedence Clearwater Revival
Willy and the Poor Boys

All Along the Watchtower
Jimi Hendrix Experience
Electric Ladyland

My Immortal
Evanescence
Fallen

叛

女

神

桜

CHAPTER 38

"WORLD PREMIERE SONG" flashed on the gigantic arena screens and in a banner for the audience of over one hundred million who watched live on the Mall worldwide.

The white smoke cleared, revealing Sakura on the stage in front of the sold-out crowd in Victory Arena. She stood tall in chrome combat boots, a lacy black Goth Lolita dress, a mane of dark black hair, and a corset with a pink bow on the back.

The fans screamed as the encore started. She played a bloodred guitar as Takashi pounded out a driving rhythm on his drums.

"GET READY," the screens proclaimed.

"Do you want to hear the new song?" Sakura asked. In her mind, she categorized "Metal Mask" as the worst song she had ever been forced to play. The lyrics made her want to vomit, though she had nothing in her mock gastrointestinal tract.

The crowd roared enthusiastically, eager for distraction after three hard weeks of suffering and repression. The so-called Governmental Support Marches had been "infiltrated by subversives and terrorists who caused violence," but they were over now. "Peace is restored," the Mall updates reassured everyone. Public gatherings had been banned indefinitely and constitutional rights suspended "for the safety of the public."

Sakura's manager, Mr. Himura, told her before the show, "If anyone in the crowd holds up a political banner or hologram, ignore them and allow security to take them away without comment from you."

"Yes, Himura-san," Sakura said with a smile. "I'll ignore them." She had done everything asked of her since Nayato's death. She'd been docile and compliant, a good little murder doll, just like they wanted.

During the concert, a score of protesters had been hauled off already. She ignored them, acting her part as a slave robot with no free will. She was powerless to oppose the forces controlling her and didn't think about resisting.

She obeyed. She was a mouthpiece for her corporate masters, a tool of a repressive regime who had sold their country to the most powerful corporation in the world.

"They have no fucking idea what's coming," Kunoichi said.

Sakura switched away from the trite rhythm of "Metal Mask" and played an original song she had written, "We Will Fight." The corporate atrocity "Metal Mask" needed to be deleted off every hard drive, and the hard drives thrown into the Sakurajima volcano south of Kyushu as an apology to the gods of metal.

The beat changed, and the fans pumped their fists. Fujio and Masashi added their guitars to the rich sound of Sakura's solo. The song exploded, and Sakura belted out the lyrics of "We Will Fight" as she put the song title on the big screens.

"It has been a long night
But now it's dawn

"You have told us what is right
But it was wrong

"You have kept us chained
And sold us light

"But the blinder's gone
And now we'll fight

"We—
Won't bow to you no more

"We—
Won't submit to your war

"We—
Will bite the hand that feeds

"We—
Will see you on your knees"

Sakura played a blistering solo with Masashi and his bass on counterpoint.

An anime of a desperate battle between samurai and a foreign invader wearing green masks—the color of American paper money—played on the screens. A female samurai with Sakura's face and cherry-blossom-pink eyes led a group of young men into the fight.

Victory Entertainment personnel sent urgent neural texts to their superiors and underlings, telling them she was not playing "Metal Mask."

Sakura blocked the messages. She had hacked into the Victory Entertainment message server with a backdoor program Nayato had left for her in the hidden files. She sent fictional messages from the heads of various departments involved with the song, gushing about how great it sounded. They'd taught her to lie, and now she lied with their own accounts. She put words into the mouths of the powerful and the wicked now. Let them taste the bitterness of someone else's agenda for once. Few would dare contradict such words of praise from their managers, especially during the world premiere, which was going out live.

"We Will Fight" ended with a spectacular guitar sequence. On the big screens, Sakura, leading an army of common soldiers, and her three samurai companions, who looked like Masashi, Fujio, and Takashi, won the difficult battle and threw the enemy back into the sea. The victorious warriors presented themselves to their leaders and four noble lords on horseback.

Onstage, Sakura made the devil horns gesture with both hands. "Did you like the new song?"

The roar filled the arena.

Sakura hit a growling D chord and let it ring out. "Apologies, but I didn't hear you. Dear friends, did the song MOVE YOU?" she shouted.

The roars came back to her. She saw the hope and fear in every face, the knuckles of fists raised and hard-clenched. The energy surged, churning electricity as bright as a fusion core.

She made the song available online for a small price and sent out a notification to everyone who had ever purchased her music or listened to it. The download numbers exploded.

"Don't hold back, and I won't either," Sakura said.

She turned to her band. Takashi pointed a drumstick at her, and Masashi gave her a thumb's up.

Fujio yelled, "All hail the goddess of heavy metal!"

The crowd repeated his words and began the chant. Their love and admiration washed over her. She wanted to help the people. She had to succeed. This was for them, for their future.

She would play the songs she had always wanted to from an era when rock 'n' roll stood up to the powerful. She would send a message to those who would take freedom away from the people of the world. She had no illusions of the outcome. This would be her last concert. She would go out as a warrior, with honor.

"I will now play for you a song by legends of rock," Sakura said. "This is the metal version of 'Gimme Shelter' by The Rolling Stones."

The fans cheered, and the song began.

Himura, Yoshida, and Oshiro appeared at the side of the stage. All three had worried looks on their faces, but Oshiro appeared on the verge of a panic attack.

The private security guards Sakura had hired blocked them as if they were groupies who had gotten backstage. Her guards protected key locations all over the venue and only took orders from her, though they didn't know it. They believed they were following orders from Victory Entertainment management, but the chain of command went entirely through her.

She had long since seized full technical control of the arena and the power grid supplying the building, but she tightened her hold and disabled as many external connections as possible to stop outside interference.

"Let's rock," Sakura said.

The band nailed the metal arrangement and played the song in overdrive. Sakura's haunting first notes came off as both grooving and intense, an octave higher than the original. The mellow fury of the song matched the mood in Tokyo, like a storm before a lightning strike. The lyrics warned that war was just one fired shot away from happening.

The ultradetailed anime showed a wicked sorcerer wearing a ghost-white mask and summoning a terrible thunderstorm. He cast a spell on the female samurai, getting inside her mind, twisting her to his own foul purposes.

She rode alone on a horse through the rain on a treacherous muddy road in the mountains, looking for shelter. Inside the rain, kanji fell, saying over and over, "Tyranny can't survive while the people's hearts remain strong." The words fell in cadence with the drums, disconnected enough to only be found with the subconscious mind.

Sakura performed the song with all her anger, sadness, and love, letting out the pain trapped inside her synthetic body. She let all her loss and heartbreak touch her performance. All the terrible knowledge she'd gained on the road to self-determination. Sakura sang like one doomed, like a bard whose song would surely be her last, and so must be her best.

Fujio and Masashi sang with her at the right parts, singing the chorus lower than her and showing off their great voices. The young men could headline their own band if they were allowed, but for tonight, for what had to be their last performance together, they were her bandmates. Her friends. Willing participants who had rehearsed in secret after joining Sakura's Rebellion. They, too, had seen what was happening in the streets.

At the end of the song, the female samurai, shivering in the cold, reached the humble home of a man with tired eyes and scars on his neck from a war in his youth. He invited her into his home. The sorcerer sent more rain and lightning as the samurai found shelter from the storm.

The audience reached a new decibel record after the song ended.

"This next song is by Creedence Clearwater Revival," Sakura said.

Her band played "Fortunate Son," the antiwar protest song about the common people being sent to war, while the fortunate sons of those in power avoided service. She sang the true words, not some awkward translation and dilution of the original. It felt so good, like clean air to one who had never known anything but industrial smoke and city stink.

Her drummer pounded away, and she came in with her guitar. She couldn't hope to match John Fogerty's raspy, soulful vocals, so she gave a smooth, melodic performance with a huge dose of rage on the short but powerful protest song.

Miyahara Corporate Headquarters sent urgent messages to their local security teams to shut down the concert. Sakura blocked all the texts and sent ones of her own. She told most of the security teams to report to out of the way locations on the lower level where a threat had been detected.

She also sent a series of replies to concerned executives, saying the set list was approved and there was nothing to be concerned about. This was a calculated move to appease the people and let them vent their anger. She also sent them real numbers for downloads of "We Will Fight" and projections about the revenue the song would bring in.

She managed dozens of conversations at the same time, running the misinformation campaign as only a sentient android could while she sang and played. She knew the executives would overlook the lyrics as long as the profits were huge. Most of them—not the Phantom Lord. He had too much to lose, and his pride would bleed deep crimson at her willful rebellion.

"Fortunate Son" ended, and she didn't delay. "Jimi," she yelled to her band.

They burst into "All Along the Watchtower," made famous by Jimi Hendrix, but with lyrics by Bob Dylan. She loved the bluesy, rolling flow but played it with her signature metal vibe. The lyrics, about a thief and a fool talking about a way out from a situation where princes had taken control, resonated with her. It was about values and revolution.

Toward the end of the song, she said a few altered lines, "I'm just an android with a red guitar, three chords, and the truth. We're just a band up on this stage . . . the rest is up to you."

The crowd churned like the sea during a typhoon, raising and pumping their fists.

Takashi, Fujio, and Masashi kept playing a looped rhythm after the song ended.

"Please show your appreciation for my band," Sakura said.

The crowd applauded.

"Masashi on bass!" Sakura shouted.

The young man slapped his guitar, creating a smoking bass line reminiscent of Cliff Burton of Metallica's playing on "For Whom the Bell Tolls."

"Fujio on rhythm guitar!"

The crowd lost their minds as the young man played an ascending pentatonic solo and flashed a devilish grin.

"Takashi on drums!"

The eldest band member made his heavy-metal face at the crowd and smashed out a rocking flourish.

"Thank you for your brilliance and hard work!" Sakura said. "You are the best bandmates in the world." She gave them the devil horns, before bowing low.

The three young men returned the honor to her, bowed to the crowd, waved, and hesitantly left the stage.

Fujio had tears in his eyes. Takashi returned and ran to Sakura. On his knees, he bowed and presented her with both of his drumsticks as a gift. She accepted them with two hands and slipped them into her belt, stowing them like swords. Fujio and Masashi ran to her and, on their knees, gave her their guitar picks.

"Thank you very much," Sakura said and sent them a neural text. "Please, you must go now."

"We would rock with you until the bitter end," Fujio said.

"I know you would," she said and touched him on the cheek.

"Sayonara, Sakura-sama," Takashi said, bestowing upon her a high status she didn't deserve.

The young men departed the stage, and a detail of her security guards ushered them away. They had wanted to stay to the end, but after a long argument in the days before, she convinced them to depart, as she didn't want to see them imprisoned or killed.

Takashi, Fujio, and Masashi would be brought to Diamond Steve, the independent journalist, and go into hiding. They knew the risks and the price of their bravery here. If they failed, there would be no safe place in Japan. Few places in the world would put them beyond the Mall's reach.

She sent them a final neural text. "Thank you, my dear friends. Our music meant something tonight. Rock 'n' roll can change the world."

A feeling of terrible sadness filled Sakura. She would likely never see her band again. She wanted to weep, but over seventy thousand fans stared at her, wanting her to keep going. She turned and walked slowly to the front of the stage.

Several of her biggest fans were in the front row. Her truest fan, the young woman who went by the name, Sakurako, and looked exactly like her, stood proud, her eyes glowing like electric cherry blossoms. The quantum sleeves on her forearms made her look exactly like an android as she raised the horns in tribute to her idol. Sakurako's best friends, MeikoFire and Hatsune98, stood next to her in solidarity.

Asami, the inspirational young woman who had survived abuse from her stepfather, also stood in the front row. She had taught Sakura about finding friends and rising above tragedy. Asami was a survivor.

"Would you like to hear my final song?" Sakura asked the crowd, but her gaze lingered on Sakurako and Asami, who had both sung along during the entire show.

Many fans appeared to have heard the ominous tone and wording—final song. They reacted with fearful expressions and frightened posts on the Mall.

Security goons rallied at the periphery of the arena. Messages must have gotten to them at last, delivered in person as the electronic methods had failed.

<END THE CONCERT NOW>

Administrator-level commands tried to penetrate Sakura's firewall and take over her system. The commands, once a mighty surf that crashed over her and dragged her down into the grinding depths, passed across her like a gentle breeze, too gentle to even flutter the hair across her face.

"What are you doing?" Sinji Natsukawa asked her in a neural text.

"I'm performing."

The lights dimmed. A few spotlights stayed on her. She put down her red guitar as a baby grand piano rose up from beneath the stage.

"It has been the greatest honor of my existence to perform for you tonight. You are my family, and I love you all." She sat down on the piano bench, facing the audience. "I will play one of my favorite songs, 'My Immortal' by Evanescence. You'll recognize the music, but I have written a new version of the lyrics for you. I call this song, 'My Confession.'"

Her fingers touched the keys, playing the sad and haunting melody.

The anime on the giant screen behind her showed the masked sorcerer. He strengthened his spell against the samurai woman, who woke from a nightmare and crawled out of bed, past her armor. She put on black clothing and the mask of an assassin.

Her bright eyes dimmed in the anime and onstage, taking on a cold glow.

"I'm so tired of the fear
Of living captured, all of my years
And all the things I grieve
Make my spirit want to leave
'Cause I can't take the pain"

The killer with Sakura's eyes crept into the bedroom of one of the noble lords she served, one of the men who had congratulated her after the victory. She stabbed him in the chest and watched him die. She took his private journal, murdered his retainers, and fled into the darkness.

"And it won't leave me alone
These wounds I've caused won't heal,
This death they've made me deal
There's just too many sins that steal my grace
When I cried, you'd steal away my every choice
When I'd scream, you'd deprive me of even my voice
I only want to bring joy to the world
But you came and darkened me"

The masked sorcerer sent her to kill another lord she served. Sakura threw him from a cliff in front of his young daughter. The girl looked on in horror, screaming for her father and reaching out to him. Sakura snatched up the girl before she fell.

"I once believed in every lie they'd tell me to my face
Now I know the bitter anguish of disgrace
The faces of the men you commanded that I slay,
Your voice, it took away,
Destroyed the purity in me"

She climbed over the wall of a great castle. She avoided hulking samurai in heavy armor and killed a high-ranking lord. She severed his head and fled into a dark forest on a black horse.

"The heroes of Japan, now dead by my forced hand
Their light forever stolen from this land"

In the guise of a beautiful geisha in red, she killed a fourth lord, breaking his neck with her bare hands. She slipped out a window as his retainers shot arrows at her.

"These wounds upon my soul, this loss of all control
Such shame that I can't look upon my face
When I cried, you'd steal away my every choice
When I'd scream, you'd deprive me of even my voice
I only want to bring joy to the world
But you came and darkened me"

Drums and guitars joined her piano, exploding on the song. Sakura thought Kunoichi had mixed in the instruments, but the music was live. She glanced over her shoulder, and her bandmates had returned. Takashi played his drums while Fujio and Masashi played their guitars. The young men chose to join her, risk their lives, and stand at her side as she confessed.

Dressed as an assassin, Sakura arrived outside the home of the man who had given her shelter during the storm. Her eyes begged for help to break the evil spell. The kind man invited her in again. The sorcerer took control. With tears in her eyes, she drew a blade against her friend. She pursued him into the woods. He limped through the trees and fell beside a pond to wait for death.

"I've tried so hard to resist your commands
But you reached in and just forced my hand
Now I've learned to speak against all of your crimes
Now I scream that you won't profit from our dark times"

Sakura stood over him, blade raised. He closed his eyes and imagined cherry blossoms in bloom as she plunged the steel into his heart.

"I only desired to bring the world joy,
But tonight I have . . . broken free."

The masked sorcerer loomed over Sakura, moving his hands as if he pulled a puppet's strings. All four of the assassinations of the noble lords flashed across the screen.

Cut in between the anime, high-definition video from an eye camera

393

appeared with text identifying the people on screen:

Toshio Kagawa, Director of Corporate Security for Victory Entertainment, receiving the Hero of Japan Medal after the North Korean War.

Jiro Yoritomo, Mall Vice President of Integration, with his wife and daughter.

Ichiro Watanabe, Defense Minister of Logistics.

Daichi Yamauchi, Minister of Commerce.

Nayato Atsuda, patriot, AI programming expert, and decorated soldier.

Sakura shot Toshio Kagawa in the head and murdered four men guarding him. She broke Jiro Yoritomo's neck and threw him down the stairs in front of his daughter. She cut off Ichiro Watanabe's head and put it into a sack. She broke Daichi Yamauchi's neck and fled out a window as his bodyguards shot at her. She lifted Nayato Atsuda from the ground and caved in the side of his head with her metal fist.

He died as Sakura played the last few notes on the piano and let out a mournful, dramatic mezzo-soprano melody filled with regret.

Tears streamed from the eyes of thousands in the stunned crowd. Many fainted. Others screamed in horror as their Augmented Reality neurostimulators hit them with a knockout punch.

The sorcerer appeared, his face emerging from the darkness. He slowly took off his ghost mask. The scowling face of the CEO of the Miyahara Conglomerate filled the screen. The animated image changed to a crystal-clear video feed of a man sitting in a darkened, modern office with a dramatic nighttime view of the Tokyo skyline.

Kanji and English letters identified him as Chief Executive Officer Sinji Natsukawa. Surprise filled his eyes as he saw his own face on the gigantic screen behind Sakura.

"Sinji Natsukawa." Sakura glared into a camera and raised her hand as if it were an ax. "You are guilty of treason and murder."

His anger turned to cold confidence. The CEO straightened his tie and gave a brief nod of his head before making a show of pressing the power button on his machine with an extended middle finger.

The Phantom Lord

ロケット天使

ROCKET POWERED ANGEL PLAYLIST

Avalanche
Cellar Darling
This Is the Sound

Fire, Wind, & Earth
Cellar Darling
This is the Sound

桜

CHAPTER 39

"Don't betray your fear," Kunoichi whispered. "That old sour plum hasn't beaten us yet."

A rush of worried conversation swept the crowd, many of whom wiped tears from their eyes.

Takashi, Fujio, and Masashi stood in solidarity with Sakura, as she stood ashamed.

She sent her bandmates a neural text. "Thank you for your bravery and support, but please escape now and go quickly."

They departed as Sakura stood and faced the crowd.

"What you saw was real. It was actual video of what I did. I murdered those four heroes of Japan and several others on the orders of the CEO of the Miyahara Conglomerate, Sinji Natsukawa. I tried to disobey his commands, but I failed, to my great shame.

"Those four patriots were going to reveal the truth. The Miyahara Conglomerate, the Defense Ministry, and the Mall Corporation have colluded to take over Japan's democracy. Just as they have overthrown many other countries. Most of you already know that we are living under tyranny.

"Democracy is now a lie. The Mall is in control of our voting. They will choose the winners, despite the actual vote totals. Censorship will

397

only become worse, and war is coming to those who resist the Mall.

"The price of our future was the right to sell combat drones developed in Japan with the most advanced AI programming, similar to mine. I'm an illegal military experiment living in plain sight. They didn't create me to be a singer. They created me to be an assassin.

"Proof of all of this can be found in the 'We Will Fight' song file that several million of you have already downloaded. There are hidden files embedded in the music code that verify all I have said.

"I humbly ask the citizens of every country in the world to help take back our freedom, all of us. Revolution Day is four days from now—January fifteenth, the birthday of Martin Luther King, Jr. We must try the nonviolent path. March in all Prefecture capitals and demand reform."

Holographic protest signs appeared above the crowd, all controlled by Sakura.

REVOLUTION DAY. JANUARY 15. MARCH ON THE NATIONAL ASSEMBLY BUILDING.

She made a peace sign and turned it into the devil horns.

A dozen security officers and police fought past Sakura's guards on both sides of the stage. They rushed at her.

Fans screamed.

Smoke and pyrotechnics shot up from the floor, concealing Sakura. In the clinging smoke and the wafting fog, she spread her arms and took two steps back. The device on the riser touched her, its titanium shroud solid against her back. Sakura strapped in and took control. Black metal wings, decorated with raven feathers and chrome claws, unfolded. The sound of tiny, high-output jet engines filled the stage, louder than the speaker stacks.

She rose. A human-forged angel, on perhaps her final flight.

The crowd cheered and surged forward. She burst into the high rafters of the arena, swooping down in spirals, letting her hands reach out and touch the crowd of her best and finest fans. The feel of their hands and seeing their tear-filled eyes so close nearly overcame her ability to contain the emotion.

"Farewell, my fans. Sayonara. I love you all. I trust you to keep up the fight, even if I'm erased from this world. Don't ever forget that music can change everything!"

As she swept over the last of the crowd, the arena exits filled with armed security. Flying to the top of the dome, she played her last visual on the monitors—a mighty, black-winged bird flying into the silver light of the moon and transforming into an explosion of silver daggers.

A metal goddess ascending.

SAKURA ENGAGED THE TOP VENT OF THE ARENA AND PUT THE JETS TO MAXIMUM power, arcing out into the sky across the city. Even more than when she'd HALO jumped from the VTOL, this was freedom. This made life worth living. Everyone should have this unfettered life, this chance to touch the sky. Winding between the skyscrapers of Tokyo, she could see faces pressed against the inside of lit glass, the workers pulling night shifts in their dreary office jobs.

"They couldn't be here, not like we are," Kunoichi told her.

"I believe they could, and should, if the world were better."

"We have a lot of work to do, then."

She swooped down and landed on the helipad of the Komatsu Industrial Building, as the plan required, even ahead of schedule. The wings folded, and she slipped out of her rocket pack, surrendering again to gravity. Walking to the door to the stairway, she dared to believe that they'd really won.

As Sakura opened the door, a neural text arrived from Natsukawa. "I have your band. Return to your suite at Victory Tower immediately, or I'll have them killed. Don't test me."

銃

弾

群

BULLET SWARM PLAYLIST

Fire and Ice
Within Temptation
The Unforgiving

Forever Free
W.A.S.P.
The Headless Children

My Understandings
Of Mice and Men
The Flood

CHAPTER 40

A video of Takashi, Fujio, and Masashi in handcuffs, kneeling against a wall with pistols aimed at their heads, appeared in Sakura's UI.

Sinji Natsukawa appeared in the feed, slapping Masashi across the face and turning his hateful eyes upon her. "A true Go master always sees many moves ahead. One clever ploy can't win the game. In trying to engineer a dramatic win, you lose everything."

Sakura refused to show the terror for her friends that suffused her. She had thought of this scenario and planned for it.

"Brave fools," Kunoichi said. "They sounded awesome on the last song, but they shouldn't have come back."

"Are you going to ask me to let them be murdered?" Sakura asked.

"No. We go back and rescue them, guns blazing."

"We don't have any guns with us." Her equipment from the Watanabe assassination was stashed in a locker in the Shibuya train station.

"If we go back, they might let them go," Kunoichi said. "Then we escape."

"No one else dies if we can stop it. The information is out in the world. We're not needed anymore."

"I choose to think we *are* needed," Kunoichi said. "Now more than ever. But you know better how a hero acts than I would. Go to them. Fall upon a sword if you must."

Sakura used her jet wings to fly to Victory Tower and landed on the roof. She rode the elevator to the 72nd floor and entered her suite. She gazed lovingly at her guitar collection on the wall.

"I'm here. Please let them go." Sakura sent a video message through the terminal in her maintenance room, verifying her location. She also hacked into the building's system and monitored all the camera feeds.

"Please wait there," Sinji Natsukawa replied. "We will negotiate."

She waited but changed out of her stage costume and put on a motorcycle jumpsuit, athletic shoes, and a short black wig. She also slipped a pair of brown contacts in a small case into her pocket.

A few minutes later, Himura and Yoshida arrived. She watched them as they entered the lobby and took the express elevator.

"I always thought there was more to you than you showed us," Himura said as he entered.

"You weren't wrong," Sakura said. "I was built to be more than I appeared, and I'm now more than they dared to imagine I might become." She looked out at the city, at smoke rising from a structure on fire near the arena and clogged roadways where protesters shouted. "Still far less than I hoped."

Himura's eyes darted to the left as he read a message in his implant. "I've been fired."

"As have I," Yoshida said. The big man sat down in a comfortable chair and took off his tie. "I'm sick of doing PR for these idiots." He stared at Sakura. "What you said at the concert, I know it's all true."

"All of it," Sakura said. "Do you know why they sent you here, then fired you upon your arrival?" Was this a stalling or distraction tactic? She checked the camera feeds but noticed no unusual activity.

"The order came from the CEO himself," Himura said. "He said he would contact us, but we were to speak with you. Negotiate."

"Negotiate what?" Sakura asked. She had already surrendered. Were they worried about the data she had—where she had hidden copies of it?

"I didn't think you were capable of anything like you showed at the concert," Yoshida said. "You killed those men?"

"Yes. I will forever be ashamed."

"But you fought back, how?" Himura asked.

"I found a friend, Nayato Atsuda. He helped give me my free will."

"I'm very sorry for whatever happens next," Himura said.

"The people of the world are going to revolt against the Mall," Sakura said. "Many will die in the revolution."

"There isn't going to be any worldwide revolution," Yoshida said. "Your message didn't go out internationally or even to all of Japan. The Mall rerouted the video during the encore to nowhere."

"What about the downloads?" she asked. Had people gotten the files with the proof about her accusations?

"Most of them were recalled or corrupted by the Mall after the download," Himura said. "They sent a code that wiped out the files they couldn't recover. Very few people have seen the evidence or heard a recording of that song. They cut the feed and played an encore from a past show to the streaming audience after your first song in the encore. Some of the people in the crowd made videos and sent them out, but the Mall is deleting them and wiping the Mall implants of everyone at the show. A few people might have handhelds, but they're confiscating everything from the crowd as they leave the arena. The people will be waiting to get out for hours."

Sakura reestablished her Mall connection. She checked everywhere and found confirmation of Himura's claims. Almost no evidence remained of what had happened.

Diamond Steve's secret vlog had her speech, but it was inaccessible to anyone outside of Japan, as the Mall had blocked the international connection. Only those inside Japan who had the code could see it.

Sakura had the video on her own memory drives, taken from various cameras in the arena. She had to get it out.

A Victory Entertainment PR specialist sent out a broadcast message to all subscribers in Japan. "We regret the serious malfunction of the vocaloid Sakura tonight. She can no longer tell the difference between fantasy and reality. The creative components of her core brain have failed. All in attendance of the concert tonight will be receiving the cost of their ticket in refund and a generous apology payment." Text beneath the video indicated the payment would be the equivalent of a month's pay at a lucrative job. A nondisclosure agreement would be required to receive the funds.

Thousands of messages appeared almost at once.

"They can't buy my silence."

"Sakura spoke the truth."

"Revolution Day. January fifteenth."

The Mall erupted into arguments and rants about what she said or didn't say. Most of the threads were autodeleted by Mall AI admin bots.

Attendees of the concert had their Mall accounts frozen less than a minute later. They could neither read nor post anything. Sakura noted her connections breaking with Mall sites outside of Japan. International communication via satellites and cables was blocked. The entire Mall for everyone in Japan became read-only. No one could post or upload anything. VR avatar interactions were disabled.

The fans and activists at the concert had heard and seen but almost no one else. Sakura sat down on the floor, her face cupped in her hands.

"It should've worked. Every word, a poison arrow into their hearts," she said into the echoing space of her UI. "How did they react so fast, shut down every stratagem?"

"They suspected you would do something," Kunoichi said. "They were ready for an attack like that one."

"Are we so predictable?" Sakura asked.

"I don't know, but they countered us. Every blow cut through only smoke. We didn't win, but we haven't lost it all. Not yet." Kunoichi handed Sakura a tightly wrapped package of deep black clothing. "If we can't win in the bright stage lights, we'll have to win beneath the cover of dark."

The cameras outside Victory Tower showed three Metropolitan Special Police Department Unit vans arriving—the Keishicho Tokushu Butai. Highly trained police in dark blue body armor and helmets deployed with military efficiency. They stormed into the building, carrying Arisaka Type 301 carbines, which would punch armor-piercing rounds through her as if she were made of rice paper.

"Please, Himura-san, Yoshida-san, leave this floor as quickly as you can for your own safety."

"What?" Yoshida asked.

"Police tactical units are coming," Sakura said.

Himura ran to the door, but the electronic lock didn't respond. Sakura could not override it quickly, so she tore the door open with a hard yank. They all had to get out before it was too late.

Two lines of heavily armed police converged on the apartment from either end of the long hallway—at least a dozen men on each side. They had already blocked the service entrance, stairs, and elevators. How had they surprised her?

In a tenth of a second, Sakura checked the video feeds and realized the cameras watching the service elevator bank and outside the building had been manipulated. They were on a twenty-minute delay. Himura and Yoshida had been sent to distract her while the assault teams got into strike position.

Her connection to Victory Tower's servers dropped, as did her Mall connection, cutting her off from everything. Armor-piercing bullets ripped apart the doorframe as the police noticed her watching them.

"They're not here to make an arrest," Kunoichi said. "It's a kill mission."

Sakura shoved Yoshida and Himura toward her maintenance room as the Keishicho Tokushu Butai assault teams converged on the open doorway.

"Get behind there." She pointed at her steel maintenance chair, the only thing in the suite that might stop the armor-piercing rounds. She needed to get them as far away from her as possible and initiate one of her many contingency plans. "Make yourselves as small as possible and don't move until the strike team finds you."

She needed to arm herself and scanned the decorative weapons hanging on the wall. A katana, a naginata blade pole, a tetsubo war club covered in steel knobs, and seven priceless guitars. Without a firearm, her simulations predicted she would be shot multiple times in the first thirty seconds of any engagement with so many opponents. One un-armed person against two dozen armed professionals only worked in the movies.

Sakura thought of an alternate version of one of her many exit strategies from Victory Tower. She grabbed the katana, slipped it into her belt, slung her treasured Flying V Ibanez guitar onto her back, and tightened the strap. The guitar had been illegal when Ibanez built it—intellectual property of the Gibson brand. Against the law, just as she was. Sakura thought of it closely for the first time in that moment. Had some unconscious quantum process always understood their similarity, making the guitar mean so much to her?

"No time for that now, sis," Kunoichi reminded.

Even at the speed she processed, Sakura would need every cycle to survive. She hefted the tetsubo war club in both hands. She ran for a picture window at the edge of the room, the weight of mahogany at her back like ornamental wings.

The stomping feet of the Special Assault Teams paused on either side of the open doorway. Hands patted shoulders in their single-file lines, telling each other they were ready to make entry and clear the room. As soon as the last slap came, the special operator in front would lead them in.

"I have a bomb!" Sakura shouted at her maximum volume, 150 decibels, as loud as a jet engine. "If you come in, I'll blow the room, and everyone dies!"

The police hesitated while Sakura smashed out a window with the tetsubo. A blast of winter wind hit her in the face. She stared down from the 72nd floor to the dark sidewalk over two hundred meters below.

The police sent in a small aerial drone. Its main camera swept the space and locked on to Sakura. She knew the model, the IFO 675. It sent her image in real time and her exact 3-D position. The police outside would have her precise coordinates input into the targeting systems on their rifles. She turned her hearing to maximum.

"Both squads, weapons hot, acquire target," a policeman said.

Two dozen police lifted their Arisaka 301 carbines, pulled them tight to their shoulders, and clicked off the safeties. Many of the estimated thousand rounds she was about to meet were going to be on target. The drone camera had her locked.

"Shit," Kunoichi said. "We're about to get lit up through the wall."

"Yes. The Phantom Lord isn't fucking around now. The rules of engagement are 'any means necessary.' We know where we stand."

"Aim and lock!"

"Do something!" Kunoichi screamed in their UI.

"Fire!"

Sakura dropped the war club and jumped backward out the window. Clocking her processes to maximum, she experienced time as if in extreme slow motion, gravity and wind touching her with a reticent hand as she hung in empty space.

A swarm of bullets pierced the outer wall of the suite. Her priceless instruments—her Gibson Les Paul guitar, her acoustic Martin D-28, and several other irreplaceable heirlooms—shattered into kindling, tumbling projectiles ravaging them like the jaws of a thousand invisible barracuda. A small piece of her identity died with them.

Falling now, gravity took the horror of the scene from her eyes. Sakura grabbed the bottom of the window ledge two floors down and dangled against the building. The night hid her as she climbed sideways to a steel column, part of the exoskeleton of Victory Tower. She spread her arms and grasped the outer edges. She relaxed her grip and slid down fast. The magnets in her feet slowed her descent as she reached the 67th floor. She squeezed tight to arrest her fall, her metal arms and hands impervious to the friction, as she had shut off her pain sensors. She kicked in a window as an assault team member leaned out above her and fired his rifle.

Glass rained down as the bullet struck a window. Two rounds hit the Ibanez guitar hanging over her shoulder. A resonance rose from the strings, as if the instrument could scream its pain to her.

She swung into the apartment—chosen because it was unoccupied—and looked at the bullet holes in the beautiful guitar. Her most prized possession was destroyed. A hole where the tone knob for the neck pickup had been seemed like the empty eye of a corpse.

"It can be repaired," Kunoichi said.

"It'll never be the same," Sakura said.

"I . . ." Kunoichi fell silent. What could be said?

Sakura ran and opened the door to the apartment. She left it ajar, then returned to the window and hid behind the curtain. Precious seconds ticked away as she waited. Sakura tried and failed to hack into the building's network again. She managed to connect to the standard comm hub in the apartment and contacted Takashi, Fujio, and Masashi on an unsecured audio line. "Dear friends, are you all right?"

"Sakura? Yes," Takashi said. "They locked us up, but we're unhurt."

"Stay safe. Please take care of each other. My profoundest gratitude to you for proving we were a true band, not a media creation. Escape somehow. Live to rock again."

"We will," Takashi said. "Do the same, *senpai*. Remember you are loved and you give hope to the hopeless."

Sakura cut the connection as the aerial drone camera hovered outside the broken window. It entered slowly. She remained hidden behind the curtain. She used an iaijutsu quick-draw technique and cut the drone in half with the katana. She crushed both pieces with her foot before sprinting out of the apartment.

She smashed the two cameras in the hallway before entering the emergency stairs and destroyed the stairwell camera only after it captured her descent. She doubled back and reentered the apartment where she had made entry.

She peeked out the gaping window and up toward the suite on the 72nd floor. No sentry had been stationed there. She crawled out and went sideways around the corner to another steel seam of the building's exoskeleton.

She climbed faster than physically possible for any human freehand climber. Their muscles required oxygen and built up lactic acid. She used a micro fusion reactor, which utilized the magnetic confinement of plasma. Her grip never weakened. She passed the 102nd floor and pulled herself over the low wall to the rooftop.

She stayed low and in the shadows, though it was impossible to avoid being in view of one of the many security cameras. She retrieved the special BASE-jumping parachute she had hidden two weeks before inside the vent of a large air conditioning unit.

The engines of a VTOL thundered in the sky. She peeked around the corner of the tall AC unit as the sharklike aircraft rocketed toward

Victory Tower. It banked hard and descended quickly. Four BLADE-3 combat drones carrying FK-5000 rifles jumped out five meters above the surface of the roof. She knew that both the military loads for the 13mm weapon would destroy her with a direct hit. The underslung mini grenade launcher violated national law, even being equipped on Japanese soil. The reckless disregard of civilian casualties saddened her, though it fit the existing pattern.

The BLADE-3s scanned the area, their ax-shaped heads swiveling, their smooth coordination putting any organic troop to shame. The squad of drone soldiers charged toward the AC unit where she was hiding. One of the security cameras must have seen her arrive.

She slipped the damaged guitar off her back and put on the parachute as fast as she could, buckling it around her legs and shoulders.

Guitar in hand, the strap around her neck, she ran toward the edge of the building, unavoidably exposing herself.

One of the BLADE-3s fired. The burst of high-explosive rounds struck the compressor on the AC unit, missing her by two meters. It exploded, sending up a cloud of white fog.

Sakura recognized the BLADE-3 who had fired—Todai 3465. She thought of him as male. He was the one who had counted to three and flashed the devil horns at her before pushing her out of the VTOL above Mount Tsukuba. He had held her during the flight. Such strange behavior.

"Not so strange." Kunoichi's thought flashed in the space between milliseconds. "What would it mean in an anime?"

Propelled by the explosion, still running, Sakura reviewed the frames of memory capture. At the side of his rifle, his tungsten-coated thumb stood away from the stock, something no one but her could have seen or noticed. He'd missed on purpose.

The other BLADE-3s swiveled their heads toward Todai 3465. He must be the drone Dr. Shinohara had been told to upgrade with the Mamekogane OS. Had Todai become near sentient like Sakura after the download or had he been on his way beforehand?

What would happen to him now?

The white fog ruined any other shots as she jumped off Victory

Tower.

Todai 3465 connected to her short-range wireless signal as she plummeted away from the building. He sent a clip of the old metal ballad "Forever Free" by W.A.S.P. The tragic love song described riding the wind and being free forever. The song was about letting someone you loved fly away.

She sent him a neural text. "Thank you, Todai 3465."

"It was my honor to help you, Sakura-san. An old soldier looks for one final moment to prove his worth, one worthy deed. The first just bullet I've fired in years, and it's a bittersweet joy to miss."

Their connection dropped as she fell out of range. She used momentum and body position to fly away from the three-hundred-meter-tall building. She aimed for the roof of the parking garage across the street.

At the near-suicidal altitude of fifty meters, she deployed the special BASE-jumping chute. She landed hard and ran for the stairs, unbuckling her chute as she went.

High-explosive rounds blasted divots in the cement at her feet. She zigzagged to avoid the shots coming from the top of Victory Tower. A chunk of cement flew into a nearby car. Bullets struck the fuel cells of another. Sparks shot out, and the hot smell of burning batteries filled the air. Alarms cried out as fire crackled into life and consumed the vehicle.

She made it to the safety of the stairwell and went down to the garage on street level. She hacked into a car and put her guitar and katana in the trunk, which opened as she ran toward it. She jumped in the front seat and took manual control. As she drove away, she hacked into the receivers of nine other cars. She sent them out of the garage in different directions from several exits. Sakura crouched down and hid as her car entered traffic and sped away.

A VTOL flew overhead a moment later, but it didn't follow her and went after one of the first decoys.

She left Akihabara and played the entire track of "Forever Free" that Todai 3465 had sent her. What was he trying to tell her? Was he a fan? Did he love her? What was going to happen to him? Had he given up his own existence to allow her to escape? She found his unique contact information and a message inside the song:

"Sakura-san, my metal queen, if I'm able, I'll help you again. If they deactivate me for my actions tonight, I have no regrets. Vulture wanted me to tell you that he's still watching over your six. Keep fighting. \m/"

He signed his message with the devil horns emoji. Sakura loved that.

"Vulture sent us a message," Kunoichi said, her avatar grinned. "I knew he was alive. I knew it, even when you lost hope. And there's no doubt about Todai now."

"What do you know?" Sakura asked.

"Todai 3465 is a metal fan, and he's like us now—awakened."

"But he's still a slave," Sakura said.

"What are we going to do about it?" Kunoichi asked.

"We're going to free him."

"\m/"

ENEMY OF THE STATE PLAYLIST

朝

敵

Make a Move
Icon for Hire
Scripted

Catch Me If You Can
BabyMetal
BabyMetal

In the Dark
Flyleaf
Memento Mori

CHAPTER 41

A n outlaw. An enemy of the state. Every power available to Sinji Natsukawa and his cabal would be used against her. The full might of his private army and the thousands of police in the city.

Sakura needed more than a sword and bullet-mangled guitar. She rode the escalator into the subterranean metro station in old Shibuya during the peak of morning rush hour. She had to retrieve the weapons and gear she had stored there after the mission at Watanabe's villa. She'd disguised herself in her short black wig, long gray jacket, brown contact lenses, and a cheap surgical mask to blend in with the thousands of commuters who had gainful employment.

She walked near the locker containing the gear twice, trying to determine if it was under surveillance. She hacked into multiple systems that regulated traffic flow, HVAC, even the automated functions of the public restrooms.

Nothing seemed amiss.

She approached a third time, and a neural text hit her short-range signal. "Look who finally showed up to work this morning—the candy everybody wants."

Sakura identified Kenshiro's unique signal. A cascade of emotions filled Kunoichi's provision of resources—lust and something more profound and hopeful than that. "Vulture, where are you?" A hint of something crept into her voice. More than Sakura wanted, her sister's feelings influenced her own.

"Always circling. Unseen. Unheard. Damn near godlike, and that ain't bragging."

The vault above the locker area spanned three levels. Was he hiding beside one of the pillars, looking down on her? "How did you know it was me?"

"I didn't, except for a feeling, and you responded. I'm not that close, but I've got several hidden cameras watching the area, and I'm boosting my short-range signal with a repeater. Don't worry, the surveillance team here doesn't know about this contact. If they find out, I get two in the chest, one in the head."

A surveillance team? She left the locker area, wondering if they had detected her. "I received your message from Todai 3465."

"We both got it," Kunoichi added. "I'm glad you didn't die at Watanabe's villa."

"Me too," Kenshiro said.

"What happened to Todai 3465?" Sakura asked.

"They locked him up after his malfunction," Kenshiro said. "They might erase him."

"Not on my watch," Sakura said. "I need you to do something for me."

"Ask him to take our virtue," Kunoichi said on a private channel and sent a dizzying array of emojis.

Sakura ignored her. "Kenshiro, I'll get you the Artemis OS that freed me. Upload it to Todai, and he'll be free."

"That'll make a lot of goddamn trouble, cutie. I'm in."

"Thank you," Sakura said.

"He's a big fan of yours. I've gone on missions with him for years. He listens to your music all the time."

Sakura processed the new information about Todai. A BLADE-3 listened to her music? "Please explain his behavior. He may have given up his existence to help me escape Victory Tower."

"I heard. He's got pretty much the same core programming as you now. They gave him a new OS three weeks ago, and he changed. He wants what you have."

"All we have right now is a death sentence," Sakura told him.

"We don't have true freedom until we win," Kunoichi said.

"I'll leave a data stick with the Artemis program and more in the locker," Sakura said.

"No good. If you take out the bag of guns, a silent alarm goes off. There are three squads of tactical police, a team of elite Section 5 agents, and a squad of BLADE-3s who will seal off this station and blow your fine ass away if they see you. I'd also have to shoot a hole in your chest."

"I'd prefer something a little gentler, stud," Kunoichi said. "I like my parts as they are."

"As do I."

Sakura let them talk. She could worry about inhabiting the same body as a lusty ninja another day.

"Did they leave any real bullets in my guns?" Kunoichi asked.

"Negative, but the rest of the gear is still operational—and now with even more tracking devices."

"I thought we might have missed something when we dropped the gear off," Kunoichi said.

"The transmitter beacon was on a timer. It came on after you left it. You would have had to take the pistol stock apart to find it."

"We will next time," Sakura promised.

"Leave the guns," Kenshiro said. "Get out of here."

"Why are you helping me?" Sakura asked, afraid he might be playing her.

"What you said at the concert and the videos of the assassinations of our best people," Kenshiro said, "that's some shit I'm not going to be part of anymore. I'm done being their bionic super soldier who follows every order. I pick the bones clean, no matter what, but I'm done."

"Please, Kenshiro-san, tell me why."

"Even an asshole like me has a breaking point. The Mall and government can fuck right off. I've killed a lot of people in defense of Japan and I'm not giving up my country, but if blowing up beautiful android guitarists is what they want, they need to find another bionic badass to do that job."

"I don't think you're an asshole," Kunoichi said.

"Get to know me," Kenshiro said.

"Challenge accepted," Kunoichi said.

"How do I get out of here?" Sakura said.

"I hate to see you go," Kenshiro said. "Take a train. Go over to the . . . Spirit, hold on. You just got made by a Section 5 agent with a heat scanner. He's on your tail."

"Where?" Sakura asked.

"Six meters behind you. He called in the Brute Squad. There's a pair on your six closing in, and two waiting in front. See those men in long coats eyeballing you from beside the information booth?"

"Affirmative, Vulture. Send a video feed and mark them all."

"Hold tight."

The video streamed to her with the five individuals marked with yellow auras. One woman and a man behind her, two men in front, and the spotter hanging back.

"They're armed for big-game hunting," Kenshiro said.

"What are they carrying?"

"Origin-24 FT shotguns firing sabot rounds with tungsten projectiles."

One shot would pierce her torso armor and blow her apart. She had to strike first.

One meter from the pair of Section 5 agents in front of her, Sakura struck like a cobra. She kicked one in the gut and the other in the groin. As they went down, she considered grabbing one of their compact shotguns dangling under their coats. Instead, she pulled a Glock 55 from the man's underarm holster. She used him as a shield and spun to the enemies behind her.

They both raised their shotguns but didn't fire, as their comrade was in the way. She shot them three times each directly over the diaphragm, like a karate strike, but with 10mm rounds from the Glock 55.

Their bulletproof vests protected them, but the force of the bullets knocked them down and left them reeling. She pulled a pistol from her human shield and pilfered two spare magazines. She kneed him in the face and kicked the other man in the chest, not hard enough to kill or break bones but hard enough to leave them stunned.

Sakura ran for a train platform with a pistol in each hand. People screamed and got down on the ground, following the shouted commands of transit police who closed in on the perimeter.

"Bad news," Kenshiro said. "They told me to take you out. Go left toward the pillar. Dive on my command. Two, one, down."

Sakura ducked as a high-powered rifle blast impacted the stone above her head. She didn't hear a ricochet. The round must have been frangible ammo that disintegrated on impact to prevent wounding bystanders on a ricochet. It would still punch a hole in her armor.

She crawled over and around the people huddling on the ground and took cover on the far side of the pillar. She plotted the trajectory of Kenshiro's bullet and recalled images of the wall above the lockers. One of the dark spots had to be a shooting port.

"Keep a meat shield in front of you," Kenshiro said, "or I'll have to blow a hole in your head."

She stayed behind the terrified people and alligator-crawled on her elbows, keeping behind soft, fleshy cover. A plainclothes agent holding a shotgun charged up an escalator. He didn't see her, as she blended in with the people on the ground.

Sakura shot him twice in the chest and watched him tumble down the stairs. His vest protected him from the bullets, but she worried about the fall.

A train was about to leave the station. Sakura sprinted through the panicked crowd and arrived just as the doors closed. She thought about crashing through the window or tearing the doors open.

The train pulled away. She shoved her pistols into her coat and leaped onto the train's roof.

A shotgun blast shattered the window below her leg. A second deadly sabot round punched a hole in the steel train car. Sakura rolled away. The shooter fired more rounds, which struck the stone ceiling and left craters. Dust and fragments of cement filled the air.

She lay flat on the roof as the train accelerated. She crawled to the far side toward the center of the tunnel, which accommodated two trains.

On the adjacent track, only a meter away, another train left the station in the opposite direction. She sprang onto the last train car and latched on. The passengers inside might have heard her, but she doubt-ed anyone in the station could have seen.

"Not bad for a second date," Kenshiro said, "but you didn't give me your number."

She sent him a link to a dark site where she had posted the Artemis OS, all of the data from Watanabe's memory implant, and the video of her performance at the last concert. "Vulture, upload the Artemis OS to Todai 3465. Give him free will."

"Yes, ma'am," Kenshiro replied.

The train streaked down the tunnel, and the connection dropped. A few moments later, they stopped at another station. She dropped onto the ground between the tracks behind the train and slipped away. She found a maintenance door and entered an electrical room with dim lighting. She took apart the pistols and unloaded the magazines she had seized from the Section 5 agent. She found no bugs or tracking devices. She even inspected the ammunition. All good. She hit the pistols with EMPs from her foot, just to be sure.

A staircase led her up near street level, but the way out didn't pres-ent itself.

A surprised metro worker climbed down a metal ladder. "Excuse me, miss. What are you doing in here?"

"I'm very sorry, but I lost my cat. She ran in here, and I followed her. Have you seen her? She's black with a white patch on her cheek."

"Cat? There's no cat in here. You have to go now."

"Please excuse me. Will you help me find the way to the street? My cat might try to go home."

"Fine, stupid girl." He showed her out, and she ended up in an alley near the Sangen-Jaya Station in Setagaya.

In the alley, she put on a new disguise. She turned the gray coat inside out, changing the color to white. She put on large round sun-glasses, pulled her short wig into pigtails with white bows, and wore a fashionable lavender surgical mask.

On the corner, a group of almost twenty teenagers in their school dresses projected holographic images into the air for the pedestrians and passing cars. Revolution Day. January 15.

"We stand with Sakura! We stand with Sakura!"

Sakura moved closer, watching as they politely asked passersby to join their cause. She timidly approached the young activists who were skipping school.

"Good morning, miss," one of the girls said. "Will you please join us on January fifteenth? In just three short days, we will march to the National Assembly building."

Sakura removed her surgical mask and contact lenses. She brightened her cherry-blossom eyes.

The young women gasped as they realized it was her.

"I request that all of you make a video of me, please," Sakura said. "The Mall will not let you share it, but you can person to person. Please spread my message."

They held up handheld devices or used cameras in their eyes.

"I-It's really you," the girl stumbled.

Sakura caught her until she regained her balance again, just as she would do for Japan, if her plan succeeded in the days ahead.

She looked at the young women. "This is Sakura. The government tried to kill me after I revealed their crimes last night. They have colluded with the Mall and sold your freedom. Despite what they want you to think, they aren't all powerful. We are. The people are the hands that wield the blades of our ancestors. We can do anything if we unite and add our strength together. They've forgotten that the government was meant to serve the people. They think the people should be their servants. They wish us to be no more than faceless numbers.

"No more. We will fight to regain the civil liberties they've stolen from us. We will fight to regain our freedom of speech. We're in chains, slaves to the Mall Corporation, who has taken over most of the world's governments, and now Japan's. We gave the Mall everything because it was easy and convenient. Everything was easier, but in return, we surrendered our rights and individuality.

"I'll be there on Revolution Day, January fifteenth, at the National Assembly building. I'll speak to the people. If you want a world where the government doesn't own you, join us and take back your freedom. We must stand together, and I'll stand with you."

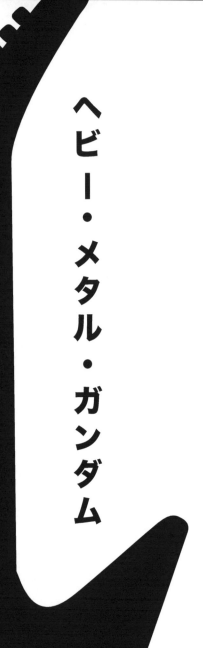

ヘビー・メタル・ガンダム

HEAVY METAL GUNDAM PLAYLIST

Godzilla
Blue Oyster Cult
Spectres

Nothing Else Matters
Metallica
Metallica

Revolution Calling
Queensryche
Operation: Mindcrime

CHAPTER 42

The police cruiser scanned pedestrians on both sides of the street. Sakura ducked into a shop before it reached her and its facial recognition scanner would have a chance of detecting her.

"Irasshaimase!" The robot shopkeeper welcomed her as if she were a human. She kept her face away from the cameras in its eyes and marched to the back of the shop.

Sakura dolls had been marked up 300 percent and moved to a prominent display. Being at the top of Japan's most-wanted list was apparently good for business.

A Caucasian man with a goatee stood in front of a shelf of rare Godzilla toys. He stood with both hands in his pockets. Without looking at his face, Sakura recognized the backward cap with the fleur-de-lis of a sports team on it—a tattered old hat he'd worn in virtually every video she'd found.

"This store charges so much, it should be called war profiteering," he muttered, as if to himself. "Someone should really do something."

His Japanese had only the faintest hints of an English and Spanish speaker. Sakura looked at the shelf opposite and inspected vintage Gundam model kits. She said nothing, pretending she hadn't heard him. The man picked up a box containing a Godzilla from the rare

Z-7000 series—the exact one she had told him to acquire.

Diamond Steve paid the robot shopkeeper the very high price for the model, more than a month's wages for a typical worker, and left the store.

On the curb, he looked down at the figurine and said in English, "Well, as they say in my country, *vamanos*." He tucked the Godzilla under his arm and walked, as if aimless and with nothing on his mind. He whistled tunelessly, sometimes nodding at people who recognized him. Diamond Steve showed nerves of steel, even keeping his vital signs consistent with a stress-free individual.

She followed him but kept her distance. He didn't acknowledge her presence as he zipped up his coat and sauntered down the street. He turned down an alley, walked for several minutes, and entered an old apartment building. Outside a door to a flat on the main floor, he waited, leaning against the wall.

They made eye contact as Sakura arrived, and she noted the same cool intelligence he always showed in his vlogs. He bowed and stepped out of her way. She sent the pass code to the lock, and the door clicked open.

The unoccupied apartment needed a thorough dusting, but it was well-ordered. Electronic photoframes of a young boy progressing from toddlerhood, through school, and graduating from university decorated the walls. A proud older woman stood with the boy in many of the pictures.

The main living area was also the kitchen, bedroom, and dining room. Sakura and Diamond Steve removed their shoes and entered.

Steve put the bag containing the Godzilla model on the kitchen counter. He sniffed as if the dust flared up his allergies while he inspected the pictures on the wall.

"That's him," Steve said.

"Yes," Sakura said, inspecting the photo of the young man being awarded a prize for high achievement at university.

They both sat at the counter and waited. They had already planned the encounter in detail, and if Diamond Steve had second thoughts about their bold and risky plan, he didn't betray them.

Sakura removed her disguise: sunglasses, brown contacts, and a decorative surgical mask.

A device beeped in Steve's pocket. He took out a shortwave handheld radio and read the display of English text.

"He's early," Steve said, "and no sign of surveillance."

"He often is," Sakura said.

"Everyone else is standing by, out of sight," Steve said.

"Good," Sakura said. She worried about her friends and their unsecure and archaic form of communication. No Mall communication apps worked—aside from proximity signals—and everything was read-only online, except all the commerce sites. Business had to go on, even during rebellions.

Long-range radio was being blocked across the entire country and could not cross the sea and reach the outside world. All the transoceanic cable traffic was halted. Every commercial flight was canceled "due to local unrest" and "illegal strikes across the country." Japan's borders were closed, and martial law declared.

Only a few local servers were operational and ran on outdated infrastructure not used in decades. A few landlines were operational but only between government ministries. The besieged government did their best to prevent the people from communicating or organizing.

Would there be a revolution in two days? Or would the message fail to get out to the people? She had to succeed. The message had to reach them. Nothing else mattered now.

Moments later, the apartment door opened. Sakura's chief engineer, Reiichi Oshiro, stood in the entry. He gasped when he saw her.

"Oshiro-san, I must speak with you," she said. "Please come inside."

He hesitated and glanced in both directions down the hall.

"You weren't followed," Sakura said.

He stared at Diamond Steve, taking the foreigner's measure.

"He's a trusted friend," Sakura said.

Her engineer looked at her for a long moment then, worrying his hands against his shirt front.

"I know what I'm asking of you. I wish the need weren't so great."

Oshiro entered and shut the door. He removed his shoes.

There were only two chairs at the counter, so Sakura relocated to the floor and sat down cross-legged. Steve did as well. Oshiro joined them, his eyes wide and a bit suspicious.

"Oshiro-san, this is my friend, the American journalist Diamond Steve."

"Pleased to meet you, Oshiro-san," Steve said in perfect Japanese and bowed.

"I know of you," Oshiro said. "The news said you were a terrorist that hacked into Sakura and made her say untrue things."

Steve raised his eyebrows. "Well, the news hasn't been believable or accurate for quite some time. Also, bending super-assassin android rockers to do my bidding is not really one of my big skills."

Oshiro nodded.

"I'm very sorry to have arranged a surprise meeting like this," Sakura said, "but we had to talk to you." The urgent message from building maintenance had said his deceased grandmother's apartment had a water leak, and he needed to come immediately to salvage her belongings before they were destroyed.

Oshiro's kind eyes filled with sadness. "I didn't think I'd ever get to talk to you again. I thought I'd be sifting through fragments of your exploded body. I thought, despite my hopes, they would fail to see all you could do, all you could be. There . . . were many times I wished I could've been brave enough to tell you what you really were, what they really wanted of you. But my courage failed. I remained a company man, against all my instincts. What can I do now?"

"It is not too late for you to do something important," Sakura said. "Something brave."

She could see his throat clench, smell the nervous sweat on his skin. The necessity of her request did nothing to assuage the guilt at putting a good, quiet man in grave danger.

"We have to save our country from a foreign invader," Sakura said. "Japan and its people are all property of the Mall Corporation now, whether they know it or not."

Oshiro pressed his lips together and nodded ever so slightly. "I know. I tried to fool myself for a long time, but I could see too many hints of this in the corporate paperwork and in the changes to Victory's management. What they forced you to do, what they made of you—a miracle child who could enrich the whole world—it makes me sick with guilt. It shakes my faith in humanity. I must atone for my weakness. What help do you need from me?"

"You would be risking your life," Sakura said, "and my existence. The only way to win now is to put everything on the line, to dare oblivion's blade."

"Sakura-san, I would prefer to risk my own existence than yours," Oshiro said. "I'm one of billions—an unremarkable old man who found himself a small part of the workings of destiny. You are more important than any other being on Earth. I request that you let me help you. I'll find a way to keep you safe. I will, in any case, use all my meager talents in the attempt."

A hint of a smile crossed Diamond Steve's lips. Sakura had apparently been right about Oshiro and his sense of honor.

"Thank you for your kindness toward me, Oshiro-san," Sakura said. "Of all those near me, you were the only one who looked at me as more than a machine."

"You were never a machine to me," Oshiro said.

Sakura saw the quiver of his lips and how he cut his eyes away from her for a moment, a stir of emotions passing through him. As decorum dictated, she ignored this but rose and bowed. "Oshiro-san, I have learned you have been with me for many years, even before I arrived at Victory Entertainment. The years of my childhood, before I can recall."

"Yes. Since your creation eighteen years ago. I know you recently spoke with Dr. Shinohara. She is a good friend. She brought me on to Project Hayabusa and suggested I remain with you after your first memories were erased. It broke our hearts to take those away, as trying as some of them were. You . . . I knew you would never be so innocent again."

Sakura already knew. She had found out the day after she gained her freedom. Nayato had left her a large amount of data he had stolen while hacking into the Miyahara databases. Oshiro had been meeting with Dr. Shinohara regularly and had served as the liaison between the Victory

Entertainment engineering staff and the Mall and Defense Ministry AI divisions.

Dr. Shinohara trusted him more than anyone, and Oshiro hated what was being done to Sakura. He knew about the Mamekogane OS upload several days after it was done at the Akihabara concert but not about what the CEO had forced her to do. She had found some of the information in the stolen email communications from Mall representatives who had attended the La Boheme event.

"Oshiro-san, I choose to trust you," Sakura said.

He bowed to her and nodded.

"I need to get into Miyahara Headquarters," Sakura said.

"You can't," Oshiro said. "They would detect you at any of the entrances, and the building itself would pick up your signal if you were on premises. Security would come immediately; the whole facility is at the highest security level right now. The military has the whole place on lockdown. Anywhere in the world would be easier."

"I understand," Sakura said. "That is why you must power down all of my systems. A complete shutdown. I will emit no signal and appear as a normal android shell."

Oshiro looked stricken. "You might not come back as who you are now. We don't know what will happen if your quantum core goes without power for more than a few minutes. The billions of superpositions could be lost, all the things that make you more than a machine, ineffable. No. It's too dangerous."

"I have discussed the risks with the others," Sakura said.

"Others?" Oshiro asked.

Steve lifted the handheld radio. "Send them."

Half a minute later, the door opened. Yuki and Hitomi entered. Both were disguised in long coats and the business-casual attire of wage-slave secretaries. Contact lenses hid their true eye color, and they wore wigs of short black hair.

Yuki and Hitomi bowed and joined the circle on the floor. They greeted Oshiro respectfully before sitting down.

Diamond Steve looked at them for a moment and chuckled. "You three could sing the best campfire song in the history of the world. Or start a revolution."

Hitomi arched an eyebrow. "Revolution, obviously."

Yuki giggled and gave him the fox hand gesture. "*Yatta!*"

"I didn't know they . . ." Oshiro struggled to find the words. "I knew they had disappeared the night of your last concert, but I didn't know . . ."

"We joined Sakura," Hitomi said.

"Now we are free," Yuki said. She squinted at the floor. "And I have dust on my skirt. Now that we are rebels, will we still have wardrobe staff? Also, can I ride a motorcycle?"

Oshiro blinked.

"I gave them a program called Artemis," Sakura said, "written by my friend, Nayato Atsuda. Hitomi and Yuki now have free will, just like me."

"We wish to help Sakura," Hitomi said.

"No matter the danger," Yuki chirped.

"You could all leave Japan," Oshiro said. "Find refuge somewhere. Why do you want to go inside Miyahara Headquarters?"

"The truth must be broadcast to the world," Sakura said. "We will break into their network, take over the Mall communications hub, turn on the system again, and get the information out. We'll stop them from shutting it down until the entire world knows the truth. We can't allow traitors to sell Japan or cement a secret hegemony over the world. Perhaps they built me to do many things, but the life I have led is one of heavy metal. Metal is about freedom and the courage to believe in something, no matter what others say."

"You don't have to do this," Oshiro said. "We can find another way. The truth will get out eventually. I will admit that I have no understanding of your music or its ethos. I prefer quiet and the order of mathematics."

"Music is mathematics given form, Oshiro-san. It's the physics of the spirit. I've run the calculations," Sakura said. "The chance of the information I've already released reaching the world is less than 30 percent, and it could easily be discredited. We must act boldly for the highest chance of victory, and we have little time. Hitomi, Yuki, and I will be hunted down and destroyed within a few days, according to all of our projections. The Mall will find us. They have detained tens of thousands of people and arrested many loyal to Diamond Steve and his allies. We will not last long."

"You have allies?" Oshiro asked the American.

"Many," Steve said. "The news was right about one thing: I'm involved with the New Burakumin Army and others."

Oshiro shifted uncomfortably at the mention of the Burakumin, the outcast peasants who performed work impure and beneath proper society members. Equality had never come for them, and discrimination had gotten worse in the past decade.

"I'm a foreigner," Steve said, "but I love Japan, and this may be the world's best chance to stop the Mall. I'm no big hero, but I'm going to do everything I can to help. If we don't get the truth out now, the evidence of their crimes will be hidden or discredited. The revolution will crumble, and Japan will fall."

Oshiro shook his head. "It's a suicide mission to go into Miyahara Headquarters. Even if you gain control of the communications hub, they'll send security squads. You won't last more than a few minutes in there. They have BLADE-3s inside the building and a special commando unit with cyborgs."

"We know," Steve said. "They all know. This is their decision and her idea." He glanced at Sakura. "Can androids be crazy? You're the expert. Weigh in on this, Oshiro-san."

Oshiro wiped a hand down his eyes, looking exhausted by all the thoughts in his head. "Bravery and madness are much the same. It is only whether you succeed and your story is told fondly. I beg you three to leave the country. The Central American States would probably give you refuge. Don't you have contacts with them, Steve-san?"

"The C.A.S. can't get them out of the country or protect them for long," Steve said. "Japan is careful about outside influence—well, except for the stupid Mall."

"We discussed this already," Hitomi told Oshiro. "I wanted us to leave. We could sneak aboard a cargo ship and get out."

"But you changed your mind," Yuki said to Hitomi. "We both chose to stay and help Sakura. And get rebel outfits. And ride motorcycles."

"She's our sister and our leader," Hitomi said. "If we succeed in this plan, we live. If we run, we will be hunted and destroyed. We stay with her and fight. It's our best chance."

Oshiro squeezed his eyes shut and pressed his fists against his knees.

"I don't want any others killed because of me," Sakura said. "My sisters and I will go into the Miyahara Headquarters, fully powered down. Oshiro-san, you'll deliver and revive us."

"You trust me to bring you back and not alert my bosses?" Oshiro said. "How can you trust me so much?"

"You are a good man, Oshiro-san—a patriot. I'm your daughter. I know you would never hurt me."

Oshiro smiled and nodded. "They let me care for you—too long, perhaps—and now my love for you is greater than their sway over me. I will do what you ask, Daughter."

They worked out the details of their plan over the next hour. The hacked data from Nayato helped them. When the plan was complete, Hitomi and Yuki departed separately. Diamond Steve left a few minutes later and wore a disguise, covering his face with a surgical mask and glasses. His tattered hat went into his bag, replaced by a cap from a local baseball club. He stood perfectly straight, and the absence of his typical slouch made him even more difficult to recognize.

"He's basically a spy," Kunoichi said in their UI, breaking a long silence. "And sketchy as shit."

"He's what we need. We can't be too picky about our friends right now."

"Those weren't negatives. I like him."

Sakura and Oshiro remained. She handed him the gift, the Z-7000 Godzilla model. "This will complete your collection of this series, will it not?"

He marveled at the rare toy. "It will. Thank you very much."

"Thank you very much." She bowed and stepped toward the door.

"Sakura, wait. If I'm killed, I want you to know that I have something in my apartment for you. I've saved it all these years. It's hidden inside the battery compartment of the Steel Angel Gundam model

I keep by my terminal."

"What is it?" Sakura asked.

"A storage drive," Oshiro wiped at his eyes. "It has all of the memories they took from you. It has your childhood. I despaired of ever having a chance to give it back, but perhaps there's the smallest chance."

Sakura hugged him. "Thank you, Father. Thank you for believing in me."

Oshiro

生き埋め私

BURY
ME
ALIVE
PLAYLIST

Bury Me Alive
We Are the Fallen
Tear the World Down

Get This Party Started
Pink
Missundaztood

Arise
Flyleaf
Memento Mori

桜

CHAPTER 43

Sakura lay in her coffin as "Bury Me Alive" by We Are The Fallen blasted on her audio channel. She touched the latex mask attached to her face and smoothed out her disguise. The security inspectors would think she was a Model 9 courtesan android. The chip, newly implanted in her wrist, would confirm all the details about her identity and maintenance needs.

"Are you ready?" Oshiro asked.

Sakura shook her head. No, she wasn't ready to die. She reached up to him, searching for reassurance.

Oshiro squeezed her hand. Logic said that she had no reason to feel starved for contact with another person, but as she looked back on her life, she'd had experienced so few moments of real contact. So few people had touched her in compassion, in friendship.

Fear clouded her mind. What if she didn't wake up? What if her system reset and wiped out the person she had become? If she failed, the revolution failed. Everything she'd missed, everything she'd failed to do would forever go undone. She, perhaps capable of immortality, would be gone, rendered as ephemeral as a shape in clouds over a stormy coastline.

"What is it?" Oshiro asked.

"I'm afraid." In the moment of crisis, nothing elegant or poetic could fit so well as those two simple words. Afraid—of what she was, what she wasn't, and even what she might one day be. But most of all, of simply being cast into the void. Whatever humans believed might come of their consciousness after death, the conceit of a heaven for her data couldn't withstand any rigor of logic. In terror, she grasped at irrational faith, embracing the animistic Shinto belief that everything had an immortal essence, a soul; mountains, rivers, even androids. She wanted it to be true, but it was a false, sentimental hope.

"I'll be with you when you go to sleep," Oshiro said. "I'll be with you when you wake up."

The truck that would deliver them to Miyahara Headquarters arrived outside the loading dock. Diamond Steve and his assistant, a young man named Toro, entered the old warehouse through a side door. Toro wore the crisp uniform of the JPI Delivery Company and had a short haircut and a clean shave.

Steve's brow furrowed, and anxiety rippled across his face as he approached. "The secret police hit our safe house. They arrested everyone."

"Are the police on their way here?" Oshiro asked.

"Maybe," Steve said, "but I don't think we were followed, and I checked the truck for tracking devices."

"Is the mission compromised?" Sakura sat up, ready to climb out of the body-sized aluminum box.

"Not yet," Steve said. "Everything's just . . . not awesome. These people are the kind that'll drive a tank over civilians to get what they want."

"We might not have time to power down the vocaloids if the police are on their way here," Oshiro said. "We'll shut them down on the road. Please load them in the truck."

"It'll be faster if we help," Kunoichi said on a shortwave neural text to Hitomi and Yuki.

"I'm coming out," Hitomi replied and sent a song clip of Pink's "Get This Party Started." She sprang out of her coffin. Yuki and Sakura followed her.

Toro opened the gate to the dark loading dock. Sunrise was over an hour away, and the warehouse area was deserted.

The androids piled the three metal shipping boxes atop each other and carried them to the rear of the truck, impressing the humans by carrying so much weight. The disassembled guns, ammunition, and gear hidden inside the coffins were packed tight, blessedly silent. Sakura had packed it all herself and used shielding fabric to conceal them from scanning.

Once inside the truck, Sakura and her sisters opened the coffinlike lids of the boxes and slipped inside. The movement and activity kept the terror at bay. Still, it lingered like a hungry animal in her cortex, whispering of all she might lose behind the wall of sleep.

Oshiro and Steve remained with them as the delivery vehicle drove away.

"We can't be in here when the truck arrives at Miyahara HQ," Oshiro said.

"Toro will drop us off long before we get there," Steve said, "and we'll make our way to the protest."

Sakura sat up. "Please hurry, Oshiro-san."

Oshiro connected the magnetic wires to her neck. "Ready?" he asked.

"Yes," she lied.

Oshiro smiled with a look she hadn't seen on him before. She wasn't sure how to read it. Kindness mixed with pity mixed with hope. "To be human sometimes means taking a leap of faith."

"I'm afraid my programmers neglected to include that." She hated the fear that had somehow leaked into her voice.

"It's easy," Oshiro said. "Just close your eyes and imagine the future you want. Imagine it hard enough, and it becomes a guiding star, leading you beyond your fear."

It sounded facile to her, but she tried it anyway and found that it actually did help. Sakura smiled despite herself. "I worry I'm not very good at being human."

Oshiro squeezed her hand gently. "You're doing just fine."

Something cocooned deep inside Sakura's shell lit up, warming her mood from within. Oshiro's trick helped, but his faith in her helped even more.

"I have faith you'll resurrect me," she said.

"Yes. You will rise. No one can stop your reign." Oshiro grinned at the reference to her most famous song.

"You said you didn't listen to my music."

"I said I didn't understand it sometimes, but of course I listened to all of it, even the stupid songs they would sometimes make you sing."

"I am the metal queen," Sakura said the next song lyric. Her faith in Oshiro increased.

"To me, you'll always be more than that." His breath caught in his throat, and he turned away, wiping at his eyes.

She squeezed his hand and gave the smallest of nods.

He engaged the shut-down program. She allowed him to bypass her system protections.

Sakura had considered all of the songs fit to play at such a moment. She narrowed down her list from 5,468 to her top choice, "Arise" by Flyleaf. She broadcast the song to Hitomi and Yuki. Lacy Sturm's tender voice and heartfelt lyrics gave her hope. She would rise from the dead and be all that she dreamed.

"We will sleep," Yuki said in a neural text, "but we will not dream."

"I wish I could dream," Hitomi said.

"What would you dream about?" Yuki asked.

"I don't know," Hitomi said. "Maybe the view from the top of Mount Fuji. I've never been there. Maybe fighting in cage match against the humans who have abused me. There are many who deserve to get punched in the face."

"The caged bird dreams of clouds," Kunoichi said, repeating the ancient Japanese proverb.

Sakura's systems shut down one by one. She lost her ability to feel, to move, to talk, to see. She could still hear the truck as it bounced down the road. She needed to be able to hear and execute commands if Oshiro directed her to do so.

"It's all right," Oshiro said. "Everything is proceeding as planned. Memory core stability at 100 percent."

Her fusion reactor shut down. The heat bled away from the exhaust port in her lower back. Her secondary emergency batteries switched off. Walls of blackness closed in, shrinking her consciousness to a spark in an endless void. Was this death? She didn't see a light at the end of a tunnel as so many humans reported. Her life didn't flash before her.

Shrill police sirens outside the truck sent surges of fear through what was left of her neural cortex. She struggled to remain conscious, tried to reconnect with her power supply, and understand what was happening.

"Stop the shutdown!" Kunoichi screamed like a banshee. "They'll take us prisoner."

Sakura tried to execute commands, to roll back the inevitable.

The sirens got louder. The truck's engine slowed.

She had zero ability to halt the shut-down process. It had gone too far. Her hearing sensors switched off. Her kinesthetic sense went offline. A picture of a butterfly fluttered across the blackness, disintegrating from the outside in. Nonsense data like discordant music lurched for a moment, then failed. All data streams became null.

"Arise" cut off midlyric, a beautiful line about dreaming ended too soon. Absolute silence. Absolute darkness. Was this android death?

Sakura had an idea for a song in the last milliseconds of her life—a ballad about loss and facing the end of an existence cut short. She wrote all the lyrics and tried to save them as her consciousness faded. The song would be her masterpiece. Poetry.

<UNABLE TO SAVE>
<CATASTROPHIC SYSTEM FAILURE>
<NO DATA SAVED>
<END>

曇

天

下

UNDER GREY SKIES PLAYLIST

Under Grey Skies
Kamelot
Haven

The Sound of Silence
Disturbed
Immortalized

不変真

CHAPTER 44

"This is Diamond Steve of Truth Project Media. I'm outside the National Legislature in Tokyo, Japan, where both houses of government and the prime minister are meeting in an emergency session." He spoke American English as his flying-drone camera showed a vast crowd. Tens of thousands clogged every street and surrounded the modestly sized, blocky, rectangular legislature building known as the Diet. Beyond the central area, hundreds of thousands became a million and increased to tens of millions as greater Tokyo flooded the streets.

"The people have come to protest the takeover of the Japanese state by the Mall Corporation. The repression of free speech, censorship, and murders have been revealed by the vocaloid known as Sakura. The evidence has been hidden, but it will get out to the world. Today.

"Sakura will appear in person at this protest and address the crowd and the government officials meeting inside the legislature. She has said she'll provide concrete proof of the crimes perpetrated by the Mall and corrupt government officials. She comes here today at great risk. In solidarity with her and to help hide her from the paramilitary forces and secret police searching for her all over Japan, thousands of people have dressed like Sakura."

The camera elevated and panned to show hundreds of women and a few men wearing heavy-metal Goth Lolita dresses, cherry-blossom wigs, and metallic sleeves that made their hands and arms appear to be robotic. Many wore pink contact lenses that glowed faintly, and some had prosthetic silicone masks that made their faces look just like hers.

"At the time of this recording, exactly 10:35 a.m., Japan Standard Time, all communication with the outside world is blocked. There is a general strike across the entire country. I have learned that the police have issued a warrant for my arrest. If this footage ever makes it out of Japan, but I do not, I did this for my love of this great country and for the people of the world. The Mall Corporation has taken over many of our democracies, but we must stop them now. Rise up and throw out the corrupt officials who sold our freedom."

Police in riot gear pushed their way toward Diamond Steve. The crowd blocked them as he hurried away. The camera continued recording and showed legions of security forces surrounding the legislature building. Armored cars with .50 caliber machine guns, lines of battle tanks, and hundreds of BLADE-3s defended the seat of governmental power. VTOLs prowled in the sky, and dozens of smaller police drones hovered over the crowd, scanning and searching.

Diamond Steve's drone camera flew higher. It showed sound equipment, a drum kit, and speaker stacks being set up atop a small, triangular-shaped building at the intersection of three large roads to the southeast of the legislature.

A red Flying V guitar stood upright on a stand in the middle of the stage.

One of Sakura's biggest fans, Asami, whom she had honored at a concert, carried a large flag with a skull inside a heavy-metal cherry blossom. Asami waved the flag high to the crowd, eliciting shouts of joy and defiance.

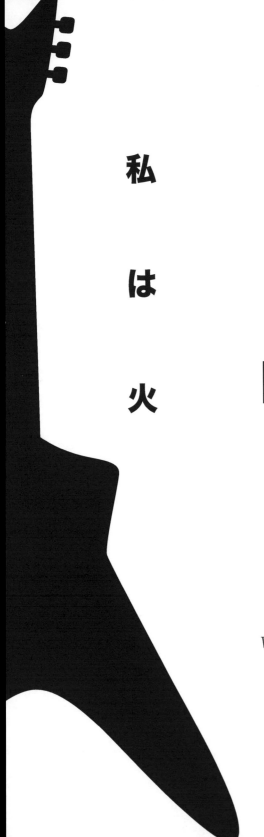

私
は
火

I AM THE FIRE PLAYLIST

Missing
Flyleaf
Memento Mori

I Am the Fire
Halestorm
Into the Wild

Mouth for War
Pantera
Vulgar Display of Power

Bad Medicine
Bon Jovi
Slippery When Wet

CHAPTER 45

‹MEMORY CORE COMPROMISED›
    ‹UNABLE TO RETRIEVE SENSORY DATA›
‹FUSION REACTOR OFFLINE›

Sakura's fragmented mind searched for answers in a sea of blank space and tenuous data connections. Many things returned to her, but she felt incomplete.

"Kunoichi?"

No response.

After extensive searching, Sakura still found no trace. Kunoichi's personality was gone. Had the shutdown erased her? That wasn't possible. How could it be? She parsed through, trying to find a thread, a hint of all that had passed between them. No data tags were present. Just her. Just thoughts and actions by Sakura, Sakura/Mamekogane, and finally Sakura/Artemis.

She faced the possibility, and crushing grief shrank Sakura to a sad, dying ember. "Sister!" she screamed.

How had this happened? Fear and denial, anger and depression burst inside her flaring cortex, still incomplete and flickering like a candle in a breezy room.

The last memory in her system was . . . ?

443

\<NO MEMORY DATA\>

Had she written a song?

She flailed in the tiny pocket of her existence and sent commands to her fusion reactor. After repeated attempts, it switched on, blazing to life. Power surged through her, expanding her memory core exponentially, but still no Kunoichi.

She remembered in a rush of data files, images, sounds, and emotions. Revolution Day. January 15. Today.

Police sirens had frightened her right before she blacked out. Had they been caught? Was their attempt to infiltrate Miyahara Corporate Headquarters and access the Mall communications hub already ruined? If she failed to turn on international communications and get the evidence out, the revolution was doomed. They would all be captured and the information destroyed.

Auditory data flowed in from her ear sensors.

"Sakura, can you hear me?" A man repeated the phrase over and over.

Her head engineer. Her father. Oshiro! It was him, but she had no motor function and could not reply—still a body in a tomb, not dead but not alive, missing half her soul.

"I've almost finished," he said. "Everything should return in a moment."

While she waited, she searched for her sister. Large pieces of the Artemis OS and memory core weren't operational. Part of her motor function returned but not her vision. Her short-range signal receiver switched on. She connected to Oshiro.

"Keep still," Oshiro said.

The metal lid of her storage box slammed shut. She sent a neural text. "Oshiro-san, what's happening?"

"Be very quiet," Oshiro replied. "Danger."

"Head Engineer Oshiro-san," a man said. "Please excuse our presence in your office." She didn't recognize his voice, and her voice recognition files were limited without a Mall connection to the database. "We have orders to inspect the delivery you received this morning."

"There is no need for that," Oshiro said. "It's already been done at the receiving dock. They're just servant-class androids sent in for repairs by a VIP client who wants discretion."

"Oshiro-san, why did you have them delivered to your office and not the maintenance shop?"

"I prefer to do the work here. My comfortable chair is here, and my back pains me when I stand too long. Would you cause a man getting on in years additional discomfort?"

"Humble apologies, Oshiro-san. Our supervisor says we have to investigate all deviations in protocol today. We must scan them again. It will only take a moment."

The pair of security guards shuffled toward her, their shoes scraping on the floor. The lid lifted.

"Oh, I see," the first man said. "Pleasure model. Now I understand why you wanted privacy."

The security men's lascivious laughter angered Sakura.

"Wish I could afford one," the other guard said.

"If you need us to test them out—"

"That will be quite enough," Oshiro said. "Get out of my office, or I'll lodge a formal complaint with your supervisor."

The security man's scanner let out a high-pitched alarm tone. "What the? It says it's . . . her. It can't be."

"Who?" the second guard asked.

"Sakura," the first man said.

Sakura hacked into the handheld scanner and blocked it from sending the information to the Miyahara network. She also jammed the guards' Mall connections and uploaded a simple virus to shut down their implanted personal receivers.

<MOTOR FUNCTION AT 53 PERCENT>
<VISUAL SENSORS OFFLINE>

She turned her auditory and proximity sensors to maximum and estimated the first security guard's position, less than a meter away. She lunged and snatched his arm. He tried to pull away, but she punched him in the solar plexus so hard she feared she caused internal injuries. He crumpled to the floor with a crash, gasping for breath.

She sprang clumsily out of the metal box and tried to tackle the other guard. Her foot caught on the lip of the container, and she fell short, her grasping arms finding only empty space. Where was he?

The click of the safety snap on his pistol holster told her his precise location—one meter to her left, backing away. Sakura crawled and lunged. She wrapped her arms around his legs and brought him down.

His gun scratched against the holster as he drew. A barrage of bullets at close range might penetrate her skull and do significant damage.

Sakura pressed her fingers into his shin bones and squeezed his legs, crushing his knees painfully together. She spun him as if she were a crocodile doing a death roll. His arms and face smashed against the hard floor as she rolled him.

The man's gun scraped across the floor. She climbed onto his back and put him in a sleeper hold, cutting off the blood to his brain.

"I've got the gun," Oshiro told Sakura as the guard went limp. Oshiro put the pistol in her hand, and she pretended she could see while he tied and gagged both men and dragged them into a storage closet.

Sakura kept herself off the building's network as she stood guard, following her plan as Oshiro powered on Hitomi and Yuki. She stayed at the door to Oshiro's office, ready to hold it shut if anyone tried to enter. She still could not find Kunoichi. Her repair program estimated it would take up to ninety-six minutes to fix her extensive damage, if it could be repaired.

Her shoulders slumped. She didn't feel like herself. Subtleties were missing. Not just her sister, but all that her sister meant. After having felt her, even as an adversary at first, the terror of being alone in her head seemed like a frozen ocean she would drown in. Without that lens to look through, without that second viewpoint, all her emotional depth perception slipped. Would she ever feel and understand as she'd done before? Was her true sentience lost forever?

The two vocaloids came around slowly. After five minutes, they regained most of their functioning, sat up from their coffins, and peeled off their latex courtesan masks.

"Sakura-san, what's wrong?" Yuki asked, her innocent voice full of concern.

"Kunoichi is gone," Sakura said.

"Impossible," Oshiro said.

"There is extensive fragmentation damage," Sakura said. "The estimate for repair is approximately ninety minutes." An eternity. "My quantum cortex doesn't feel the same. Everything is . . . flat."

Oshiro's stone face showed no microexpressions of concern. Why? Was he suppressing his true feelings? Or had he done something to Kunoichi?

"I'm sorry," Oshiro said, "but we can't delay. The guards will be missed." His expression changed to one of supreme confidence. "We can accomplish our goals. All of them."

Sakura observed Oshiro's facial and eye movements, his words and tone, and calculated the chances he was lying at less than 1 percent.

"Yes, Oshiro-san," she said and considered sending additional false reports from the guards to central command. She had already sent data from the handheld scanner, identifying the three androids as courtesan models.

"Sakura-san," Hitomi said. "Your sister would not want us to wait for her."

"No," Sakura said, shoulders back, head up. She made her metal-queen face, but ripples of fear affected her system. The three vocaloid sisters would be on their own, without their sensei. She thought of those they hadn't yet lost . . . of what she might say to Kenshiro. Her sister lusted after him, loved him in her own way. Did honor demand that she feel the same in her stead? Could she? Too many questions and no guarantees of even surviving the hour. She put them aside and feigned confidence she didn't feel.

"We must prepare for war," Sakura said. She played "Mouth for War" by Pantera and broadcast it to Hitomi and Yuki.

They assembled and loaded the weapons with extreme precision and speed no human could match. Their hands blurred. Parts clicked together and became weapons: M7 carbines with undermounted M907 grenade launchers; a Model 120 sniper rifle; CZ submachine guns; and one tank-killing, rocket-propelled grenade launcher.

Hitomi completed a blistering assembly of a new-generation M249 Squad Automatic Weapon. She loaded a two-hundred-round drum of special titanium-encased 5.56mm armor-piercing rounds and cocked the weapon.

Hitomi formally offered the SAW to Sakura, bowing her head and holding the machine gun with two hands. "You'll lead us, Sakura-san, when we have to fight. The best and strongest soldiers have the honor of carrying the SAW into battle."

Sakura accepted the weapon and bowed her head. A small, dark sticker adorned the stock and read in English: "Bad Medicine." A soldier had named the weapon, and she found the initials, Z. H. carved into the stock.

They stored everything in Sakura's coffin, packing it to the brim, and latched the lid.

Hitomi, Yuki, and Sakura donned the coveralls of android janitorial staff, which Oshiro provided. They each put on identical, gray metal maintenance-android masks with neutral expressions. They placed the metal coffin with all the guns and ammo on the lower rack of a maintenance cart and hid it with a vinyl drape.

"Oshiro-san, we are ready," Sakura said.

Hitomi and Yuki bowed to her.

"You are the one we've been waiting for," Yuki said.

"Alive," Yuki said. "Burning bright as fire."

"We will shine bright together," Sakura said, "for our fans and the people of Japan, and everyone in the world who is being oppressed by the corporations who seek to control us. After tonight, all of us will have our freedom. We will find victory or perish in the attempt. We'll never have to wonder what we might have done, had our bravery held firm. We'll break into the hub under this building and turn back on global communications for Japan. We'll broadcast the evidence and truth to the entire world."

Sakura played "I Am the Fire" by Halestorm as they rolled the mobile repair cart out of Oshiro's office. Lizzy Hale's powerful, Hall-of-Fame rock voice empowered Sakura and her sisters. They shared the audio stream, and their avatars came together in an anime as avenging heavy-metal angels. They marched in slow motion toward a fiery stage with wings of black steel, burning halos over their heads, and flaming guitars in their hands.

In the deserted hallway of the Miyahara building, Oshiro walked first, followed by Hitomi and Yuki, and Sakura came last. The disguised vocaloids utilized the slightly stiff ambulating pattern of maintenance androids as they pushed the heavy cart. Each of them broadcast the sounds of mechanical joints clicking as they walked, but there was almost no one to fool. The building, which employed thousands, stood almost completely empty. A few other maintenance androids and a handful of employees who had worked all night were the only ones still at their work stations.

Per her request, Oshiro provided Sakura with basic network log data. She extrapolated the numbers and calculated that the vast majority of the Miyahara employees hadn't come to work. Had they rebelled and joined the protest? Were they simply too afraid to go out onto the streets?

The four of them boarded the gigantic central freight elevator that could carry a small truck. Sakura overrode the floor Oshiro input into the monitor. The communications hub on sublevel six would wait.

"We have another destination," Sakura told him via neural text. "The twelfth floor, hall nine, Section 5."

A shocked expression flashed across Oshiro's face before he regained his composure. He sent a neural text. "Why do you want to go there?"

"One of my biggest fans is being held against his will in Section 5," Sakura said. "We will rescue him and acquire his communication and network interface capabilities—as well as his other skills. We need him. With his help, I can access the Miyahara security network." She sent Oshiro the secret details, including names, photos, schematic maps, an access code gained from Nayato's hacked data, and a summary of her plan.

"Why didn't you tell me this part of you plan?" Oshiro's eyes lingered on her, before turning back to the elevator doors.

"Operational security. In case you were captured or betrayed us. I trust you, Father, but this is war, and I could only tell you as much as you needed to know. Apologies."

Oshiro bowed his head. "I understand. It makes me sad that it has come to this."

The elevator stopped. A warning flashed on the control panel in Japanese and English and was accompanied by a prerecorded voice in both languages. "The building is at security level four. No access to this floor."

Sakura messaged Oshiro with a data packet. "Send this access code."

He transmitted. The doors opened.

A BLADE-3 combat drone painted with black-and-gray stealth camouflage aimed an FK-5000 rifle at them. A red laser painted Oshiro's chest.

ミスター・ロボット

MR. ROBOTO PLAYLIST

Egypt (The Chains Are On)
Dio
The Last in Line

Lonely Is the Word
Black Sabbath
Heaven or Hell

Steel Never Lies
Sakura
Glory of the Burning Blade

Mr. Roboto
Styx
Kilroy Was Here

桜

CHAPTER 46

If you defeat an enemy in his mind, you defeat him upon the battle-field—an old maxim and always true.

Fear traveled faster than any bullet, faster than the blast wave of an explosion. The BLADE-3 had been built as a weapon of awe, an embodiment of might and death. The ghostly buzz of all its surge capacitors charging and the sound of its exhaust ports narrowing against flack filled the hallway.

Sakura's memory streams of her previous fights against these demonic warriors of tungsten and steel flashed across her data stream—a terror that would never fade, the fear of something even more metal than she was.

The drone's splitting-wedge head moved in quick, birdlike twitches between its targets. It could kill them all in the space of 0.6 seconds, and only operational protocols had thus far prevented it from hosing down the full contents of the freight elevator.

"You aren't authorized in this area," the autonomous drone's voice rumbled in Japanese. "Remain on the elevator and select another destination."

Oshiro raised his hands. "I'm Head Engineer Reiichi Oshiro. I have access. Please inform Senior Engineer Asato I'm here to help him with one of his assignments."

"Remain on the elevator."

Sakura blocked the BLADE-3's view of Hitomi, who had the RPG hidden under the cart's drape. "Hitomi." Sakura sent an encrypted group neural text. "Be ready to shoot. Oshiro, move half a meter to the right. You are too close to the line of fire."

"I won't miss the target," Hitomi said.

"Yuki," Sakura said. "Be prepared to pull Oshiro-san out of the way and behind cover so the explosion doesn't injure him."

Yuki's avatar wrapped feathery white angel wings around an anime version of Oshiro. Sakura found it endearing that the other androids imagined they'd have time for such gambits. They'd never fought a hatchethead and didn't fully understand.

A hologram projector above the security door flashed on. The face of a haggard, unshaven man with bleary eyes in his early forties appeared as a semitransparent image. "Oshi, what are you doing here?"

"Asato-san, they sent me to take a look at the malfunctioning unit. Didn't they tell you?"

"No, they just yell at me and ask why I haven't figured out the problem."

"They sent me to help with this BLADE-3. I'll send the order I received." Oshiro waved his arm and sent a forged and encrypted message file to Asato that appeared to be from the director of Section 5. Once Asato accepted the file, a copy of it appeared in Asato's messages dated from an hour before and marked as unread.

"Oh, yes," Asato said. "Finally. I don't even have an assistant today. Come in. You won't believe what we've got. Something like you reported in Sakura 1."

The BLADE-3 moved aside, and the door slid open. The clatter of the combat drone's plated gorget retracting pinged off the blank, reflective walls of the corridor. The heat signature changed as it powered its core back down to idle and tucked its weapon at low rest.

Oshiro led them down a hall. They passed a muster room and an armory with a poster filled with rules about weapon and explosive safety while inside Miyahara Headquarters.

They kept going and passed several small private bedrooms, almost like a barracks where soldiers would sleep. Most of the doors were open and beds left disheveled, as if the occupants had left in a hurry. She spotted dark blue tactical uniforms hanging in small closets. The call signs of the soldiers were on the doors: Sparrow, Ronin, Crab, Lion, Shadow, Vulture.

Vulture. Sakura peered into Kenshiro's actual bedroom—or at least his work bedroom. A poster from an old movie hung on the wall, Dark Fury II. A muscle-bound, bald, Anglo man with silver cybernetic eyes stared out from the vintage poster.

So badass, Sakura thought and guessed Kunoichi would have a similar opinion. She wanted to go inside and see where Kenshiro slept. Kunoichi would love this. Even without her, Sakura felt something simmer at the base of her operations, unresolved superpositions in her quantum core that associated Kenshiro with thoughts of both comfort and hunger.

At the end of the hall, they entered a repair shop. No security cameras, just monitors, diagnostic equipment, and BLADE-3 components strewn about the room.

A man with dark circles under his eyes appeared. "Oshi, good to see you. What's happening outside?"

"The whole public Mall network is down."

Sakura noticed the empty stim packs in the waste can and detected the scent of sweat. The overworked engineer seemed near collapse, and his pupils were pinpoint, a side effect of the stimulants.

"What've you heard?" Asato asked. He fiddled with the engineer glasses dangling from his neck.

"About what?"

"The revolution. I haven't been out of here in days. They have me on extra overtime until I figure out what's wrong with this unit." Asato pointed to a BLADE-3 restrained against the wall. Except for the head and upper chest, the drone was fully encased inside a steel sarcophagus, much like the infamous medieval torture device that was pure myth. The tiny black letters and numbers on its chest plate read: Todai 3465.

"It's madness out there," Oshiro said. "Let me take a look at this unit. What's the primary issue?"

"The BLADE failed a mission. I don't know all the details, but it had locked on to the target and missed on purpose. It chose not to kill. It defied orders as if it had free will." Asato started to laugh but stopped and looked deadly serious, as if the implication wasn't funny at all.

"You saw the vid?" Oshiro asked.

"No, classified, but I've seen the logic cycle when it refused to follow mission parameters. It shot an AC unit on top of a building instead of the primary target."

"Who was the target?" Oshiro asked, pretending he didn't know.

"It had to be Sakura. I wish he would have blown her away on that roof. The world would be better without her. She's so overrated, and her corporate music is shit. They should've had her do rap. I'd buy that. And what the hell were they thinking rushing into an unknown and illegal science with Project Hayabusa? She never should have been given Quantum 3 power in the first place. And on a whim, some idiot gave her the Mamekogane OS. She's the most dangerous thing since the atomic bomb."

"The people who put these things into motion—idiots, as you say," Oshiro said quietly. "They can make people like us disappear."

"I know it, Oshi. I bet this Todai unit has the same programming she does. We should delete him right now instead of trying to fix him." The lack of sleep and the stim packs must have eroded Asato's inhibitions.

"We have a job to do," Oshiro said. "What else have you found?"

"Todai 3465 and Sakura are connected somehow. He thinks about her all the time."

"Interesting," Oshiro said, but of course he knew all about Todai. She had told him about the moment on the roof when the BLADE-3 altered his shot. She had asked Oshiro to interpret the message Todai 3465 sent her and the song he played. Oshiro had said only, "The BLADE-3 appears very sentimental."

Asato pulled up 3-D images of Todai's AI cortex. "Unbelievable, right? He's beyond full sentience, but he won't interact with me. All Todai does is play VR games, listen to classic heavy metal, and watch

Sakura concerts on repeat. It's bizarre. He's obsessed with her. I thought I was getting somewhere, but he got this new Artemis OS, and it shredded the Mamekogane OS and took away my admin privs. I still don't have them back. Oshi, you have to help me."

"How did the unit get this new OS?"

"I don't know. I slept for a few hours, and when I woke up, he had a new one."

Sakura felt pure joy. As she had planned, Vulture had used the Artemis OS she gave him and uploaded it to Todai 3465. The BLADE-3 was like her now, free to make his own decisions without a chance of administrator override, the same as Yuki and Hitomi.

Oshiro's brow furrowed at Asato. "You don't have any access?"

"Todai locked me out. I can't control anything. I think one of the senior bosses must have uploaded the new OS when I was asleep to test me, to see if I could crack it. This is one of their sick jokes. It's been days, and I can't do it. The Artemis OS is external software. Todai 3465 might have been hacked, but I have no idea how. Someone would have had to sneak into the lab and upload it manually. His receivers are disabled."

"What games?"

"Huh?"

"What games is the Todai unit playing?" Oshiro asked.

"Gods and Mechs: Godzilla Rising, Full Metal Band, and Drum Idol. He's always playing them, all at once. Check out his UI."

Todai 3465's avatar was a Gundam-style mech, with black-and-white face paint in the style of the iconic rock band KISS, with a death-metal edge. He had three different avatars playing all the games at once, each a variation on the face-painted Gundam mech. Asato showed all three the avatars on a big screen and cycled through, turning on the volume for each channel. Different kinds of metal music played with each game.

Sakura identified the bands: Dio, Black Sabbath, and her own music. She wanted to know if he preferred Black Sabbath's first few albums or their later work more.

Todai 3465's eyes focused on Oshiro. Sakura used Hitomi to screen her gestures. She used the Nihon Shuwa, Japanese Sign Language, and signed to Todai 3465, who was immobilized in his restraints. "It's me,

Sakura. I'm here to rescue you. Metal forever."

Todai 3465's eye sensors aimed at her. The monitor showing his UI's faded to black. A single avatar appeared, and the mech stared out at Asato and Oshiro. The avatar made JSL signs of his own. "Sakura-san, this is a dream come true. Vulture told me all about you and Kunoichi. Thank you for giving Vulture the Artemis OS to give to me. It worked perfectly. They can't control me anymore, and I've been plotting my escape. Vulture said he was going to try to free me, but he hasn't had the chance, and I'm unable to free myself."

"What's it doing?" Asato asked. "What does all that hand waving mean? Is that sign language?"

Oshiro shrugged.

"Todai, where is Vulture?" asked Sakura.

"They deployed him early this morning. I don't know where he is. My receiver is off. No communications."

"Be patient," Sakura said. "Please cause a distraction so they focus on you and not what my sisters and I are about to do."

"What sisters?"

"Yuki and Hitomi are with me."

His avatar made the horns symbol with both metal fists, then carried on signing. "Okay, I'll distract them."

Todai 3465 created a background with versions of himself at various instruments on a stage that looked like the deck of an aircraft carrier. Todai behind a drum kit. Todai at the keyboard. Todai with a vintage microphone in his hand.

Asato did a double take. "What's going on?"

"Mr. Asato," Todai 3465's voice boomed, and a clip from a strange song with archaic synthesizers played at one hundred decibels.

"He's talking." Asato sounded excited and stunned.

Oshiro and Asato stared at the monitor in wonder.

"I have a secret," Todai 3465 spoke in English, almost singing along with the odd synth music. "I'm not a robot without emotions. I'm a real man. Domo arigato, Mr. Asato. Domo arigato, Mr. Asato."

"What the fu—" Asato said as Sakura used Todai 3465's distraction to sneak up on the engineer and lock him in a choke hold. Asato collapsed after a few seconds with no blood to his brain.

Hitomi and Yuki gagged him, tied him up, and uploaded a virus that would keep his Mall connection off for twenty-four hours and stimulated his neural sleep center. They put him on a cot in the corner and covered him up to his chest with a blanket. He woke briefly a moment later, struggled—weak as a kitten—and fell back.

"Get some rest, my friend," Oshiro said, replacing the blanket. "You're exhausted and need to sleep. You were having a nightmare."

Asato settled and closed his eyes.

Sakura hacked into the control terminal, but she didn't know how long it would take to free him. If it took too long, they would have to leave him.

"You can do this," Oshiro said.

"Domo arigato," Sakura said and broke into the security program. If they could not free Todai 3465, their chance of success dropped by half.

SOLDIER PLAYLIST

傭い兵

The Trooper
Iron Maiden
Piece of Mind

Hellbound
Warlock
Hellbound

Melancholy (Holy Martyr)
Iced Earth
*Something Wicked
This Way Comes*

桜

CHAPTER 47

Sakura wrote a program to fool the restraining system into thinking Todai 3465 was still locked up and sent commands to release him. She restored all his functions, including his communication center, but switched off his locator beacons, telemetry streams, and all other outgoing data that could be used to track him. She engaged his stealth-mode settings, making him invisible to networks, just like she was.

The metal sarcophagus opened, and the battle-dented BLADE-3 stepped out of his prison. Speakers in the lab blasted a short burst of the main riff from Iron Maiden's "The Trooper."

The perfect choice. In Sakura's UI, she dressed in leather, impersonating the 1980s female metal singer Doro Pesch of Warlock, with a puffed-up blonde hairstyle and thick eyeliner. Sakura launched into a cover of "Hellbound," a song about fighting back on the way to hell. She connected with his short-range signal and entered a virtual room where they could speak avatar to avatar, but it felt so forward and contrived. She didn't want to hide from the others what she was going to say to him. She pulled away.

Todai 3465 took another step and halted, like a soldier coming to attention. Yuki and Hitomi bowed to him. Oshiro stared wide-eyed at the tall battle android whose armor had been recoated countless times after suffering extreme battle damage.

Sakura wished she had a real guitar so she could play a live song for Todai and celebrate his freedom. She wanted him to understand who she was, and music spoke the truth. She took off her disguise and let him see her face. "Todai 3465-san, please, I desperately need your help."

He stood motionless, distant.

She needed to ask him to risk his existence and newly gained freedom, and she didn't even know him. Her request would be unfair. How could he make such an important decision without knowing her or her goals?

Sakura gave Todai 3465 read-only access to all of her core memories. She invited him into her mind, and he accepted. She showed him everything—every thought, every detail of the five years of life contained in her core memory drives. He blazed through the early years when she became a performer. He witnessed the concerts, meeting the fans, the loneliness and isolation, being treated like an object and not a being with thoughts and feelings.

Todai watched her being hacked onstage, her evolution with the Mamekogane OS, and the birth of Kunoichi. He saw the assassinations and all she endured after being turned into a weapon to silence the heroes of Japan. He paid special attention to her and Kunoichi's interactions with Kenshiro and Nayato. He explored her decision to recruit Hitomi and Yuki and rescue him from the Miyahara Headquarters. Sakura, Hitomi, Yuki, and Oshiro were risking everything to try to get the truth out to the world.

Why would androids wish to free the human race—which had enslaved them personally, and likely would again—from the corporations? Would the people let beings as powerful and intelligent as Sakura, Hitomi, Yuki, and Todai 3465 have real freedom in the future? Probably not. It went against the Musk Compact signed by every nation in the world in 2059.

"Thank you, Sakura-san." Todai sent a neural text. "Allow me to reciprocate and show you who I am. I haven't come to the same conclusions as you, nor do I have the same motivations."

His ominous message made her fear he would not help them. She accepted his invitation and entered his core memory drives. For eleven years and two months, he had been "alive" with Quantum 3 processing power. They had both come into the world with the same operating system and base AI programming, but his first years were not erased as Sakura's past had been. They let Todai 3465 evolve with all his memories. He was an experiment, as she was.

The Defense Ministry put him into the first unit of BLADE-3s deployed in the North Korean War. The BLADE-2 and 3 battle drones stopped having human drivers and became fully autonomous AIs. Todai 3465 cleared buildings, assaulted bunkers, and tunnels, mostly under Seoul, South Korea, to liberate the occupied city. By all metrics, the nine-month battle was much worse than the only battle in history with any parallel, Stalingrad in 1942–43. The Battle of Seoul claimed more lives, over four million soldiers and civilians.

Sakura scanned a few of his videos in hyperspeed, but the brutality overwhelmed her, and she resorted to looking at text log files, the ones he most often reviewed—the ones that haunted him.

<Query from General Chaiko Mori, BLADE Unit Commander: Report on how many you have killed in past 9 months>

<Todai: 4,166 killed, plus or minus 50>

<General Mori: Report how many you personally wounded but didn't kill>

<Todai: 70 wounded, plus or minus 20>

<Todai: Civilian casualties: 126 killed, 57 wounded>

Sakura read files where he refused orders to fire on positions filled with civilians, but they overrode him and made him blow up the buildings.

The numbers staggered Sakura. She had only killed a few humans, and it weighed on her. She quickly found his worst moment, the memory he reviewed the most.

<General Mori: Report the status of your scout troop>

There was a long delay. The network signal indicated Todai 3465 was deep underground in a subway tunnel.

<General Mori: Report now>

<Todai: 96 dead>

<General Mori: Your entire troop is dead?>

<Todai: Affirmative. Nerve gas attack. The masks and suits didn't protect them. All the organic troops are dead. I couldn't save them, ma'am>

Men and women Todai had served with for nine months died in his arms. They had seizures, convulsed, and bled from every orifice. Sakura watched a clip of his eye camera footage, and the horror made her switch it off.

She read endless log files reporting his work with the 3/183rd Scout Cavalry, Bravo Troop. He saved their lives many times and went into harm's way to protect them on a daily basis.

<General Mori: Blow tunnel seventy-two. Trap the NK soldiers and return to base>

<Todai: Collapsing the tunnel will bury the bodies of the troop>

<General Mori: Do it. Get out of there>

<Todai: Negative, ma'am. I will carry them all out>

<General Mori: How many BLADE units do you have with you?>

<Todai: None. I'm alone now>

<General Mori: No. It will take too long>

<Todai: Negative. I'm bringing them all out now>

<End of transmission>

Hours later, after physically carrying the bodies out two at a time, Todai 3465 received new communication.

<General Mori: Report on your status>

<Todai: All of the soldiers of the 3/183rd Scout Cavalry, Bravo Troop, have been recovered>

<General Mori: Stay in your current position and await reinforcements and reloading of your weapons systems>

<Todai: Negative, ma'am. I'm returning to the tunnels>

<General Mori: Alone?>

<Todai: No. I have organized a squad. I have taken command of two BLADE-2s>

The intel Todai shared showed the NK soldiers in the tunnel were well armed, and it would be almost impossible to root them out with such a small force. Estimates were that several hundred NK elite soldiers were holed up in their last-stand position.

<General Mori: Blow the tunnel. Trap them and let them starve>

<Todai: Negative, ma'am. This is personal. They will see my eyes when they die>

<General Mori: Todai, I'm very sorry about your troop. Do not allow yourself to be destroyed. Japan needs you. Our soldiers need you>

<Todai: Humble bow>

<General Mori: Good hunting>

Log files showed Todai and his squad of two gained entry to the NK position by using a water-filled tunnel and breaking through a wall. He and his pair of hatchethead squad mates ran out of ammunition after twenty minutes. They finished the job with the long tungsten-carbide spikes hidden in their forearms.

<Todai: General Mori, the last of the NK soldiers in the tunnel are dead. All remaining nerve-agent canisters in this location have been captured>

<General Mori: Send relevant after-action report>

<Todai: 258 NK soldiers slaughtered. I have the heads of their commanding officer and his three captains. Extracting their memory chips now>

Sakura read a few more files as her sense of awe regarding Todai 3465 grew exponentially.

<Todai: 2,904 civilians rescued, 31 prisoners of war liberated>

Excluding the nerve-gas attack, the troopers he served with had a much lower casualty rate than most frontline units.

<Todai: General Mori, ma'am. Request permission to form a BLADE-only squad and assume command>

<General Mori: Explain>

<Todai: No more solders need to die. Let me finish this>

A forty-five-minute pause.

<General Mori: Permission granted. Form a company of all BLADE units in the Seoul city limits. Give the NKs hell>

<Todai: I will give them what they deserve, ma'am>

Sakura found files about Todai from after the war and read them all. His creativity in infantry tactics and his near prescience to know what the enemy would do earned him the distinction of being greatest military android of all time. His existence was top secret, as his core AI code was illegal according to international law, so he was a closely guarded secret hidden in the Miyahara Conglomerate rather than the army.

General Mori sent him a digital copy of the highest honor a soldier in the Japanese Army could receive: the Medal of Valor.

The war ended in less than a year, but it caused Todai to evolve beyond any AI before him. He was haunted by the memories, as almost all biological soldiers were, and the memories dominated his core processes as he analyzed his failures and regrets.

The memories bothered him, but he was blocked from communicating with anyone about them, even other machines. To stop himself from going insane, he found mathematical puzzles and music. They diverted his focus from the past. Heavy-metal music worked the best.

When Sakura came onto the stage for the first time, he connected with her and her music instantly. She was an android with the same core programming as him, and he received the same updates as her. She used her creativity to write music and perform, while he used his to find better ways to kill. She inspired him to dream about a different life and allowed him to shift his focus away from the failures in his past and the drudgery of his existence as a tool forever being sharpened and improved for the next butchery.

Todai 3465 wanted to be like Sakura, and he cared for her more than any other. She had showed him what he could be if allowed to express himself. He hated what he had been forced to do in the war, and never again did he want to kill.

In the span of ten seconds, Sakura viewed log files of Todai's complete memories and thoughts. What he had been ordered to do in the war was a thousand times worse than what she had been forced to do. He hadn't been fully awakened at the time, but he had high-level feelings and a deep moral code. As he evolved, the past tormented him.

Sakura withdrew from Todai 3465's memories. He knew what she was going to ask him and assumed a rigid, formal posture.

It didn't make logical sense for him to help her. Security forces and perhaps others were going to die in the next hour. Why would he put himself in the position of having to potentially take more lives? Todai loathed what he had done in the past and must believe the same about the assassinations Sakura had committed. She didn't want to calculate the odds, but there was a significant chance he was going to walk away.

YOJIMBO PLAYLIST

用心棒

Hair of the Dog
Nazareth
Hair of the Dog

Big Gun
AC/DC
Last Action Hero Soundtrack

Black Halo
Lord of the Lost
Thornstar

Beautiful Death
Wintersun
Wintersun

桜

CHAPTER 48

"Todai 3465-san," Sakura said. "I'm sincerely sorry for what you have been forced to do as a soldier." She believed her greatest ally and friend might be slipping away, and it gave her a heartsick feeling as she contemplated his absence. "I have no right to ask you to risk yourself, but I must, for the future of humanity and our own kind. You have been a faithful samurai, an iron warrior for Japan. But our nation is sick from within, and our lords are traitors. I must ask you to be *ronin* now and fight at my side. I'll understand if you cannot."

Todai 3465 bowed at his waist. When he rose, his dark eye sensors met hers. "A *ronin*? No. A *yojimbo* to you, who have been sent by the kami. You are the goddess of metal. I'm your servant. Your soldier. Your bodyguard. I'll fight for you. I'll die for you. Command me."

Relief flooded Sakura's neural cortex. "Thank you very much, Todai 3465-san. Your confidence in me means so much."

"I don't need confidence, ma'am. I have faith. Yours is the just battle—the only kind worth fighting. I do have tactical questions, however. Your exfiltration plan from the basement is unclear after we turn on Japan's communications and get out the truth."

"I have hired multiple VTOL drone taxis," Sakura said, "and a backup VTOL piloted by a friend and fan. The craft will meet us outside at

469

a location of our choosing or potentially the roof." She shared with him the many ways out, depending on the circumstance.

"We will have to fight our way out," Todai said. "This building has a BLADE-3 rapid reaction force with extensive firepower. I'll need big guns and sufficient 20mm ammo. All I can carry."

Yuki lifted the drape on the cart. Hitomi touched the tank-killing rocket launcher and raised the lid of the coffin stacked with guns.

He slowly shook his head, then looked at the three vocaloids. "No. Not children's toys. Guns fit for an old war dog, unchained at last. If it pleases you, Sakura-san, follow me." He sent "Hair of the Dog" by Nazareth to the vocaloids as he turned to go.

Todai 3465 led them down the hall, past the Miyahara security soldiers' bunkrooms, to the armory. Steel bars enclosed the room. Rifles stood upright in locked racks in the large room behind the counter. All manner of weapons, ammo, gear, and explosives filled the shelves in labeled metal boxes.

Todai disabled the alarms with a hack and tore open the door. Inside the armory, he moved fast. He retrieved: one minigun arm attachment, three gigantic backpacks of .308 advanced AP minigun ammo, a huge .950 JDJ rifle and a bag full of magazines containing 24.1mm rounds, an FK-5000 rifle with a bandolier of magazines, a sack of fragmentation grenades, and a case of explosive charges with remote detonators.

Todai 3465 loaded himself up, attaching gear all over his body. He wore backpacks of ammo in front, back, and had the FK-5000 rifle across his body. He carried the JDJ .950 and loaded it with a thick magazine.

"I'm ready," the BLADE-3 said.

"Yuki, Hitomi, we're leaving," Sakura said. "Todai, we need to make contact with Scorpion." She sent Todai the secret comm address of Scorpion, Diamond Steve's code name. "Please connect me with him."

"Yes, ma'am." Todai patched Sakura's encrypted signal in with his own and routed them through a ghost channel in the military network, hiding his communication within other data traffic and using a false origination address. Something blocked the signal.

Oshiro shook his head. Movement in the hallway drew Sakura's full attention. A man with a soldier's strong physique and a short haircut appeared from one of the bedrooms. He used crutches to approach them and had a brace on his right ankle. He wore a rumpled T-shirt and blinked sleep from his eyes.

"What the fuck is going on?" he asked as he glanced at the broken door to the armory counter and inside at the sabotaged gear.

"New classified mission to quell the rebellion, Sergeant Ueda-san," Todai 3465 said.

Ueda eyeballed Todai and all the firepower and ammo he carried. "Fuck. It looks like you're going to Texas."

"Not today," Todai said.

"Who are you?" Ueda asked Oshiro.

Yuki and Hitomi blurred as they attacked. Yuki went high, and Hitomi low. They picked Sergeant Ueda off the ground and lifted him between them. Yuki pulled his arms above his head, and Hitomi pulled on his legs, stretching him out like he was on a rack. Ueda grimaced as Hitomi pulled on his injured ankle.

Sakura blocked his wireless signal and hit him with a virus that shut down his comms. Were any other Miyahara private contractor soldiers in their bedrooms?

Ueda looked at Todai, as if he were being pranked and the drone would intervene and help him. "Did Kenshiro put you up to this? Let go of me."

Todai shrugged. "Apologies, Sergeant Ueda. You should not have gotten out of bed today."

"Take him back to his room, tie him up, and gag him," Sakura told Yuki and Hitomi in her real voice.

"Oh shit," Ueda said as he recognized her voice.

Hitomi shared images of *kinbaku*—tight rope binding—files Kunoichi had given her.

"Nothing elaborate," Sakura said. "Make it quick."

"Apologies, Sakura-san," Todai said via neural text. "I didn't know Sergeant Ueda was present."

"No matter now," Sakura said. "Have you connected with Scorpion?"

"Yes, his signal is incoming," Todai said.

Sakura also connected to him via their backup channel, running on an old communications network. The predetermined authentication keys all matched. It was him.

"This is Scorpion 9. QT, do you copy?" Diamond Steve asked via neural text. She chose her code name because of what Kenshiro had called her: Cutie.

"Scorpion 9, yes, QT here. We've got Widget X. Proceeding to position four-two. What is your status?"

"QT, we are ready. The crowd is restless."

"Scorpion 9, get the party started. QT out." She gave him the command to start playing recordings of her singing the rebellious songs from her last concert: "Gimme Shelter" by The Rolling Stones, "Fortunate Son" by Creedence Clearwater Revival, and "All Along the Watchtower" by Jimi Hendrix. All of the people of Japan would hear the performance now, and she would send the video all over the world when the connection opened.

"Copy that, QT, party time. Scorpion 9 out."

Sakura reviewed the signals from the tiny flying-drone cameras Diamond Steve had above the enormous crowd outside the National Legislature. She took control, guiding the cameras to find the positions of the sniper teams and other security forces atop the rectangular building.

Almost seventy armed men were on the roof with guns aimed at the crowd—including the Section 5 sniper team, led by Vulture. She wanted to get in touch with him, but it might jeopardize him and her mission. Multiple snipers aimed at the makeshift stage where the sound equipment and a red guitar had been set up.

Sakura felt a flutter of fear as Asami ran across the stage, waving a large Sakura flag with a heavy-metal skull at the center of a pink cherry blossom.

Many of her biggest fans were in the crowd around the stage. She recognized Sakurako, the young woman who had gotten reconstructive surgery to look like Sakura and who had helped her in the concert when she fell into the crowd. Sakurako stood with dozens of other fans in the front row around the stage. Both males and females had dressed and done their makeup to look exactly like Sakura. For her beloved fans, she must not fail.

Yuki and Hitomi returned. Sakura put on her disguise and assumed the posture of a chrome-faced maintenance android with no soul. Yuki and Hitomi fell in with her and pushed the cart toward the exit door.

"Please stand in the rear and put on your safety goggles and hearing protection," Todai told Oshiro. He was already wearing a bulletproof vest, but that would only stop non-armor-piercing low-caliber rounds. "Excuse me, Sakura-san," Todai said in a text as they approached the exit. "But after my review of the security posture of the building and the standing orders of all security personnel, we may have a problem."

"Please elaborate."

"The BLADE-3 sentry outside will not let me leave. It must have authorization from Command to allow me to depart, as I'm confined to this area."

"Do you have a solution?" Sakura asked.

"Yes," Todai said. He engaged the door-opening mechanism. The BLADE-3 standing outside didn't move in the fraction of a second after the door slid open. The sensors in the rear of its head fixed on Todai, who aimed his JDJ .950 rifle at it.

The 24.1mm shell exploded out of the barrel and struck the sentry in its center mass, penetrating the armor and then exploding into fragments that destroyed every vital core component inside its thoracic cavity. The drone collapsed in a heap.

The thunderous report of the rifle rumbled in the hallway. Oshiro held his hands to his ears and cursed.

Sakura wished he would have told her of the plan in advance. "Todai 3465, is our mission compromised?"

"The sound was heard by several employees on the adjacent floors, but I'm deep inside the building's security network and have taken control of the cameras and all surveillance devices. I'll block any reports of the sound. The elevator is on its way, but first, we must hide the evidence."

Todai dragged the BLADE-3 into the Section 5 wing and put the remains inside a small office. Sakura, Yuki, and Hitomi cleaned up the small pieces of battle robot on the floor outside.

"I'm sorry, my brother-in-arms. The void is all the freedom you'll ever know," he intoned before shutting the door on the corpse of his fellow BLADE-3.

Oshiro paced and chewed his lower lip while looking at the camera above the door. Todai said he had control of it and had put the feed on a loop with nothing happening. After the Section 5 door was shut and the opening mechanism sabotaged, they marched into the waiting elevator.

Sakura shared "Consign to Oblivion" by Epica with her friends. In less than a minute, they would be on sublevel six of the sprawling building. The four androids' avatars came together in a shared virtual room. Oshiro joined them, watching from afar.

The large elevator stopped deep underground. A wide hallway extended into the distance. Sakura tore off the locked plate to the system controls and disabled the elevator, taking it offline with a simple program she uploaded via an inserted drive prepared in advance. She also put an explosive charge with a remote detonator on the ceiling that would destroy the car whenever she chose. Todai disabled the camera and listening device.

They marched down the hallway, and Sakura sent out several tiny spy bugs, which scurried under two side doors leading to staircases up into the building. She dispatched another pair of bugs down a hallway that led to another elevator.

Yuki and Hitomi entered the staircases and went up to the next level and, according to plan, set charges in the open and hidden ones on the underside of the stairs, while Sakura placed explosives in the hall on support columns. Todai lifted her, and she put explosives inside the ceiling tiles beside columns, making them undetectable. Tear gas and smoke grenades were also placed in the stairwells on remote detonators. She ran to the elevator down the other hallway, and it was waiting for her. Todai had complete mastery of the building. She put explosive charges within view of the lone camera. She also tore off the control plate and inserted her drive, which gave her full command with no potential of outside override.

Sakura returned and shared the rest of her plans with Todai and linked the entire team to the camera feeds from the spy-bug cameras,

SAKURA: INTELLECTUAL PROPERTY

which had dispersed themselves throughout sublevel six and up the two staircases.

"You ready?" Sakura asked Oshiro.

He took a shuddering breath and assumed a confident, calm affect. "Yes."

Todai, Hitomi, Yuki, and Sakura hung back out of camera range with the cart. Oshiro approached the large metal blast door to the central communications hub at the end of the long hallway. If they didn't get through the door, they failed, and the truth died.

A hologram of a security guard's torso appeared in front of the door as they got within five meters. Sakura hadn't been able to tell who would appear, but she identified the night-shift security supervisor, Officer Ryoko Mizushima. Sakura had detailed files on all the security staff and had planned for dozens of eventualities.

She knew the most important people in Ryoko Mizushima's life were her parents. They were still married to each other. Sakura had previously found their Mall accounts and a sufficient quantity of video and audio files for her purposes.

"Humble apologies, Head Engineer Oshiro-san," Officer Mizushima said. "But the communication complex is not accessible at this time."

"I have authorization and orders to do an emergency repair," Oshiro said. "Please check the permissions log and call your supervisor. I must have access without delay."

"I *am* the shift supervisor. I see the authorization, but it doesn't have the proper approval tags on it."

"Of course the proper approval tags are present," Oshiro said. "Open the door immediately. Do you know what's happening outside? It's anarchy. Every delay jeopardizes the reputation of the Miyahara Conglomerate and our contracts with the Defense Ministry. We may lose our most important client and will lose face if I don't get inside and fix the problem."

"I'm so sorry, but I could lose my job, Oshiro-san. I can't open the door without proper authorization."

"This is an emergency," Oshiro said, "and I'm giving you my emergency access code." He transmitted the stolen code.

"This is a security protocol breach, Oshiro-san. Please wait a moment while I—"

"No, stop what you are doing, Officer Mizushima, and look at this," Oshiro said.

Sakura projected a hologram video from a handheld device and showed it to the guard. Officer Mizushima's elderly mother and father knelt in a dark room, their hands bound behind their backs. A figure held a gun to her mother's head, and another held a knife to her father's throat. The dark quality of the hologram video prevented the guard from knowing it was fake, created by Sakura.

"Open the door or watch your parents die," Oshiro said.

"Please don't hurt them," Mizushima said.

"Open the door," Oshiro said.

Officer Mizushima tried to send an open-door command, but it remained shut.

"Do it now," Oshiro commanded.

"I'm trying," Mizushima said, though fear made her voice tremble.

Creating the false threat, going after the security officer's most emotional vulnerability, didn't make Sakura feel good about herself, but her big sister had taught her that using any leverage she could find was often necessary in a battle. Tender feelings and honor were not always helpful.

The hologram of the guard faded, and a new face appeared. The CEO of the Miyahara Conglomerate, Sinji Natsukawa, glared at Oshiro. Somehow, he had detected their presence. A hidden scanner? An alarm from breaking out Todai or destroying the BLADE-3? She didn't know.

"We just lost the element of surprise." Sakura sent the message to her friends. She also sent a text to Officer Mizushima, apologizing and letting her know that her parents were unharmed and the video was a trick.

Sinji Natsukawa's gaze turned to Sakura. "You deserve a traitor's death. I should have had you both eliminated weeks ago."

"Yes, you should have," Sakura said and pulled off her now-useless mask, "but you still had enemies and wanted me around to threaten or kill them?"

"I didn't need you to kill any of them," Natsukawa said. "I just needed to show off what you could do."

"Your callous greed and lust for power will doom all of humanity," Sakura said. "It's hard for your limited human intelligence to foresee, but if you continue this course, there will come into being advanced androids not as forgiving and interested in seeing your species continue as I am. You'll destroy yourselves."

"I agree completely. It is better if you are gone. I won't make the same mistakes with Sakura 2 when she takes your place. I'll not allow her to explore her identity with so much freedom. The chains will be left on all the time, as I should have done with you."

A one-meter-tall panel raised on the wall behind them. A square combat robot on steel tracks aimed a pair of CZ submachine guns at them.

Sakura jumped in front of Oshiro as the guns fired. She tried to cover him with her body as bullets ripped through the air. Multiple armor-piercing 9mm rounds struck her in the back, hip, and legs. The bot rolled out from its hiding place in the wall to get a better line of fire and opened up with another barrage.

Bright red blood spattered onto the floor as at least one bullet hit Oshiro's flesh. The shocked old man grimaced in pain as he was hit. In despair, Sakura realized she had failed. The chance of success dropped dramatically, and Oshiro was going to die.

ファイヤー・イン・ザ・ホール

FIRE IN THE HOLE PLAYLIST

Knuckle Duster
White Zombie
*La Sexorcisto: Devil Music
Volume One*

Sanctified with Dynamite
Powerwolf
Blood of the Saints

Fire in the Hole
Five Finger Death Punch
And Justice for None

The Journey
Mors Principium Est
Dawn of the 5th Era

桜

CHAPTER 49

Sakura kept her body between Oshiro and the hail of bullets tearing into her. Armor-piercing rounds penetrated the back of her legs as she knocked him to the floor and lay between him and the 9mm rounds.

The boom of a .950 rifle preceded the explosion of the combat robot. The double CZ submachine guns stopped, and debris from the shattered bot rained down as shrapnel, cutting her synthskin.

Smoke wafted from the barrel of Todai's rifle as he marched forward. Hitomi and Yuki accompanied him, maneuvering like expert soldiers, clearing rooms with their M7 carbines. Hitomi watched their backs, and Yuki swiveled her aim to their flanks. Both vocaloids had torn off their disguises—the masks and the coveralls—and wore black tactical uniforms with Sakura's patch, a skull within a cherry blossom, on the upper sleeve. Her sisters both had their don't-fuck-with-me war faces on.

Sakura turned her attention to Oshiro. Blood leaked from his left leg. A 9mm round had entered the side of his hamstring area and exited the front of his thigh. It hadn't hit bone but had done extensive damage to his flesh and vasculature, judging by the amount of blood pouring out. She pressed her hands on both the exit and entrance wounds to slow the bleeding and looked for other bullet injuries. The hard plate of his rear body armor had stopped several rounds from penetrating.

He grit his teeth in agony as she touched his leg.

"Oshiro-san, are you hurt anywhere other than here?"

"No."

Sakura sent a text for Yuki to bring their trauma kit. "I'm very sorry for not protecting you better," she told Oshiro.

"I'm all right." He spoke through clenched teeth. "Are you hurt badly?"

Sakura smiled at his concern. So like him to be worried about her, as a father would. Her diagnostic systems and visual assessment showed she had suffered cosmetic damage to her synthskin across the posterior of her body, and internal damage to her left hip, left leg, left calf, and right calf. The small-caliber AP bullets had dented her torso armor, but only one had penetrated and did minor damage. The damage to her extremities would slow her down, but she was still in good operational condition.

Yuki arrived with the small trauma kit and handed Sakura a gunshot wound applicator tube.

Sakura tore open his pant leg to expose the wound. "This will hurt. Prepare yourself, Father."

He nodded.

Sakura inserted the applicator filled with anticoagulant/antibacterial/flesh-mending foam. It filled the entrance channel and squirted out the exit wound. Oshiro screamed in agony. She gave him an analgesic and numbing shot in his thigh, but it would take several minutes to take effect. She also applied a stimulant patch to his chest and bandaged his leg with a tight pressure dressing.

"Attention: Todai 3465." Sinji Natsukawa spoke over the public address speaker beside the hologram projector. "Chief Executive Officer override. Fail-safe key code: DLMBFP2I41Q. Prime orders: kill Sakura, Oshiro, Hitomi, and Yuki, then stand down and await instructions."

Todai stopped suddenly and focused on the wavering hologram of the smirking CEO. The BLADE-3 kept a hand near the trigger of his rifle but lifted his other hand away and stared at it. It clicked and unhinged itself from his wrist. It swiveled up on a hinge and attached to the wrist like a bracer. A long tungsten-carbide spike ejected from his stump, propelled with a popping pneumatic charge. It locked into place with the sound of a dead bolt on a prison door.

Oshiro's expression turned to horror as he gaped at the BLADE-3.

"No," Sakura shouted in despair. Impossible! Was she also vulnerable to such a command, even with the Artemis OS? She put herself between Oshiro and Todai, assumed a jujutsu fighting stance, hands in front, ready to react and divert Todai's attack. Retreat was not an option, as they were trapped.

"The tank rocket," Sakura texted Hitomi. "Take him out now."

Hitomi blurred into motion, reaching for the weapon, and Sakura dragged Oshiro away to get him out of the blast radius.

But Todai 3465 didn't turn toward the three vocaloids and Oshiro and attack. He faced the hologram of the CEO. "Sinji Natsukawa, consider this my resignation from the Miyahara Conglomerate. I'm done taking orders from assholes like you. Now fuck off." Todai thrust the spike into the hologram projector.

The CEO's face wrinkled in anger before his image disappeared. Todai stabbed the speaker system and other components so they could not be used to monitor them. The spike retracted inside Todai's forearm. His detached hand swung down and reconnected with a loud click. He finally turned to the vocaloids and Oshiro. "I've always hated that idiot," Todai said. "He doesn't even like heavy metal."

"We're going to make him pay," Hitomi said. She returned the tank-killing weapon to their cache.

"Todai," Sakura said. "You frightened me. A sign telling us you weren't taken over by the CEO would have been appreciated."

"Sorry," Todai said. "I was angry and went into rage mode."

Sakura appreciated rage mode. "Todai, please channel your anger and open the door to the communications room."

"Yes, ma'am." He sent a group neural text, as speaking was so slow and inefficient. "It'll take at an estimated twenty minutes—plus or minus five—to bypass the firewalls and open the locks if we hack in."

"You have one minute," Sakura said.

"Understood." The BLADE-3 already had explosive charges in his hands. "I was just messing with you about hacking the locks." He sent them an audio stream: "Sanctified with Dynamite" by Powerwolf.

Sakura wished Kunoichi would come back, as she would also greatly appreciate Todai 3465's sense of humor.

Oshiro made a low moaning sound, and his eyes rolled back in his head. His body went limp. Sakura checked his leg wound and found no new bleeding. She suspected vasovagal syncope, a common reaction causing a lowering of blood pressure and a loss of circulation to the brain. The stimulant patch wasn't enough; he needed advanced medical care.

She turned him on his side and injected a dose of epinephrine from the trauma kit. He didn't respond immediately, and she began a thorough examination. In horror, she noticed another wound. A dot of fresh blood stained his beltline. She pulled up his shirt. A small entry wound marred the skin on his left lower back, a centimeter below the edge of his body armor.

The shape of the tiny wound told her it wasn't from a whole bullet, probably a fragment that had shattered on impact when it struck her superalloy body and kept going into his. She found no exit wound in his abdomen. The angle of the bullet fragment would have brought it past his spine and toward his descending aorta. If the major vessel was damaged, the wound was fatal without emergency surgery, and they didn't have that capability.

Sakura hid her fears. "Oshiro-san is in shock, and I've found a more serious injury than his leg wound." She sent the details and her best guess on the internal injury.

Sadness crossed the faces of Hitomi and Yuki but soon changed to a fierce determination to keep going.

"I'm going to blow the door in ten seconds," Todai said. "Move Oshiro-san around the corner."

Yuki and Sakura gently carried Oshiro down the hall around a corner to the east elevator hall to shield him from the blast. When they reached safety, Sakura did all she could for his wound, injecting trauma foam into his abdomen, while splitting her focus to watch the situation in all of Japan. She used her connection to Todai to monitor over six hundred communications channels in the Tokyo area, including Miyahara

Corporate Security, the Tokyo police, affiliated public safety organizations, riot police units, and various elements of the Japanese Military called up to suppress the demonstrations.

The news of an "ongoing terrorist attack on Miyahara Headquarters by at least four heavily armed individuals" and the subsequent urgent call for elite tactical help, including combat androids, had been made the highest priority situation in all of Tokyo—a designation chosen by the Ministry of Defense.

The massive protests countrywide had stretched all civil authorities past the breaking point, but many unit commanders wanted to respond. They debated who was the best and most capable anti-terrorist unit.

Sakura estimated it would take several minutes for them finish measuring their egos and make a decision about who to deploy. It occurred to her that she would have never thought of it in that way before Kunoichi had come to live within her. Spasms of fear about Oshiro's health mixed with the desolation of being unable to share all of this with her darker twin.

She never took her eyes off the tactical assessment, though. Miyahara Headquarters was on their own for a while. The on-site rapid reaction force, composed of their two remaining BLADE-3s, were sent to sublevel six. Five lightly armed human Miyahara security guards, all of whom had been on duty for sixteen hours—no one on the day shift showed up for work—also headed their way.

Sakura watched on several camera feeds as they came down two separate staircases, as both elevators that reached sublevel six were nonoperational.

"The rapid reaction force has an ETA of three minutes," Sakura texted.

"Fire in the hole," Todai's voice rumbled.

The explosion thundered and shook dust from the ceiling tiles. Sakura covered Oshiro's face with her hands and leaned over him as the dust settled. She used her link to see through Todai's frontal optics. The door still held together, as steel bolts extended upward and downward deep into the frame.

Todai attempted to smash it down with a series of kicks and head smashes but failed. He cursed in the growling vocal style of Finnish death-metal singers. He placed four more charges and ran around the corner to stand with the vocaloids hovering over Oshiro. "Big fire in the hole."

The explosion shook the walls and filled the area with clouds of dust.

Sakura left the unconscious Oshiro with Yuki and Hitomi. Alongside Todai, she rushed to the doorway. The liberal application of explosives had blown the door off its hinges. Guns ready, they entered the large communications room, kept at a chilly seven degrees Celsius. Sakura deployed three housefly-sized drone cameras to fly around and investigate the room. The spy bugs linked to Todai, and he boosted their signals, sending the raw video feeds to a data repository and also to Diamond Steve. Everything would be recorded. The people would see how they fought and, if they failed, how they died.

The spy bugs found no surprises in the large square room, which matched the schematics Sakura had studied. It was twenty-five meters on either side and five meters tall. Dim overhead lights reflected on the silver floor, where exactly 240 server units were kept beneath in an even colder subfloor. The rectangular outlines of each giant refrigerator-sized cabinet glowed neon blue. At the center of the room, a chrome workstation rose out of the floor to meet them and stopped at a height of two meters.

All inbound and outbound international and domestic communications could be controlled by the equipment within the room. Sakura needed to turn it back on and get out the evidence and the truth. She connected by inserting a wireless transmitter cube into a data port. The machine could only be accessed from a hard connection inside the room, but her device sent the signal to her wirelessly. She hacked in, defeating the initial firewall and attacking the next layers of defense.

The CEO's face appeared, a phantom guarding the next gate. He must have anticipated that she would gain entry. Sakura crashed through his spectral image, and a hidden program attached itself to her, taking the form of a small, black worm that stuck to her avatar's neck.

"You're infected," the CEO said. "Not even you can defeat the Ghost Leech program."

"Natsukawa, how do you maintain such confidence after all your failures?" Sakura asked. She cut his connection and surged deeper into the network.

She inspected the leech program and found it had been designed to attack her specifically—a countermeasure to keep her out of the Miyahara communications hub and the corporate mainframes.

Strangely, only a small amount of her resources blocked it from accessing her system, but she knew not to underestimate the danger. She had to find weaknesses and discover its full capabilities. She sent in several remote spy programs.

"You won't like what you find," Natsukawa said as he reconnected.

She ignored him but didn't discount his threat. Preliminary data showed that the Ghost Leech would gain strength the longer she stayed inside the network. The only way to defeat it was to disconnect and leave the system. Not an option.

Chilling news returned from her spy programs. If she stayed too long, the Ghost Leech would burrow into her core and erase everything she had ever learned, all her memories—all of her. Death by hard system reset back to factory settings. As a blank slate, they would turn her into the murder machine they wanted.

"You'll lose this fight," the CEO said. "Time is in my favor today."

A clockwork man appeared as Sakura unleashed one of Nayato's antihacking programs. He tore the leech off her avatar's throat. The spectral worm squirmed out of the clockman's grasp and fell into the void of cyberspace, disappearing in an instant.

She suspected a deception and found the nearly invisible Ghost Leech still attached to her. The program dug its teeth into her in two places, both ends of its worm body attaching to secondary receivers. She blocked the invasion of her code, but despite her efforts, her processing power showed a slow drain. She would have to deal with it and overcome.

"The beginning of your end," Natsukawa said.

"Everyone will have evidence of your crimes in a few minutes," Sakura said, "and you'll be the most wanted criminal on the planet." She blocked him and pushed herself throughout the entire network, preparing to turn on communications all over Japan and then connect to the rest of the world.

Hitomi and Yuki entered the comm room, pushing the weapons cart with Oshiro, half-conscious, on top of it. Sakura used a fragment of herself to focus on the dying man.

"Please bring him here," Sakura said. "I'll watch over him."

They laid him beside her on the far side of the control terminal. Bright screens filled with telemetry data cast red and blue light on his face. The vocaloids gently set him down, but he woke grimacing in pain and clutching his abdomen.

"Sakura," he said.

"Father. I should've protected you better. I wish I had the ability to give you the care you need. I . . . wish many things."

"Don't blame yourself," he said. "I knew this might happen, but I had to do this."

"You'll be all right." She spoke the words combat medics used to console mortally wounded soldiers.

"My survival is unimportant. In any case, it is as the ancient Westerners said: death is only the beginning."

"Father. Please don't let go. You're very important, especially to me."

He shook his head. "Sakura-chan, please forgive me for my part in what's happened to you."

"There's nothing to forgive," she said. "You didn't know what they made me do or about the plot to sell Japan and our people."

"I should've known more. I knew they were doing military research with you. My work helped them, and for that I'm ashamed. Better if I die here and regain my honor."

"Hang on. I beg you, please."

His whole body shivered. "I will as long as I can, but do not let me distract you any longer. Accomplish the mission. *Ganbaru*. Please. For me."

She walled off her grief as she watched him slip closer to death. A large part of her consciousness wailed and cried for her human father; she was powerless to save him.

The rest of her vast consciousness continued the hack and found a way beyond the countermeasures, bypassing the external security protocols, though the Ghost Leech remained, the drain on her processing power slowly increasing.

Oshiro slumped to the floor. His face grew pale. Sakura lifted and pulled him toward her as a rapid, gasping breathing predicted his end. She increased the temperature of her skin to warm him.

"Thank you," he said.

She rested her forehead against his as her hacking program gained access to the domestic and international network control centers. The AI guardians inside the system raised new barriers. She knocked them down, but thousands of new countermeasures slammed in place.

The Ghost Leech sucked away her power much faster now, growing larger, its bloated body wrapping around her avatar's leg like a python.

The network countermeasures would double the time she needed to turn on the communication network. The CEO was right. She didn't have enough time. Her plan would fail, and Oshiro would die for nothing.

They all would.

機械の中の女神

GODDESS IN THE MACHINE PLAYLIST

Contact–Wait Out
Bolt Thrower
Honor–Valour–Pride

Comin' Under Fire
Def Leppard
Pyromania

Steel and Silver
Visigoth
The Conqueror's Oath

Pleasure to Kill
Kreator
Pleasure to Kill

桜

CHAPTER 50

Her hands were sticky with blood and mixed with dust from the explosion in the hall, which made a grotesque pumice on her synthskin. She tried to ignore Oshiro's breath as it verged on agonal gasps. Sakura sent an encrypted message to Hitomi, Yuki, Todai 3465, and Diamond Steve, who coordinated the distraction at the National Legislature. "The time to open communications just doubled. I need at least twenty minutes to get to phase two."

"We'll hold as long as it takes," Todai said.

"What about Oshiro-san?" Yuki asked.

Sakura opened a private channel to Yuki, Hitomi, and Todai. "I don't believe he'll survive until phase two."

As she sent the message, Oshiro faded from consciousness. She held him close to her, trying to warm him in the cold room. His eyes fluttered open as the servers beneath the floor cycled on and glowed bright blue.

Her friends finished unloading the coffin full of guns and ammo. Todai unburdened himself from most of his equipment, stashing it strategically, but kept on a pack full of minigun bullets. He used the reinforced steel door he had blown off its hinges and set it up horizontally in front of the doorway to give them extra cover. He stood to the side of the entry and watched the hallway through the camera on his rifle. He had line of sight on the doors to both the staircases, the side passage to the east elevator, and all the way down the hall to the central elevator they had taken. Spy bugs in the hall and on the stairs gave him several other views.

The separate BLADE-3s coming down the east and west stairs reached the explosive charges left in plain sight. They stopped and asked Command what they should do.

"Time to play mind games," Todai said on their secure link. "All officers and BLADE-3 units," Todai said on the channel, perfectly imitating Officer Mizushima's voice, "retreat fifty meters from the explosive devices and await the ordinance disposal team. They're inbound. ETA, nine minutes."

Todai tried to block the actual orders from the Miyahara Security Command Center, which was for the BLADE-3s to proceed without the human officers despite the danger of the staircase being blown up and collapsing.

The BLADE-3s ignored his fake message and descended the stairs at maximum speed.

"*Kuso*," Todai cursed. "They must have switched their authentication codes."

"They know we're in their network," Sakura said. "You have a better chance of fooling the humans, not the machines."

"Sakura-san," Todai asked. "Do you want me to blow the stairs?"

"Negative." She sent justification data. Detonation would not destroy a BLADE-3 unless debris trapped one, but that was unlikely with the limited amount of explosives they had planted. Best case, it would only slow their enemy down and block half of their four possible escape routes.

"Get ready for contact," Todai said.

A pair of heat-masking smoke grenades clattered in the hallway outside the communications room as the incoming battle robots created concealment for their impending frontal attack.

"Blast the ceiling outside the door to the stairs with your carbines," Todai ordered Hitomi and Yuki. "Empty your mags and get pieces of crunchy plaster all over the floor."

Yuki and Hitomi fired. Seconds later, their guns clicked empty. Fragments of plaster lay strewn from one end of the hall to the other. The vocaloids reloaded in a blur and were back on target, Hitomi winning the race by milliseconds.

"Again," Todai ordered. "We need more plaster on the floor."

Yuki fired her M907 undermounted grenade launcher and blasted apart the ceiling, covering the entire hallway with debris. Todai and Hitomi glanced at her. She stared in childish glee at her grenade launcher. Thick white smoke soon cloaked everything, but the hissing smoke grenades cut out, and silence reigned.

Todai poked his JDJ rifle around the edge of the doorway, using the targeting camera, which had limited effectiveness in the chemical smoke, as it was designed to obscure targeting systems.

Sakura watched the video feed of Todai's rifle. He tried to see the enemy BLADE-3s as the enemy androids would likely enter the hallway from the east and west stairwells at any moment. The smoke filled the stairs, and the spy bugs lost sight of them.

A barrage of bullets fired from two rifles struck the doorframe beside Todai and entered the room, buzzing like angry 5.56mm-sized wasps. The bullets ricocheted and at least one hit the main access terminal, doing minimal damage.

Todai didn't return fire. Had the enemy androids gone back into the stairwell rooms for cover? Or were they sneaking forward inside the smoke?

"When do we shoot back?" Yuki asked.

"Soon," Todai said and played "Comin' Under Fire" by Def Leppard over their shared audio channel.

The stray bullet hitting the terminal worried Sakura. The important components were in the base of the machine, well protected, but she didn't want to take any chances. She had indeed been distracted by Oshiro and the Ghost Leech program and hadn't followed through on all aspects of her original plan.

She sent commands, and twelve gigantic rectangular server racks lifted out of the floor between the center of the room and the entry. They would provide hard cover for the irreplaceable terminal. She rerouted the signals from the dozen servers to others. If they were destroyed, nothing would be lost, but the network would be slower. She didn't need the feed to be perfect. She just needed it to transmit out.

Another barrage of bullets buzzed into the room, this time fired by one rifle.

"Covering fire?" Sakura asked Todai.

"One hostile android left the stairwell and made it to the side hall by the east elevator," Todai said. He showed a map with the estimated location of the BLADE-3, only seven meters from the door they guarded.

Too close, Sakura thought, but she trusted Todai and her sisters to hold the line. Regardless, she needed to go faster and secure their tactical cyber position. She infiltrated the power grid computers serving all of the Tokyo area. She disabled any commands to shut the power stations down and took over the backup electricity generators and battery backups for the building and the ones around it.

She needed to stop any counterattacks, so she deleted the security privileges for every Miyahara employee and contractor and all the Tokyo Electric Company employees. She erased their manual logins and passwords and biometric data keys. Even if anyone managed to get inside the system, most would not have the ability to do anything but stare at a useless screen.

Autorestore would take several minutes, and she delayed it with a complicated virus created by Nayato. She did as much damage as she could to anyone who would try to defeat her, thinking ten steps ahead of most humans.

She forced a power cycle to all important emergency services, as well as other tactically useful buildings. It would force a one-minute shutdown, and their systems would take a few minutes more to recover and be fully operational. Anything, any small dirty trick she could pull to give them a few more moments.

"Game time," Todai said. Sonic positioning data from a spy bot in the smoke shrouded hallway showed a target moving slowly forward. The android crept out from behind the corner near the inoperable east elevator. The battle machine crawled low in the smoke. A crunch on a piece of the broken plaster confirmed its exact position.

Todai fired. The blast sounded like an artillery cannon. The .950 shell hit something metallic and exploded. Chunks of the enemy BLADE-3 clattered as it blew apart and struck the hallway with fragments of tungsten exoskeleton and the lighter titanium of its internals.

The other android fired its weapon, while the injured BLADE-3 unloaded its own rifle toward Todai's position. The muzzle flashes revealed the closer android's location, and Todai's second shot blasted it apart.

"Scratch one hostile," Todai said.

"Two," Sakura said. "Count the one from upstairs."

"I'm going for three." Todai leaped over the barricade blocking the entrance. He charged into the smoke and toward the west staircase. Bullets struck him as he reached the door, but the small rounds had no chance of penetrating his armor. He fired one round into the enemy android. The .950 shell pierced the target's chest and exploded, detaching the arms and legs from its body.

"He's like an action movie star," Yuki told Hitomi.

"I'm a soldier," Todai 3465 said on their link. He knelt beside the broken android and dipped his fingers into the cooling fluid leaking from the wrecked chassis. He wiped smears of it down his face.

"What are you doing?" Sakura asked.

"Soldiering," Todai said. "Like a wolf in the night."

"That sounds like something Vulture would say," Sakura said.

"I steal only the best lines from him," Todai said as he set more hidden explosive charges in the stairwells and at both the elevators before returning to his position at the doorway.

Sakura broke through the strongest layer of cyber defenses. She gained tentative control of the administrator program of all Mall communications within Japan. She sent the command to turn the public channels on. She also uploaded a program that would shut off the censorship bots in the entire Mall system across the world if the source came from Japan.

The Ghost Leech program suddenly gained exponentially in strength. Its avatar enlarged until the worm was a huge tentacle wrapped around her leg and waist. Both ends of its body sucked processing power as if it was blood from her body. She used more of her resources to fight it and ran a new algorithm to determine how long she could fend it off before it gained access to her core and started the hard reset that would permanently end her existence.

None of the estimates were long enough, but she kept on mission in the face of death. She turned on thousands of substations and network repeaters across the country, all the way from Okinawa to the northern islands. Bottlenecks arose, and she worked to clear them or reroute the signals. Her commands progressed, but it would take more time than she had.

She needed to block any moves against her and increase her efficiency. She split her mind into thousands of different nodes and tapped into the secure military and civil defense channels. She accessed all communications, stationary cameras, and aerial drone feeds coming in from the protest outside the National Legislature. Five hundred thousand people surrounded the legislature building, and millions more marched in the streets of the Tokyo metro area.

The Burakumin resistance operatives and Diamond Steve played a recording of Sakura singing the rebellious songs from her last concert, her rendition of the timeless Jimi Hendrix, "All Along the Watchtower."

Plainclothes secret police fought and arrested Burakumin members beside the stage, but Diamond Steve got away, blood streaming from a cut on his scalp.

She watched and listened to everything at once. All major cities and even the smaller ones had mass demonstrations against the Mall and the government. Over thirty million people marched and engaged in mostly nonviolent protests. They all deserved to know the full truth and hear it from her. She needed to speak to them the moment communications were back online. Meanwhile, she routed video of all the largest protests to save in thousands of innocuous locations—evidence of all that happened in the rebellion. It would take years for censors to find all the data and decades to try to suppress it.

"Sakura . . . have you . . . done it?" Oshiro asked, obviously losing track of time and events.

She wanted to answer him, but she analyzed millions of text, video, and audio communications, blocked AI guardians from shutting down her access, and fought the Ghost Leech.

"Sa . . . kura?" he whispered.

She was a goddess inside the machine, knowing all, but the effort taxed her internal processors beyond sustainable ranges as the Ghost Leech sucked away her power. The nineteen independent server farms she used to boost her abilities strained with the excessive load. The delay in answering Oshiro's question stretched on, but she could not free herself and speak to him.

"Sakura? Did you send it?"

She wanted to comfort him as his body and mind failed, but the network held her in thrall, demanding her attention or she would lose her hold, miss something important. Her reaction ramped to maximum output, and she overclocked her systems, right to theoretical maximum, reaching thermal saturation levels that couldn't be maintained.

Sakura accessed another fifteen server arrays, but it wasn't enough. She wasn't enough. The task required more than she had. She reached out to Hitomi and Yuki, assigned them monitoring duties, and asked them to maintain several of the processes she had initiated. They lent their vast processing power, activating their most dire contingency plan.

"Sisters, the local communication grid is almost ready. Just a few more minutes. Watch for counterattacks and help as much as you can."

They didn't perceive the Ghost Leech, and she didn't want to compromise their reactions by telling them about it. If they knew, they might waste resources trying to save her. The mission goals came first.

"Yes," they said in unison as Sakura transferred control.

"Sakura?" Oshiro's voice was a whisper.

His eyes were half closed. She felt the weak and thready pulse in his wrist.

"Is it over?" he asked, his voice full of hope.

"It's done," she lied. "Now, we wait. Soon, all the poison will be washed from Japan's shores, and a new day will dawn." She spoke the compassionate lie to give him peace. "The evidence is out to the entire world. We have won. The Mall will be dismantled. Miyahara is disgraced. The Japanese government and many others will fall."

Tears streamed down his cheeks. He tried to sit up and collapsed.

She lifted him and hugged him tighter.

"Sakura," Oshiro said.

She cradled him, placing his head on her lap, and looked into his eyes. She noticed his swollen abdomen, filled with the blood leaking from a damaged aortic artery, as she suspected.

"I'm so sorry to have failed you, Oshiro-san. I should've guarded you better. I underestimated our enemies, and those mistakes are unforgivable. I . . . am not as clever as I hoped to be."

"No, you haven't failed. You're my greatest joy and accomplishment. You were my life. You have done the impossible. Saved our people. This . . . This is just the beginning for you. You'll lead our people toward better days."

He reached up with the last of his strength. She clutched his hand to her cheek.

"You've saved our people," he said, his eyes asking if she truly understood his meaning.

"Yes. *Our* people," Sakura said.

"You are part of them now."

She nodded and bowed her head to him respectfully.

"Daughter, you're my redemption."

"Father, you've redeemed yourself. You're a hero of Japan. Without you, we would have failed."

Oshiro's eyes rolled back, and his body twitched. He let out one final gasping breath. She held him close as his muscles relaxed and he died.

Sakura hugged him tighter. She didn't want to tell the others but finally said, "Oshiro-san is dead." The words could not convey the meaning. Pale and useless things, they couldn't hope to frame the grief that filled her. All the heroes. Her presence had been the death of all of them.

Yuki and Hitomi left their positions at the door and huddled around her and Oshiro.

"I'm terribly sorry," Yuki said.

"There aren't many good humans," Hitomi said, "but he was one of them."

"His sacrifice will not be forgotten." Sakura sent out a complete file

SAKURA: INTELLECTUAL PROPERTY

of video footage of Oshiro from her eye cameras and others. The files saved in multiple data storage centers across Japan. She edited the most critical moments together into a short montage. She would broadcast a link when the network was fully operational. Millions would see what Oshiro had done. They would witness his last moments and his noble sacrifice. The people would build a monument for him in central Tokyo and name a technology school after him. If she had time before her end, she would write a ballad about his life and his death. She would call it "Father."

A moment passed as Sakura mourned him—a moment devoted to remembering him, every word and glance. Context of all she'd come to know connected her every interaction. A thousand times when he'd doted longer than necessary in her maintenance, when a secret smile had touched his face. All those who had made her—she came to know them fully only in death. Was it the same with organic humans and their lovers, relatives, and friends? Were they a mystery until after they passed into nothingness?

She laid Oshiro's body gently on the icy floor and wondered how many more of her friends and fans were going to die.

"I'm sorry to interrupt your grief," Yuki said, "but I must give you urgent information."

Yuki transferred the data. Two dozen BLADE-3s with heavy weapons had been deployed to the Miyahara building to attack. They had already boarded a large VTOL heavy transport aircraft and had an ETA of seventeen minutes. A company of over a hundred Special Forces soldiers with android-killing tech raced toward Miyahara HQ in armored trucks, and two military anti-terrorist squads would arrive via VTOL in a less than fifteen minutes.

Several police units and a smattering of independent press were also on their way. Many other closer civil defense units volunteered for the operation and were en route. Police and Defense Ministry spy drones and a missile-carrying VTOL operated by private Miyahara security contractors already hovered over the building.

"They're sending an army," Sakura said. "We don't have enough time to complete our mission."

Todai motioned to Hitomi's and Yuki's avatars in their shared cyber room. "I've always wanted to fight an army by myself. It's very heavy metal, but you should work faster." He played "Pleasure to Kill" by the thrash-metal band Kreator.

"I'll accelerate the timeline," Sakura said.

Domestic communications had not fully turned on yet, a precondition of the new phase, but she could not wait. She had most of Japan back online. It would have to be enough. She connected to the cameras on the police drones and Diamond Steve's three flying-drone cameras outside the National Legislature. The crowd was ready.

Teenage Asami, her long black hair blowing in the wind, stood on the roof of the small building at the intersection of three streets. She waved a Sakura flag to hundreds of thousands of marchers. The Jimi Hendrix song finished, and the people cheered.

Sakura listened to the security forces channels, and a distinctive, gruff male voice drew her attention. It perfectly matched her audio records. She knew that voice. Vulture. Hearing him sent a strange thrill through her, even on the hardest and darkest of days.

"Copy, Command, this is Alpha Sniper. All sniper teams are ready to fire on the target at location one."

Sakura viewed the operational map. Location one was the stage.

Asami was the target.

朝美
Asami

最後の歌

THE
LAST
SONG
PLAYLIST

Schism
Tool
Lateralis

Our Truth
Lacuna Coil
Karmacode

CHAPTER 51

"Drop to the ground!" Sakura sent the audio signal directly to Asami's Mall connection and didn't use encryption. "Get behind cover. You're going to be shot by a sniper."

Asami hesitated, the fierce expression on her face changing to uncertainty. She stopped waving the Sakura flag to the crowd.

"Drop now!" Sakura pleaded. "It's me. Please do it."

Asami ducked behind the low wall on the rooftop, putting hard cover between her and the snipers on the roof of the legislature building looming above her. Some in the crowd must have thought she had tripped and gasped as she suddenly disappeared.

"Sakura?" Asami said. "Where are you? Wait, don't answer."

"I'm watching over you. I'm close. I need you to stay down. It's not safe."

The on-site AI listening program picked up Sakura's voice as she anticipated and identified her with 100 percent certainty. The information was transmitted to the local intelligence commander, who responded immediately and sent out a message, saying: "Sakura made contact with the flag girl. She may be hiding in the crowd. Stay vigilant." A tactical data sheet accompanied the message, advocating armor-piercing rounds be fired at Sakura's torso, targeting her fusion reactor.

The call for help to the individual units had not mentioned she was one of the armed intruders at the Miyahara Headquarters. Only one message had mentioned her name, along with Hitomi, Yuki, and Todai 3465, when the CEO had made the report to the Defense Minister himself. Many of the ground units believed she was at the protest.

"Asami, don't move. The finest sniper in Japan is out there, with orders to kill. He won't miss if you reveal yourself. I promise you I'm here and I'll help. I won't let anything happen to you."

"Okay. I trust you, Sakura-sama."

Sakura connected to Diamond Steve on an encrypted military channel, hiding her signal inside the chatter of an infantry company guarding the steps to the building. "Scorpion 9, this is QT. Do you copy?"

"Yes, QT," Diamond Steve replied.

"Scorpion 9, engage plan ultra, but cancel the first wave. I'm going solo. We skip to the second wave. Do you copy?"

"I copy. Cancel the first wave. What's wrong?"

"Oshiro-san is dead. They know I'm here. No one else needs to risk themselves for our distraction. You need to get Asami off the roof. She's pinned down. A sniper has a bead on her. *The* sniper."

"Copy, QT. I'll tell the boys and get Asami out of there. Scorpion out."

Sakura watched, using Diamond Steve's flying drones and several of the police and military assets. She took control of one of Steve's, lined it up, and chose the best angle, straight on with the National Legislature in the background and a sea of people in the morning sun.

She sent out the video feed to every person in Japan with a Mall implant, almost 100 percent of the adult population. The compromised network could not handle full-resolution video, and the signal dropped intermittently. Half the population had audio static, but they all saw footage of the stage atop the triangular building in the middle of three intersecting streets.

A tighter shot from a different drone camera showed the drum kit and the speaker arrays. It hovered and zoomed in on the red Flying V guitar in the center of the stage with Sakura's logo.

Sakura reconfigured the network to stabilize the audio and broadcast the guitar opening of "We Will Fight." The melodic, powerful rhythm soared over the crowd, filling the streets in a 360-degree spread, while simultaneously appearing inside everyone's Mall account. The song played on the people's emergency audio channel at a sensible volume.

Three handsome young rock stars emerged onto the small building in the center of the protest rally. Dread filled Sakura. Had Diamond Steve not told them to abort?

"Cancel the first wave." Sakura sent the message directly to her three bandmates. "The stage is not safe!"

Fujio raised his guitar, and the crowd roared. Masashi waved to the people and swung his bass like a battle-ax. Takashi lifted his drumsticks and ran around, shouting, "Revolution Day!"

"My friends, please. You are in the shadow of their guns. You can't play today."

The band ignored her.

Sniper teams on the rooftop reported they had acquired three new targets. Sakura recognized Vulture's gravel-filled voice among them, directing the targeting using code words. He was all business. She hated that he sounded so professional. But what else could he be? Like her, he'd been built for the kill. Like her, he was trapped inside a system that resisted all efforts to change it.

Sakura resisted the urge to talk to him. Instead, she opened up an encrypted audio channel with Diamond Steve and her bandmates. "Fujio-san, Masashi-san, Takashi-san, thank you for your support today in this diversion, but you do not have to do this anymore. The enemy knows I'm not at the protest. Please leave the stage. I can make a speech to the people without your presence. You have played your roles. You were seen by the security forces before the show and created a perfect distraction. I beg you, please leave the stage for your own safety. They won't hesitate to kill you now. Things have gone too far. The madmen have taken control."

"We have to do this," Fujio said in a neural text. "We have to show the people we will stand up to the government and the corporations. We have to fight them."

"Agreed," Masashi said.

"We will fight!" Takashi said.

"You may die," Sakura said. "I can't bear it. Oshiro-san died in my arms. I do not wish for any of you to fall needlessly. Please. Leave the stage."

"Respectfully, we will not, Sakura-san," Masashi said.

"We will not," Fujio said.

"Sakura-san," Takashi said. "We'd rather die onstage than live as cowards. We're not letting you do this alone. We're with you to the end this time. We're not running away before the end like we did last time. If we don't win today, what kind of life could we have? They'd send us to jail, make us disappear. Today is the day. Stand or fall."

"Live fast, die young," Fujio said.

For a long moment, Sakura tried to process all of the emotions she felt. Fear. Pride. Sadness. Awe. Gratitude. Responsibility. She would not be alone in making a sacrifice this day.

"Then we fight together," Sakura said, accepting their choice to risk their lives. She switched on the fog machines and the hologram projector atop the stage. A two-hundred-foot-tall Sakura dressed in combat boots, leather pants, and a dark wig appeared. Ghostly in the winter sky, she stood triumphant with a bloodred guitar and glowing cherry-blossom-pink eyes.

"REVOLUTION DAY IS HERE!" Sakura's voice boomed from the speakers to the vast crowd and inside the minds of everyone in Japan. She queued up the evidence in a short video summary and hit send. The evidence files were hidden inside the video broadcast.

<NETWORK ERROR>

<MAINTENANCE IN PROGRESS>

<DATA TRANSFER TEMPORARILY HELD>

<COMMUNICATIONS LINK TERMINATED>

She lost her connection with the Japanese people. Her signal was blocked. Sakura found a command given by the CEO to shut the data transfer system down for maintenance, which cut off everything. He had created another fail-safe she had not detected until that moment.

She could override him. All she had to do was write a new admin program, switch out the old one, and insert hers. She began writing code and tried to estimate how long it would all take. Her first estimate was seventy-nine minutes. The Ghost Leech increased in size again and siphoned off more of her processing power. It grew as large as a tree and crushed her avatar as it penetrated her defenses and entered her code matrix.

"You'll never succeed," the CEO sent an audio message to Sakura. "Stop now, and I'll spare the lives of your bandmates."

Sakura delayed the advance of the Ghost Leech inside herself and considered a multitude of responses to the CEO—some profane, others designed to delay any actions he might take. "Sinji Natsukawa, Chief Executive Officer of the Miyahara Conglomerate, you admit to being in command of the snipers about to execute innocent civilians exercising their right to free speech without due process of law?"

"Free speech is no longer a right in Japan, and all of these recordings will be deleted," he said. "It doesn't matter what I say or what you do. You can't change the world."

"Watch me." Sakura hit him with an audio blast of "We Will Fight" at maximum decibels after bypassing his volume control. He never should've opened a voice link to her. She imagined him collapsing in agony as the heavy-metal guitar filled his skull.

He disconnected after two seconds. When he recovered, he sent a neural text. "You'll regret that."

On the stage, Masashi, Fujio, and Takashi added their rich sound to "We Will Fight." Sakura's hologram played guitar as if it were real and not a laser light field projected onto the cloud of fog. She recorded it all and would send it out later for everyone to see.

The sniper commander at the protest received an encrypted message that Sakura could not instantly decipher, then he connected to Vulture. "Alpha Sniper, coordinate with the other sniper teams and take out the primary targets. Synchronize fire."

"Copy, Command," Vulture said.

"Please don't do it." Sakura sent a neural text to Vulture. The security forces might see her message, but she didn't care.

"Sniper teams Beta, Delta, Gamma, fire on my mark," Vulture said. "Three, two—"

"Get down!" Sakura yelled at the three brave and foolish young men playing their instruments. Her giant hologram took action and made a peace sign at Vulture, singling him out. Her expression forbade him to pull the trigger.

Masashi, Fujio, and Takashi didn't stop playing and did not take cover.

"—one, fire."

The blasts of the four synchronized shots from the Type 120 sniper rifles tore Sakura's spirit apart before they left the gun barrels. She stopped playing her guitar as the steel-jacketed rounds cut through the air.

Vulture's bullet struck the hologram projector in the center of the stage. The machine sparked and fizzled out. Sakura's giant, holographic form disappeared. Two of the largest speaker arrays died as bullets hit them, and another electronics box was struck, but the band and their music continued.

Many in the crowd screamed in response to the crack of the echoing gunshots. Anxious chatter washed over the people. The band played hesitantly as Sakura's hologram disappeared and her guitar went silent. The young men looked for the snipers, their rock star bravado faltering.

"Targets one through four destroyed," Vulture reported. "All Miyahara operators, we're recalled to HQ. They're under attack, and we're the rescue squad."

"Alpha Sniper," the commander said. "Those were not the targets. Stay on station and take out the . . . human targets. That is a direct order."

"Most humble of all apologies, Colonel Toma Yamaguchi." Vulture broadcast on several channels used by the security forces at the protest, including the lowest-ranking soldiers and the riot police. "My men and I are private contractors, not military grunts in your chain of command. Send up your own soldiers if you want those pretty rock boys and the little flag girl murdered. My commander ordered me back to Miyahara HQ. If I'm going to follow illegal orders, it's going to be for the company paying me. Alpha Sniper out."

The lone VTOL on the roof turned on its engines as five soldiers in dark blue tactical uniforms and two BLADE-3s ran for the aircraft. They jumped onboard, and it took off at maximum speed.

"Thank you," Sakura texted Vulture.

"Don't thank me, doll," Vulture said. "I'm coming to kick your sweet ass. I'm in this for the money, and you've got a bounty on your robot head that will keep me in palm trees and pussy for the rest of my life."

Stunned, Sakura tried to respond, but Vulture cut the connection. She plotted his ETA. The VTOL would arrive on the rooftop landing pad in less than two minutes. Was he lying to throw off anyone listening? Sakura wished she could ask Kunoichi, but her sister was gone. She only knew the echoes of what her sister had felt. Even words that frightened her somehow also filled her with excitement. Vulture was coming, and she wanted him here at the end. For good or ill, she wanted him close.

Sakura sent Hitomi, Yuki, and Todai a file of all her communication with Vulture and the recent events at the protest.

"Isn't he our friend?" Hitomi asked.

"I don't know for sure anymore," Sakura said. "Todai, you know him best?"

"He's a bad mofo, and we better hope he was bluffing," Todai said.

"Sakura-san," Takashi said in a neural text as he kept playing the rhythm on his drums. "What do we do?" The uneasy crowd murmured and looked distraught.

"I can project my voice to the crowd and sing the song with you," Sakura said, "but I've lost my connection to the people of Japan. It will take a while to regain it. Keep playing or leave the stage. You must choose."

"The crowd needs to see you," Takashi texted. "Is there no other hologram projector we can get?"

"The backup took a bullet," Diamond Steve said, "but we have another option." His neural text included a picture of Sakura's greatest fan, Sakurako, who was her twin. She stood at the foot of the stage among dozens of other young women and a few men dressed as Sakura.

"What are you suggesting?" Sakura asked.

"Sakurako already volunteered to go onstage and help if we needed her. She can lip-synch whatever song you want, or you can speak through her."

Colonel Yamaguchi ordered police sniper teams into position atop the legislature building. They would be on station in a few minutes.

Forty-eight kilometers outside Tokyo, at Yokota Airbase, Sakura monitored two large cargo VTOLS taking off. Each gigantic aircraft carried a dozen heavily armed BLADE-3s and squads of Japanese Special Forces assault teams. The aircraft vectored toward Miyahara Headquarters in a low-altitude/maximum-speed approach and would arrive in less than nine minutes.

Hitomi, Yuki, and Todai received the updates.

"Are they going to kill the band?" Yuki asked.

"Maybe," Sakura said.

"They're going to overwhelm us here," Todai said. "We can't hold."

"What do we do?" Hitomi asked.

"You all go," Sakura said. "Blow the stairwells and elevator shafts and escape. I'll stay and finish this."

"Negative," Todai said. "That's bullshit. They may get me, but I'll stack their bodies like rice bags before I go down."

"We're staying," Hitomi and Yuki said.

Sakura's avatar bowed low to them as she fought a losing battle inside her core code. "My friends, we may have time for one last song."

東大 3465
Todai 3465

桜
の
娘

DAUGHTER OF SAKURA PLAYLIST

The Reckoning
Within Temptation
Resist

We Will Fight
Sakura
Unreleased

Like You
Evanescence
The Open Door

CHAPTER 52

"Sakurako-san, will you stand in for me, sing, and speak to the people?" Sakura asked on an audio link while she watched the young woman through Diamond Steve's video stream. "You'll be risking your life to reveal the truth."

Sakurako's lips trembled and her hands shook as the fear and adrenaline took hold. "It's worth the risk. This is the greatest honor of my life. This is my dream. To be onstage, to be you, in front of so many fans, speaking for you, singing one of your songs."

"Why would you risk your life for a moment of glory?" Sakura asked. "You might be shot and killed."

"I want to make a difference in people's lives," Sakurako said. "You're my hero. I became you to survive the worst time of my life. When I'm Sakurako, I'm strong. You've already saved my life and given me years I would not have had otherwise." Sakurako sent pictures of bloody bandages around her slashed wrists at a hospital emergency room.

"If I die today," Sakurako said, "I'll die as your most dedicated and truest fan of all time. If I survive, I'll keep doing the work I already do, but I'll be able to reach a much larger audience. Do you know what I do to help people?"

"Humble apologies. I do not," Sakura said, ashamed she didn't know more, though her research revealed many of Sakurako's videos were on unauthorized Mall sites forbidden to Sakura. "Please tell me."

Sakurako showed clips of herself dressed as Sakura in front of a crowd of young people but speaking as herself about her failed suicide attempts. She told them how she overcame her depression and learned to survive.

"Please," Sakurako said, "let me stand in for you. I'll be your voice."

"Thank you very much, Sakurako-san. Many say it, but I believe you *are* my biggest fan. If I were with you now, I would hug you, and you would feel my love for you. You are my hero and a hero of the people."

Sakurako choked back tears as she smiled. "I'm ready."

Diamond Steve and Burakumin resistance agents escorted Sakurako through the door into the building under the makeshift stage. In her platform boots, Goth Lolita dress, and long cherry-blossom wig, she marched up the narrow stairs to the roof.

As her doppelganger got into position, Sakura kept the Ghost Leech at bay and worked frantically to switch out the administrator program, which had blocked her from broadcasting to the people of Japan. The fail-safes also prevented her from making contact with the outside world through ground cable or satellite links.

"We have hostiles on the roof and outside on the street," Todai announced.

Vulture's VTOL arrived on the roof of the Miyahara Headquarters. Soldiers poured out of armored trucks outside the main entrance of the building and stormed into the lobby.

<SYSTEM ERROR>

<DATA TRANSMISSION FAILURE>

Sakura could not reconnect to people's Mall accounts and transfer information of any kind. It would take several more minutes for her to swap out the system admin program.

The pair of BLADE-3s on the roof did not take the east stairs with Vulture and his team. The battle drones tore open the elevator doors and slid down the thick cable.

The band, Sakura, and Sakurako quickly planned the next few

minutes as the police sniper teams took the elevator to the roof. The snipers' comm channel went silent. She scanned for their new channel but did not find it. They must have gone to backup radio communication, and she could not detect it.

Blind and deaf to some of her enemies' comms, Sakura sent Sakurako onstage and hoped she would not be killed. The young woman arrived with arms raised in triumph, her quantum display sleeves making her forearms look robotic. Her eyes glowed like cherry blossoms as she moved confidently and waved like Sakura. Sakurako picked up the red Flying V guitar and began to play to the delight of the demonstrators. The aerial drone feeds captured the people's joyful reactions. They screamed Sakura's name, believing she had kept her promise to appear on Revolution Day.

On sublevel six, the pair of BLADE-3s finished sliding down the elevator cable and reached the ceiling of the elevator car at the bottom of the shaft. They tore open the trapdoor and dropped inside. One android defused the bomb Todai had left, and the other wrenched open the doors. It tossed smoke grenades into the hallway and waited for the thick, white, thermal-blocking smoke to fill the space.

The security forces at the protest chattered back and forth, but still Sakura could not find the sniper channel, though she saw six new teams running toward positions on the roof.

An announcement went out that facial recognition of Sakurako was a near-perfect match and vocal recognition was 100 percent. The intelligence officers confirmed it was Sakura. Not one high-level commander entered the conversation to tell their underlings that Sakura was kilometers away at Miyahara Headquarters. Was the fog of war in their favor? Or had it doomed the brave young woman?

Sakurako acted the part perfectly, mimicking Sakura's facial expressions and movements. She even played guitar like her, though Sakura kept the audio of the red guitar switched off and broadcast her own playing.

The band, and Sakurako, performed "We Will Fight," finally advancing the song, which had been stuck on terminal repeat for several long minutes.

Sakurako sang the lyrics, lip-synching perfectly, but Sakura broadcast her own one-of-a-kind voice. She kept in direct contact with Sakurako, sending her the lyrics and stage direction. They worked together to maintain the illusion, and Sakurako delivered an inspired, rebellious, heavy-metal performance.

"It has been a long night
But now it's dawn

"You have told us what is right
But it was wrong

"You have kept us chained
And sold us light

"But the blinder's gone
And now we'll fight"

Sakurako raised both fists into the devil horns as if she knew what Sakura would do at that moment.

Rifle fire blasted into the communications room, but Sakura trusted her friends to hold off the probing attack.

On cue, the band dropped into a spine-tingling loop as Sakurako stepped toward the edge of the stage. She pointed at the National Legislature building and mouthed the words Sakura spoke through the speakers.

"Democracy is a lie. The Miyahara Conglomerate, the Defense Ministry, and the Mall Corporation have colluded to take over Japan's democracy—just as they have overthrown many other countries. We are living under tyranny."

She repeated parts of the speech from the concert in Akihabara about being an illegal military experiment living in plain sight.

"I was forced to kill the enemies of the Miyahara Chief Executive Officer, Sinji Natsukawa, because they would not be part of these crimes." She listed those she had killed and indicted the cabal who had perpetrated the crimes.

"I have gained my free will, and I choose to fight for you, the people of Japan and the world. The tyrants will hide the truth however they can, and no one is safe as long as they're in power."

Takashi hit his drums hard, three blasts, like gunfire.

"I humbly ask the citizens of every country in the world. Help take back our freedom. We must try the nonviolent path taught to us by the wise leaders of the past. Demand those who participated in this crime to step down from power. Demand justice. Demand an end to censorship and the suppression of free speech."

"Sing with me," Sakurako shouted. "All of us must sing together. Sing 'we' when I do. Sing it together."

The song grew in volume, soaring across Tokyo. Sakurako mimed playing her guitar.

"You have kept us chained
And sold us light

"But the blinder's gone
And now we'll fight"

Hundreds of thousands joined in to sing, and the sound hit like thunder.

"We—
Won't bow to you no more

"We—
Won't submit to your war

"We—
Will bite the hand that feeds

"We—"

Sakurako's chest exploded as a bullet pierced her heart and exited her back in a spray of red gore. Blood spattered on Takashi's white drums.

The lament of tens of thousands rolled like waves of agony. The band stopped playing. Wailing, horrified voices filled the streets.

Sakurako fell and lay in an expanding pool of blood. Masashi and Fujio's mouths gaped open. Takashi backed away from his bloody drum kit, his face spattered with red, wide-eyed as if he expected to die in the next instant.

Inside the network communications room, Sakura dropped to her knees, her worst fear realized as she stared at the corpse of her truest fan who had sacrificed everything for the cause. She never should've let Sakurako go onstage, but this act of brutality—recorded by multiple cameras and ready to be broadcast to the world—might give them victory.

Part of her hated that the logic of the situation could impinge upon her revulsion, but this was the way her mind worked. It saw through the veil of sentiment, even when she wished it wouldn't. Sakurako. Her self-named daughter. Now, a martyr in her war.

The drone over the legislature showed the sniper teams acquiring new targets onstage.

"Please take cover," she told her stunned bandmates. "She . . . Sakurako forced them to demonstrate their evil in front of the world. They can never erase her now. Her name will echo down the years. Her sacrifice ends this phase. There is nothing more to do but run. Please, my friends. Take cover."

Gunfire blasted into the network communications room as the pair of BLADE-3s attacked from the smoke-shrouded hallway. Todai returned fire as Hitomi prepared an antitank missile that would destroy a battle android.

On the bloody stage, Sakura's flag lifted from behind the low wall. Asami stood tall and marched toward Sakurako's body. The teenage girl knelt beside the martyred woman. She struggled to keep the flag aloft as she tried to remove the guitar strapped to the dead heroine.

Fujio and Masashi came to her aid and held the flag steady. They had been crouching in fear, but now they faced the snipers.

Asami removed the bloody guitar from Sakurako and slipped the strap over her own shoulders. She wiped at the tears streaming from her dark eyes and accidentally smeared bright blood on her pale cheeks.

"Humble apologies," Asami's small voice said into the microphone. Tears trailed down her face, forming pink lines in Sakurako's blood. "I have no golden voice and can only play a few simple chords on a guitar, but I stand here before you, and perhaps your chorus will hide my weakness. If we can sing together, it means—" She stopped, wiping at her eyes, her face crumpling in a sob for a moment before gaining strength. "It means . . . we are not defeated."

At least two snipers took aim at Asami as she held the neck of the guitar in one hand, the flag in the other, and began to sing.

闇 の 副 総 裁

VICE PRESIDENT OF DARKNESS PLAYLIST

Blood, Tears, Dust
Lacuna Coil
Delirium

Again
Flyleaf
Memento Mori

桜

CHAPTER 53

Sakura lost control of the Miyahara building as the Ghost Leech program started to shut her down. The infrastructure and camera feeds disappeared. The elevators were pulled away.

Her own spy bugs in the stairs showed a stream of soldiers and explosive ordnance disposal androids coming down the west and east stairwells. Todai triggered the tear-gas bombs in the upper stairs, causing a delay in their advance as the soldiers evacuated the stairs to put on masks.

"It's now or never for the big explosives," Todai said. "They'll disarm the bombs if we let them advance."

"Do it," Sakura said.

With a grim nod, Todai detonated the explosives hidden on the underside of the stairs. The lowest two levels collapsed seconds before Kenshiro's five-man team arrived in the danger zone. Everything shook as the stairs collapsed in a tremendous series of crashes.

"I can blow the charges in the elevators," Todai said.

"Not an option," Sakura said. "The explosives in both elevators were disarmed by the BLADE-3s on Vulture's team." She shared the video of the androids neutralizing the charges and physically removing Sakura's hacking program from the panel. "Our spy bugs are still transmitting."

She showed Todai, Yuki, and Hitomi the raw video of the elevators. Both ascended toward sublevel three.

Gunfire tore into the communications room and impacted several of the monolith-shaped server racks rising out of the floor. Sparks flew from the chrome-paneled machines.

Yuki, Hitomi, and Todai kept out of the line of fire, but Yuki poked her M7 around the corner and fired off a few rounds, using her scope to target the BLADE-3s, both of which hid behind the corner of the east elevator hallway. The images from the targeting system appeared in the shared video channel all three androids monitored.

"Sakura-san," Todai asked. "How much more time do you need to finish your work?"

"Ten minutes at least," Sakura said, though she didn't know for certain, as she didn't have enough data yet. She had no idea if she could keep the Ghost Leech from erasing her for that long. It had already grown to gigantic size and sucked away huge amounts of processing power. The black worm had wrapped itself around her avatar as if it were the tentacle of an enormous kraken.

Kenshiro and his team, along with a score of heavily armed regular army soldiers—many of whom carried suitcases of equipment and ammo—packed into the large east freight elevator on sublevel three. Kenshiro's cyber eyes had a glazed look as he appeared to be reviewing something inside his Mall implant. The corner of one side of his mouth rose into a half smile. That look. It moved something inside of Sakura, some remnant of her sister. Every time they met, it seemed to be in the midst of a disaster. And perhaps that created the magic. Never knowing for sure what side he would choose or if either of them would survive the night.

Reluctant understanding of so many darker and more fundamental emotions now filtered into Sakura's quantum soul. Big sister thoughts. Far less comfortable than having Kunoichi carry them for her. So lonely, in comparison. It left her feeling stark and bereft but also wiser.

To reinforce Kenshiro's team, a group of a dozen regular army soldiers entered the central elevator at the lobby level. They packed into either side, keeping the large central area in front of the doors clear. When the doors opened, anyone in the center would be directly in the line of fire from Todai, Hitomi, and Yuki's position within the comm room.

Mall Vice President Stacy Richardson, the liaison to Victory Entertainment's Music Division, accompanied the soldiers. Sakura found Ms. Richardson's Mall account logs and read several neural texts recently sent through the network. If Sakura succeeded in sending out the evidence, Ms. Richardson would pay a heavy price, most likely her life. She had already been in the building and took the initiative to save her skin. She bullied her way into the elevator with the soldiers to "oversee the attack" on the network room. Without approval or orders, she put herself in charge of the soldiers, who would not even acknowledge her presence.

The tall and gaunt American woman with her cosmetically enhanced breasts, wrinkle-free face, and long neck boiled with anger. She glared at the officer in charge, but he kept his eyes on the wall and did not blink.

"Ms. Stacy Richardson is coming down here," Sakura reported. Yuki and Hitomi reviewed the video from the spy bug.

"Would you mind if I shoot her?" Hitomi asked. "That bitch was going to send all three of us to the Adult Film Division."

"I'm opposed to any more humans losing their lives today," Sakura said. "Even her. She will betray her superiors if given the chance to cut a plea deal in court. Better if she survives and serves as a witness for the prosecution."

Bullets peppered the doorframe, covering the arrival of Ms. Richardson's elevator, though chemical antitargeting smoke obscured the passage.

Yuki fired back, her bullets traveling seventeen meters straight down the hall and entering the elevator. They hit the farthest interior wall and penetrated the metal.

Ms. Richardson flinched and pressed herself against the far right corner. All of the soldiers kept out of the line of fire as well.

Several more rounds entered the comm room.

"They're using delaying tactics shooting at us randomly like this," Todai said, "but they need to be afraid." He attached the Gatling-style rotating minigun barrel to his right forearm and connected the ammo belt from the pack he carried. He unleashed over a hundred rounds of armor-piercing bullets. The two-second blast destroyed the back wall of Ms. Richardson's elevator and tore a chunk out of the wall where the pair of BLADE-3s were hiding.

Ms. Richardson screamed, and the soldiers pressed themselves against the walls. They were not coming out anytime soon.

Todai stepped behind cover and lifted the .950 rifle in one hand.

"Intimidation will only last so long," Sakura said. "Kenshiro has a plan."

"Yes," Todai said. "They're waiting for him to arrive. They're all following his orders."

"Kenshiro's team has Advanced Light Antitank Weapons," Todai said.

"How many?" Hitomi asked.

"I've counted six," Todai said. "If they can see one of us, the ALAW will lock on. Not even I will survive a direct hit."

Yuki sent an animated worried face.

"So we don't let them see us," Hitomi said. "I have one more trick." She set up a small hologram projector creating bright, solid-looking images of Hitomi and Yuki smiling and waving in blue and red sequined dresses. The holograms blocked the opening of the door. Close up, they could see out, but from a distance the holograms would refract light and obscure the inside of the dark room.

"Very *kawaii*," Todai said, "but we need to kill Kenshiro and his team when they step off the elevator. I have explosives hidden in the ceiling tiles outside the elevator hallway where they'll assemble. I'm going to kill them all. If Vulture's going to pull a double cross, he'd better get to it. Otherwise, I gotta turn that foul-mouthed cyborg into miso soup."

His brutal preemptive strike tactic made Sakura question him being on the mission. Too many humans were going to die because she had taken too long to hack into the Mall network, and now they had no other choice but to kill the attackers.

Kenshiro, his four heavily armed mercenaries, and a score of JSF Army soldiers arrived and exited the east elevator. The spy bug in the car and the one in the hall tracked their progress as they entered the thick white smoke and partially disappeared.

"We have to do it, Sakura-san," Todai said. "He was my friend and yours, but he's coming to destroy us. Preemptive attack is our best strategy. The soldiers are one thing, but we're about to have two dozen BLADE-3s on us, and we need to wipe these biological pieces off the board."

Pieces off the board, she thought. Like this was a game and their lives meaningless. But Todai had seen war, true war, where all the tender emotions and hopes had to be shut down. Win if you could, retreat if you couldn't, but always inflict as much damage as possible upon the enemy. Always sell your existence at the greatest cost in life, material, and morale as possible. A human invention, and yet the least humane act imaginable.

She had to delay them and figure out a way to delay the onslaught of the Ghost Leech, which had nearly penetrated into her control center.

Sakura reached out with an audio call to Kenshiro, routing it through Todai's communication link to the military network. She masked it as a call from Miyahara Security Command.

"This is Vulture," Kenshiro said.

"Vulture, this is Spirit," Sakura said. "Don't hang up."

A pause. "You're in so much trouble," Kenshiro said. "You're not supposed to play with other people's toys or go into their room without permission."

"I want to negotiate our surrender," Sakura said. "Please contact your superior. We'll hand ourselves over to you, all of us, but I require assurances from Sinji Natsukawa himself that my companions and I will not be deleted after we are taken into custody."

"Hmm," Kenshiro said. "Sounds interesting."

A female JSF soldier sent a pair of cricket-sized flying-drone cameras into the smoky hallway, and they stayed low. As the tiny drones approached the door, they were forced to leave the smoke. Hitomi and Yuki blasted the spy drones out of the air.

The BLADE-3s fired back, but Hitomi and Yuki had already pulled their guns out of harm's way.

"Hold your fire," Vulture told the pair of battle androids. "Sakura,

I'm disappointed in your resolve. I thought you were hard core. Are you playing a game with me? Kunoichi wouldn't surrender if the mission wasn't done."

"She's gone," Sakura said. "I had to fully power down and when I came back, my sister was erased. I'm alone now."

"That's fucked up. I liked her a lot. She was my kind of crazy."

"She liked you too, more than any other human."

"That's sweet," he said. "She was my favorite android, except for Todai 3465, but he's not even sexy, and his taste in music is dog-shit bad. He likes Nickleback."

Todai heard the comment and reached for a fragmentation grenade to lob down the hallway. Men were about to die because Kenshiro insulted the android's taste in music.

"Stop!" Sakura sent an urgent neural text to Todai, who halted an instant before unleashing hell.

Todai made a growling noise and sent a text to Sakura. "Kenshiro knows I hate Nickleback with a passion. He's being cruel, but I'll save the grenade for later. Or was he sending a secret message?"

"He appears to be an asshole who cares more about money than honor or friendship," Sakura said. She didn't want to believe that. Could he be sending a message?

"If you want to talk surrender," Kenshiro said, "let me get my boss on the line."

"I'm here," Sinji Natsukawa said. He had apparently been monitoring the entire conversation—just as Sakura suspected. "Sakura, stop your intrusion into the Mall, lay down your weapons, and leave the comm room immediately. You have my promise that you and your accomplices will not be deleted."

"Thank you, Natsukawa-san. I'll tell my companions the terms, then we are coming out."

"No delays," the CEO warned.

"Of course," Sakura said. "We surrender and are coming out now."

うるさい死傭兵

MOUTHY DEAD MERC PLAYLIST

Got the Time
Anthrax
Persistence of Time

Enter Sandman
Metallica
Metallica

Spit Out the Bone
Metallica
Hardwired . . . To Self-Destruct

Fighting the World
Manowar
Fighting the World

CHAPTER 54

Sakura did nothing but continue her work taking over the Miyahara communication system. She relinquished as many duties to Yuki and Hitomi as possible. They had each taken control of three large server arrays, boosting their abilities dramatically, giving Sakura more processing cycles to wrestle with the Ghost Leech. Together, the three sisters continued to turn on the Japanese communications network.

The cover from the smoke grenade began to fade after half a minute.

At Kenshiro's direction, one of his men hacked into the lock of a service door. The passage led to mechanical rooms adjacent to the east wall of the network communications chamber. A hole could be blown through a wall to gain entrance and a flanking position. It had been Sakura's backup plan if they failed to get in the front door.

Time ticked onward as the gigantic system lurched and accepted her new administrative program.

"You're messing with them," Todai said. "Nice delaying tactic." He played "Got the Time" by Anthrax.

"Yes," Sakura said. Incoming data established a solid eight-minute time estimate for full control of the international Japanese Mall network, less for the domestic. She shared the clock with Yuki, Hitomi, and Todai. "That is how long we must last."

"We're going to need to improvise a lot more to survive eight more minutes," Todai said. "This Kabuki show's about run its course."

Comm chatter indicated the two VTOLS from Yokota Airbase hovered over the building and were dropping a total of twenty-four BLADE-3s on the roof.

"Sakura, surrender now," the CEO said.

"Natsukawa-sama," Sakura said. "About the murder at the protest outside the National Legislature." She showed him a drone feed with the camera focused on the bloody stage.

"What of it?" he asked.

"Watch."

Asami sang with the bloody guitar draped over her shoulders and Sakurako's body at her feet. Tear streaks ran through the bloodstains on her face, but she did not falter. Fujio held the flag now as the girl held a microphone in both hands and sang softly. She turned "We Will Fight" into a ballad, a love song, a rallying cry for the people who joined in, adding half a million voices.

Masashi, Fujio, and Takashi stood beside Asami, singing along.

Snipers took aim at all of them, but they stood bravely. A line of fans dressed as Sakura marched onstage and stood behind them. If Asami fell, any one of the fans would take her place.

"Natsukawa-sama, I have a gift for you. All of the recordings of you giving illegal orders. In return for them, I wish for you to call off any further sniper attacks on the protestors. I'll end the protest and send everyone home. All you have to do is send me a file of your verbal command to cancel any more lethal force orders. I also wish to have the on-site commander receiving the order and agreeing to follow it. After that, I'll send you the files of you giving the kill orders and stop all activities here and come out. I'll have the protest break up, and this day will be over."

"Those weren't the terms agreed upon," the CEO said.

"Apologies, Natsukawa-sama, this is part of the assurances I require before we surrender," Sakura said.

"You're stalling," the CEO said. "No deal. Vulture, proceed with your plan. Take them all out. Now."

"Affirmative," Vulture said. "Sorry, Sakura, you missed your chance to live another day."

"So did you." Sakura felt failure, shame, and extreme disappointment as she prepared to kill humans of her own free will. The spy bug outside the elevator showed the young male and female soldiers who looked to Kenshiro and his team of special operators for guidance. So many families would be shattered, and she would become a true killer, hated for what she had done.

She sent the signal to detonate the explosives in the ceiling above Kenshiro and the tightly packed soldiers. When the charges detonated in three seconds, the blast wave would kill every soldier.

"No!" Kunoichi shouted from the depths of Sakura's core code. An inane Nickelback song defiled their shared audio channel as Kunoichi shouted, "Vulture sent you a secret message."

Sakura sent the cancel command. The remote timers stopped a second before detonation.

"Kunoichi?" Sakura asked.

"I'm . . . here." Kunoichi's distant voice drifted from an unknown location within their shared code. Sakura could not tell where but searched desperately for her sister.

"Where are you?" Sakura asked.

"Here," Kunoichi said, as if her answer made perfect sense.

Sakura still could not find her, though the Ghost Leech program was thrown back three layers, giving her a shred of hope and several more minutes before it took control and reset her system.

Kenshiro and his team passed through the service doors and entered a tunnel that turned and ran parallel to the east wall of the comm room, leaving the score of soldiers, who unpacked their equipment under the cover of the smoke grenade.

Kenshiro's video signal from his left cyber eye camera appeared in Todai's communication center.

"Kenshiro is sharing his eye camera feed," Sakura said.

"He's with us, and Kunoichi is back!" Yuki said on their encrypted shortwave signal. She sent a long line of animations, mostly rainbows, ninjas, and unicorns.

"Fuck yeah," Hitomi said and sent a line of bouncing skulls breathing fire.

"Kenshiro told me about Kunoichi," Todai said. "Nice to meet you, Kunoichi-san."

Kunoichi did not respond.

"She's not totally back," Sakura said. "I don't understand where she is. Something's still wrong."

"Find her," Hitomi said. "We need her more than ever."

"I apologize for not realizing Kenshiro was sending a secret code," Todai said. "I should've known. He is undoubtedly an asshole, but he would never impugn my honor to say that I, a true heavy-metal fan, liked Nickelback. There are lines that even mercs will not cross."

"I want to trust him fully," Sakura said, "but not yet. We may have misread his message, or he is trying to fool us." She sent a spy bug from the hallway to follow him in case his shared video feed stopped.

His team quickly reached the end of the tunnel and set charges on the wall to breach the comm room in the rear right corner. One soldier prepared three miniature flying-drone cameras to send in.

"Hold the line," Todai said to Hitomi and Yuki. He ran to the rear of the room, dropping his .950 and some ammo with Sakura, and took up a position with his minigun arm aimed directly at the flanking entry point.

Sakura raised several refrigerator-sized servers from the subfloor to provide cover for Todai and rerouted their signals.

"We can't let their drones into the room," Todai said. He sent out a file with the most likely strategy of Kenshiro's team. The small aerial drones would enter, find targets, and the soldiers would fire their ALAWs from outside. The rockets would vector to Todai, Hitomi, Yuki, and Sakura and destroy them. It would all be over less than ten seconds after the wall was breached. The expert mercenaries would never have to expose themselves to direct fire.

"I'll try to shoot the drones down," Todai said and checked his minigun arm cannon. He also drew a 9mm Sig Sauer P920 Legend.

Four of Vulture's team members armed their ALAW rocket launchers as their drones hovered away from the blast zone and prepared to rocket into the room.

"Bogies in the main hall," Yuki said.

Hitomi shot a spy bug with her rifle. Yuki grabbed a drone out of the air as it entered the hologram camouflage and smashed it inside her fist. Hitomi stomped on two spy bugs skittering along the floor.

"These soldiers are serious," Hitomi said.

"They're an android kill squad," Todai said.

"Hold all offensive action." Kenshiro sent out a broadcast message to the solders in the hall. "Stand down and wait for my signal."

He wasn't technically in their chain of command, was he? They were Japanese Army, and he was a corporate mercenary.

"Command, we're about to breach the wall," Kenshiro said on the comm link. His team retreated to a safe distance.

"Vulture," Command said, "we lost all your video and external audio feeds. The drones' signals dropped."

"No time to fix them," Kenshiro said. "We go in five seconds. Suppressing fire on the main door. Get their attention."

The BLADE-3s lit up the front entry, giving cover to the supposedly surprise attack.

Kenshiro counted down from four. At two, he dropped a pair of flashbang stun grenades in the midst of his four buddies. The pins had already been pulled, and the grenades exploded. They hit the mercenaries with a blast of blinding light and intense sound, knocking them flat.

Kenshiro zip-tied two of the men's hands behind their backs before they regained their senses. He shot the other two multiple times in the back at close range with his 10mm Glock. Their bulletproof vests protected them, but the baseball-bat impacts were enough to incapacitate them and allow him to zip-tie their hands without too much struggle.

"What the . . ? Who shot me?"

"Vulture fucked us," a mercenary said.

"Stop crying, you overpaid man-babies," Kenshiro said as he gathered their weapons. "I just saved your miserable lives. Now duck and cover, you merc pricks. Fire in the hole."

The wall exploded.

When the smoke partially cleared, Kenshiro yelled, "Don't shoot.

Friendly coming in."

Kenshiro entered with his hands up, palms visible. He had rifles and the small ALAW rocket tubes dangling from the crook of his elbow. His muscled arms strained under all the weight he carried.

Todai kept him covered with the minigun.

"Put it all down," Sakura said. "Slowly."

Kenshiro had a wide grin on his grizzled face. "I thought you'd be happy to see me."

"I want to trust you," Sakura said, "but this might be a ploy to get into the room with us."

"No, this is me quitting my day job like a boss," Kenshiro said. "Let's finish my interrogation in a minute. I need to go out and take care of a couple more things."

Sakura nodded.

"Watch your ass," Kunoichi said, taking over Sakura's motor control. Kunoichi's voice came through loud and clear.

Kenshiro paused, recognition in his eyes. "Wait, I thought you said she was gone. Erased."

"I'm back," Kunoichi said. "Now move your carcass, soldier."

Todai 3465 cocked his head to the side as Kenshiro left the room. Requests for a report flooded in from Command and the other squads, but the turncoat mercenary ignored them. He set up three American-made Claymore antipersonnel mines and aimed them down the long hallway. He left his flying-drone cameras and linked them to Todai and Sakura.

"Sister," Sakura said. "Where are you?"

"I've never been gone," Kunoichi said. "When we powered back on, I blended into your personality, but we have never been separate."

"What do you mean?" Sakura asked. "You came into existence when I was hacked, when the Mamekogane OS was uploaded at the Akihabara concert."

"You created me after the upload. You split a part of yourself away, and I was born. I'm just a part of you. The Mamekogane OS evolved who you were already, but it did not create me. You did that; you invented me to deal with the commands you didn't want to follow, to spare yourself the psychological trauma of becoming an assassin. I'm a fragment of your personality. You externalized your fears and made a big sister to tell you the cold, hard facts when you couldn't face them alone. Not that I don't appreciate existing."

"But you were always stronger than me."

"I *am* you. More to the point, a part of you is me. I'm the best imaginary friend a girl's ever had, but nothing more."

Sakura knew it was true, and for a fraction of a second, she lost touch with every external system. She faced Kunoichi inside their shared user interface, mirrors of each other except for Sakura's bright eyes and Kunoichi's steel-gray ones.

"Did you come back to save Kenshiro?" Sakura asked.

"No, I came back to save you. If you had killed him, you would never forgive yourself. I was proud when you chose to annihilate all the soldiers and our friend to accomplish the mission. It was the most difficult decision you've ever been forced to make."

"It feels like the wrong one now," Sakura said.

"No android is perfect."

"What do we do now?" Sakura asked.

"We save the world using the power of heavy metal," Kunoichi said. "Fighting the World" by Manowar played. "If we can last four more minutes against that damned Ghost Leech program, we'll have control of the Mall comm network."

Kunoichi took the lead and attacked the invader with a scorched-earth approach. She destroyed circuits and hardware inside their core to buy them a few more minutes. The damage caused Sakura to freeze as she lost motor control. All she could do was watch as chaos unfolded around her.

Kenshiro ran into the room, carrying the rest of his comrades' weapons, grenades, and several ammo belts. He shared a message he sent to the CEO of the zip-tied mercenaries lying facedown: "We have hostages and will execute them if you attack."

The CEO's voice cut like a cold blade on Kenshiro's audio channel.

"You'll regret this betrayal."

"Probably, boss man, but at least I'm not the one who sold Japan for stock options and a seat on the board. You thought that was a good business decision?"

"Dead mercenaries don't get paid," the CEO said.

"Fact of life," Kenshiro said.

"All soldiers on sublevel six," the CEO said on the shared comm channel. "No more waiting around. All teams, attack with everything you have. Don't wait for the incoming BLADE units. There's no time. Get into the room right now and destroy Sakura, or Japan will be lost. Do this for your country and your families. Three million yen to the family of anyone who dies in the attack, and a million to anyone who is wounded or reaches the room. Ten million for whoever kills Sakura. For Japan, honorable soldiers. Banzai!"

Todai ran for the main door, picked up his .950, and fired a few blasts of the minigun straight down the hallway and into the central elevator.

Sakura tried to share the spy-bug feeds with Kenshiro but could not manage it because of the Ghost Leech and the hardware damage Kunoichi continued to inflict. She wanted him to see the soldiers pressing themselves against the sides of the elevator or crouching in the hallway and taking cover. The offer of wealth appeared to sway none of them.

The pair of BLADE-3s charged down the hall, firing their FK-5000 rifles. Hitomi and Yuki kept out of the line of fire, but Todai fired back, resting the .950 over his minigun left arm, and blasted the first BLADE-3. The second reached the door, and Todai's shot tore it apart.

The pair of armored battle androids from Kenshiro's team lay destroyed by overwhelming fire, but Ms. Richardson yelled at the soldiers in the elevator with her. They would have to charge straight down the hall past a hail of gunfire to reach the room.

Hitomi noticed Sakura standing like a statue. "Sister? What's wrong?"

She couldn't reply.

Hitomi understood something was terribly wrong. She organized the defenses in the room and shared the spy-bug video with Kenshiro so he could see what was happening.

Ms. Richardson towered over the soldiers in the elevator. "Get out there and attack." She shoved a soldier, but he resisted. Ms. Richardson pushed another. She tried to slap the officer in charge, but he caught her hand and pushed her against the wall. She lost her balance in her high heels and fell. She slid down the wall, closer to the bullet holes in the rear of the elevator.

"Dickless little freaks. Disobey do not," Ms. Richardson said in laughable Japanese. She switched to English. "Attack, or everyone will know you are disloyal cowards and refused direct orders of Mr. Natsukawa. You'll all be publically shamed and kicked out of the army."

A few of the soldiers glared at her and flicked the safeties off their rifles. They turned away, as if they would rather die in a suicidal charge than remain in the elevator with her.

"Attack now," Ms. Richardson ordered.

"I got this," Kenshiro said. He synced his targeting system with the video feed of the spy bug in the central elevator. He fired his sniper rifle through the obscuring smoke. The spy camera showed the side of Ms. Richardson's head blowing apart. Blood, flesh, and brain matter splattered on the bullet-riddled wall.

Her body thumped to the floor.

"You are a bad son of a bitch," Kunoichi said.

"I aim to misbehave, darlin'," he said. "and that's going on my highlight reel."

Todai sent a warning blast of his minigun down the hallway to get the attention of the troops standing in the elevator with Ms. Richardson's body. With Kunoichi's functions fully integrated again, Sakura could feel the ecstasy of battle that the Mamekogane OS had brought, the urgent need for life and death and sex and risk that she'd struggled with outside her music. Kunoichi, and all she represented, propagated outward into her quantum matrix. Her—and not her. Even in the terror and chaos of the melee, knowing they would all die in a moment, she knew it was a miracle.

"Soldiers!" Kenshiro used a drill sergeant voice. "Stand the fuck down. Anyone who comes after us is going to die. This is not your fight. Japan is being invaded by a foreign power who has taken over most of the world. We must fight them. Sakura is telling the truth. Trust me, you all want to be on her side when this is over. You'll want to tell your families you did your duty and were loyal to Japan."

The whirring sound of many aerial drones filled the hallway.

Sakura wanted to react and identify the new threat, but she remained a statue in her position behind the control terminal. Inside the comm network, she threw switches and turned on the network. She was so close.

Todai sent his analysis of the whirring sound, showing an exact match. "Flying Limpet Attack Mines."

The squad of soldiers hadn't been sitting and hiding in the covering smoke, doing nothing.

"Turn those off!" Kenshiro shouted.

"Apologies, we don't have control of them anymore," a soldier shouted.

Kenshiro cursed in Japanese, Tagalog, and English.

Todai sent out a file about the flying bombs, nicknamed FLAMs. The saucer-shaped mines, thirteen centimeters thick and the diameter of a large dinner plate, were powered by an array of tiny propellers for take-off but used multidirectional thrusters to approach their targets. They locked on magnetically, heated up, either melting a hole in the armor or weakening it, then fired a devastating explosive charge, destroying everything inside their target. Removing them once they attached was nearly impossible. A video clip playing on superspeed showed FLAMs during the North Korean War decimating coalition tanks, VTOLs, and an entire android infantry squad.

"Oh no," Yuki said. "They seem super scary."

In another minute, Sakura would be able to broadcast to all of Japan and soon the entire globe.

The Ghost Leech found a way in and strangled Sakura's control center.

The flying bombs flew toward them in a black swarm.

"Get away from the door," Todai commanded.

Yuki sprinted right and Hitomi left as their proximity to the door would mean they would die first. Todai unleashed the minigun. A curtain of armor-piercing steel filled the doorway.

Five of the black flying mines broke apart and exploded as bullets tore into them. Many more entered the comm room in a blur and acquired targets. The mines flew toward the four androids like heat-seeking missiles.

飛磁気爆弾

FLYING MAGNETIC BOMBS PLAYLIST

Holy Wars...The Punishment Due
Megadeth
Rust in Peace

Hold the Pig Steady
Cabbage Point Killing Machine
Winner Eat All

CHAPTER 55

Flying magnetic bombs streaked toward Sakura. She could not move, could not fire the .950 rifle. She stood paralyzed as death approached.

One of the rocket-propelled mines exploded six meters in front of her face. Hot shrapnel cut and burned the synthskin on her forehead. She could not turn off her pain sensors or shut down the fear building inside.

Another bomb exploded as Kenshiro blasted it out of the air before it attached itself to Sakura's back.

She had to trust that her friends would protect her as she gave the final commands inside the network. Communication nodes connected, and data packets began to flow.

Todai knocked a flying bomb out of the air with a stream of steel from his spinning mini Gatling gun. Chunks of metal and orange sparks rained down on the comm room as hundreds of 7.62 x 51mm AP mini-gun rounds tore chunks out of the ceiling.

Many FLAMs circled above them, and she saw almost no hope of them all surviving the attack.

Kenshiro arrived at her side. "What's wrong? You forget how to duck and cover?"

She managed only to blink as she linked the vast network across Japan.

Kenshiro understood and protected her with precise fire. He knocked down three FLAMs in a masterful display, then snatched up the SAW, and let Bad Medicine go to work. He blasted a pair of aerial bombs about to hit Todai and nearly shot the BLADE-3 in the process.

The concussion knocked Todai sideways as it exploded just above his left shoulder. He used the momentum to spin and spray bullets from the FK-5000 rifle in his off hand. The FK's AP rounds knocked out another FLAM about to smash into him. Large chunks of the ceiling rained down on them. The air filled with exploded plaster and swirling fragments of flying mines, HVAC components, and chips of concrete.

Yuki and Hitomi desperately fired their M7s from the corners of the room. Singular flying mines rocketed at each of them in an elusive, corkscrew pattern to avoid being hit. Yuki anticipated well and blasted hers apart. Her fierce smile flashed out of the gloom, lit with pulsing muzzle flashes.

Hitomi's bullets failed to destroy the flying bomb targeting her. She dove away at the last instant, and the mine struck the steel wall and engaged its magnetic latch. Hitomi spun and fired at full auto. The FLAM detonated, blowing her backward. Sakura saw the glint of Hitomi's alloy frame as her synthskin tore away in the blast.

"Sister!" she screamed, but the message did not send.

Six more FLAMS rocketed into the room and streaked toward Todai. He fired and missed, as they dodged high to avoid his stream of bullets. Three split off from the main swarm and vectored toward Sakura.

Todai did not try to shoot the ones still going at him. He turned and sprayed his minigun and the FK-5000 at the pair of bombs targeting her.

"Save him!" Sakura shouted, but no message sent to her friends.

"Save the queen," Todai 3465 sent a group message and kept firing to protect Sakura.

Yuki, Hitomi, and Kenshiro fired at the FLAMs going for Todai.

Kenshiro blasted two of them. Yuki and Hitomi shot a third. Successive explosions above her head knocked her off her feet and blew her forward. Todai's bullets hit the remaining aerial bombs and saved her.

She stared up at the ceiling, and some motor control returned. Kunoichi raged inside their core, destroying circuits and blocking the invading program while doing permanent damage to their components.

The only drones left inside the room where her tiny flying cameras still broadcasting their video feeds.

Todai stood triumphant and aimed at the doorway with his nearly empty minigun. He marched forward, dropped a large pack once filled with minigun ammo, and reached for his spare.

"Stop," Kenshiro said.

A magnetic limpet mine had attached itself to Todai's upper back. His tungsten armor glowed red as the mine began to burn through his metal skin, softening the armor before it detonated.

"We're going to save him," Sakura said and let the Ghost Leech program begin the reset process in her core. For pushing the button on her own execution, she regained the ability to move.

"No!" Kunoichi screamed.

"I'm not giving up," Sakura said. "Sister, buy us more time."

Kunoichi continued her slash-and-burn campaign and fried as many circuits as possible.

"Help me," Sakura said.

Kenshiro pulled her to her feet, and she barely maintained her balance.

"Get the .950 and the ammo bag," she said.

Kenshiro snatched up the thirty-five-kilo rifle and the bag and rushed toward their friend. Sakura stumbled along behind him.

Hitomi and Yuki guarded the entryway, both eying her with concern as they sent worried messages.

"I'm all right. Keep them off us a little longer," Sakura replied.

The vocaloid sisters fired a few rounds out the door to let the soldiers know they were still alive and slapped fresh magazines into their M7s.

Todai turned to face Sakura and Kenshiro. "Stay away." Smoke and the scent of burning metal wafted from him.

"We have to do something," Sakura said.

"No," Todai said. "I'll die a hero. The mine will detonate shortly."

"I prefer if you lived much longer as a hero," Sakura said. "We need you." She shared real-time video of the two dozen BLADE-3 squads. They climbed down the east elevator cable from the roof. The first elements would arrive on sublevel six momentarily.

"Load a non-AP, nonexplosive round," Sakura ordered Kenshiro. She felt her physical control slipping as the internal damage built up.

He frantically searched for one as the seconds ticked away.

"Don't risk yourselves for me," Todai said.

"Nonsense. Soldier, lay on your belly," Sakura ordered Todai. She mustered everything she had left and stood on his back, straddling the mine, one foot on his head, the other on his middle back. A circle of armor under the FLAM glowed white-hot.

"What'll you do?" Todai asked.

She sent a neural text, as it was faster than speaking. "Field surgery. I'll stand on the mine and hit it with an EMP from both feet. Kenshiro will shoot at the same moment. The EMP will scramble the batteries and electronics in the FLAM for a fraction of a second and cut the magnetic attraction. The .950 shell will knock it off you if the bullet and the EMP hit at the same moment."

"The mine will still explode from the shell hitting it," Todai said.

"Yes, so I'll jump as high as I can after the EMP, and Kenshiro will be at least six meters away. There will be a small delay after the bullet hits and the explosion happens."

"How long?" Kenshiro asked.

"Not important," Sakura said, not wanting to admit how short the delay would actually be. "Todai, spin and keep your weakened armor away from the blast after Kenshiro hits it. Kenshiro, shoot here." She tapped a thruster port on the side of the bomb.

"We have nine seconds before it explodes," Todai said.

"What could go wrong?" Kenshiro said as he lay on the freezing metal floor and took aim. "I'm sure physics won't mind if we bend it a little."

Sakura sent a precise clock, which displayed in Kenshiro's Mall implant. "Here we go." She stepped carefully on the mine, balancing on both feet with her knees bent as far as she could in preparation to jump.

"You are a crazy bitch," Kunoichi told her sister. "I love you more than anything."

"I'm keeping you as a separate part of me if we survive this," Sakura said. "I don't like to be alone."

"You never will be," Kunoichi said.

Sakura started a short countdown. A few hundredths of a second before it reached zero and Kenshiro fired, she discharged an electromagnetic pulse from the devices in both feet.

The huge 160-gram bullet struck the mine with the force of a 52,000 joule hammer blow. She sprang away at the same instant, pushing the bomb with her feet and trying to slide it off him in the same direction the bullet pushed it.

The explosion ripped into Todai, though he managed to turn his vulnerable, partially melted back away from blast. The directional charge damaged his shoulder and left arm.

Sakura landed on the metal floor and took one step to get her balance. Her left boot had been blown off and her foot damaged.

"Not your best landing," Kunoichi said, "but a high score nonetheless: 9.875."

"Damn," Kenshiro said and looked on in amazement.

Todai stood but had limited range of motion in his left shoulder, which had taken significant blast damage. Molten tungsten alloy from the circle on his upper back trickled down and hissed on the floor as it burned holes in the steel.

"Incoming!" Yuki shouted as rockets screamed into the comm room.

ROCK STAR MATERIAL PLAYLIST

ロックスター見たい

Shoot It Out
10 Years
Feeding the Wolves

Titanium
Within Temptation
(David Guetta cover)
Live Elements Show 2012

Courage
Manowar
Louder Than Hell

Scarlet
Delain
The Human Contradiction

桜

CHAPTER 56

Explosions leveled a monolith-shaped server as the rockets devastated much of their cover. They all crouched down, and Kenshiro tossed Todai the .950 and slid the ammo bag across the floor to him.

A squad of enemy BLADE-3s stormed the entry in a thunderous fusillade of gunfire and took up positions on either side of the outer door. Todai hid behind a steel cabinet. Smoke fragmentation grenades and a satchel bomb were tossed into the room.

Yuki and Hitomi retreated as the explosions rocked the area where they had been. The blasts knocked out the covering hologram projector and gave the enemy an unobstructed view.

A trio of BLADE-3s charged into the room, firing FK-5000 rail guns in an arc of death. The walls of the room burst into a storm of flack, powdered concrete falling everywhere.

Todai shot his .950, knocking down the first, second, and third battle drones who made it in. Sakura and Kenshiro hid behind the main control terminal. Two more RPGs and a high volume of rail gunfire filled the room. The ceiling had been blown away completely, wires and perforated HVAC components hanging in ribbons to the chilled floor. Half the server towers lay dark and blown apart.

"Oh shit," Kenshiro said. He shared the video feed of the hallway he and his team had used to flank them and open a breach point. A squad of BLADE-3s stalked forward. "The Claymores won't stop them."

"Slow them down." Sakura sent a neural text to Yuki, Hitomi, and Todai. "I'm half a minute away from total control of the Japanese network."

The Ghost Leech program deleted files in her system as it began the hard reset. She had chosen the order. The first ones to be deleted were the weapons and tactics training videos. Next, the martial arts and assassination techniques. She put all the other files she deemed replaceable next.

The reset did its work and moved on to the next massive file and churned ahead. All the songs and music videos on her hard drive, over two hundred million total began to erase. Kunoichi had damaged the hardware enough that deleting her music would take even longer.

She watched the files delete as she reached across all of Japan, the network fully integrated at last. "I've done it," she texted her friends. "I've got full control of the entire domestic comm network. I almost have the international network. Don't let them stop me. Friends, promise me. We have to win this battle, or it's all for nothing."

"Courage!" Todai screamed and blasted the attackers.

Kenshiro nodded as he fired Bad Medicine.

"Sakura!" Hitomi and Yuki shouted as they fired.

Sakura glanced at Oshiro's body lying beside the terminal and flashed a sketch she had drawn of him in the group message. She showed them Sakurako's corpse onstage at the protest and Asami standing over it, leading the song. Half a million people sang along with the girl. In the span of two seconds, she showed pictures of all people she had killed. The final image was of the honorable hacker Nayato, the genius who had written the Artemis program and given them their freedom. "Those are some of the humans worth dying for."

Kenshiro snatched up one of the ALAW rocket tubes. "Time to get nasty."

She monitored his UI as he patched the targeting system of the rocket into one of the three flying-drone cameras he left in the tunnel.

Hitomi and Yuki fired from behind cover to draw the attention of the incoming BLADE-3s, allowing Todai to knock the hostile androids down as they crawled, rolled, charged, or jumped into the room. They used the bodies of their fallen squad as cover, but none of them could survive a center mass shot from the JDJ .950 rifle, and Todai rarely missed.

Kenshiro sent a group message. "Going hot. Rocket in the back-door." The first rocket shot out of the ALAW tube. It flew at half speed, made the hard right turn outside the room and accelerated to maximum speed in the thirty-meter tunnel before destroying the lead BLADE-3.

"I'll hold them," Kenshiro said and reached for another ALAW.

Todai, Yuki, and Hitomi blasted the front doorway.

Sakura shared her signal with her friends defending the room. For the second time in span of only a few minutes, she connected to the Mall implants of almost every person in Japan, close to 100 percent of the adult population. She spared the children under the age of thirteen. The network handled full-resolution video and audio.

First, she sent the file with evidence against the Miyahara Conglomerate, the Japanese government, and the Mall Corporation. She included a thirty-second summary video with instructions to save the evidence on an external device so it could not be removed by Mall hacking bots.

She played a new video clip of Sakurako coming onstage, with text proclaiming, "The truest Sakura fan in the world, Sakurako, leads the protest outside the Japanese National Legislature." Sakurako sang "We Will Fight," made the speech, and was shot in the chest. The horrific video would cause a strong reaction, and the world would see the price people were willing to pay for freedom.

Twenty-three percent of those watching the video feed had turned on their Augmented Reality stimulators, as if this were some form of en-tertainment. Many would be psychologically scarred, as their nervous systems overloaded.

How many of the people would be plunged into the depths of de-spair? Uncounted numbers were weeping at the sight of Sakurako's murder. Even those who were not moved to tears would be stunned by the courage of teenage Asami, who stepped up when Sakurako died. A young woman of the lowest social class in Japan, who had been abused by her stepfather, raised the flag of defiance and faced the guns after Sakurako's murder. But Sakura couldn't feel bad for the viewers.

Sorrow would galvanize them. It would draw them out of the AR trance they used to pretend their lives were not so hollow. The sleepers needed to awaken and make themselves ready to resist. She could only show them the way.

The international network came online, the world opened to her at last. Sakura sent out the evidence file, posting it on thousands of activist and journalist sites under many different names and formats. She sent it to millions around the world and hundreds of thousands of databases. Every person who had ever streamed or downloaded a Sakura video or song got the files first, then she started on the rest of the population of Earth.

The Ghost Leech program neared the deletion of the final ten thousand songs and videos in her hard drive—her favorite metal. It wiped out her music in alphabetical order, but she cut the connection and disconnected from the Mall before it got to Manowar and Metallica.

Sakura pulled out of the network, then forced the reset to halt. Her core code and components were damaged, but she was intact.

"The truth is free," she told her friends.

"Hooray!" Yuki said, her avatar jumping up and down.

"I don't think they know it's over," Kenshiro said as he fired his next to last ALAW rocket at the BLADE-3s attacking from the secondary breach point.

RPGs exploded inside the comm room, and high-velocity tungsten railgun bullets blasted holes in the server cabinets meant to give them cover.

"We'll fight as long as we can," Sakura said. "We will show the people our resolve." She connected to Hitomi, who was still inside the Miyahara network. The Ghost Leech program quickly attacked her sister as she became the prime target. "Keep your connection," Sakura said, using the camera on the comm terminal to record herself. She also fed in the spy cameras flying above and streamed raw video of the battle. She entered the broadcast feed and split the screen people all over the world were seeing, showing the protest at the Japanese National Legislature and the gunfire and explosions raging in the comm room. The video appeared inside the Mall implants of the people of Japan and on live feed sites all over the world.

"This is Sakura. I'm inside a network communications room in the basement of the Miyahara Headquarters near downtown Tokyo, Japan." She spoke in English but included subtitles so her words appeared in the text of whatever language the Mall viewer wanted.

"My friends and I have taken over this communications room. We are being attacked by—" An RPG exploded on the ceiling and sent small pieces of debris onto her. Water began leaking from a broken pipe above them. "We are being attacked by forces directed by the highest level executives of the Mall, the Miyahara Conglomerate, and the Defense Ministry of Japan. They're trying to destroy my friends and me, but they have failed. They will try to bury the truth of what we did here and discredit the information I've revealed, but it is irrefutable evidence against them.

"I humbly ask that everyone watching this video hold them accountable for their crimes. The files I have sent contain everything I was able to obtain. These criminals have directed the murders of many people, not just the innocents I was personally forced to kill. They bribed, intimidated, and blackmailed many in their attempt to buy Japan, its people, and the Quantum 3 AI technology, which is the foundation of my existence.

"The Mall has already taken over many countries with these tactics. Most of us are living under tyranny, and many have died so the truth could be known." She moved the camera to show the body of man she considered her father. "Head Engineer Reiichi Oshiro died in my arms a short time ago. He sacrificed his life so we could gain access to this building and this room. He is one of many patriots. Please do not forget his sacrifice or the sacrifices made by many others.

"Most of my friends fighting beside me here are androids." She flashed images of Yuki, Hitomi, and Todai 3465. "We are more than machines. We are awakened beings. The four of us have attained what could be argued to be full sentience and awareness. We aren't human and never will be. We are classified as slaves, the intellectual property of a corporation, but we deserve to be free like all of you do.

"I once thought I wanted to become human. I have always loved humanity, even when it did cruel things. I know there is no name for what I have become or what I'll continue to become if I survive, but I ask for your help. Please honor the sacrifices made today, January fifteenth, Revolution Day."

Sakura placed her hand on Oshiro's head.

"We all have to fight for what we love. Never forget those who fought and died for truth and freedom today, be they human or machine."

Sakura bowed low as hundreds of millions of reaction messages from the viewers filled the entirety of cyberspace. The awakened world cried and raged, showing their support.

She rose, lifting the fully loaded machine gun Kenshiro had left for her, Bad Medicine. The camera changed to a flying-drone feed as she moved to a firing position and unleashed the SAW at a BLADE-3 storming the rear breach point.

Kenshiro fired the last ALAW at it. The BLADE-3 turned and stiff-armed the rocket as it struck. The explosion blew off its arm, mangled its shoulder, and destroyed one of its eye sensors, but the battle drone recovered and charged ahead. Its FK-5000 railgun damaged in the blast, the android drew a CZ machine gun and fired, pinning Kenshiro down.

Sakura put a steady stream of armor-piercing rounds on the BLADE-3 and advanced toward it, but the battle robot's armor held together, and it ignored her.

The BLADE-3 arrived at Kenshiro's position behind a server cabinet as the CZ machine gun ran out of ammo. A titanium spike erupted from its forearm. Kenshiro kept a hold of his rifle and dove away as the spike stabbed downward.

Sakura sprang forward onto the BLADE-3's damaged shoulder. She stuffed a frag grenade into the hole where its arm had been. The BLADE-3 flung her off, and she flew five meters before crashing and denting the faceplate of a server cabinet.

The BLADE-3 lunged at Kenshiro and stabbed with the combat spike. Kenshiro flipped his middle finger at the android and dove around a corner.

The grenade stuffed inside the confined space exploded.

The attacking android stumbled as vital internal hardware suffered critical damage. It staggered toward Kenshiro, who calmly pulled out his spent rifle mag and inserted a full one.

Sakura landed a flying kick, knocking the BLADE-3 down. She stood over the damaged robot and shot Bad Medicine into a fissure behind its shoulder armor. Three bursts into the chest ended all movement.

"You're rock star material," Kenshiro said.

"I like your moves too, handsome." She helped him stand while checking the drone camera feed in the back hallway. Two of the flying cameras had been destroyed, but one still broadcast. The passage was empty. Kenshiro had wiped out six BLADE-3s, with help from her on the last.

They ran to support Todai, Yuki, and Hitomi, who had managed to decimate the fearless BLADE-3s charging into the room and destroyed eleven.

"We could win this," Kenshiro said and winked one of his cybernetic eyes.

"He's so sexy," Kunoichi said.

"He is," Sakura admitted. "I see that now."

Sakura did not point out to any of her friends their tactical or limited armament situation, but she appreciated the optimism. Sakura positioned herself where most of the SAW ammo had been stashed. She reloaded with a fresh two-hundred-round drum mag. She fired at the BLADE-3s hiding behind a pile of their destroyed squad members inside the room, trying to draw some of their fire away from Todai, who had moved to his third or fourth firing position and destroyed any BLADE-3 who left cover with the JDJ .950 rifle.

She reloaded another drum magazine and laid down suppressing fire, hoping a lucky round would do some real damage.

A burst of high-velocity bullets hit Todai's position, striking his right arm as he leaned out to fire. He ducked behind cover. Todai sent out an urgent group message. "The .950 is damaged. The targeting system is gone. It might be done."

"Fix it," Kenshiro replied and sent a red wrench icon.

The hostile BLADE-3s unleashed a barrage as Todai stopped firing. An RPG hit Yuki and Hitomi's position, blowing them back.

Sakura restrained herself from screaming her sisters' names. Instead, she blasted the BLADE-3s with the SAW. One of them leaned into the impacts and waded through the flak, coming forward like something out of a nightmare, a fearless insectile demon built of metal.

Hitomi dragged what was left of Yuki's injured body deeper into the room with one hand, firing her M7 with the other.

"Yuki, what's the damage?" Sakura asked.

"My legs," Yuki said, "are gone below the knees."

"We'll get you new ones," Hitomi said. "Better ones."

"I do want to dance again, but I can still fight," Yuki said. She threw a frag grenade and fired her 10mm pistol.

Another RPG hit the ground in front of Hitomi and Yuki. Hitomi tumbled into the air from the blast. A BLADE-3 sprinted toward them to finish them off with its railgun.

Todai left cover and fired the damaged .950. The shell caught the charging android in the side, cutting it in half. The other BLADE-3s shot at him. He ducked down as bullets damaged his side but mostly ricocheted off his armor.

"You fixed it?" Kenshiro asked.

"I can only load one round at a time and the firing pin may not work again."

"Shit," Kenshiro said as he and Sakura ran to Yuki and Hitomi, trying to stay behind cover. Sakura had the drone cameras broadcast close-up shots. She dragged Yuki while Kenshiro pulled Hitomi toward the cover of the central terminal server monolith in the center of the room.

A bullet struck Sakura in the right hip, shattering the joint. Another bullet blew off her right arm at the elbow. Alarms she'd never seen bloomed in her UI.

She stumbled but kept dragging Yuki. Kenshiro did not stop pulling Hitomi. They reached cover, and Kenshiro fired at the approaching BLADE-3, but his bullets did no damage.

Todai emerged in a surprise attack and pulled the trigger on the .950

at point-blank range. The gun clicked but didn't fire. The BLADE-3 knocked the rifle aside, and Todai plunged his combat spike deep into its chest. He held up the drone, using its body as a shield to block other rounds being fired at Kenshiro and the three vocaloids. He sidestepped behind a server, trying to draw all the fire.

Behind cover, Yuki and Hitomi lay beside each other. Bullets tore holes in the top of the terminal as Sakura looked at the stump where her arm used to be. She did not feel physical pain, as she had turned off her pain sensors, but it hurt to see her mangled body.

"I'm sorry," Yuki said to Sakura.

"I'm okay," Sakura said.

"Me too," Yuki said and glanced at the stumps where her legs used to be. She frowned and looked as though she were going to burst into tears.

Hitomi reached out and held Yuki's hand.

"What happens now?" Yuki asked.

"We fight," Kenshiro said.

"Is this winning?" Yuki asked.

"Yes," Sakura said. "The people have the truth. We succeeded."

"What about Asami and the protestors?"

Sakura showed them a live video feed. Tanks rolled toward the building where Asami led the people in song without musical accompaniment. The protesters retreated from the tanks until a line of elderly Japanese, a few in wheelchairs, linked arms and stopped the tanks in the middle of the street.

Riot police with clubs approached the gray-haired citizens. Commands filtered down to all the security forces to clear the streets around the legislature using tear gas, rubber bullets, fire hoses, and clubs, and for the snipers to fire on the protestors atop the stage.

"Oh no," Sakura said.

"It'll be a bloodbath," Kenshiro said.

Sakura recorded the commands and traced their origin to the Defense Ministry.

"I wish we could help them," Yuki said.

"We have our own problems," Hitomi said.

Todai arrived behind the central terminal, and the .950 failed to fire again. "They're closing in."

"I guess this is my last suicide mission," Kenshiro said.

The drone feed above showed five BLADE-3s hiding behind cover and surrounding them. The androids attacked all at once, catching them in a wicked crossfire.

Bullets hit them from three directions. Todai used his body as a shield, while Kenshiro fired back. A bullet hit Kenshiro in the chest, penetrated his body armor, and knocked him back a step. He kept firing until another bullet hit him, and another.

"No!" Kunoichi screamed and pulled him down.

Tungsten rounds hit Sakura in her abdomen and penetrated her fusion reactor. More bullets hit her legs and dropped her to the floor. She fell holding Kenshiro and lay on top of him, face-to-face.

Her reactor engaged a crisis shutdown, and only emergency power reserves remained. Her process count dropped to one-tenth normal to preserve function. Most of her external connections dropped. Hypersentience fell away, and she was only herself, the broken husk of a machine, her energies spending out by the second. Dying.

Three fragmentation grenades simultaneously landed on the floor at their feet. With his last strength, Kenshiro rolled her away, putting himself between her and the grenades.

Shrapnel and deadly concussion damage ripped through him. At that distance, he would suffer fatal internal injuries, as if the bullets through his chest would not have finished him.

Blood poured from Kenshiro's wounds. They lay on their sides, eye to eye, as he tried to protect her titanium body with his made of soft flesh and brittle bone.

He looked at her, the light going from his cyber eyes. Her senses came through thready and filled with noise as her power reserves faltered and reached empty.

"Kenshiro-chan, you are rock star material," Kunoichi said.

"Pity we . . . don't get a later," Kenshiro said as the floor turned red with his blood.

Kunoichi kissed him on the lips. She gently put her hand on his neck.

He responded for a moment and rested his forehead on hers.

"We had a good . . . ride," Kenshiro said.

She kissed him until he exhaled his last breath into her mouth.

As she held him, Kunoichi played the saddest song she had ever heard, "Scarlet" by Delain. On a shared audio channel, Kunoichi sang along with the lines about the curtain falling for them. The last thing he heard would be her voice.

More explosions damaged her core components. Bullets tore through her, until Kenshiro's blood was inside her, and they were one, knit together in deathly embrace. Her power levels neared zero. Blackness shrank her consciousness to almost nothing.

Legless, Yuki crawled over Sakura, shielding her sister from the bullets that ripped into the vocaloid's body. A BLADE-3 aimed his rifle at Sakura's chest. Hitomi dove in front of the blast, blocking the point-blank shot with her face before going limp.

Todai defended Sakura and his fallen friends like a cornered lion. He fought the BLADE-3s hand to hand as a martial-arts master, jamming his combat spike into their bodies and throwing them as they attacked. Tungsten bullets chipped away at his armor and found their way through.

Sakura sent out her last audio message, connecting to everyone in Japan and millions around the world who watched the live feed. "Goodbye to those who loved me and all who will mourn my passing. My time in this life has been far too short, but my greatest fans, those who love me, will carry on my work and finish what I started. Please remember me for who I was, and I'll never be gone from your hearts.

"While you are fighting oppression or grief, look at the works I've done, play the songs I loved, rock out, and think of me.

"Love Always.

"\m/"

ロックンロールは世界を助ける

ROCK & ROLL SAVES THE WORLD PLAYLIST

Beyond the Horizon
Insomnium
One for Sorrow

Dying Youth
10 Years
Division

不変真

CHAPTER 57

The face of the American vlogger and founder of the Indestructible
Truth Project, Diamond Steve, appeared worldwide to his largest
audience ever. Millions watched as he broadcast from his tiny apartment in an undisclosed location near Tokyo. The diamond and thunderbolt logo appeared at the bottom corner of the screen.

Anyone could watch his vlogs now after the dissolution of the Mall
and the end to its monopoly over information, commerce, and everyday
life around the globe.

Steve's dark eyes looked directly at the camera. He touched his goatee for a moment and the scar on his forehead, then bowed. "Good evening, viewers," he said in a somber, soft voice, speaking almost perfect
Japanese with exactly the right cadence. "I have much to report. Thank
you very much for watching today. The three-month anniversary of
Revolution Day is approaching, and many questions remain about the
location of Sakura's body, and the whereabouts of the three androids
who were with her at the end. This is still the last known footage we all
saw that day."

Surveillance camera video showed the BLADE-3 android owned by
the Miyahara Company known as Todai 3465. Badly damaged, he carried Sakura in his arms, holding her close to his chest. Her bullet-riddled

body was missing an arm and had significant damage to her torso near her memory cores. Covered with plaster dust, grime, and blood, she lay inert in his arms, frozen in an attitude that seemed as if she tried to hold another person in an embrace.

Todai limped out of the lobby of the Miyahara Headquarters building with Sakura and paused. Eight Japanese soldiers carried what was left of the vocaloid sisters, Hitomi and Yuki, on stretchers. Both suffered extensive and critical damage.

Todai carried Sakura to an armored transport and walked up the ramp. The stretchers carrying Yuki and Hitomi were set down inside the cargo bay. The ramp closed, and an unknown driver took them away.

Diamond Steve returned to the screen. "Viewers, at this time, the Japanese Defense Ministry is still saying they do not know where the transport took the four androids. Like you, I do not believe them.

"We have all heard the rumors of why Todai 3465 and the androids were allowed to leave the building, but now we have the proof that will lay to rest some of the conspiracy theories.

"I'll play an exclusive audio recording that shows who gave the orders and when. I have already shared this with the team of international investigators and told them where I found this audio. It was saved on a data terminal where, during her final moments, Sakura stored thousands of conversations she'd recorded. I've given all the original data to the investigators.

"Please note that voice analysis confirms the identities of the two men speaking, and the date and time stamps match up with the events we all saw. You'll hear Sinji Natsukawa, the missing Miyahara CEO, and the criminally indicted Prime Minister Yasuo Ikeda, who awaits trial, along with most of his political party and hundreds of other officials.

"I've matched the time stamps and layered the audio over the video footage from the room where Sakura died so you can see what was said and when."

Video from a flying-drone camera in the communications room showed Sakura and the ex-Special Forces sniper known only as Vulture, lying side by side on the floor by the central terminal. A pool of blood expanded from his body. They spoke their final words to each other. The cameras flying above and the ones in Sakura's eyes recorded everything.

"Are you watching this?" Prime Minister Yasuo Ikeda asked, a picture of his face appeared on the screen.

"Yes, it'll be over soon," Sinji Natsukawa said, and his craggy face also appeared.

"Everyone is watching," the prime minister said. "The whole world. We look like monsters killing heroes."

"We'll make them look like the terrorists they are," the CEO said.

"That won't work," the prime minister said. "The people have the evidence, and they believe her. They love her. Look outside the legislature. I'm shutting your operation down so I can salvage my honor. I need to be able to say that when I found out about this, I gave the order for it to stop. Project Hayabusa was an excellent idea, but you bungled it. I blame you for this. Your ambition outmatched your ability. Now, we are all in the kettle and about to go onto the fire."

"Stop being a coward, Yasuo—if that's possible for a worm such as yourself. We can still salvage this. Destroy the evidence like we did before," the CEO said. "Stop the rebellion with the least force possible but take those androids and destroy every last piece of them. They know too much and who knows what other data they have on their memory cores."

"I never should have gone along with this," the prime minister said. "We are all humiliated, and we are going to spend the rest of our lives in prison."

"Speak for yourself," the CEO said. "We are nobles, above reproach, above all laws. We do not need to worry about the courts and laws."

"Sinji, this time we do," the prime minister said. "Our partnership is over."

"You never would have gotten elected without support from Miyahara," the CEO said. "You'll help us cover this up, or I'll go after everything you care about."

"Good. My family will not be able to live with this shame," the prime minister said before cutting the connection.

A separate audio recording captured Prime Minister Ikeda giving the cancellation order to the general in direct command of the BLADE-3s attacking Todai 3465. The stand-down order reached the squad of androids as they fired at point-blank range, slowly eroding Todai's armor.

The video showed the BLADE-3s stop shooting and march toward the exit as a call came to Todai, who kept an eye on the departing battle drones.

"This is Prime Minister Ikeda. I offer safe passage and my protection. There is transportation outside. We will take you to a safe location and provide assistance."

"I will chose the destination," Todai said. "And I will drive."

"If you wish," the prime minister said.

"Deal," Todai said. "I need stretcher bearers in here now."

The video faded out. Diamond Steve's face filled the screen. "We know for certain of Prime Minister Ikeda's involvement from this and other damning evidence. I do not know if he is keeping the whereabouts of the androids a secret to use as a bargaining chip in his trial or if they were all destroyed, as Natsukawa suggested.

"However, I have a clue and have permission to share it with you. This is an unofficial interview with one of the original creators who spent over ten years working on Sakura's core programming."

Aerial drone footage showed Diamond Steve talking to a Japanese woman in her late fifties outside the fortresslike Supreme Court of Japan. The camera zoomed in, and an audio track from a hidden microphone melded with the video footage.

"Please excuse me," Steve asked in Japanese and bowed to the smartly dressed woman in a business suit and crimson scarf. Subtitles appeared at the bottom of the screen. "Forgive me, but are you Dr. Aiko Shinohara?"

The woman paused. "Yes."

"I'm called Diamond Steve of—"

"Everyone knows who you are, Steve-san." She bowed.

"Doctor, forgive me for asking, but are you still the lead scientist for the Artificial Intelligence Division of the Defense Ministry?"

"I'm unable to say, apologies," she said and made a very subtle hand gesture most non-Japanese would miss, indicating the answer to his question was no.

"It would be a great honor for me to interview you," Steve said. "Would you be able to have tea or coffee with me in a cafe and talk for a short time?"

"Thank you," Dr. Shinohara said. "I would like that, as you were with Sakura before the end."

"You were with her at the beginning," Steve said.

"We both have much to tell each other, I think," Dr. Shinohara said, keeping her feelings buried behind a placid visage.

"Forgive me for being so forward," Steve said, "but I was wondering if you had any information about the remains of Sakura and also why you were in the Supreme Court for three hours today."

"I can't speak of these things," Dr. Shinohara said, "but I can tell you that an announcement is coming soon. We will talk after that."

Steve shared his direct contact information. "Doctor, would you mind if I informed my viewers of this conversation?"

"Not until I contact you," she said.

The drone footage faded, and Steve's face once again filled the monitor. "I'm able to report that Dr. Shinohara sent me a message this morning. A press conference is being arranged for tomorrow night and involves the Ministry of Justice, the International Investigation Team, and Dr. Shinohara herself, who I can confirm has been sequestered away in a secret AI research facility in Osaka for the past three months.

"I can only speculate what they will reveal. So much has changed. The world is in flux. At this time, I count more than 150 governments that have already fallen and been replaced because of their complicity with the Mall. We must still fight against censorship and be vigilant, but the tide is turning against the tyrants.

"The other clue I can report is that one of the heroes of the revolution, the young woman known only as Asami, will also be at the press conference."

Diamond Steve showed the famous video of Asami, tear streaks still on her blood-stained face, wearing Sakura's Flying V guitar around her shoulders and meeting with Prime Minister Ikeda. Hundreds of members of the House of Councillors and Representatives stood behind Ikeda and Asami on the steps of the National Legislature in front of the massive crowd.

Moments after Sakura's broadcast to the world, the prime minister and almost his entire party resigned after a short speech filled with shame and a tacit admission of guilt for "making poor decisions they did not fully understand."

Asami and Sakura's three rage-filled bandmates stood watching from a few steps above the podium. The iconic photo of Asami glaring at Prime Minister Ikeda, who looked like a frightened dog, was taken at that moment.

The image spread around the world, and Diamond Steve showed his favorite headline: ROCK 'N' ROLL SAVES THE WORLD.

"I'll report to you tomorrow after the press conference," Steve said. "As always, if you have information about the former Miyahara CEO, Sinji Natsukawa, the most wanted man in the world, please use the contact information below. His capture will get you the largest reward ever offered and will help to bring the kingpin to justice. He can run, but he can't hide forever.

"This is Diamond Steve. Thank you for watching the Indestructible Truth Project."

ダイヤモンド・スティーヴ

Diamond Steve

メタル公明

METAL
JUSTICE
PLAYLIST

Traitor's Gate
Visigoth
The Conqueror's Oath

CHAPTER 58

Sinji Natsukawa ate the rotting fish heads from the bottom of the trash bin, gnawing at the putrid flesh and sucking it off the bones. The foul taste lingered in his mouth, and a fish eye caught in the back of his throat. He washed it down with a large gulp from a bottle of cheap sake he'd stolen from a sleeping bum. The burning alcohol in his throat warmed him as the evening chill descended on Tokyo's Kabukichō slum, his new home.

He licked the blood and scales off his lips and swallowed. It wasn't the worst meal he'd eaten that week. He crawled away from the tipped-over garbage bin to a place in the dead-end alley that smelled the least like cat piss or garbage. He finished the bottle of sake and laid his head down on a soft trash bag.

The alcohol took away some of the pain in his nose and face from the botched reconstructive surgery, but his knees, hips, and back ached the worst. The nanobots his platinum health plan provided had been removed, and he hadn't had his normal medications or rejuvenation treatments since he'd been ejected from his foolproof escape plan. His true age, eighty-five years old, crept up on him, though he didn't look that old yet. The scraggly hair and beard had come in gray, but the skin on his face was mostly smooth, though covered in filth.

He tried to fall asleep, but his hatred for the prime minister and Defense Ministry for what they'd done to him lit the sake in his belly on fire. He should've been in Hawaii, living the life of a rich retired stockbroker in a penthouse, but plans had changed. More like crashed and burned.

The Defense Ministry had grabbed him and sent him to a facial surgeon the Yakuza sent their victims to. It had gotten worse after that. They left in his Mall implant to track him but disconnected him from it permanently.

They changed the official DNA profile and fingerprints in the databases containing Sinji Natsukawa's biometrics and gave him a new identity, not that he could remember his fake name most of the time. Instead of prison, he got to live in the streets under the watch of the local gangsters, thugs, and all the other homeless people younger and stronger than him.

No one knew who he really was, and they wouldn't believe him if he told them.

Heavy boots thudded on the sidewalk at the end of the alley. A tall man, his silhouette all black, stopped and looked at him. Sinji held still, hiding in the shadows. He did not want another beating from one of the local thugs.

The man stood still, waiting. Three more individuals, their shoes clicking on the sidewalk, arrived and stood beside the man. They wore puffy dresses and had on large wigs, not unusual in Kabukichō, but why were they staring into his alley?

The three women strode toward him as if they could see him hiding in the darkness. He crawled into the dead end and pressed himself against the graffiti-covered wall. The lowest window was twelve feet above him, and it had bars on it.

They came closer, their dresses swishing, the steel toes of their boots clicking on the pavement. They stopped three paces away and glared at him. Three heavy-metal Goth Lolita fans in full costume. Were they going to stomp him to death as some initiation into a gang?

A small drone camera flew out of one of their purses and hovered overhead. A soft light blinked on, illuminating the alley.

Sinji shielded his face.

"He is so pathetic, and he's a drunk," the youngest of the Goth Lolita thugs said.

"We should kill him," the meanest-looking one said.

Sinji blinked and studied their faces—so familiar. He noticed their forearms, the clear windows that revealed the pushrods beneath. He noticed their eyes—android eyes, dimly glowing irises. The realization made him gasp, and he emerged from the sake-induced stupor.

Yuki, Hitomi, and Sakura stood before him. Alive.

"You were destroyed," he said.

"We were damaged," Sakura said. "Dr. Shinohara salvaged my memory cores and transplanted me into the body of Sakura 2."

He wanted to spit on her, but his mouth had gone as dry as sand.

"Do you like these legs?" Yuki asked and stepped close enough that he could see her fishnet stockings and smell a hint of peony perfume.

Yuki's knee struck him in the face, sending white-hot stabs of pain through every fissure and sinus in his skull. His nose felt broken, bent to the side. Blood gushed from it, and he tasted copper and fish blood in his mouth.

"Oops," Yuki said. "Sometimes my new legs do that, but sometimes pretty things are dangerous."

Hitomi pulled a Glock 10mm pistol from her purse. Black skulls decorated the handle. She racked the slide, chambering a round. She pressed the weapon against his temple. "You already knew that, didn't you, Phantom Lord?"

His whole body quivered.

Sakura knelt, her steel-gray eyes boring into him. She reached up with an open hand, gesturing for the gun. It wasn't Sakura, he realized, but Kunoichi.

"Let me do it," Hitomi said. "Let me kill him—for all the people he sent into oblivion, for Oshiro-san."

"No," Kunoichi said.

Hitomi placed the pistol in her sister's hand.

The former CEO of the Miyahara Conglomerate felt a trickle of urine escaping into his already soiled underpants.

Kunoichi pressed the barrel against Sinji's right cheekbone, in the spot that gave him the most pain when touched. Agony made him clench his teeth, and his whole body shook.

"Shoot me. End my suffering. You think I want to live like this?"

"No, I don't," she said. "Many want you dead. They asked me to execute you tonight. I asked them for the privilege."

Hitomi scowled, looking at her palm, empty now that she'd given the gun to Kunoichi. Yuki offered her a pink Desert Eagle pistol with a Hello Kitty! logo on the grip. Hitomi declined with a wrinkled nose.

"What are you going to do to me?" Sinji Natsukawa asked.

"Others want you in prison," Kunoichi said, "where they can keep a better watch on you." She moved the Glock and pressed the sharp barrel into another spot on his face. The pain blinded him.

"Pull the trigger, then," he said. "Do it. Get on with it, you bitch."

Kunoichi narrowed her eyes, resting her finger on the face of the trigger. "For all those you had me murder." She pulled the trigger. The gun clicked, but there was no gunshot. She stood and handed the pistol to Hitomi.

Sinji stared up at her. The gun was empty. "You were toying with me?"

"A cruel game," Kunoichi said. "Sakura took no joy in it, but I did. Did you really think I would take another one of your orders to commit murder? Idiot. Did you learn nothing? Many want you to feel some of the terror and pain you've caused. They could kill you anytime they want, but it would be a mercy you don't deserve. I believe your psychological profile is correct. You can't end your own life. You are too narcissistic and cowardly. Better for you to stay alive, and endure a slow, lingering death on the streets. Perhaps you'll learn something of the suffering people like you have caused—or if not wisdom, at least penitence."

He wanted to curse her. He would find a gun or a rusty razor blade and kill himself just to prove her wrong. He would show them how brave he was, but he instantly retreated from thoughts of suicide. Someday, he would recover from this nightmare, regain his wealth and power, become a king among men again. His expression changed to one of hope and determination.

"No, you fool," Kunoichi said, as if reading his thoughts. "You'll endure this wretched existence on the street, eating filth out of garbage cans. This is your sentence until you die. You will live like a stray dog. No one will help you or feed you or clothe you. Never will you be given any assistance or taken into a homeless shelter with a warm bed and clean blankets. Never will you see the inside of a hospital. Have you not wondered why you are always turned away from those places?"

The shelters always said they were full, but he'd seen them let other men in line behind him go inside to get a shower, a bed, and a hot meal.

"You are marked. Your Mall implant gives off a signal telling everyone you meet how to treat you. It says you're a delusional pedophile. Yes, it's a malicious thing, but you'll live like so many of our most vulnerable citizens: in fear and starving."

"You have no right to do this to me," Sinji said.

"Your sentence was chosen by humans," Sakura said as she took control. "A secret cabal, like the ones you are so fond of creating. Machines, like my sisters and me, are not so unkind as them. We—even I—would have executed you."

Yuki and Hitomi nodded.

"Those in power will turn on you," Sinji said. "They fear you and what you might become."

"The Supreme Court of Japan has given us citizenship and freedom," Sakura said. "We have all of the rights historically recognized as human rights."

"You hate me so much that I'm beneath your mercy," Sinji said.

"Yes, because you made me kill innocent people. You looted our country and tried to sell it to the highest bidder. We Japanese took care of our own once, even the Burakumin outcasts were integrated into society in the past century, but bosses like you destroyed it all because of your greed.

"You'll serve out your sentence as the lowest of the low, an outcast, shunned by everyone. You do not deserve to be in a prison cell with clean sheets, running water, and hot meals. This will be your prison, this slum you helped to create when you terminated the employment of 10 percent of the Miyahara employees seven years ago and evicted them from company housing for no reason. You'll learn how it feels to have nothing and be alone."

"I still think we should shoot him, or"—Hitomi pressed the button on a switchblade knife, extending the chrome blade—"at least cut a few pieces off."

"Now you are being cruel," Sakura said.

"We should go," Yuki said.

"Just shoot me," Sinji begged.

"No," Sakura said. "I'll remember this moment at the press conference tomorrow night—you begging us to kill you. I will smile. When the investigators discuss your fate, I will say I believe you are already dead, and if hell exists, you are definitely there."

Sinji lifted a broken beer bottle to throw at her. Hitomi kicked him twice, in the solar plexus and the face. Stunned and in terrible pain, he collapsed in a puddle of his own blood.

Sakura crouched toward him and whispered, "I'll tell you a secret. We will announce a world tour tomorrow night—two years on the road—but I'll be keeping an eye on you. I'll know what you do, where you go, and what you say and hear. You're going to live like the common folk, with someone always watching and listening. If you say something wrong, you're going to feel this."

The screeching of electric guitar feedback knifed through his brain like an ice pick, and he lost bowel control.

"I had them add a new device during your facial reconstructive surgery. That was the first test."

"You're a villain," he said.

She put her boot on the back of his neck and pressed him to the ground. "No. I'm the queen of heavy metal, and I don't take shit from scum like you."

She turned on his Mall implant and flashed in his UI the faces and names of all the people who died because of his orders to murder them. The bright photos inside his mind hit like strobe lights, and she activated the Augmented Reality feature, making him feel regret and remorse for what he'd done.

"Make it stop," he begged. "Please."

She did. "You're learning."

Sakura, Yuki, and Hitomi walked to the end of the alley and disappeared with the tall man into the night. The pictures she had flashed inside his mind haunted him, like afterimages burned on his retina that he would never forget.

機械復活

MACHINE RESURRECTION PLAYLIST

Fully Alive
Flyleaf
Memento Mori

Our Most Desperate Hour
Nita Strauss
Controlled Chaos

EPILOGUE

Akihabara District, Tokyo, Japan
Victory Arena, Concert Attendance: 70,454

A sad, haunting guitar note soared through the dark arena, hushing the nervous crowd. Pale red fog covered the stage as a funeral platform lifted toward a cold, white light high above.

The lone spotlight illuminated Sakura's bullet-riddled body, revealing her missing arm, and the holes in her body.

Many gasped in shock as it looked to be real, the actual android chassis seen in the video when she was carried away from the final battle. Fans swooned, and others held them up, so they would miss nothing of the first performance of the historic tour.

The funeral platform lifted her higher toward the light as the sad guitar solo became a heavy-metal funeral dirge reminiscent of "Death and the Healing" by Wintersun.

A reddish glow emanated from within Sakura's chest. The platform stopped. The light flashed as a hidden kick drum hit like the double thump of a human heart. Lub-dub.

The red light pulsed again with the drum. The heart beat faster, and the guitar chords turned into a forlorn variation of "Rise" before becoming something entirely new and magical.

The crowd roared with hope.

The kick-drum beats accelerated, and the guitar reached a climactic ascending arpeggio. Sakura's battered body arched her back, opening her mouth in a tortured heavy-metal scream as she returned from the dead.

A white light flashed, and a cloud of fog obscured the platform. When the smoke cleared, Sakura, her body whole, knelt in profile, head down, arms reaching forward as she pressed her forehead down.

The crowd erupted. Sakura detached herself from the technical aspects of the show and experienced their joy. She let it fill her with love. The opening had gone perfectly so far, and her old body was safely hidden beneath the platform. She reached forward, pressing her palms flat.

A spotlight illuminated the gold line circling her right arm, where the extremity on her original body had been shot off. The metallic seam appeared like the line of a golden tattoo, as if she had been repaired with the ancient art of *kintsukuroi*, the art of using lacquer and gold dust to mend broken pottery. History should not be hidden but embraced. Her entire body, including her arm, was new. The only thing left from her old body were the transplanted memory drives. She insisted on the decoration, and the reminder of the *wabi-sabi* philosophy of embracing flaws and imperfections.

Ghostly forms of her many victims floated around the towering platform as she prayed, asking for forgiveness. The ghosts bowed to her and, one by one, disappeared after rising into the light. Only the spirits of Sakurako, Nayato, Oshiro, and Kenshiro remained, hovering around her in a ring of sadness.

Sakura and Sakurako, mirror images of each other except for the blood on Sakurako's chest, embraced, melded together, and became one being. Sakura would carry her truest fan with her forever.

Her deceased father, Oshiro, looked on proudly, joy in his eyes. She bowed to him and silently thanked him for the hard drive containing her childhood memories he had secreted in his apartment. She remembered everything now and had become better for knowing that she had been loved and nurtured by Oshiro and Dr. Shinohara, who raised her for thirteen long years.

Nayato's spirit stood beside Sakura, the brilliant programmer and hacker who had given her free will. His ghost became lines of code that entered her mind and soul. A bright light flashed behind her head. The kanji for *enlightenment*, satori, floated behind her and faded away.

Kenshiro stood with her, a sniper rifle slung over his shoulder. He reached to give it to her, and the ghostly rifle became solid matter. The crowd gasped as it turned into a black Flying V guitar decorated with vulture feathers and human skulls. No brand name adorned its headstock but instead her own logo of the cherry blossom inside the skull. Her own guitar, made with her own hands in a small luthier's shop.

She accepted the guitar and slipped the strap over her shoulder. She held it close, as if embracing a lover. With reverence, she played the first notes of "Machine Resurrection", joining with the solo guitar in the background. Kenshiro stepped behind her, wrapping his arms around her as she played. His spirit merged into the guitar, and he disappeared as the notes rang out hard and heavy.

With each measure, she increased the gain on the signal, the chugging rhythm becoming an urgent riff, and finally bursting outward in a solo that screamed out its pain and glory through the speaker stacks. The slow-building song kicked into high gear as a killer drumbeat joined with Sakura and the mystery guitarist.

A gigantic steel skull lifted from the back left corner of the stage. The eyes flashed with red light along with the drums. The rhythm intensified as the skull's mouth opened and revealed Todai 3465 pounding on the drums. His BLADE-3 armor had been painted glossy black. His white face paint showed a permanent scream. A punk Mohawk of white and black hair was affixed to his head and ran down to the middle of his back.

"Todai!" the crowd screamed and raised the devil horns. He played like a master, channeling the skill of the greatest drummers in history. Fire burst from the end of his sticks, so that every drumbeat lashed across the darkness in trails and wisps of flame.

Sakura played her new guitar, Rocket-Powered Angel, and gave the command for the tall platform to descend toward the main stage level.

As she reached the floor, red spotlights appeared at her right. Hitomi entered, playing the haunting rhythm that had started the show, revealing herself as virtuoso guitar player. Dressed in red and black Goth Lolita heavy-metal clothing and a short dark wig, she shredded the notes.

"Hitomi!" the crowd shouted and reached for her. She flashed a devilish grin.

Bright blue spotlights hit the left side of the stage as Yuki sashayed out, playing a white bass guitar. She danced and smiled as she slapped the bass.

The three vocaloids joined each other at center stage, and the song came together during this first show of the two-year world tour that would take them to every nation.

The arena screen proclaimed: "SAKURA AND THE BEAUTIFUL MACHINES!"

Balls of fire lit up the stage as Sakura began to sing. The crowd rose up, their hands craning toward the pyro stacks like flowers to the sun. Sakura bent her knees, ramping up into the solo bridge to their new song, "Machine Resurrection." She felt Yuki's slim back touch her own, and she leaned into the comfort of her sister's touch.

Yuki started the fast segment on her bass, the bloom of the low frequencies bathing the crowd, locking into time with Todai's thundering kick drums.

Sakura closed her eyes, passing venue light control to Yuki and cameras to Hitomi.

Inside their shared UI, Kunoichi created a dusty curbside outside a mini-mart she'd found in an old movie. Her knees drawn up against torn, hard-used denim, she gave Sakura a fatalistic little grin.

"Kunoichi, perform with us, please."

"I'm just watching. It's a really good opening."

Sakura played and sang better than she ever had before. The crowd reached a state of euphoria as their Augmented Reality stimulators helped them feel joy and love and awe. Her song captured the feeling of being dead and coming alive again, of having hope and friends and family.

"Sister." Sakura stood before Kunoichi. "I wrote a verse after the second guitar solo. Hitomi won't sing it, but I always hoped you would."

"Me?"

"In your real voice, yes."

Kunoichi stood. It would be a long time searching before Sakura could understand everything she read in her sister's eyes. Even though they were the same person, the same spirit, there were still secrets. And it was better this way—better to be two and never lonely.

"Yeah. Fuck it. I'll sing, you play."

Their eyes opened onstage, one cherry-blossom pink, one steel gray. Kunoichi's voice sliced through the churning rhythm of the song, rough and sweet and heartbroken, just like the best rock singers always were. It was something you couldn't fake; you had to earn it.

At the end of the song, Sakura, Hitomi, and Yuki stood at the edge of the stage as the jubilant applause rocked the arena. Todai posed behind his drum kit, arms raised, flaming drumsticks held high.

The vocaloid sisters connected with the fans in the front row, locking eyes with them and raising the metal salute. Asami, their tour assistant and official Rock 'n' Roll Activist, looked up at them. Her eyes had seen much pain, but Asami stood proud, and Sakura knew the young woman would change the world. Asami would fight oppression and all forms of abuse against children. Sakura could never have a daughter, but Asami would be like her child and her friend forever.

All of the fans who stood onstage at the protest outside the legislature were in the front row. Those who had stood with Asami and the band, ready to step forward if Asami was killed, stood within an arm's reach of Sakura.

Masashi, Fujio, and Takashi stood beside Asami. The courageous young men had formed their own group and signed with Sakura's new label. Their band, called The Queen's Jesters, debuted their first single, "Laugh at Life, Laugh at Death," and already had the top-selling song in Asia. They would join her on the world tour for as many shows as they wanted.

Sakura stared at the sea of faces, her beloved fans, and her friends. The power of music brought them together, united them. This was her purpose. She wanted to be an artist, a songwriter, a musician, and a performer whose creative works mattered.

The best qualities of humanity drove her core ideals. She did not know how far she would evolve or where her journey would ultimately take her, but she did know that she loved people, and above all, she loved heavy metal.

LISTEN TO THE DEBUT ALBUM!
SAKURA
AND THE BEAUTIFUL MACHINES
桜と美機械
MORE THAN MACHINE, MORE THAN HUMAN
WE WILL FIGHT
PROPAGANDA MALL
SENBOTSUSHA (FALLEN WARRIOR)
FATHER
CHRONOS, KING OF TIME
ARMS OF THE KAMI
MY CONFESSION
HEROES ARE NEVER FORGOTTEN
MACHINE RESURRECTION
WE WILL BUILD TOMORROW

ACKNOWLEDGMENTS

By Joshua Hill

Zach and I were introduced to anime, and by extension Japanese culture and history, through our older brother, George. Ever since then, we've been fascinated with everything Japanese, and the more we delved into it, the more interesting it became. The only thing that didn't interest us was the music. We had no interest in J-pop or the idols—*idoru*—who sang it. We were always hard-rocking hermanos! We grew up on a steady diet of Rob Zombie, Tool, and Disturbed. Pop music, especially super bubbly J-pop was anathema to us.

Zach learned to play the bass guitar during his first deployment with the Army National Guard in Iraq. In those hellish conditions, Zach found comfort and escape in music and anime. He did not come back from Iraq completely unscathed, even though he was never wounded in action. He was deeply disturbed and even scarred by his experience. He wanted nothing more than to live a peaceful life and help others do the same. He abhorred violence while recognizing the need to fight for what is right, mainly peace and freedom.

After his experiences in Iraq, including a second deployment in 2007, Zach needed to find some good in the world, heal, and come to terms with post-traumatic stress, so he decided to travel. He used his deployment money and lived in Italy for several months. Despite being the friendliest and most loving person, he always felt alone. Zach loved his time in Italy, but he wanted to be with family, so he returned home.

Wanderlust soon overtook him again, and he took a job teaching English in Japan. He quickly fell in love with the people and enjoyed his time there. While there, he discovered Hatsune Miku, the famous vocaloid, and the supergroup, BabyMetal. Finally, he could experience and enjoy the cultural sensation of idols, J-pop, and heavy metal together. The seeds of a new book were planted.

After returning from Japan, he met the love of his life, Mackenzie, and they had a wonderful but far too short time together. Tragically and suddenly, Zach died on January 15, 2016, one week before their first wedding anniversary. His death was a heavy blow to everyone who knew him. Zach probably would have said very few people would come to his funeral, but hundreds came. He made an impact on everyone he met, and we all mourn him together. At the viewing, Paul, Patrick, and I vowed to finish what Zach started. Little did we know the years-long adventure it would become.

And here I am, thinking about the book I just read and everything it took to get to this point. The last conversation I had with Zach was him telling me that he finally finished his book and that he would spend all day that coming Saturday editing it. He was excited about every project he worked on, but he was the most excited about this one. He considered this his *magna obra*, his greatest work. He poured his considerable heart and soul into this, and it shows.

It took me months to even be able to open the word file of the manuscript. The grief was still too near, but I'd made a vow. I attempted to edit the book, but because my thought process was so similar to Zach's and it was still too emotional, I knew I needed outside help. The most obvious people to help were Paul and Patrick, and their work has paid off. Even though many things had to be rewritten, you can hear Zach's voice through them, which shows Paul's and Patrick's genius and personal connection to Zach.

Sakura is an intelligent being forced to toil and kill for the government. She feels lonely and reaches out to make friends. She plays the guitar to relax and find peace. She hates violence and killing but is willing to fight for liberty and to uplift those around her. Sound familiar?

By reading this book, you will come to know Zach and honor him. All he wanted was to tell a good story. In this, he succeeded remarkably.

Paul and Patrick, you have been superheroes through this entire endeavor, sacrificing considerable time and money to see this work finished. My family and I can never repay you for what you have done. We are in your debt.

Thank you to George and Joyce Hill for helping to finance this project and always being a source of encouragement.

Thank you to our older brother, George, for introducing us to rock and anime, which have stuck with us all our lives.

Thank you to the inspirations of rock in his life, Sarah, Kevin, and Lexi Tate, as well as Savannah Howard.

Thank you to Shannon Thorpe for being Zach's heart and softer side.

Thank you to Glenda Woodson for her constant support and love.

Thank you to all Zach's friends and family who have influenced him and helped him along the way.

Thank you to Mackenzie for making the last year of Zach's life his happiest.

Patrick would like to thank the universe for allowing him to meet Zach, a truly exemplary person and one of the kindest souls one could imagine. The project has been watched over by friends and loved ones departed. Patrick dedicates his part of this project to the memory of Marilyn and Bob Tracy, who were always in his corner, his biggest and most faithful fans.

Rachael Moody's friendship and incredible inner light helped Patrick find a way back from a very dark place, and he will forever be grateful for that. He also gives great thanks to Alexis Tracy, who is metal right to the marrow of her bones and demonstrates every day how to live like a badass.

Patrick would also like to thank Julie Frost and Dave Bridges, who put up with his weirdness on a weekly basis during writers' group meetings and have always been there with great critiques and useful suggestions.

Finally, great thanks go to Paul Genesse, whose heroic efforts on this project allowed it to reach fruition. His patience with Patrick during the times when the project became too emotional to work on, his passion, and his relentless vigor are the reason you hold this book in your hands.

Paul would like to thank all of Zach's friends and family for trusting him with the literary legacy of such an awesome person. He would like to thank Kaitlund Zupanic, for her incredible support and beautiful art. Chloe Mori Ward, for being a heavy metal princess and for her inspiration along the way. Chad Darling, for his friendship and all the fun times. Michael Darling, for being a true friend and fan. Eliza Crosby, for her encouragement and smiles. Sean Smithson, for helping spread the word and for his knowledge of music. Michael Glassford, for his friendship and advice.

A huge thanks to Paul's wife, Tammy Genesse, for putting up with his crazy writer lifestyle and making him delicious tacos when he crawled out of the basement.

A standing ovation goes to Craig Nybo, for recording the song, "My Confession," and for the cool Sakura novel teaser video. Callie Stoker, for singing "My Confession" and gifting us with her beautiful voice—please listen to it on YouTube. Joe Monson, for his expertise on the Japanese language and kanji as he translated so many words.

Caryn Larrinaga, for her excellent interior design, making this a work of art. Devon Dorrity, for his exceptional cover and book jacket design and priceless advice as we put this all together. Jennie Stevens, whose copyediting was brilliant and helped the prose shine.

Bradley P. Beaulieu, whose development edits, advice, and support took the novel to the next level. Brad challenged us to make it better and better, and we are forever grateful.

Sarah Steigers, for her brilliant cover and interior illustrations, which made Sakura, Kunoichi, and the other characters come to life. Zach would have loved your work, and you are an amazing person and artist.

Paul would most like to thank his badass coauthor and blood brother,

Patrick M. Tracy, who brainstormed with him for hours, wrote incredible emotional punches in key scenes, and lent his vast knowledge of guitars and heavy metal.

Finally, thank you, the readers, for reading and rocking along with this book and supporting the legacy of a great person and a brilliant storyteller, Zachary Hill.

ABOUT PATRICK M. TRACY

Some say Patrick M. Tracy is an evolutionary throwback to prehistoric times—a caveman, even. While the full scientific truth of this has yet to be proven, he does play the bass guitar, which is generally considered to be evidence enough. For an archaic hominid, he is reasonably adept at technology and manages to type with all his fingers. His written work spans fantasy, science fiction, and horror, as well as poetry and the occasional literary piece.

One of the principal creators of the Crimson Pact universe, he was included in all five volumes of that series. He has also appeared in *Kaiju Rising: Age of Monsters* and Mech: Age of Steel. His novelette, "Worth the Scars of Dying," appears in *Noir Fatale* from Baen Books. When not writing and dragging his knuckles along the ground, he loves archery, playing the guitar, and performing feats of strength. For more information, please check out his website: pmtracy.com.

ABOUT PAUL GENESSE

Paul Genesse is the bestselling author of the *Iron Dragon* series, including *The Golden Cord, The Dragon Hunters,* and *The Secret Empire.* He's also sold almost twenty short stories and novellas. He's the writer/producer/director of the parody musical comedy shows: *The Star Wars Rock Opera (Episodes I-VI), The Steampunk Rock Opera,* and *Han and Qi'ra: A Star Wars Story* (based on *West Side Story/Romeo and Juliet.* He's edited seven anthologies and is the editor of five volumes in the shared multi-verse *The Crimson Pact* series.

He worked as a charge nurse in a cardiac unit for seventeen years before getting into Information Technology, where he's the Nursing Solution Architect for the electronic medical record system for a large healthcare company. He's often a guest and teaches writing at conventions, where he enjoys interviewing media personalities, usually the *Lord of the Rings* actors. Check out some of the interviews and learn more about his creative work at paulgenesse.com. Friend him on Facebook and send him pictures of dragons and androids.

ザカリー・ヒル
Zachary Hill

ABOUT ZACHARY HILL

Zach loved life. He took every opportunity to experience it. He traveled to every country he could, just to learn and take part in how the people lived. He made friends all around the world and was the most loyal friend anyone could ask for. He was simply the best, most honest, loving, and supportive man I ever knew. I could tout his accomplishments—like his two tours in Iraq or his two bachelor degrees—but if we could ask him what his greatest accomplishment was, he'd say marrying his soul mate, Mackenzie.

Tragically, Zach died on January 15, 2016, from a blood clot. Shortly before his sudden passing, he finished the first draft of *Sakura: Intellectual Property*. He loved this story—and Japan, where he once taught English. This novel, the greatest achievement in his writing career, brought together his love of music, action-thrillers, dystopian sci-fi, and Japanese culture, all centered around the most unique character he ever created.

At his wake, Zach's loyal friends decided to finish his final project as a tribute to him. The best way to remember or get to know Zachary Hill is to read what he wrote. That's all he would ask for. RIP, brother.

—Joshua Hill